HUNTING RABBITS

HUNTING RABBITS

A NOVEL

MARK GILLEO

ALSO BY MARK GILLEO

Out of Tupelo
Terminal Secret
Favors and Lies
Love Thy Neighbor
Sweat

2020 Press, LLC.

Copyright © 2022 by Mark Gilleo

Visit the author's website at www.markgilleo.com

ISBN: 978-0-9990472-6-2

ISBN: 978-0-9990472-7-9 (ebook)

First trade edition: June 2022

ACKNOWLEDGMENTS

I WOULD LIKE to thank the following people for their input and/or editing assistance: Dave Allen, Tim Davis, David Dutil, Sue Fine, Scott Forrest, Michele Gates, Dan Lord, Clark Neily, Doug Rippey and Sheridan Snedden. Additionally, I would like to extend gratitude to my editor, Nora Smith, for her skill and professionalism.

Last but not least, I would like to thank my wife, Ivette, for all of her support.

CHAPTER 1

DETECTIVE SANDRA BROOKS removed her sunglasses and ducked under the yellow police tape stretched across the entrance of the Walgreens. She stepped inside and paused to survey the drugstore crime scene through piercing blue eyes. Slowly shaking her head, she walked around a sea of merchandise strewn across the floor and spotted a uniformed officer at the farthest cash register.

"Detective Brooks," the officer said with a dose of deference as the detective approached. At five foot two, the redheaded detective commanded respect despite her diminutive stature. It was respect that had grown after a video of her using a trashcan to disarm a six-foot-five suspect high on PCP had gone viral.

"What do we have?" Brooks asked, gesturing toward the overturned merchandise.

"Assault and attempted robbery."

Brooks pulled out her small black notebook and flipped it open. She scribbled across a blank page and added the date. "Attempted robbery? Nothing was taken?"

"No. Thanks to a bystander. The suspect pulled a gun on an employee at the register and demanded money. A customer stepped in and, shall we say, diffused the situation."

"A good Samaritan?"

"That's what it looks like."

"Any leads on the perp?"

"Not much at this point. He was wearing a ski mask."

"Can't beat a ski mask for full concealment. And you can roll it up and slip it in your pocket when you're done. Any other description?"

"Black male, between six foot and six two, faded jeans, burgundy T-shirt. We know the weapon was an older Glock 19 because he left it behind."

The uniformed officer pointed his nose in the direction of the nearest pile of merchandise. "The weapon was found under the remains of the battery display. Standard 9 mm with fifteen-shot capacity. The serial number on the gun had been removed. Forensics and ballistics will see what they can determine."

"Any chance for prints?"

"There's always a chance. It's been tagged and bagged."

"What else?"

"You should check out the surveillance video. It's short and sweet."

"Let's see it."

Detective Brooks followed the uniformed officer to the back of the store where a plain clothes police tech with thick glasses was seated in a chair next to the store manager. A bank of small security screens clung to the wall.

"I hear we have an interesting security video," Brooks said.

"Just finished making copies," the tech replied.

"Can you run it from the beginning?"

As the video played, the police tech emceed the recording he had clearly already watched several times.

"The suspect entered the store at 1:23 in the afternoon. He was wearing a ski mask with a large single hole that stretched across both eyes. He seemed to walk a little stilted. Maybe a bad leg. Maybe he's older. At any rate, he immediately brandished a firearm from the waistband of his pants and ordered the employee behind the register to open her cash drawer. As you can see, there were no customers in line at the time. This feed is from the camera behind the registers."

"It's a little on the grainy side," Brooks said.

"Yes, it is," the police tech replied.

"I already told him that we're due for a security system upgrade," the store manager countered. "But you know how it goes when you're dealing with a big company and headquarters. Everything takes twice as long as it should."

The police tech responded. "And I explained that a security system upgrade won't produce a better image unless more memory is added. Good quality video takes up a lot of memory. There's a reason law enforcement releases surveillance images of suspects and asks the public to help identify them. For most businesses, it's too costly to save high-quality video that runs twenty-four seven."

Brooks' eyes moved back to the screen and the tech continued with the surveillance recording. "The store also has overhead shoplifting cameras. The image is clearer, but the angle of view is less useful."

Brooks pointed to the screen as the perpetrator waved his weapon in front of the girl at the register. "Our perp is a lefty, assuming he held the weapon with his dominant hand. Good news for us. That narrows it down to ten percent of the population."

"Yep. Next, the perpetrator orders the female employee at the register to fill a Walgreens bag with cash."

"Can you pause it?" Brooks asked and the police tech complied. "Did the girl at the register notice anything about the way the suspect spoke? An accent? A left-handed perp with an accent would reduce our suspect pool to a select few."

"Nothing about an accent."

"Continue."

"As the female employee begins putting cash in a plastic bag, our good Samaritan appears from aisle three with a handheld shopping basket."

"He looks like an average middle-aged white guy with a goatee and baseball cap," Brooks said.

Heads nodded in agreement.

"When the good Samaritan steps out from aisle three, the suspect turns his attention away from the register and points his weapon at the man.

The man places his shopping basket on the floor, raises his hands, and stares straight ahead. He remains unmoved and compliant until our suspect pistol whips the employee behind the register, who apparently wasn't filling the bag fast enough. At this point, we can see the good Samaritan says something to our suspect. The security footage doesn't have audio, but the employee behind the register seemed to think he said something like 'that's unnecessary.' Understandably, she wasn't sure, given that she'd just been assaulted with a handgun."

Brooks watched the screen as the perpetrator stepped away from the register, walked back to the end of aisle three, and shoved the gun in the face of the good Samaritan.

"Here comes the good part," the police tech said. "The man responds to the gun in his face by putting his hands even higher into the air. But when the suspect looks back toward the employee at the register, it's the beginning of the end. The man lands a solid right to the perp's face. The perp recoils but doesn't drop the weapon. The next view of the suspect is the bottom of his shoes as the man hip throws him into the candy display."

"Karate? Judo?"

"Something. Surprisingly, the perp gets right back up, then the struggle continues at the expense of the store's merchandise. The batteries and gift card endcap is knocked over next, followed by several shelves of chips and salsa. The perp's ski mask is pulled to the side in the scuffle and we see a little more of his face, but not enough to identify him."

"And somewhere in that melee is where the suspect lost his weapon?"

"That's our assumption. The suspect and the man grappled down the aisle until they reached the bottled water. The good Samaritan loses his cap at this point, and the best surveillance feed switches to an overhead shoplifting camera. From this angle, it appears that the suspect realizes he's in trouble, and he pulls a knife from his back pocket. Unfazed, our hero seizes the hand holding the knife, moves his body to position the suspect's elbow on his shoulder, and pulls down."

The video showed the perpetrator's elbow being bent in the wrong direction.

"That had to hurt," Brooks said, wincing.

"No doubt," the tech replied. "The suspect grabbed his injured arm, stumbled through the debris on the floor, and headed out the front door of the store. He was reported to be heading north toward Gilpin. We're in the process of trying to corroborate that intel."

"Was a BOLO issued?"

"Yes, ma'am."

"How many employees were on the clock when the suspect entered the establishment?"

"Three, not counting the pharmacist. One employee was at the register, one was stocking paper towels in the aisle furthest from the entrance."

"I was here in the office," the store manager added. "I came out when I heard the commotion and immediately called 911."

"How long was the suspect on the premises?"

"The entire incident lasted fifty-four seconds," the police tech responded, pointing at the time stamp in the corner of the screen.

"Witness statements?" Brooks asked.

"We had a married couple perusing dental hygiene products in aisle six. They hustled over and took a peek at the fracas from the end of the aisle before retreating to the back of the store. They provided witness statements but nothing to help identify the suspect. A student from VCU was evaluating condom options at the rear of aisle eight. He also provided a statement and contact information, but nothing useful to assist in identifying the suspect."

"What about our good Samaritan?"

"Nothing. He chose to leave the scene before the police arrived."

"Then let's get started collecting surveillance videos from neighboring establishments and knocking on doors in Gilpin. See if anyone can help find our perp."

*

Brooks answered her phone, her voice cutting through the early morning silence of Richmond's Major Crimes Unit.

"I'll be right down," she said, hanging up the phone in her cubicle and checking the time. She took an elevator to the basement and wound her way through the windowless halls to forensics. She stepped through an institutional gray door and spotted a lone latent print expert in the corner.

"Over here," the LPE said, raising one hand while using the other to click the mouse next to his keyboard.

"Tell me you got something good, Jimmy," Brooks called out to the LPE in a loud voice as she crossed the room. When she arrived at Jimmy's desk, she took a quick glance at the young man's ear gauges, which had stretched his earlobes well beyond normal proportions.

"I'll call it good news," Jimmy replied, positioning two images side by side on the screen and then sliding over for Brooks to get a better view. "Take a gander and tell me what you see."

"Fingerprints," Brooks replied.

"Technically, yes, but I was asking about their similarities."

"I think you should tell me."

"You're obviously not a morning person," Jimmy replied with a smile.

"Just tell me what you've got."

"Well, as you know, guns are designed with rough surfaces to improve grip and reduce accidental drops. It makes getting prints off a gun a little tricky. With that in mind, this gun actually produced three prints. Quite a bonanza, really. Two prints on the magazine and one on the slide. Neither location is a surprise as they're two of the smoothest surfaces on a gun. I ran all the prints through AFIS, which identified a probable match for one of the three."

"Only one of the three prints matched?"

"That's right. A partial print off the slide of the gun resulted in a match. Of course, all potential matches are subject to human judgment and a second verification."

"I assume you're the human doing the judging."

"I am." Jimmy pointed to specific locations on the prints. "We have a solid arch and whorl match. A little less accuracy on a loop. In total, we have six matching points, which is on the low end, but passable. Another LPE will be in shortly to verify the initial findings with AFIS."

"Any chance the matching fingerprint came with a name?"

"No name. But it did come with an interesting history. The partial print pulled off the slide of the gun matched a partial logged as evidence in a thirty-five-year-old cold case."

"You're kidding."

"I'm not. Have you ever heard of the Matoaka murders?"

"Just the name."

"That's better than I did. I'm from Wisconsin and before this morning I'd never heard of the case. I read up on it after I saw the old case reference. The Matoaka murders were a series of unsolved killings in Williamsburg, near the College of William & Mary. The only piece of evidence in that case was a print pulled off a Sony Walkman. That's the partial you see on the right-hand side of the screen."

"Incredible."

"That was my thought as well. Incredibly lucky."

Brooks mulled over the implications of the fingerprint results. "Who knows about the matching print and the connection to the cold case?"

"So far, you and me."

"Let's keep it that way until I run it by the captain. If the press catches wind of a print from a cold case, this place will turn into a circus."

"Will do."

"And email me those images," Brooks said, pointing back at the screen.

"I already did," Jimmy replied.

*

Detective Brooks knocked on the frame of the open door and waited for her boss to respond. A gold plaque and a myriad of other commendations adorned the wall behind him, the accolades indicating the man inside was the captain of Richmond's Major Crimes Unit.

"Come in. Have a seat," Captain McFarland replied from across the office, closing the folder he had been reading and placing it on the desk. The captain stood, towering over Brooks as she settled into a chair at a table on the other side of the room.

"Good morning, Captain. Thanks for making the time."

"It sounded urgent."

"It may be. Better safe than sorry on this one. We found intriguing forensic evidence from the crime scene at the Walgreens on Broad Street."

"The attempted robbery and altercation?" the captain asked for confirmation.

"Correct."

"Do we have a suspect?"

"Not yet, but we did pull a partial print off the weapon used. Forensics hit on a probable match in AFIS. No name, just a match to a print from another crime, in another jurisdiction. A cold case, as it turns out."

"How cold?"

"Thirty-five years."

"Antarctica cold."

"Actually, Williamsburg cold."

The captain's eyes seemed to jump. "What was the case?"

"The Matoaka murders."

Captain McFarland leaned back in his chair and muttered unintelligibly about somebody's mother. "That's not an easy case to forget."

"I only vaguely remember hearing about it. I was nine years old at the time."

"Well, I can assure you any teenager or college student who lived between Richmond and Virginia Beach at the time remembers the case. Four murders in six months. 1986-1987. I believe three of the murders occurred in the immediate vicinity of Lake Matoaka. That's where the moniker came from. Most of the victims were found on the running trails near the lake, adjacent to the William & Mary campus."

"Did the authorities ever name a suspect?"

"No. The state police aided Williamsburg on the investigative side, but I don't think they ever named a person of interest."

"Did the FBI get involved?"

"The FBI didn't start investigating serial killings until the mid-nineties. I believe they offered a behavioral criminal profile, but profiling was in its infancy at the time. Also, DNA wasn't collected as a matter of course until the following year and the first DNA database wasn't created until a few years after that. And most of the early cases involved rape. None of the Matoaka victims were sexually assaulted."

"So the investigation fizzled?"

"I don't know if 'fizzled' is the right word. But I do know it was a scary time. For almost a year, the city of Williamsburg and the College of William & Mary were on high alert. And then the killings stopped."

"And it's been quiet ever since?"

"Pretty much. The chief of police in Williamsburg keeps the case active. He has some personal interest in the murders."

"How's that?"

"He's from Williamsburg. And his sister was one of the victims."

"You're shitting me."

"Nope. His younger sister. The chief was in law school at UVA at the time of the murders. He took a year off, returned the following fall, and graduated near the top of his class. Then he took his fancy degree back home to become a cop."

"Sounds like you know him."

"We've met a few times over the years. I know his story. He's sharp. Knows his way around the legal system." The captain wrung his hands together. "How sure are we about the print?"

"It's on the low end for the number of matching characteristics. We're confident but we're going to run it again for verification. Prints analyses aren't infallible."

"I agree. Have we had any luck with security cameras?"

"We've collected surveillance feeds from a dozen businesses in the blocks surrounding Walgreens. One of the supplied feeds indicated the perp took off his ski cap after he rounded the corner, but we only have a shot of him from the rear. We have a lot more videos to go through. I feel good about our chances that one of the feeds will provide an image that can help us identify the suspect."

"Let me know if you require more manpower. We need to find this guy or know where he got the gun."

"Yes, sir. Do you want help from the public on this one?"

"Not yet. And let's keep the bit about the cold case to ourselves. That stays within these walls."

"Yes, sir."

"Have we contacted the hospitals to see if they've received anyone with a serious elbow injury?"

"We have calls into all city hospitals and urgent cares. We've heard nothing yet."

"Let's expand the range on that request. Contact the hospitals in Charlottesville, Norfolk, and Fredericksburg. Our perp is going to need a doctor if he wants to use his arm again."

"Yes, sir," Brooks replied, unsure if her walking orders were complete.

The captain pensively stared at his phone. "Come back in five minutes and let's make a call."

CHAPTER 2

CHARLIE GATES STOOPED down and pulled a green pod off a soy bean plant. He shuffled his feet through the rich soil and stopped at a row of tomatoes. He gently spun one on the vine until it released into his hand. His eyes moved from the skin of the ripe tomato to the half-acre of corn stretching to his left. He checked his watch and looked up at the graying eastern sky. Then he headed inside, leaving the rest of the farming duties to his father, the impending rain clouds, and God.

He entered the mud room at the back of the house, set his tomato on top of the washing machine, removed his farming boots, and stepped into his black work shoes. He sauntered into the kitchen, grabbed a seat at the table, and leaned over to tie his shoes, brushing dirt off the cuffs of his pants before sitting up to finish his morning coffee.

Barbara Gates came into the kitchen with a phone to her ear. Charlie stood, his ironed uniform adorned with a badge on his chest. Smiling, Barbara finished her conversation and set the phone down. She put her hands on her husband's shoulders and gave him a kiss.

"How are things looking out there?" she asked.

Charlie stepped back into the utility room and returned with the harvested tomato, placing it on the counter. "Tomatoes are coming along. Soy looks good. I think the corn will be happy with the rain we have coming. I'm guessing Dad will be out there working at some point today."

"I'm sure he will. And the corn will turn out fine. It always does."
Charlie nodded.

"I have a faculty meeting after my lecture today, so you and your dad
are on your own for dinner tonight. There's leftover lasagna in the fridge. If
that doesn't work, then you'll have to figure something else out," she said.

"We'll manage."

"I'm also on the schedule to churn butter on Saturday."

"That always sounds a little naughty to me."

"Oh, I'm sure it does, Chief," his wife replied, rubbing her hand across
his derrière. For Dr. Barbara Gates—a William & Mary history professor—
the historical reenactments at Colonial Williamsburg, including churning
butter, was a volunteer gig close to her heart.

"Your father is scheduled to work on Saturday too. So you'll have the
place to yourself."

"I'll find something to keep myself occupied," Charlie replied. As his
wife left the room, his mobile phone began to vibrate, and he pulled it
from his pants' pocket.

"Charlie speaking."

"Chief Gates?"

"One and the same. Who's calling?"

"This is Captain James McFarland, from the Major Crimes Unit here
in Richmond. We've met a couple of times over the years. I'm here with
one of my detectives, Sandra Brooks."

"Good morning. How are things in the big city?"

"Busy enough for job security. I'm sorry for hunting you down. I called
the station first and they said I could reach you on your cell."

"No problem. What can I do for you, Captain?"

"Actually, I think it's the other way around."

"I didn't know I had anything cooking in Richmond," Charlie said,
his curiosity piqued.

Captain McFarland cleared his throat. "Well, Chief, fair warning, what
I have to say may come as a surprise."

"I'll consider myself warned."

"We pulled a partial print off a weapon used in an assault and attempted robbery yesterday at a drugstore downtown. And that print came back as a match to the partial print left behind in one of the Matoaka murders."

"You're kidding . . ." Charlie replied, steadying himself with a hand on the counter as he absorbed the news.

"No, sir."

"I'll be there before lunch."

*

When Barbara Gates came back into the kitchen, her husband was staring blankly at the stack of napkins between the salt and pepper shakers on the table. When he looked up, she saw the glistening remnant of a tear that had already fallen from his square jaw.

"What happened?" she asked. As the wife of a career law enforcement officer, she understood the limitless possibility of answers to her question.

"Richmond PD called. They might have a lead on the Matoaka murders."

"Oh my God."

"I'm heading over there now. I'll be back when I'm back. Don't mention anything to Dad. When we have something concrete, I'll let him know."

CHAPTER 3

CHIEF GATES SAT with Captain McFarland and Detective Brooks at a long table on the third floor of Richmond Police Headquarters. Through the windows, the clock tower of the Jefferson Hotel reflected the late afternoon sun. The James River disappeared around a bend in the distance. At the front of the room, a police technician lowered the lights and swiped a remote control off the table. A frozen image of the surveillance feed from the Walgreens robbery illuminated the flat screen on the wall.

"What you're about to see is the attempted robbery of a local Walgreens. During the attempted robbery, the perpetrator is disarmed, leaving his weapon on the ground. That weapon had several fingerprints on it, one of which is a possible match to the evidence collected from the Matoaka murders."

Chief Gates nodded at the summation and the police tech started the video. When the video reached its end, Detective Brooks glanced over at Chief Gates.

"Do you have any questions?" Brooks asked.

"Can we take another pass at it?"

"Sure."

Chief Gates scribbled on a yellow legal pad and waited for the encore presentation. Another fifty-four seconds passed, and the recording ended for the second time.

"What do you have for leads?" Gates asked.

"We still haven't identified the suspect. The perpetrator was last seen walking in the direction of Gilpin. It's a neighborhood a few blocks over. Traditionally it's been urban housing. Gentrification is just beginning to get a foothold."

"Any more info on the gun, other than the prints?"

"The registration number had been removed. Ballistics indicated the gun was used in a robbery last fall at a popular Italian restaurant called Mama Zu's. A single shot was fired into the ceiling. The suspect left the premises without taking anything."

Gates's attention moved back to the screen on the wall. "A black-market gun. No registration. No sales history."

"That's the way it looks," Brooks confirmed.

"A needle in a haystack," Gates mumbled.

Captain McFarland interjected. "The gun isn't the only avenue to pursue. We've been collecting security surveillance videos from establishments throughout the neighborhood. We've got forty hours of feeds already and have five times that amount coming in. Hopefully it will lead to something solid."

"Would it be possible to get copies of the surveillance feeds?"

Captain McFarland quickly volunteered his detective. "Absolutely. Detective Brooks will make sure you get copies of everything. We can put what we have on a drive for you and send over anything else we get."

The captain flicked his head in the direction of the door and Brooks rose from her seat. The police tech followed her from the room, leaving the two senior law enforcement officers alone at the table.

"I know this is personal for you, Chief Gates, but rest assured, Brooks is a good detective. A bulldog. She'll make sure you get everything. And on the off chance you're not getting what you need, call me directly. Day or night."

"Thanks, Captain."

"Absolutely. Do you have anyone from your side who you'd like to get involved? It sounds like a lot of material to sift through. As the chief of police, I'm sure you have other tasks."

"I do, and I do," Gates replied. "Detective Luis Millares will take the lead from the Williamsburg PD side."

"Luis Millares," Captain McFarland confirmed, writing it down.

"But everyone calls him Quags," Chief Gates added.

"Why is that?"

"I think it's short for Quagmire. I may be the only one who still calls him Detective Millares."

"Any experience? I realize investigative chops can be hard to come by in smaller localities. I know Williamsburg is a quiet jurisdiction."

"It is. But Detective Millares worked fifteen years as a homicide detective in Miami before heading north."

"Miami to Williamsburg?"

"That's right."

"Interesting. Years ago, I read that Burlington, Vermont, regularly hired retired New York City detectives. It seemed like a win-win situation. Detectives with experience looking to wind down their careers in a quiet city, and a quiet city using experienced detectives to keep things quiet."

"In my case, Detective Millares was looking for a change of scenery and he had family in the Norfolk area."

"Has it worked out?"

"We haven't had a homicide since he joined the Williamsburg PD."

"Maybe you should keep him around as a good luck charm."

"He's luckier than you know."

"How's that?"

"Before leaving Miami, he was shot five times, center mass, by a drug cartel."

"And obviously he's still alive."

"He is. My wife says Millares working for the Williamsburg PD is like having a Ferrari to drive to the grocery store."

"Sounds like it's time to take your sports car out on the highway. Let it breathe a little."

CHAPTER 4

CHIEF GATES PAUSED at the doorway across from his reception-ist's desk.

"He's in there," the receptionist offered. "I helped him find a few things, but he's been banging around for a while now."

"Thanks. And thanks for staying late. Take tomorrow morning off if you want."

The receptionist smiled. "Thanks, Chief. I've been meaning to get my nails done."

"Check in after lunch."

"Call me if you need me before then," the receptionist replied, flicking off her computer monitor and grabbing her purse.

"Will do."

Opening the door, Chief Gates watched Detective Millares finish hang-ing a map on the wall. A second map was already attached to the opposite wall, red push pins marking the locations of four thirty-five-year-old cold cases. Files were stacked in separate piles on the table in the middle of the room. A whiteboard was in the corner, partially blocking the only window and making the small conference room feel even more claustrophobic.

"Good evening, Chief," Quags said, turning toward the door, sleeves rolled up to his elbows. His dark hair was ruffled, his five o'clock stubble thick. His badge and gun hung on his belt.

"I see you've been busy," Chief Gates replied.

"You said to pull out everything we have in the files. This is it." Quags took a sip of water from a bottle, the veins on his thick forearm visibly pronounced.

"Take a seat. Let's talk," Gates ordered.

Quags sat, and Chief Gates lowered himself into a chair at the end of the table, a pile of boxes on the floor to his left.

"What's the word? I'm guessing there's been some movement on your sister's case," Quags surmised.

"Potentially. When was the last time you read through these files?"

"A week ago," Quags replied, seeming to tread carefully. "You told me this case was a priority when you hired me. I never presumed that changed."

"And when was the last time we had a lead in the case?"

"Five months back. The woman out near Kiwanis who claimed she remembered seeing something thirty-five years ago. At the end of the day, it was nothing more than booze, boredom, and suggestive TV programming creating memories for her that didn't exist."

"And how's your memory?"

"I'd like to think it hasn't slipped yet. It'd be a serious liability for a detective. When that starts happening, it'll be time to move to traffic enforcement."

"We have a couple of openings for crossing guards. If this investigation doesn't work out, you can have your pick," Gates replied.

"Then I guess it better work out."

Chief Gates summarized his day. "The Richmond Police pulled a partial fingerprint off a weapon used in an attempted robbery of a drug store. It matched the fingerprint evidence from the Matoaka murders."

"Jesus, Chief. A fingerprint? That's good news."

"Potentially. The Richmond PD has provided us with some surveillance videos to go through. Between the videos, the fingerprint, and the case file, hopefully the pieces will fall in place and we can find our perp. Put this thing to bed."

"Yes, sir."

"Additional surveillance videos should be coming in tomorrow. So, if you need to go over the details of the cases, do it before you dig in."

Quags tapped his temple. "In all seriousness, my memory is fine. I'll start on the surveillance tapes first thing in the morning. Early."

"Go over the Matoaka case files again, anyway. Consider it a refresher course," Gates insisted.

Quags paused, stood from his seat, and stepped toward the map on the wall. Then he turned to face Gates as he pointed at one of the red pins pressed into the map.

"The first victim was Jennifer Costa. Found on Monday morning, October 13, 1986. She was senior at William & Mary and an avid runner. Her body was discovered on the northwest corner of Lake Matoaka, just off the running trail. Throat slit. No weapon recovered. The medical examiner estimated she had been killed the night before. A shoe print was found near the scene. A men's size nine running shoe. A Nike. An impression was made with the assistance of Virginia State Police, who had better technology at the time."

Quags pointed at the next pin in the map. "Our second victim was found a little over a month later, during Veterans Day weekend. Kara Shields. A graduate student. Her body was recovered on the east side of Lake Matoaka, opposite from where the first murder occurred. She wasn't a runner, though Kara's boyfriend said she walked the trails regularly. The boyfriend was out of town at the time of the murder with a solid alibi. Cause of death was determined to be blunt force trauma. No weapon recovered. The ME suspected a rock could have been used as the murder weapon, based upon the fracture pattern on the skull. The victim's ID was found on the ground near the body."

"Our third victim, Amber Nelson, was the only victim not found near Lake Matoaka. Amber was a junior. Murdered over Christmas break. She was from Northern California and didn't fly home because she was saving money for a spring break trip south of the border. She was working over Christmas break at Sal's Pizza here in Williamsburg. She was found in the woods not far from her apartment. Groceries and a receipt in her car indicated she had just returned from the store. Her driver's license was found on the passenger seat of her vehicle. Cause of death was strangulation. No weapon found."

"The fourth victim was your sister, Heather Gates. Stabbed to death on a park bench on the edge of Lake Matoaka on an unseasonably warm Sunday morning in February 1987. The murder took place sometime before lunch. Extremely brazen. In the commission of that crime, the killer left a bloody fingerprint on your sister's Sony Walkman. Model number 983403."

Gates nodded.

"All four of the victims were brunettes. All four were taller than average," Detective Millares added.

Chief Gates closed his eyes and asked a painful detail. "How many times was my sister stabbed, Detective Millares?"

Quags paused before offering the final gristly detail. "Eleven."

"Suspects?"

"There were two trains of thought on that front. The first was that the suspect could have been another student at W&M. The Williamsburg PD interviewed over a thousand students, as well as most of the staff at the time. When the murders stopped at the end of the school year, it only lent credence to the theory that a student had been responsible.

"The second theory was that the killer was law enforcement. Based on the fact that two of the four victims were found with their IDs nearby, it suggested the possibility that either someone from law enforcement, or someone impersonating law enforcement, had asked to see the victims' IDs prior to their deaths. In the end, neither theory bore fruit."

"Anything else of note?"

"The shoe impression that was collected from the first murder scene disappeared shortly after its existence was disclosed by the press. Reports indicated that the shoe impression went missing from the state police evidence room."

Chief Gates nodded again. "Impressive memory, Detective. Impressive."

"It's a limited gift. I wish I remembered everything as well as I remember case details."

Chief Gates took a deep breath, giving himself a moment for his emotions to subside. "Let me ask you a question. Do you miss it?" Gates asked.

"What?"

"Murders. Solving murders."

"I'd be lying if I said I didn't miss the chase. And I'll always miss the feeling of taking a killer off the streets."

"Well, I hope you have it in you to take at least one more out of circulation."

"I'll do my best."

"As of this moment, we have no ID on the perpetrator associated with this new fingerprint. So until I tell you otherwise, this is the only thing I want you working on."

"I'm flattered you're trusting me with this, Chief."

"We both know you're the only detective I have who's ever worked a real murder case."

"I'm still honored. I'll give it all I've got."

"Good. I'll check in on you in the morning. See how you're doing after you've watched a few hours of video."

"Sounds like I need to find a large-screen monitor and a comfortable chair."

"Buy them if you have to. Submit the receipts."

"Yes, sir."

"And it may help to get a map of Richmond on the wall. Just to get our bearings."

CHAPTER 5

MORNING COFFEE IN hand, Chief Gates pushed open the door to the small conference room. Quags looked over, a pair of sunglasses perched on the bridge of his nose. A chewed cigar protruded from his clenched teeth.

"Too bright in here?" Gates asked.

"Eye strain. I've been watching videos for several hours," Quags answered.

"Then you were here before the cock crowed."

"I was here before the cock did anything."

"Do the sunglasses help?"

"I like to think they do."

"Well, it's time for a break. Richmond PD called. They found a body that may be our perp. I told them we'd head over. You're driving. Bring the car around and I'll meet you out front."

*

Quags kept the needle nipping at ninety and Chief Gates kept his grip on the handle above the passenger door.

"Do you always drive this fast? You did hear me say the guy is dead, right?"

"I did."

"And I don't see any reason for us to join him."

"Sorry. Old habits die hard. Everyone drives fast in South Florida."

"Not everyone. I've been to Miami. I saw plenty of senior citizens puttering around."

"Trust me, even the blue hairs get testy if they're late for an early bird special."

Quags dropped his speed to eighty and Chief Gates seemed to relax. "Have you ever spent time in Richmond?" Gates asked.

"A little. I know a *mamacita* who lives in the Museum District. But I haven't seen her in a while. Three or four months. She's probably moved on."

"*Mamacita*? Doesn't that mean 'hot momma'?"

"The direct translation is 'little mama.' But 'hot momma' is a close approximation."

"My Spanish could be better. I studied French for five years. My mom said it would be useful. It hasn't been. You can be my Spanish translator."

"Fair enough, Chief."

"I think my Spanish would be better if Williamsburg had a larger Latino population."

"Williamsburg has Latinos, they just lay low."

"Maybe so. Either way, I'm sure Williamsburg has been a big change from Miami."

"It has. But I like the area. My brother retired from the navy after twenty years and lives down in Norfolk. My parents moved to Virginia Beach a year later. My brother and I get together regularly to fish. Something we've been doing since we were kids. The winter here sucks compared to Florida, but I can take my boat out on the York River and the Chesapeake."

"And no drug cartel is trying to kill you."

"And that. Getting shot isn't fun, regardless of what you hear."

"Rehab and recovery must have been tough."

"It wasn't easy. But it changed me for the better. The way I figure it, everyone has to go through something in life to know they're actually living. It could be a serious injury. It could be a divorce. For me it was being shot five times."

Gates nodded without responding.

"And I figure, for you, maybe it was the death of your sister, Heather," Quags added, staring straight ahead through the windshield.

"If I subscribe to your theory, then my sister's death counted as a proof-of-life event for a lot of people. For me. My parents. Her friends. Grandparents."

"No doubt."

The two men paused, both seeming to ponder their lives as the scenery raced by outside the windows of the police cruiser.

"I can only imagine how you feel about this lead," Quags said, breaking the silence.

"As a homicide detective, you can imagine better than others."

"Not on this one. Thirty-five years is a long wait for justice. It's a lifetime."

"It's been a life sentence for my family. My mother never recovered. She lived until a few years ago, but life lost a lot of meaning for her when my sister was killed. My sister and my mom were very close. That was one of the reasons that Heather chose to attend W&M. She wanted to be near our mother."

"And your father?"

"He handled her death the old-school way. By keeping everything bottled up. He moved in with us when my mother passed. Actually, he moved into what we call the Dad Shack behind the house. It's a renovated one bedroom that used to be slave quarters. It's nothing fancy, but it's not bad either. It has a bedroom, a living room, a bathroom, and a small kitchen. A couple of closets. He survives on fried eggs for breakfast and ham sandwiches for lunch. He eats dinner with us in the main house. Whatever my wife makes."

"How old is he?"

"He'll be seventy-six this year."

"Is he still with it?"

"He's slipping. Slowly, but I see it. He had a fall last summer and an undiagnosed episode after that where he couldn't remember where he parked his truck. The doctor thinks it may have been caused by ministrokes. It was suggested that he drive less and quit hunting. He agreed to the latter. We got him an iPhone and now he, my wife, and I can track each other at all times. But despite his gradual descent into old age, he still has the hearing of a bat and the eyes of a hawk."

"What did he do for a living?"

"He was a mechanic. He still toys with the occasional car, including some Williamsburg PD cruisers. He works as a blacksmith in Colonial Williamsburg once or twice a week."

"A blacksmith?"

"Yep. Dresses up in colonial garb and pounds on hot metal for the Williamsburg tourists."

"I might have seen him."

"He also does some farming."

"I heard you were a farmer."

"We have two acres that were originally part of a large farming estate dating back to the early 1800s."

Another pause filled the car.

"Have you considered what's next if this perp proves *not* to be the guy?" Quags asked.

"I'm trying not to. Realistically, I doubt I'll get another chance at finding the person responsible for my sister's murder. Father Time isn't on my side."

"Father Time is a *puta*."

"That's one of the few Spanish words I know."

"Bad words are always the easiest to remember."

"Hold that thought," Gates said, pulling his phone from his pocket. He extended his arm and read the text on the screen.

"Detective Brooks says the body is on the way to the medical examiner's office. She wants to know if we want to meet her at the ME's office or where the body was found."

"Let's start with where they located the body. It'll take a while for the ME to tell us anything definitive."

CHAPTER 6

QUAGS THREW THE car into park next to a high stone wall. The James River rumbled by a hundred yards away, rapids churning the water white. A set of high-power electric wires hummed above. Gates and Quags exited their vehicle and Detective Brooks met them at the end of the wall.

Gates introduced Quags to Brooks and the two detectives shook hands. "Nice to put a face to the name," Brooks offered first.

"Thanks for the surveillance videos. Been going through them all morning."

"Thanks for helping sift through them."

Chief Gates turned his head to scan the surrounding area. "Give us the lay of the land, Brooks."

Brooks motioned toward the edge of the parking lot. "This is the North Bank Trail. The building behind you is a Dominion Energy substation. It was once a mill. The body was found down the trail, a couple of minutes on foot from here."

"The area looks well-maintained."

"Some sections of the trail are better than others. This stretch gets a lot of foot traffic. Runners and bikers. The city has been trying to improve the waterfront. It's been slow but steady progress."

"How far does the trail go?"

"A couple of miles. It peters out at the Maymont Mansion."

"I'm not familiar with it," Quags replied.

"It's known for its Italian and Japanese gardens."

"What's up the hill to the right?" Quags asked.

"Hollywood Cemetery. Resting spot of Presidents James Monroe and John Tyler, our fifth and tenth presidents, respectively. It's also the last residence of Jefferson Davis, who many in the South consider a president in his own right."

In the distance, yellow crime scene tape wrapped around a gazebo, a loose end flapped in the breeze. A marked police car, its lights off, was next to the trail.

As they walked, Brooks spoke. "Tell me something, Detective Millares. How did you get the nickname Quags?"

"My family moved to Miami from Puerto Rico when I was ten. Westchester, actually, which is a little outside of Miami. My uncle started an import/export company, and my father went to work for him. Anyway, in school, I had a knack for finding trouble and dragging my buddies into it with me. A friend called me the Great Puerto Rican Quagmire. That lasted about a week until it was shortened to just Quags. I've had the nickname ever since. I have a lot of friends who don't even know that my real name is Luis Millares. But Latinos use a lot of nicknames. I know a family where every male is legally named Rafael, and none of them go by that name."

"That's asking for confusion," Gates chimed in.

"Not for a Latino. We're wired for nicknames. I answer to anything short of 'asshole.'"

"I'm going to hold you to that," Gates replied as they arrived at the scene and ducked under the yellow tape.

"The body was spotted in the grass behind the gazebo by a jogger. I wanted to keep the body on the scene until you got here, but it just wasn't possible," Brooks said.

"And you're sure it's our guy?"

"He fit our description and had a badly damaged left elbow. He didn't have ID on him, but a couple of homeless guys down the way said they knew him. They claimed his name was Reggie Williams." Brooks pointed down the path. The top of several blue tarps peaked over the fence along the cemetery's property line.

"Was he homeless?" Quags asked.

"Not that we're aware. One of the guys we spoke to seemed to think he worked in construction. Said he was a familiar face down here by the river. Unfortunately, heroin is also a familiar face down here by the river. It's a known issue in the camp. It's the likely reason he visited."

Quags nodded and Gates stared at the gazebo.

Brooks continued. "DMV records indicate we have fourteen Reginald Williamses, or variations thereof, within the city limits. We'll make contact and see if one of them is missing. We're also running his prints. Once we ID him, I'll be very surprised if he isn't our guy."

"How often do you get surprised?" Quags asked.

Brooks grimaced. "It happens."

*

The Richmond Medical Examiner and Coroner's offices occupied a six-story gray building at the corner of Jackson and Fourth Street. Quags followed Detective Brooks to the lot at the rear of the building and slipped into a parking spot. Two minutes and two flights of stairs later, a sixty-degree blast of air conditioning met them head on.

"*Coño*. It's cold in here," Quags said.

Brooks looked back over her shoulder.

"He's Puerto Rican. They have thin blood," Chief Gates said.

"But thick skin," Quags added.

The halls of the basement led the three law enforcement officers to the medical examiner, a woman in her fifties with white hair and thick glasses. She was perched over a body on a stainless steel table and glanced up as her visitors entered. Introductions followed before Gates and Quags focused their attention on the deceased man illuminated under the light.

"What can you tell us, Doctor?" Brooks asked.

"It's too early to be definitive, but it has the hallmarks of an overdose. He has track marks on his right arm."

"He was probably a lefty," Brooks offered.

"That makes it more likely for tracks in the right arm. And if that's the case, it would make him the eleventh fatal OD this month. But he's only been here an hour or so. I still have work to do."

Gates and Quags moved around the table, assessing the man from different views, none of which could hide the grotesque angle of the man's left arm.

"Any chance the elbow injury killed him?" Quags probed.

"Not likely. The skin wasn't punctured, which minimizes the chance of an infection. If he had a compound fracture, I would move it up the list of possibilities."

Chief Gates stopped near the head of the deceased, staring at the man's ashen face. "Do we have an age yet?"

The ME flipped through paperwork on a side table. "We won't have age verification until we have a positive ID but, off the cuff, I'd put his age between forty and forty-five."

Gates turned toward Quags. "What do you think, Millares?"

"Somewhere in there."

"Then he's not our man," Chief Gates whispered before clarifying his position more loudly. "He's probably the perp from the attempted robbery at the Walgreens, but he's too young to be the suspect in the Matoaka murders. Not unless he took up killing when he was in grade school."

"We'll know his age when we confirm his ID. It shouldn't be much longer," Brooks said.

"He's not our guy," Chief Gates reiterated. "Which leaves us with the gun and where he got it. Any known hotspots for black-market weapons in the city?"

"We have a couple. We're already kicking over rocks. Once the subject is identified, we should be able to get a better lead on where our man picked up his weapon," Brooks said.

"*Your* man," Gates retorted, the weight of a missed opportunity to solve his sister's murder seeming to settle on his shoulders. "I'm going to get some air," Gates said aloud. "Give me a call when you learn anything."

CHAPTER 7

QUAGS FOLLOWED HIS boss out of the building and into the parking lot.

"Let's take a ride," Gates said.

"Where are we headed?" Quags asked, climbing behind the wheel.

"To get some food. The only thing I've eaten today was a banana."

"I know a good Cuban place not too far from here that serves authentic food."

"I thought you were Puerto Rican?"

"I am. Sort of. I'm actually half Cuban on my mother's side, but she grew up in Puerto Rico. Got the hell out of Cuba when Castro came to power."

"What's the difference between a Puerto Rican and a Cuban?"

"As far as most Americans are concerned, 750 miles of water." Quags smirked.

"Remember, you said it first."

Quags was relieved to see the chief hadn't lost his sense of humor after their setback. "What do you say to Cuban food? The *mamacita* I was seeing in town was also Cuban and she loved the place."

"You're driving."

Pulling the car from the parking lot and onto the street, Quags tried to assuage the situation. "You know, the guy on the table back there could still be our man."

"He's too young. Mathematically, he can't be our guy."

"I'm just saying we don't know his age for sure until we have a confirmed ID and a birthdate."

"When was the last time you saw a drug user look younger than their age?"

"It's been a while."

"I dare say never."

*

The dearth of available street parking forced Gates and Quags into the SP+ garage on Marshall. Minutes later they stepped onto the sidewalk on Clay Street. By the end of the second block, both men's faces were peppered with perspiration.

Rounding the next corner, a sudden yell caused Quags to whip his head in the direction of the outburst. Through the front window of a converted townhouse, Quags and Gates paused to watch a short man in the middle of a room taking turns throwing larger men and women across a matted floor. In a steady rhythm, students in white uniforms bull-rushed the instructor only to have their weight and momentum used against them, each charge ending with an impact that momentarily shook the floor. Using the energy of the throw, each student rolled out of the fall, stood, and returned to the end of the line.

Quags's eyes ran across the shop window, the word "dojo" stenciled in peeling black letters. "You ever studied martial arts?" he asked.

"I haven't. Had a roommate in law school who was into it. What about you?"

"Nothing formal. I've fooled around with some basic defense moves."

More guttural sounds escaped the dojo through the screened front door. "Doesn't look like they have A/C. It's gotta be a hundred degrees in there."

Through the glass, they watched as the students performed their orchestrated attack with unvarying results. Moments later, the instructor yelled a series of commands in Japanese and the perpetual motion of the class stopped. The instructor stepped off the mat and returned with a wooden sword. Another command rang through the dojo and, one by one, each student charged toward their instructor, executing a roll just in time to avoid being "beheaded" by the wooden sword.

"It takes a special breed to allow someone to swing a wooden sword at your head," Gates said.

"And they're probably paying him to do it."

When each student finished clearing the gauntlet, the teacher called out additional instructions. On the next round of turns, as the instructor's wooden blade descended in an arc, each student slipped to the side of the weapon and grabbed their instructor's hand. Grasping their instructor's wrist as it held the sword, each student compelled the instructor to relinquish control of the weapon via joint manipulation.

"That move doesn't leave any room for error," Quags said, as a student narrowly missed being scalped before taking the sword from his instructor.

"Disarming a man with a sword lost all practicality with the invention of the gun," Gates added.

Quags cocked his head to the side as if considering the statement. "Let's go. We're almost there. It's just around the corner."

*

Kuba Kuba, a pseudo eponymously named Cuban restaurant, stood on the corner of Lombardy and Park in the Fan, Richmond's main drinking district and playground for the VCU student body. Quags opened the front door and Gates entered, perspiration plastering his shirt to his torso. Inside the restaurant, a passing waitress pointed with her nose in the direction of an empty booth.

Gates sat and reached for the menu standing behind the condiment holder. Quags glanced at the menu board over the counter on the far wall. Moments later the waitress scribbled down an order of *ropa vieja* and a Cuban sandwich.

"They make a dynamite Cuban espresso," Quags said.

"I try not to drink coffee this late in the day."

"One measure of a true Latino is their ability to drink coffee anytime, anywhere, and still sleep like a baby."

"Are you including yourself in that stereotype?"

"Juan Valdez has nothing on me. Caffeine doesn't keep me up."

"Does anything?"

"On occasion, the faces and bodies of past cases won't let me sleep."

"You ever talk to anyone about it? A professional?"

"Absolutely. I confer regularly with Dr. Bacardi."

"Does it help?"

"It does. We have an agreement."

"Who does?"

"Me and the departed. When the dead start to haunt me, I offer up a toast in their honor and then drink myself to sleep."

"I don't know how to respond to that."

"Not everything needs a response. Fortunately for us, a lot of suspects under questioning don't realize that until it's too late."

Gates's phone began to vibrate on the table. He glanced at the screen and then at Quags. "It's Brooks. I'm going to step outside and take this."

"I'll be here," Quags replied, eyes moving to the muted TV in the corner of the room.

*

Quags was staring at the TV, his mind churning through the likelihood that their suspect was deceased. By the time Gates returned to the table, his hot Cuban sandwich was at room temperature and the ice in his tea had melted.

Gates sat down and Quags looked over. "What did Brooks say?"

"They identified Reginald Williams. They located his sister."

"That was quick. And . . . ?"

"He was thirty-nine years old."

"*Coño.* Sorry, Chief. I know that's not the news you were looking for."

"Reggie Williams was a drywaller until last year when he injured his back and hip falling off a ladder. As a result, he doesn't move as well as he once did. Which we saw in the surveillance video from Walgreens. Over the course of his recovery from the injury, he got hooked on painkillers. From there he moved on to heroin. Gravity and addiction pulled him down that slippery slope. He's been collecting disability. He shows up at his sister's or girlfriend's house when he's not using. No criminal record."

"The attempted robbery at the Walgreens tells me his disability check wasn't enough to cover his heroin bills."

"Something along those lines. The sister didn't own a gun and she wasn't aware that Reginald had one. The girlfriend claimed the same."

"What about his prints?"

"His prints matched those on the magazine of the weapon."

"But not on the slide?"

"That's right. The match on the slide of the weapon was not from Reginald Williams."

"Then our man is still out there. Follow the gun, find our asshole."

"The Richmond PD is going to have to do the legwork on the gun. Searching for the provenance of a black-market weapon in Richmond is a little out of our wheelhouse and jurisdiction."

"I trust them," Quags said. "Brooks seems to knows what she's doing."

Gates nodded and bit into his Cuban sandwich. Quags reached over and swiped the bottle of ketchup off the tabletop. He put the bottle in his left hand and slowly grabbed for it with his right hand. He repeatedly fondled the bottle until Gates finished half his sandwich.

"I'll take the other half to go," Gates said, still chewing. "What's up with the ketchup bottle?"

"Just thinking," Quags replied, finishing his espresso and flagging down the waitress. "Could we get a box for the sandwich and the check? And a *cortadito* to go."

"You got it," the waitress responded.

"You weren't kidding about your caffeine intake," Gates said.

"A Puerto Rican-Cuban doesn't joke about coffee."

The waitress dropped off the check and Chief Gates reached for his wallet. "I got this," Quags said, placing money on the table. "I'll expense it."

Heading for the door, Quags took a parting glance at the TV as the broadcaster recapped a multiple shooting at a local Food Lion. "Chief, remind me to try something when we get back to the car."

*

Quags stood next to the closed trunk of the Williamsburg Police cruiser parked on the second floor of the parking garage. A faint squeal of tires echoed from the deck below. After several furtive glances around, Quags pulled his semi-automatic handgun from his holster. He released the magazine from the weapon and placed it on the trunk. He racked the slide and caught the chambered round as it popped out of the weapon. He confirmed the weapon was empty with a quick peek down the pipe from the safe end of the gun. He dry fired the pistol in a safe direction, then turned the gun around and pushed the grip of the weapon toward Chief Gates.

"What do you want me to do with that?" Gates asked, hands remaining at his side.

"Humor me. Take the gun. You don't have to point it directly at me, but close enough to approximate our perp and the good Samaritan's respective positions at the Walgreens."

Chief Gates squinted with suspicion before he grabbed the gun and pointed the weapon, aiming to the side, past his detective's head.

"The perp was left-handed."

Gates switched hands.

"Now, I'm going to attempt to disarm you. Try to shoot me before I do."

Gates stared down the sights of the weapon as Quags stepped slightly to the side and grabbed for the gun. The hammer on the gun clicked and Quags stepped back.

"I think you're dead," Gates said a matter-of-factly. "From this distance, you'd have to be very fast to reach the gun before I could pull the trigger. You see it done in movies, but in real life, I don't know."

Quags tried again and heard the distinct sound of another dry fire. "*Coño.*"

"Had enough?"

"One more time. Just give me a second. Quags bounced on his feet and rolled his neck in an attempt to relax. Settling into a calm stance, he nonchalantly reached one hand into his pocket.

"Ok. Let's try it on the count of three this time," Quags said.

"That's going to work to my advantage," Gates replied.

"Maybe. But I'll do the counting."

Gates stood with his left arm extended, gun ready to fire. Quags took a deep breath and began to countdown. Between two and three, he dropped a handful of loose change on the ground. As Gates's attention momentarily fell to the concrete, Quags said "three" and reached for the weapon.

"That's cheating," Gates replied, successfully disarmed.

"I was making a point. If you hesitate or are distracted, it could be done. And if you think about our perp, he was distracted. And he probably didn't have much experience with firearms. He could have easily hesitated."

"He could have."

"Let's give it another whirl."

Quags repeated the sequence several more times with Chief Gates serving as the hesitant left-handed gunman. On two additional attempts, Quags managed a reasonable gun takeaway. After each takeaway, Quags carefully examined the position of his own hand on the weapon.

"What did we prove?" Gates asked.

"I'm wondering about the print pulled off the slide of the gun. We've both watched the video of the perp being disarmed, and we know the gun was found on the floor of the Walgreens. But I think we missed something. Maybe we're looking at the wrong guy."

*

Back at Richmond Police Headquarters, Detective Brooks loaded the surveillance video from the Walgreens. Quags inched his chair closer to the monitor and Chief Gates pulled a pair of glasses from his pocket. Together they watched the attempted robbery of the Walgreens for the umpteenth time. When Reginald Williams put the gun in the good Samaritan's face, Brooks switched the video replay to slow-motion.

"Here we go," Quags said. "Keep your eyes open. Try to follow the weapon. Let's see if the print taken off the slide of the gun could have been left by the good Samaritan as he disarmed the perpetrator."

On the screen, the disarming of Reginald Williams occurred in a flash, a punch followed immediately by a well-executed hip throw.

"I don't know," Brooks replied, her piercing blue eyes focused on the screen. "The perp's body is blocking the view of the gun before things get physical."

"And we don't have a visual of the gun after the initial hip throw," Quags added. "Once the two men are further down the aisle, the overhead shoplifting camera gives us a better view. But by that time, the weapon is in the mix of overturned merchandise."

"Play the whole thing again," Gates asked.

Brooks ran through the video, pausing intermittently to examine individual frames. "Even at this speed, it's tough to get a view of the weapon."

"Let's go back to the question at hand. Is it possible that our good Samaritan left the print on the slide of the gun?"

Brooks flipped through the file in front of her. "The position of the print on the gun was likely from the person holding the gun and racking the slide. But it doesn't rule out your hypothesis."

"I know it's early, but do you have anything on the history of the gun?" Gates asked.

"Not yet. We've started fingerprinting tenants of the homeless camp down by the river. If Reggie Williams was hanging out there and using, it would be the most likely location for him to have picked up the weapon."

"Seems logical," Quags said.

A pause followed before Brooks interjected. "So, where do you want to go from here?"

"We're going to look into our good Samaritan. Hopefully the Richmond PD can continue to investigate the provenance of the weapon," Chief Gates answered.

"Absolutely. My captain has expressed his desire to assist in any way we can. He wants your case solved. So if there's anything the Richmond PD can help with, we are here for you. Whatever you need. Investigative support. Analysis—in fact, the Virginia Department of Forensic Science even has a new rapid DNA analysis machine. It's in the same building as the medical examiner. Only takes ninety minutes to determine a match."

"Thank you," Chief Gates replied. "We may take you up on the offer."

"We also have contacts with the Virginia State Police if you need an introduction to good people."

"Thank you. I have contacts of my own."

"Of course," Brooks answered.

"Are you still collecting surveillance videos?" Quags asked.

"We weren't planning to collect any more. We still have around a hundred hours that haven't been reviewed yet. Every security feed for five blocks in all directions."

"Could we request more video from a wider search area and a longer period of time?"

"How much did you have in mind?"

Quags shrugged. "All of it."

*

Back in the car, Quags turned toward Gates. "What do you think about calling in the state police?"

"Not at this time."

"They could be useful."

"Not at this time," Gates said again.

"I assume that's because the shoe print impression from the Matoaka murders went missing from state police custody. Correct?"

"It is."

"The case file says the evidence was lost. What am I missing?"

"The official file is what you've read, but it wasn't the entire story. After the shoe impression from the first Matoaka murder went missing, the state police claimed they had returned the evidence to the Williamsburg PD. They claimed that, in fact, the Williamsburg PD had lost the evidence. But at the end of the day, the state police weren't able to produce any documentation regarding the chain of evidence. Mind you, I discovered all of this years later."

"Evidence goes missing from time to time. Usually it's misplaced, stashed in with evidence from another case."

"That happens," Gates agreed. "Then again, two of the Matoaka murder victims were found with their IDs nearby. And if you consider that a law enforcement officer could have been a suspect in the murders, then you have a potential explanation for the missing evidence. Things don't just walk out of state police evidence rooms."

"Like I said, it was probably misfiled. Placed in the wrong box."

"And if it wasn't, then someone in the state police was involved. Either in the crime, the cover-up, or both."

"That was a long time ago, Chief. But it's your sister's case. I can work with whatever you think is best."

"For now, we head back home and go at this on our own. If we need help, we'll take Richmond PD up on the offer to use their resources."

CHAPTER 8

PER HIS NEW morning routine, Gates knocked on the door to the conference room located down the hall from his office and entered the makeshift Matoaka cold case nerve center. The lone window was open, and a light breeze rippled the edges of the Richmond city map now hanging on the nearest wall.

"What did you want to show me?" Gates asked.

Quags pulled his eyes away from his computer screen. "I found a couple of things, Chief. We received an additional dump of security feeds from a dozen more establishments in Richmond. Some places provided videos taken during the morning hours. Others provided surveillance feeds from the afternoon. Obviously, each business has its own procedures for saving data and overwriting previous recordings, so there's not much we can do about what was provided. Also, the quality varies a bit. At any rate, I grouped all the recordings in chronological order and started with the morning of the attempted robbery."

"Sounds logical," Gates said.

"What I found on my initial run-through led to a few more questions."

"Such as?"

"First off, did anyone from Richmond PD mention that the good Samaritan didn't enter the Walgreens through the front door?"

"Enter?" Gates asked.

"That's right. Enter. The good Samaritan came into the store from the rear entrance. Through the loading dock."

"That's the first I've heard of it."

"Well, he did."

"So he didn't want anyone to notice him going into or leaving the store?"

"At a minimum. From there, things get weirder."

"Do tell."

"On three separate occasions, prior to entering Walgreens, I saw our two witnesses being followed by our good Samaritan."

"The good Samaritan was following the *witnesses*? The married couple?"

"Yep. Following. Stalking. Measuring. I'm not sure exactly. But as our married couple from Richmond spent the morning strolling around the downtown area, the good Samaritan was lurking behind them. I have a video from outside a Starbucks. The lobby of the Quirk Hotel. In the Broadway Market Place, where they didn't buy anything. On all three stops, the good Samaritan was there."

"Curious."

"I haven't gotten to the cherry on the sundae, yet. It seems our good Samaritan, while following the couple, changed his appearance. Multiple times."

That news caught Gates by surprise. "Come again?"

"The first time I spot our good Samaritan in video, he has on a gray sun hat with sunglasses, and a beard. The second time I come across him, he's wearing some type of beanie hat with thick-rimmed glasses. Not sunglasses. He has lost the beard and he's carrying a green shoulder bag with a single strap. The third time I see him, he has a goatee and the same black backpack as seen in the original Walgreens video. But he doesn't have the baseball cap. He appears to have dark curly hair and to have gained twenty pounds of gut."

"If he's changing appearances, how can you be sure it's him?"

"He's the same height. He moves the same. Same pants and same shoes. Shoes are the most difficult attire to change on the fly. Outside of underwear."

"Sounds like you've put some thought into it."

"In Miami a few years back, we had to build a case against a drug dealer who used disguises. This hombre even went as far as dressing up as a woman. With some practice, you kind of learn to look through the disguise. A gait usually gives a person away."

Gates stared at the images on the monitor as Quags lined them up on the screen. "I don't know. If we assume this is the same guy, what was he doing with the witnesses in Walgreens at the time of the robbery? Why change your appearance, lurk in the shadows, and then go into the same store?"

"I don't know. Maybe they know each other. Either way, I'd love to hear an explanation. I say we head back to Richmond to pay our witnesses a visit. Maybe there was more going on in that store than anyone is aware of. Maybe things went pear-shaped and we only saw what they wanted us to see."

CHAPTER 9

FIFTY-TWO MILES LATER, Quags drove the unmarked Williamsburg Police cruiser through the Fan.

"I can't get over how much this area has changed over the years," Gates said. "When I was in school at UVA, we used to come to VCU to party on occasion. Back then, the Fan wasn't a safe place to walk alone. Things are different these days. I have it on good authority there's even an authentic Cuban restaurant nearby. If that's your thing."

"Lie to me and tell me you didn't like it." Quags chuckled.

"The best room-temperature Cuban sandwich I've ever had."

"*Come mierda.*"

"What does that mean?"

"The direct translation is eating shit, but it's closer to calling someone a bullshitter."

"I'll try to remember that one."

"It's useful for hanging out with Puerto Ricans and Cubans. Talking shit is one of our cultural pastimes. Along with dominoes and cigars."

"Funny how stereotyping is okay when you do it to your own group."

"Just saying how it is."

Gates pointed through the windshield. "Take a left at the next corner."

"This isn't far from my old *mamacita's* house."

"We can stop in and say hi if you want."

"She has my number. She hasn't used it."

"Any new *mamacitas* in your life?"

"Nothing steady. My brother is trying to set me up with a girl he knows in Hampton Roads. A friend of my sister-in-law. He says she's a perfect candidate for an FWB, which is about all I'm up for."

"FWB?"

"Friend with benefits."

"Ahh. Did you ever think about getting married?"

"I thought about it. But the life of a homicide detective isn't fair to a wife, or conducive to a family. No offense, Chief. I know you've been married forever."

"None taken. I was never a homicide detective."

"I'm also the proverbial dog that's too old to learn new tricks."

"Are you housebroken?"

"*Come mierda.*"

"How old are you? Forty-five?"

"Give or take."

"Hardly an old dog."

"It's not the years, it's the mileage. How long have you been married, Chief?"

"Twenty-four years."

"Did you ever want to have kids?"

"We thought about it, but it didn't work out. Had a couple of miscarriages."

"Sorry. Didn't mean to pry. But a big part of me thinks the world is overpopulated already. It certainly has more assholes than it needs."

"*Come mierda.*"

"Nice pronunciation but wrong usage. I wasn't talking shit. I was serious."

Chief Gates smirked and checked his phone for directions. "Two blocks up on the right. Just before the intersection of Roseneath."

A minute later, Quags pulled the car to the curb. Chief Gates lowered the passenger window and both men looked out.

"It's 3399, right?" Gates asked, confirming the address via the numbers stenciled on the side of the curb.

"Yeah, Chief. Doesn't look like anyone is home."

The two officers got out of the car, crossed the sidewalk, and climbed a short staircase to nowhere. A mound of earth greeted them at the end of the walkway. The rest of the lot had been flattened, trees and shrubs removed with all the finesse a bulldozer can muster. Red clay and rooted earth stretched from fence line to fence line.

"Did we get the address wrong?" Quags asked.

"This is the address from the witnesses' driver's licenses."

"Maybe they moved. They have six months to get new IDs displaying their new address."

"You'd think one of the witnesses would've mentioned they had moved when they provided their statement to the police."

Quags shrugged. "It could have slipped their minds. They were probably pumped up on adrenaline. Witnessing a violent crime shakes people up."

Gates and Quags continued to assess the implications of the flattened yard as a woman in pink yoga pants approached, pushing a stroller down the sidewalk. The child was asleep in the seat, a sun shade casting darkness on the little one's face.

Chief Gates stepped back to the sidewalk as the yoga mom neared. "Excuse me, ma'am. Do you have a minute?"

The woman stopped, a look of suspicion seeming to wash over her face. Gates noticed a can of pepper spray hanging from the handle of the stroller.

"My name is Charles Gates and I'm the chief of police for the city of Williamsburg. This is one of my detectives, Luis Millares." Gates slowly reached for his badge. Quags stepped down onto the sidewalk and followed suit.

The woman confirmed the details on Chief Gates's credentials and smiled. "How can I help you?"

"Do you live around here?"

"Yes, sir. Four houses down. I'm just taking my daughter out for a walk. Helps put her to sleep."

"Do you know anything about this lot here?" Gates asked with a flick of his head, indicating the empty lot behind them.

"There was a house there until this past winter. Prior to that, there were some young guys living there. I assumed they were students, but I never asked. They moved out before last fall, so over a year ago."

"Can you give us a better idea of when it was knocked down?" Quags asked.

"I don't know exactly, but it was cold outside. January or early February. It's been sitting like that ever since."

"What kind of house was it?"

"What do you mean?"

"Large? Small? Older? Remodeled?"

The woman pointed across the street. "It was similar to the one with green shutters, but the layout was flip-flopped."

"How about a vehicle?" Quags asked.

"I remember seeing a few different cars there. All of them were on the clunker side. Which also made me think the tenants were students."

"Do you remember the make or model of any of the vehicles?"

"I could try to guess, but I'm not good with cars."

"Fair enough. How long have you been in the neighborhood?"

"We moved in before our first child was born. He's in kindergarten now, so six years next spring."

Quags nodded his understanding then asked, "And you never spoke with the residents of this house?"

"I didn't. I waved on occasion."

"And you never saw a young couple living at this address?" Quags asked, reaching into his pocket and removing photos of the witnesses from the Walgreens. "They're a married couple."

The woman leaned forward to look at the photos and responded. "Nope. Never seen them. Mind you, I can't see this house directly from mine because it's on the same side of the street. But I pass by it almost every day when it isn't raining. My daughter won't go down for a nap unless I take her for a walk or put her in the car and drive around." The woman seemed to think for a moment. "You're looking for a young married couple who lived at this address?"

"Yes. According to our information."

"I think there must be a mistake."

"Why's that? Other than the pile of dirt where a house should be?"

"Because all the parents and younger couples in this neighborhood are pretty tight. And I'm the organizer of the weekly drink-and-sit."

"What's a drink-and-sit?"

"We close off the cul-de-sac up the block, pull out some chairs, drink wine, and watch our kids run around. Kind of like group babysitting mixed with a neighborhood happy hour."

"I didn't know that was a thing."

The woman smiled again. "Oh, it's a thing. We used to call it a sit-and-drink, but we switched it around because the drinking part became more important. You should take the idea back to Williamsburg. Start a new craze."

As the woman finished her sentence, her baby began to cry. "See what happens when I stop moving?" she asked rhetorically, rolling her eyes and then rocking the stroller.

"Well, thank you for your time," Gates replied.

"Sure thing, officer. Hope you find what you're looking for."

As the chair of the local drink-and-sit pushed her stroller down the sidewalk, the officers turned back toward the empty lot. "What do you think?" Gates asked.

"*Coño.* I've had plenty of suspects lie about where they live, but never had a witness provide a bad address."

"Two witnesses. Which makes me think it wasn't an accident."

"I could call it an incredible coincidence. But I don't believe in them," Quags said.

"Never?"

"Never," Quags answered. "I'm going back to the videotapes. I must've missed something, somewhere."

CHAPTER 10

GATES KNOCKED ON the open door and Quags looked up. "Anything?"

Quags rubbed his eyes and answered. "Two steps forward and one step back. Which do you want to hear first?"

"Surprise me."

"The demolished house that our witnesses listed as their address was a rental. It's owned, or rather *was* owned, by a rental company in Richmond. They sold the property to Evergreen last year. Evergreen is a prominent builder in Richmond, and they do a lot of teardowns."

"Did the rental company know our couple?"

"They didn't. The last tenants they had were a group of VCU students."

"So the yoga mom was right."

"Seems like it."

"What else?"

Quags adjusted the angle of the monitor to so that Chief Gates had a better view. "I started on the videos that were recorded *after* the Walgreens incident. We already know that our good Samaritan left from the rear of the Walgreens. And, if you watch the screen, you can see our man casually walks off down the alley before he disappears around the corner. Later, he shows up again in the security feeds from several other establishments as he heads in the direction of the VCU campus. All of the feeds were from exterior cameras. Once again, our man has changed his appearance since the attempted robbery. He's lost his goatee."

"He must have his disguises stored in his backpack."

"Including a second bag in the original bag. An hour after leaving Walgreens, I picked him up again heading into the Richmond Public Library. I never see him come out, but he does at some point because I run into him in another feed a little later."

"Is now the appropriate time for '*come mierda*'?"

"I'm going to regret teaching you that."

Gates turned his attention back to the screen. "What about our witnesses? Did you catch them on other surveillance feeds?"

"I have them leaving Walgreens—through the front door—and their next stop is the Third Street Diner. After that, they visit Fountain Books and spend an hour inside. For the duration of their time in the bookstore, it does not appear that the good Samaritan is following them. Based on other security camera feeds and their timestamps, he's several blocks away."

"So much for the theory that the three knew each other."

"I was ready to dismiss that assumption, as well. Then I watched the security tapes from the alley next to the convention center."

Quags pointed at the screen.

"What is that? A bus?" Chief Gates asked.

"That's right. It's a bus parked in the alley next to the convention center. And, if you stay tuned, our two witnesses are going to board it."

"The bus has a number on it. On the roof."

"Yes, it does: 418. I checked with Richmond Transportation. It's not their bus. They don't have a route or bus number 418. It's also the wrong color. Richmond city buses have green roofs and two-tone sides in dark blue. The bus in the video clearly has a silver roof. And in another feed, you'll get a better view of the side of the bus. It's light blue and silver."

"A private charter? Was something going on at the convention center that day?"

"Great minds think alike. According to their website, no. So I contacted the convention center and asked about parking in the alley next to the building. They said a permit and reservation are required. They provided the name of the company and a phone number for the bus that parked there on that day." Quags flipped through his notes. "The company is named Hampton Transportation Group, LLC. They have a simple website. I called the number the convention center gave me and left a message. I'm waiting for someone to return my call."

"It's a lead. What else can you tell me about the bus?"

"The security feed is taken from a vantage point on the side of the convention center. It's too far away to read the license plate."

Gates nodded, eyes still on the screen.

"Here comes the good part," Quags said. Seconds later, the couple walked hand-in-hand into the alley. The door to the bus opened and they boarded.

"That's definitely our couple from Walgreens."

"It is."

"What time was this feed taken?"

"Late afternoon. A quarter to five. Let me fast-forward through the next ten minutes."

"What happens during those ten minutes?"

"More people arrive on the scene and get on the bus. And then a second vehicle arrives."

"Another bus?"

"Nope," Quags replied, motioning toward the screen as a dark blue SUV pulled in the alley behind the bus. "This SUV parks, and then we have six adults appearing at the end of the alley and climbing into the SUV."

Quags paused the surveillance feed. "Recognize the guy who gets in last?"

Gates leaned in. "Our good Samaritan."

"Sure looks like it. Hat, pants, beard, glasses."

Quags worked the mouse again, scanning forward as the bus and SUV drove out of the alley. A moment later, the camera location changed, and the side of the bus and the SUV zipped past.

"Can you go back?" Gates asked. "Show me the bus again."

Quags did as he was instructed and elaborated on the provenance of the video. "This shot is from a Wells Fargo ATM near the VCU medical center. You can see the bus came around the corner and, from this angle, the vehicle looks like a school bus. With tinted windows."

The silver and blue design on the side of the bus caused Gates to freeze, his face turning ashen. "Son of a bitch," he whispered.

"You all right, Chief?"

"Anything else?" Gates asked.

"The last security feed we have is from VDOT and it shows the bus and the trailing SUV getting onto the highway not far from the Richmond Coliseum."

"Let me guess, they headed east on Interstate 64."

Quags turned toward his boss. "And why would you think that?"

"Because I've seen that bus."

"You want to enlighten me?"

"Print out the best image you have and let's take a ride. I'm driving."

CHAPTER 11

DELL WHITE'S DIESEL garage had been a mainstay in the York County, James City, and Williamsburg areas for the better part of forty years. Dell, a former Marine and the eponymous owner, was nearing eighty, leaving many to wonder why the seasoned diesel mechanic still slipped on his grease-stained overalls each morning. With no mortgage, a military pension, and a social security check, the most plausible explanation for continued employment was that his wife didn't want him in the house all day. Or so went the morning gossip at Kellogg's Diner.

*

Gravel crunched under the weight of the police cruiser as it pulled into a parking lot surrounded by pine trees. Skeletons of old vehicles were enclosed in a fenced yard with knee-high weeds. On the other side of the property, a half-dozen shiny yellow school buses were parked side by side on the edge of the lot.

"What's this guy like?" Quags asked, his eyes scanning the surrounding area, taking in every detail.

"He's friends with my father from way back. He knows everything there is to know about diesel engines, and how to fix them."

"And what makes you think he'll know our bus?"

"If he doesn't, he can probably point us in the direction of someone who does."

An arching half-barrel building cast a shadow on the cruiser as the two-man law enforcement team exited the car and stepped toward the garage. A bus sat in the building's single bay, its engine suspended on thick chains next to its open hood. Three flags hung on the back wall of the shop, indicating Dell's allegiances to America, Virginia, and the USMC. A crash of metal echoed from behind a row of shelves, followed by several salty curses.

"Dell White, it's Charlie Gates," the chief announced from a distance, walking slowly down the length of the bus.

Quags followed in his wake, taking note of Gates's cautious approach.

The sound of items banging on shelves was followed by the in-the-flesh appearance of Dell White. Moving toward his visitors, Dell wiped his hands on a red rag and shoved it into his back pocket.

"Charlie, good to see you."

"Dell, this is one of my detectives, Luis Millares."

The two shook hands. "You can call me Quags," he offered, noticing both the mechanic's grip strength and forearm tattoos.

"I'll stick with 'Detective,'" Dell replied. "How's your father doing, Charlie?"

"He's still kicking. You got a couple minutes? Is there someplace we can sit down?" Chief Gates asked.

"Work?"

"It's not a social call."

"Didn't figure. Follow me." Dell White stepped out of the building and led his guests to a picnic table on a weathered concrete slab. "Will this do?"

"Fine," Gates replied.

"Let's hear what you've got and how I can help."

"We want to talk to you about a bus. A diesel bus."

Dell spread his arms, motioning toward his surroundings. "That's pretty much all I have. You looking for one in particular? Last few years, I've had a lot of folks asking if I had any old buses for sale. Seems people want to turn them into tiny houses."

"Do you still have the maintenance contract for the school system?"

"One of them. It's enough to keep me busy. I still do ad hoc repairs for other people. All diesel work. Once in a while I play with a boat engine."

"You ever work on any Blue Bird buses not owned by the school system?"

"I get the odd request here and there."

Quags unfolded the printed screenshot of the bus and handed it to Dell. "You ever work on something like this?"

Dell reached for the pair of glasses hanging around his neck and slipped them onto his nose. "Sure thing. A couple of times."

"Was it a charter bus?"

Dell leaned back and took his glasses off. "What is it that people say about lawyers?"

"They say a lot of things, and most of them aren't very nice," Quags interjected.

Dell smirked. "I can't argue with you there. But that's not what I was thinking. It was more along the lines of 'lawyers don't ask questions they don't already know the answer to.'"

"In this case, you're half right," Gates replied. "When was the last time you had one of these buses in your shop?"

"Been a while. Year and a half. Maybe two. The last time around it was a tow and repair. Water pump was shot. Pretty common ailment for the Blue Birds once they get over ninety thousand miles on them."

"Who paid the bill?"

"I don't recall, but it doesn't matter. Because whoever they told me they were, they weren't, if you know what I mean."

Quags heard the statement and squinted, eyes moving from Dell to Chief Gates and back.

"Camp Peary?" Gates asked.

"That's what I figured. Of course, no one mentioned it by that name, or any other."

"How did they find you?" Gates asked.

"Who knows? But I'm guessing it wasn't the phone book."

"Anything about the bus that was unusual?"

"You mean like bulletproof tinted windows, run flat tires, and an odd electronic device under the hood?"

"Yeah, something like that."

"Most of the bus was standard, but one of the windows got smacked pretty hard with a chain when I was taking it down off the tow. I thought for sure the tinted glass would be broken, or at least cracked, so I took a closer look to make sure there wasn't any liability on my part. That's when I noticed the heavy laminate between two layers of glass."

"Interesting. And what was the object under the hood?"

"That was a little tougher to explain. It was a box about yea big," Dell said, holding his hands a foot apart. "It had a thick black antenna, like something you'd find on one of those old mobile phones. Back when they were the size of toasters. My first thought was that it was a radio, but there's not much use for radios nowadays. Everyone has a cell phone. Then I figured it was some kind of tracking device. Whatever it was, I know for a fact it wasn't standard equipment on any Blue Bird bus. I considered asking the guys who came out to get the vehicle when it was ready, but they didn't seem interested in chitchat."

"Anything else?"

"The bus had been fitted with several security cameras, but those are common these days."

"How did you get in touch with them after you fixed the bus? Did you get a phone number?"

"I did. When I finished with repairs, I called a number and two guys came out in a standard-issue four-door sedan. One of the guys climbed into the bus and started it up. The other guy handed me a check. And like I said, neither was interested in talking."

"You keep a record of their payment details or a copy of the check?"

"My wife does the billing, and she keeps everything. It may take a few minutes, but I should be able to find something."

"It would be appreciated."

"Can I get you some iced tea while I look?"

"Sure."

Dell stood and returned a moment later to deliver two cold iced teas in cans. "I'll be back."

*

"What's the story here, Chief?" Quags asked as Dell disappeared.

Gates pointed to the printout of the bus. "You've never seen a bus like that out on I-64? You've probably passed at least one driving to Richmond on the way to see your *mamacita*."

"If I did, it didn't stick in my mind."

"I think that's the idea. Those buses are boring by design."

"And what exactly is the connection between the bus and Camp Peary?"

"At this point, it's a hunch. Hopefully Dell can help us make that connection. But if I'm right, the bus we're looking for is used by the Central Intelligence Agency."

"No offense, Chief, but I have a hard time believing the CIA would drive school buses."

"They're not technically school buses. In Virginia, school buses are yellow by law. Specifically, they're 'school bus yellow.'"

"Creative name. But it's still hard to accept that Blue Bird buses are the best transportation the CIA could come up with." Quags stood, muttering under his breath in Spanish. "I need to walk," he said, pulling a cigar from his shirt pocket. He strolled to the edge of the gravel lot and cut the tip off. He stood with his back toward the garage until Dell returned to the picnic table. A puff of smoke drifted over Quags's shoulder as he walked back to join the conversation.

"I found the receipt and a copy of the check," Dell said. "I had to make a quick call to my wife, but she pointed me in the right direction. I'd never admit it, but I'd be in real trouble without her. God help me if I got audited and she wasn't around."

He placed the copy of the check and receipt on the table and rotated it for his guests to read.

While Gates took a moment to digest the details, Quags read aloud: "The Hampton Transportation Group, LLC."

"You know it?" Dell asked.

"As much as anyone does, I'd imagine," Gates answered.

"And it's the same phone number the convention center provided," Quags added, checking his phone.

"What exactly is going on, Charlie? I only ask because if you start poking around on our intelligence friends down the road, some people are bound to get upset."

Chief Gates ignored the warning. "The bus you see in that image could be the first real lead on my sister's killer in thirty plus years."

"Matoaka?"

"That's right."

"Damn, Charlie. You should have said so."

"I wasn't sure until you produced that receipt."

"Does your father know?" Dell asked.

"I haven't mentioned it. I don't want him to get his hopes up. And I'd appreciate it if you'd keep it to yourself for now. I need to confirm a few things before I tell him."

"My lips are sealed. But like I started to say, a lot of people around here depend on Camp Peary for jobs. People don't want to ruffle too many feathers. It's been like that forever."

"What about you, Dell? You worried I may ruffle feathers?"

"No, Chief. If I had a sister who was murdered, I'd hunt the son of a bitch down and take care of it myself."

Quags, cigar between his teeth, smiled wide and nodded in approval.

"Thanks, Dell," Chief Gates said, standing.

"Let me know if you need anything else. Anything I can do."

CHAPTER 12

GATES PULLED ONTO Interstate 64 and the traffic immediately reduced their speed. One by one, cars pulled to the right and let the police cruiser pass. As Gates gently pushed the accelerator, Quags sat back in the passenger seat and contemplated the new direction in the case.

"So we have school buses used by the CIA, lying witnesses who live in a bulldozed home, disguises in broad daylight, and the disarming of a man with a gun and a knife."

"That's where we stand. But we've made progress. We've narrowed it down to someone in their early fifties, or older, who has a current connection with Camp Peary." Chief Gates considered the implication of what he just said. "How old was the couple who gave us the false address?"

"Twenty-four and twenty-five. According to their fake IDs. Why?"

"I'm wondering if they have a maximum age for joining the CIA. We know law enforcement has an age limit."

"Give me a sec. I'll check," Quags said, pulling out his phone. His thumbs tapped on his screen. A moment later he began reading the search results. "The age limit for becoming an FBI Agent is thirty-seven. Ditto for the law enforcement function of the DHS and DOJ. The DEA is thirty-six."

"Any CIA in that alphabet soup?"

"*Coño*, I'm reading," Quags said. "Okay, here were go. The official age limit for becoming what the CIA refers to as a clandestine officer is thirty-five. Though, it says the CIA will consider older candidates who have skills determined to be in high demand, such as fluency in Middle Eastern languages."

"What does that tell us?"

"That our guy is too old to be training to become a spy at Camp Peary. Unless he speaks Farsi, Arabic, or Pashto."

"Which leaves us with . . . ?"

"Base management. Instructors. Facilities. Operations. Staff."

Gates nodded in agreement, a look of determination creasing his brow. "There's one way to find out. Let's pay them a visit."

"Who?"

"Camp Peary. The Farm."

Quags's eyebrows shot up. "Just show up at the front door and ring the bell?"

"It's a gate. And I doubt there's a bell. But, yes. We're law enforcement working an active murder investigation. They should want to help."

"I'm sure there's some sort of protocol to follow when it comes to Camp Peary, but honestly, following protocol was never my strong suit. I'm good with whatever you have in mind, Chief."

"It's always nice for a boss to hear that following protocol isn't a subordinate's strong suit."

"All I am saying is a few minutes of uncomfortable conversation is often faster than the bureaucracy of following protocol."

"For the record, *I* never said that."

"Noted."

"And, so you know, it won't be my first visit to The Farm."

"You've been before?"

"I have. Many years ago, after they built a new conference facility. They hosted a law enforcement symposium."

"What was it like?"

"We only saw the conference center."

"Sounds like a crappy tour."

"Maybe the second time around will be better. Let's drop in. Best-case scenario, we get what we need. Worst-case scenario, as Dell put it, we ruffle a few feathers."

"If you think ruffling feathers is a worst-case scenario, you need to work on your imagination."

"I can go alone if you want."

"Oh, hell no. Count me in."

*

Fifteen minutes later the cruiser crawled up the ramp of Exit 238, turned left onto State Route 143, and was greeted by a series of warning signs indicating they were about to enter a secure establishment. A U-turn section of blacktop provided the directionally challenged a last opportunity to retreat before falling under the suspicion and authority of the heavily guarded gate that loomed dead ahead.

"Look at that list of prohibited items," Quags said, reading a sign standing in the median. "No weapons, no firearms, no explosives, no alcohol, no cameras, no narcotics, no gambling."

"Sounds like fun."

"And no soliciting or distribution of handbills, whatever the hell that means."

"I'll let you ask."

The police cruiser continued past the turnaround and several MPs came out of the guard house—a red brick building with a green metal roof, tinted windows, and myriad security cameras.

"They're armed, Chief," Quags said. "Assault rifles."

"I see them," Gates replied. He lowered the window as an MP approached the driver's side. A second MP moved to the rear of the vehicle, eyes glued to Quags's reflection in the side mirror. A third MP appeared from behind the guard house and stepped into the middle of the road. Looking through the still-closed gate, Quags noted the man's finger on the trigger guard of his weapon.

"That's a lot of hardware out there," Quags whispered.

The MP tapped on the roof of the car and bent over. "May I help you?" the MP asked, seemingly assessing the car's occupants with a steely stare.

"My name is Charles Gates. I'm the chief of police for the city of Williamsburg."

The MP stoically ran his eyes over the logo on the side of the vehicle and then Gates's uniform. "And who's your passenger?"

"Luis Millares. Detective. City of Williamsburg Police Department."

"Your car and attire notwithstanding, we still need to see identification."

Gates and Quags offered their police credentials to the MP who carefully examined the IDs.

"And what business do you have with the base, Chief Gates?"

"We'd like to speak with someone in charge regarding an active police investigation being undertaken by the Williamsburg PD."

"Could you be more specific?"

"That's something we'd prefer to discuss with whoever is in charge."

The MP's glare bounced back and forth between Gates and Quags.

"Please wait here. Let me contact the public liaison officer. It may take a moment."

"Thank you."

The MP holding their police credentials entered the guard house. The other armed MPs maintained their positions, one in front of the car, the other to the rear.

Quags assessed their surroundings. "A twelve-foot security fence topped with razor wire, six visible security cameras, multiple lanes of Jersey walls, a tire-rip exit gate . . . and probably at least a dozen other things we can't see. We couldn't do anything subversive even if we wanted to."

"Sounds about right. This place is considered to be the main training facility for the CIA, after all."

"Or maybe it's all a smokescreen. Maybe this place is really a swanky resort for intelligence big wigs. Golf. Tennis. A fancy restaurant. Bird watching and massages."

"Bird watching?"

"Just thinking aloud."

"Feel free to rein in that impulse," Gates said, his voice laced with caution.

Minutes passed in silence before the lead MP returned. Seconds later, two additional MPs appeared from the guard house. One held a dog firmly on a leash. The other pushed a pole attached to a mirror on wheels.

The lead MP reached the car window and spoke. "The public liaison officer has agreed to see you. Please unlock your doors, open your trunk, and exit the vehicle. We're going to perform a security sweep and then you'll be escorted to the visitor center." The MP pointed to a second building a hundred yards away that appeared to be a larger version of the guard house.

Quags leaned across the center console to speak through the open driver's window. "Just so there are no surprises, we're both carrying loaded handguns and there are shotguns in the trunk."

"Outside weapons are not permitted on the premises by non-base personnel. You can sign in your weapons here at the gate and we'll keep them secure until you leave. Please step from the vehicle."

An MP with a handheld metal detector searched both officers and the explosives-detecting dog sniffed around the perimeter of the cruiser before traversing across the back seat. The MP with the wheeled mirror examined the undercarriage of the vehicle.

Finished with their inspection and weapon confiscation protocol, the lead MP returned the their credentials and provided further instructions. "When you reach the visitor center, please park in one of the marked spaces and remain in your vehicle until your escort indicates it is safe to exit."

"Yes, sir," Gates answered.

A black Suburban SUV appeared on the inside of the gate. The MP opened the cruiser's driver's-side door and motioned for Chief Gates to get back behind the wheel. "Please follow your escort."

"Can I ask the name of the person we're meeting with?"

"Devon Childress. Public liaison officer and chief of security."

*

Two MPs got out of the black SUV to escort Gates and Quags from their parked vehicle to the entrance of the visitor center. Following their guests through the doors, the MPs took up position near the entrance, standing at attention, posture perfect.

Quags and Gates walked around the large barren room. Historical maps and black-and-white photos of Seabees from the 1940s hung on the walls. Unmarked doors on the far side of the room gave no indication of what was behind them. After a slow, deliberate lap of the space, Gates and Quags sat down in matching chairs across from a sofa. A lone coffee table, sans reading material, stood between the limited seating options.

"I get the feeling this visitor center doesn't see many visitors," Quags said.

"You'll get no argument from me. And I'd assume we're under surveillance. Video and audio. So keep your thinking aloud to a minimum."

"Roger that, Chief."

As if on cue, one of the unmarked doors opened and a tall, thin, well-dressed, middle-aged man approached.

Gates and Quags stood and presented their credentials. Introductions followed and Quags offered the man his business card.

"Welcome to the Armed Forces Experimental Training Activity, or AFETA for short," the man said.

"Thank you for making the time to see us," Gates interjected.

"You're welcome. I understand that an active investigation has brought you out this way. How can I be of assistance?" Devon Childress asked, his large Adam's apple bouncing with each word. At six foot four, his lanky frame towered over his visitors as his eyes moved between the officers.

"Can we see some credentials?" Gates asked, the request seeming to surprise the one-man welcoming committee.

Childress patted his suit pockets and pulled out a base badge tangled in a lanyard. He passed his badge to Gates who read the front and then flipped it over.

"Your badge says you're employed by the DOD," Gates stated.

"That's correct. AFETA is a DOD establishment. And before we go any further, I don't want this conversation to start off on the wrong foot. I appreciate the efforts of all law enforcement, but I am very limited with the information that I can share regarding this facility."

"AFETA," Quags confirmed.

"That's correct."

"Why don't you call this place Camp Peary? Or The Farm? Everyone else does," Quags asked.

"Those are not the official names."

"Is everyone on the base employed by the DOD?" Gates asked.

"I'm afraid that's classified information," Childress responded with a smile.

"And your official title is public liaison officer and chief of security?"

"That's correct."

"An impressive job title. What does that entail?"

"It entails exactly what the title indicates."

Quags let his eyes wander around the room. "I see that you have no shortage of MPs on base."

"Technically, they're not MPs. They're SPOs."

"Which is?" Quags asked.

"Security protective officers. Part of the Security Protective Services. They're responsible for protecting this facility, its equipment, its people, and its secrets."

"Do they report to you?"

"That's also classified."

"But you're the chief of security," Quags prompted.

"Yes. But our security needs are atypical. It is very rare for someone to attempt to breach the perimeter of this facility. Our security directives are aimed at protecting this facility, its equipment, its people, and its secrets from exposure to nefarious elements."

"On that note, we believe that a suspect who committed a crime thirty-five years ago is now here at this facility," Gates said.

"May I ask as to the nature of the crime in question?"

"Murder in the first degree."

"That's a very serious allegation."

"It's a serious investigation. We have a partial fingerprint match and believe the person who left that fingerprint was in a vehicle that accompanied a Blue Bird bus to this facility."

Chief Gates provided the details of the good Samaritan at Walgreens in Richmond, and the subsequent chain of evidence. "Given the multiple disguises our suspect wore, we have an incomplete picture of his true appearance. Which brought us to you for assistance."

"I see. That is concerning. I'll certainly help in any way that I can."

"We'd like the names of those individuals who were in Richmond on Tuesday of this week. It should be a short list. Our suspect is a white male, between five eight and six foot. Average build. Has to be fifty or older. Given his age, it's likely the suspect is either an instructor or a member of base management. Maybe someone in operations. In addition to the list of those in Richmond on Tuesday, we'd also like the list of people currently on base who were here in 1986 and 1987."

"I understand your position and your request. And I'm sure you can appreciate the nature of our mission here at AFETA. Given their extremely sensitive nature, personnel records are classified."

"But they are kept, yes?"

"To be sure."

"And someone like yourself must have the capability to access them."

"There is a procedure."

"Why don't we bypass the process and you provide us with the list of names?" Quags interjected. "It doesn't have to be anything fancy. Just jot them down on the back of a napkin."

"Once again, I appreciate your position. The formal procedure pertaining to personnel records is that I pass your request, in writing, to our legal department. They will assess the request and make a decision."

"We're talking about a potential murder suspect."

"I understand. But protocols exist for a reason. And between us, even if I were in possession of personnel files, it would not be my decision to release them. Revealing classified material without authorization is a punishable offense."

"Murder is also punishable offense," Quags said.

Childress nodded and Quags scowled.

"Can you tell us what the group in Richmond was doing on the day in question?" Quags asked. "They appeared to exhibit unusual behavior."

"That information is classified."

"Perhaps we can speak with your superior."

"At this facility, I am the public-facing authority."

"I'm curious. Is your real name Devon Childress?"

Childress smiled again. "That's also classified."

Chief Gates tried to temper his subordinate. "What about fingerprint records? I assume all base personnel have successfully passed a security background investigation."

"Yes."

"And fingerprints are part of that background check."

"They are. But prints and other highly sensitive information are not stored locally."

"Where are they?"

"Prints are stored in a secure, off-site facility. Access to them is extremely restricted."

"So, another dead end." Quags chimed in.

Childress rubbed his chin. "Maybe we can work this out in reverse and everyone can still get what they want," he offered.

"What did you have in mind?" Chief Gates asked.

"Could you provide me with the surveillance video that has piqued your curiosity? I may be able to identify the person in question."

"We can do that."

"Also, would it be possible for you to provide me with a copy of the partial fingerprint you've obtained? I can then have it checked against our personnel files for a match. Or, alternatively, if you have the fingerprints from the original crime scene, we could also match to those."

As Chief Gates mulled over the offer, Quags stared hard at Childress, as if attempting to cut through the man's stoic exterior.

"Very well, Mr. Childress," Chief Gates conceded. "We can send you a copy of the surveillance video and the partial print pulled off the weapon earlier this week in Richmond. We can also provide you with a copy of the print from the original crime scene. Detective Millares will deliver all of them personally."

"You can drop them off at the front gate. I'll let them know you'll be stopping by."

"How long will it take to compare the prints to those in your files?" Chief Gates asked.

"A few days. A week on the outside. I'm at the mercy of formal protocols that need to be followed."

Chief Gates responded before Quags could protest. "That's fine."

"Great. We're glad to assist. I do believe this is the most expedient path for resolution."

"It's a path. We'll have to see how expedient it is," Quags said. "As Chief Gates indicated, the number of people who fit our suspect's description, and who were in Richmond on Tuesday, has to be a short list of spies, or spy support personnel."

Devon Childress clicked his tongue against the side of his mouth and shook his head slowly. "Contrary to popular belief, there are no spies here. Spies are the individuals who are recruited to provide intelligence. CIA case officers manage spies. Case officers themselves, are not spies. There's a big difference between the two."

"I appreciate the clarification. I'll be more exact in my phrasing going forward."

Childress raised a finger and removed a cell phone from his pocket. "Excuse me for a moment. I need to check this."

Gates and Quags waited as Childress scrolled down his phone screen. When he was finished, Gates restarted the conversation. "I don't want there to be any misunderstanding, so to wrap things up, we'll provide you with a copy of the surveillance videos and fingerprints, which you will match against your print records."

"That's correct."

"And you'll submit a formal request for the identification of those people in Richmond on Tuesday and those who were on base in 1986 and 1987. While we're waiting for the fingerprint comparison results, we can get a head start on a suspect list."

"I'll submit your request to our legal department. Ultimately, the decision regarding personnel files will come from my superiors. But I do understand your position, Chief Gates. And if I were in your shoes, I'd feel the same way you do. Losing a loved one to a violent crime can be traumatic. Especially a younger sibling."

Chief Gates frowned at the sudden revelation by Childress. "Did you run a background check on me?"

"On both of you. I hope you're not offended. It's standard protocol for drop-in guests."

"Then identifying our suspect should be a cakewalk for you," Gates said.

"I'll do my best. Have a good afternoon, Chief Gates. Your escort will see you back to the gate. We'll be in touch."

CHAPTER 13

DEVON CHILDRESS STOOD by the front door of the visitor center and waited until his surprise afternoon guests reclaimed their weapons from the main gate and exited the base. He crossed the floor of the visitor center, opened a door to a small office, and sunk into the leather chair. He picked the phone off the desk and punched a key.

"Did you catch all of that?" he asked Paul Paulsen, chief counsel for Camp Peary, who was seated a hundred and fifty miles north of the base.

"I did. The audio was crystal clear," Paulsen replied. "Any truth to it?"

"In this business, there's usually a bit of truth in everything. We did have a group in Richmond on the date in question. Standard SDRs. Thirty people in total. Six instructors, twenty-four trainees."

"Were you participating?"

"No. I was in meetings here on base most of the day."

"And how many of the instructors in Richmond were, as described, average middle-aged white guys?"

"Four of the six. The other two were white women."

"Not a very diverse group."

"New hires in the eighties were largely white. Consequently, most of our current instructors are as well. In another ten years, the demographics of instructors will be different."

"Any guess on which specific instructor was involved in the incident described by the Williamsburg PD?"

"Without even seeing the video, based on the information provided, I have a hunch. Ken Zara."

"I assume that's a pseudo."

"It is. Everyone calls him Zee."

"I'll need his employee identification number."

"I'll send it as soon as I'm back in my office."

"And what about this instructor makes you suspicious of him?"

"Nothing, except that he has an extensive background in martial arts. Based on the description of the incident in question, it seems probable."

"And he's a career clandestine officer?"

"Yes."

"That may be a first. A case officer who's actually skilled in martial arts."

"Don't tell Hollywood. But in this instance, that's what we have. He started studying martial arts at an early age. If I remember correctly, his father was a hand-to-hand combat instructor for the marines."

"Do you think he's capable of murder?" Paulsen asked.

"I can't say. I'd rather wait for evidence before drawing any conclusions."

"I appreciate that sentiment."

"I hope it's all a misunderstanding. Or a poor print analysis."

"Did any of the trainees who were in Richmond report seeing the alleged altercation between this instructor and the perpetrator?"

"They did not."

"Why would that be?"

"Well, I can think of a couple of reasons. But let me question the trainees and see what they have to say."

"Fair enough. Forward the fingerprint files when you receive them from the Williamsburg PD. I'll have it compared to the prints from his personnel files. I also want to see this surveillance video."

"How about a polygraph?" Childress suggested.

"That was my next suggestion. Let's run him and a few other instructors through a standard security update. Make it look innocuous. Just a run-of-the-mill polygraph with extra attention to criminal history."

"I agree with testing additional instructors. It may limit suspicion."

"It should."

"We have two polygraph examiners on permanent rotation here, but it may be better to use someone our suspect and the other instructors don't see on a regular basis."

"I'll arrange for one. We'll fly down together."

"And what about the police's request for personnel files? I have limited information here on site. Date of birth. Employee identification numbers. Official assignment. Beyond that, most of the information is in Langley."

"I'll get my hands on Ken Zara's personnel file."

"And the request for the personnel records for everyone on base who was in Williamsburg during the years of the murders?"

"Do you really think that's necessary?" Paulsen asked.

"I don't, but it was requested."

"I can't make any promises on that. As you know, personnel data is a particularly sensitive issue down in your neck of the woods."

"Fine, but the Williamsburg PD is not the only one interested in the personnel files. I'd like to know if we have a murderer in our midst."

"I'll try to get a pulse on that request, find a polygraph examiner, and arrange for travel. I'll touch base with your tomorrow morning."

"Understood."

"And to be on the safe side, let's keep an extra eye on Zara until we sort this out."

"That works for me."

CHAPTER 14

WITH THE ROAD to Camp Peary in the rearview mirror, Quags fumed. "I hate to break it to you, Chief, but Childress has no intention of helping."

"What makes you say that?"

"Years of dealing with liars. He knows who our guy is. The rest was him blowing smoke."

"He was following orders. Unlike yourself, I'm sure the chief of security for the CIA's top training facility has protocols he can't bypass."

"I'm just trying to save you from wasting your time."

"We'll send him the surveillance feeds and fingerprints and wait for the results. We'll know in a couple of days if he's going to assist."

"He's not going to."

"Time will tell," Gates said, his voice trailing off. "Have you ever dealt with anyone from Camp Peary before?"

"Camp Peary, specifically?"

"Yes."

"Not that I'm aware of. I did meet a guy last year whose girlfriend claimed he was a spy."

"His girlfriend claimed he was?"

"That's right."

"Who?"

"Just a guy I used to pass in the hall in the middle of the night," Quags replied.

Gates took his eyes off the road and glanced over at Quags. "Are you going to make me ask for an explanation?"

"It's not what you think."

"I don't know what to think."

"*Mamacita* owns a two-bedroom walk-up, and she rents out her extra bedroom. When we were doing our thing, she had a roommate. A girl named Jenny. Jenny said the guy she was dating was a spy. I don't know how true the story was. I mean, Jenny was a bartender, which made me think if she was dating was a spy, they would've been an odd couple. I always figured maybe the guy was lying to get laid. He was probably an Uber driver or something. But for what it's worth, I didn't get the impression that Jenny was making it up. So if the guy was lying, he had convinced her."

"A bartender?"

"Indeed. She had a good head on her shoulders. More tattoos and piercings than you can shake a stick at. Probably had some daddy issues. But she wasn't stupid."

"Did you ever ask the guy what he did?"

"Nope. I only met him a few times. And I didn't want him asking me about being a detective, so I didn't ask him about what he did. And he didn't offer. Besides, we weren't there to hang out with each other. *Mamacita* used to call the guy Jenny's hit-and-run. My lasting impression of him was that he could go all night. Between his stamina, Jenny's moaning, and the echoing hardwood floors, it was tough to get a good night's sleep when he stayed over."

"I'm not sure how that intel is going to be helpful."

"You asked."

"I don't think I asked for that," Gates replied.

"You know anyone from the base?"

"If you live around these parts long enough, you're bound to run into people involved in intelligence, or who were previously involved."

"We had a couple of DC spooks sit in on a drug investigation briefing once in Miami. They didn't say much. Kept their cards close to their vests."

"That sounds about right. Forthcoming with information is not one of their mottos. Around here, if you strike up a conversation with someone who says they're in town for a seminar on finance, retirement, or supply chain, chances are that you've found a spy."

"I think you mean a 'case officer.'" Quags smirked.

"Thanks for the reminder. Go ahead and get Childress the fingerprints and let's regroup in the morning. I need to run a few things by the commonwealth's attorney."

"Bow Tie Bramble?"

"One and the same."

"You want company?"

"It's probably better if I go alone. There's certain protocol to follow."

"That hurt."

"I'll bring you up to speed after I meet with him."

"Roger that," Quags replied.

"And for now, let's keep a low profile on this. No one wants to upset the goose that lays the golden eggs. After W&M and the local school systems, Camp Peary is the area's largest employer."

"Understood."

Chief Gates pulled up to the curb in front of the Williamsburg Police Department and Quags got out. "If you need me for anything, Chief, give me a call. I'm going to take a drive and check on something."

*

Chief Gates parked behind the Mellow Mushroom at Merchant Square in Colonial Williamsburg. He climbed from his car and paused as a horse pulled an empty buggy down the gravel street, hooves plodding slowly after a day of carrying tourists. A colonial block later, he arrived at Aroma's Coffee Shop, stepped inside, and removed his sunglasses. A quick scan of the room was sufficient to spot his mark in the far back corner.

"So this is where you go to get away from it all," Chief Gates said, approaching the man at the table. An open laptop rested on a stack of papers next to a large coffee cup. Sean "Bow Tie" Bramble, commonwealth's attorney for Williamsburg and James City County, looked up over his blue bow tie and smiled, white teeth topped by an almost equally white mustache.

"Only on Tuesday evenings," Bramble replied. "And only during the fall semester."

"I called your office. They mentioned I might be able find you here."

"It's my quiet time before my weekly lecture."

"What are you teaching this semester?"

"The Fourth Amendment."

"Search and Seizure."

"Indeed."

"It's been so long time since I've been in a classroom, I doubt I'd survive law school if I had to do it over."

"I think you'd pull through. And it's a different perspective from behind the podium. I find teaching law keeps me sharp. It also allows me to keep a foot in the academic world. Something to consider when I retire."

"I hate to point out the obvious but, technically, that wouldn't be retiring."

Bow Tie Bramble grinned again. "If you ever want to be a guest speaker, my podium is your podium. Or better yet, you could help run a mock trial. A career law enforcement officer with a law degree would be well-received by the students. Not to mention your personal background. We could livestream it to UVA, too, if you want. Your alma mater."

"What's the pay?"

"Pro bono," Bramble answered, motioning toward the empty chair on the other side of the table for Gates to sit.

"Pro bono? What if I send a detective who worked on drug cartel cases in Miami?"

"Absolutely. He'd work too. Just give me the word."

"I'll pass it along."

"So, what brings you out, Chief?"

Gates took a measured gander around the room before delivering the news. "We have a lead on the Matoaka murders."

Bow Tie Bramble's eyes widened. "Jesus."

Gates nodded.

Bramble closed his laptop. "Your sister's case. I can't imagine how you feel."

"You're the second person to say that. I'm trying to not feel anything yet."

"How solid is the lead?"

"A person of interest."

"A local?"

"Not exactly. The evidence indicates the suspect likely works on The Farm."

"I hope you mean *a farm*."

"I don't. The Farm, Camp Peary."

Bramble winced, took a deep breath, and exhaled. "Do you have a name for your suspect?"

"Not yet. That's the goal."

"A photo?"

"We have photos, but none of them are particularly useful. The suspect was in disguise. I'm going to try to have them enhanced."

"In disguise? Interesting."

"We have a partial fingerprint match. It was pulled off a gun used in an attempted robbery of a drugstore in Richmond earlier this week. We think the print was from a middle-aged white male who thwarted the robbery. We don't have confirmation yet, but the most likely scenario is that during the scuffle, he grabbed the gun and left a print. Which makes him a potential murderer *and* a good Samaritan."

"Not an everyday occurrence."

"That's what we were thinking as well. But the good Samaritan left the scene before the police arrived. Hence, we don't have a name."

"Are you sure it was his fingerprint?"

"Sure? No. But it's promising."

"And what evidence do you have that he works on The Farm?"

"Blue Birds. The buses, not the ones with wings." Chief Gates took a minute to explain the investigation, ending with Childress's promise to help.

When Gates finished his summary, Bramble fiddled with his bow tie and took a sip of his coffee. "I wish you would've spoken to me before going to the base."

"Probably should have."

"It's water under the bridge now."

"My detective thinks that Childress isn't going to help. That it was all lip service."

"Is this the same detective you mentioned a minute ago? The one with drug cartel experience?"

"It is."

"He deserves a raise."

"You agree?"

"Let me tell you a story."

"You've been down this road before?"

Bramble nodded. "Eleven or twelve years ago we worked the case of a CIA employee driving under the influence. Or at least we believed it was a CIA employee. The suspect was heading east on I-64 and sideswiped several vehicles between Richmond and Camp Peary. Sent one car off the road and the driver of that vehicle sustained serious injuries. Multiple motorists called 911 to report an erratic driver. A state police cruiser was dispatched to intercept, but the suspect had returned to The Farm and was on the other side of the main gate before the police arrived. And that's as far as the authorities got. They had the license plate of the car, a permanent tag, government issue, and they had a rough description of the man behind the wheel. Not a perfect case, but enough to investigate. We approached the base the following morning with a subpoena. We never made it past the gate."

"Any legitimate legal reason?"

"Legitimacy is in the eyes of the beholder. For starters, they claimed the information on the subpoena was incorrect. The CIA was specifically named in the subpoena, which turned out to be problematic because the CIA doesn't officially recognize The Farm as an installation. The base is run by the DOD."

"That point was made to us as well. What happened next?"

"We reworked our original subpoena, but at the end of the day, it didn't matter."

"Why not?"

"Let's test your legal skills, Chief. Do you recall *United States v. Reynolds*?"

"It was a Supreme Court ruling from the fifties that led to state secrets privilege."

"Very good. You get an A. I told you law school would still be easy for you."

"I got lucky."

"At any rate, from the time the legal decision for *US v. Reynolds* was made in 1953 until the turn of the century, state secrets privilege had only been invoked by the US government a handful of times. Since 9/11, however, its use has expanded exponentially. This is despite the fact that the Supreme Court originally specified that the privilege 'was not to be lightly invoked.'"

"Meaning that the courts generally favor the position of the government when they claim, 'We can't tell you for national security reasons.'"

"That's correct. Since 1953, the courts have rejected the state secrets privilege assertion by the government a grand total of four times."

"That's not promising." Gates frowned.

"No, it's not. And if state secrets privilege isn't invoked, or if it's rejected by the courts, the government has the Intelligence Identities Protection Act and the Classified Information Procedures Act. The IIPA makes it illegal to reveal the true identity of an intelligence agent and CIPA governs how classified information can be used in criminal cases."

"You learned all this from a drunk driving case?"

"I learned how Camp Peary personnel uses these tools in law enforcement matters."

"I'd hope the CIA's attitude toward a murderer would be more cooperative."

"Indictments against its employees is not a CIA priority. Espionage notwithstanding."

"If my detective is right and Childress doesn't assist in the investigation, I want to issue a subpoena for the records I need."

"How broad is the request?"

"Narrow. White male, average height, average build, who was in Richmond on Tuesday of last week."

"And who was also in Williamsburg thirty-five years ago," Bramble quickly surmised.

"Yes. If that's the case, it would simplify our investigation. We could match a name from current employee records with personnel records for 1986 and 1987. Match a name, match a print. Done."

"I can tell you without question that the CIA is not going to let you shuffle through their personnel records. They're not going to let you see their list of employees. They're not going to hand over fingerprints of their employees. Not unless they're forced to."

"I just need one name."

"You're underestimating how protective the CIA is of their agents' identities."

"Perhaps."

"Are you aware that instructors on The Farm don't know the trainees' real names? Conversely, the trainees don't know their instructors' real names either."

"How is that possible?"

"You can thank Jim Nicholson."

"The spy?"

"Traitor. But yes, one and the same. Nicholson was a career intelligence officer. At the end of his career, he became an instructor on The Farm. He was responsible for selling the Russians a list of all CIA officer trainees who were on The Farm while he was there. A full list. Complete names. Birthdays. The whole shebang. He exposed two years' worth of trainees, most of whom had to move on to other careers. It's hard to be an intelligence officer when everyone knows who you are before you even get started."

"Do you think they keep personnel records on the premises?"

"Hard to say. Compartmentalization is a key component of the Agency's ability to maintain secrecy. I know that CIA employees do not have remote access to CIA servers. If a CIA analyst or officer wants to access the CIA computer system, they have to physically be in a CIA facility. So it's possible that personnel records are not kept locally. And if they are, access could be limited, or the files could be incomplete."

"I can understand not using real names among trainees, but I'd think the instructors know each other and their true identities."

"Common sense would indicate such, but some intelligence officers have been known to use the same pseudonym for decades. It may not be that clear cut." Bramble let out a long deep sigh. "Do you know how many active CIA case officers have ever been charged with a crime and had their real name revealed?"

"No."

"Three. And here's why. Let's say we have a career intelligence officer who is now employed at The Farm as an instructor, or another job not in the intelligence field. Who knows what secrets that guy harbors? How many people would be endangered if he were publicly outed? How many years of intelligence could be spoiled by putting his face on the news? Particularly with a long-standing cold case, such as your sister's. It would garner unprecedented press coverage. The CIA won't allow that to happen. There's a reason that CIA operatives killed in the line of duty get an anonymous star on the wall at Langley."

Gates digested the less-than-optimistic trajectory of his case. "There has to be a way."

"The fact is the number of criminal cases charging people with outing an intelligence officer is far greater than the number of CIA employees charged with any crime. I wish it were different, but the data speaks for itself."

"You're describing an entity that is beyond the law."

"I'm saying they aren't going to help prosecute one of their own and they have the means at their disposal to deflect inquiries."

"And if I want to go forward with the subpoena anyway?"

"Just give me the word."

"If our friends at Camp Peary don't do what they've promised, I want to move forward with it."

"Very well," Bramble answered, leaning back in his chair. "There's something else I'd be remiss not to mention."

"What's that?"

"Given that your sister was one of the victims, you need to be very careful about your involvement in this case. You don't have a legal obligation to recuse yourself from the investigation, but if I were a defense lawyer, I would be screaming prejudice and bias. So my legal advice is to let one of your detectives handle the investigation and for you to stay away from the collection and handling of evidence."

"The only evidence we have at the moment is a fingerprint collected by the Richmond Police, which they matched against the state police database. My hands are clean on this case."

"Keep it that way."

"I'll take it under advisement."

"And my offer to be a guest speaker still stands."

Gates gave a small nod of acknowledgment. "We can talk about it after I put this investigation to rest."

CHAPTER 15

THE COMMERCIAL TAP House in the Fan served twenty draft beers on rotation. A dented copper bar, a dozen tables, and a pool table completed the interior decor. The exterior of the building boasted its history—twin wood-paneled rowhouses, stuck wall-to-wall for the last two hundred years.

Quags walked through the front door, parted a group of millennials, and found a stool at the end of the bar. He examined the available beers, the list handwritten on a chalkboard on the wall, and waited for the blond bartender with tattoos on her arms to turn around. When she did, she let out a squeal.

"Quags! Oh my God! What are you doing here? It's been a while. It's so good to see you!"

Jenny leaned over, displaying ample cleavage, and hugged Quags roughly around his neck, planting a kiss on his cheek.

"How are you?" Quags asked.

"Good. You know how it goes. Have you seen Ivonne?"

"I talked to her. She told me where I could find you."

"Are the two of you going to make another run at it?"

"I don't think either of us was seriously making a run at it."

"You know what I mean."

"We'll see. We never officially dated, and we never officially broke up either. Things just ran their course."

Jenny smiled and winked. Quags noticed the freshly shaved side of her head and an additional nose ring.

"What are you drinking?" she asked.

"Looks like I should try a beer."

Jenny waved her hand in front of the chalkboard. "Twenty to choose from."

"Get me something in the middle of the road."

"Done."

Jenny returned with a mug and put it on the bar.

"You said you asked Ivonne where I was."

"I did."

"That makes it sound like you were looking for me."

"Guilty as charged. I wanted to talk to you about your boyfriend."

"Grant?"

"Yeah," Quags said. "The guy you claimed was a spy. Ivonne mentioned you broke up."

"We did. He moved to Oregon. He opened a weed farm with his brother outside of Portland."

"So was he lying to you about being a spy?"

"I don't think so. He said he washed out of the program."

"If pot farming was his backup plan, I'm not surprised."

"He claimed the pot farm was his brother's idea. Grant never smoked when he was in training."

"In training?"

"That's what he called it."

"So he wasn't lying about being in intelligence?"

"He was either a spy, or a very convincing liar."

"I think one is a job requirement for the other."

"Maybe."

"Did he tell you anything interesting?"

"Before he washed out, he didn't tell me jack, other than he was in training. And he only told me that because I thought he was cheating on me. Caught him one day in Richmond out with a girl he claimed was a coworker. But after he washed out, he told me all kinds of juicy stuff. More than he should have. He was pissed for being thrown out after wasting over a year of his life."

"Where was he in training?"

"Come on, Quags. Everyone knows where the CIA trains its spies. All of them go through The Farm."

"Is that what he said?"

"Yep. Spent five months at Camp Peary. He also said they went to North Carolina for a few weeks. Somewhere near a swamp."

"What else did he tell you?"

"Lots. I made him watch *The Recruit* and picked his brain. Have you seen it?"

"I think. But it's been a while. Refresh my memory."

"Basically it's about a guy who was recruited by the CIA, went through training at The Farm, and then discovered his mentor is spying for the other team."

Quags nodded. "I vaguely recall it."

"According to Grant, there was a lot of truth to the movie, mixed with a bit of bullshit. The basic training course at The Farm covers things such as survival tactics, evasive driving, lockpicking, parachuting. He said he learned to use a variety of guns." Jenny paused. "You want to guess what he said was the worst part?"

"No idea."

"Writing reports. Apparently spies spend a lot of time writing reports about what they did or are going to do. And they practice writing reports while on The Farm."

"Is that why he was thrown out?"

"Not according to Grant. He said he was thrown out for violating rules during a training exercise."

"A rules violation? You mean he cheated?"

"I guess it depends on your perspective. He told me one of the unofficial mottos of the CIA is 'Lie, cheat, and steal. Just don't get caught.'"

"*Coño.*"

"So when he said he washed out for cheating, I think it meant he got caught."

"Did he say anything else about it?"

"He said they were in Atlanta. Spotting tails or following others and trying not to be spotted. Practicing how to exchange information without being detected. He said sometimes they wore disguises."

"And how did he cheat?"

"He broke the rules. Some areas of the city were off limits for surveillance and countersurveillance. He ignored the rules and then lied about it. He didn't think it was a big deal. Apparently the instructors did. Seems kind of silly, really. Grown-ups playing hide-and-seek. I mean, that's not what they called it. That's what I called it. They had a name for it, but I can't remember."

Jenny wandered off to the other end of the bar and Quags listened to her take an order for six different beers. When she returned, he asked another question. "Did your boyfriend ever mention anyone by name? Any instructors or other trainees?"

"By name? No. From what I gathered, everyone used a fake name. Grant said he called himself Gavin during training. A lot of people chose alternate names with the same first initial as their real name."

"Did you ever think his real name was Gavin and he told everyone his name was Grant?"

"I checked his driver's license. He was Grant."

"Come on. You work in a bar. You know you can't believe every ID you see."

"I never looked at it that way."

"What about the instructors? Did they use their real names?"

"I don't know about that."

"Could you ask?"

"Who? Grant?"

"Yes."

"I'd rather not."

"Things didn't end well?"

Jenny dropped her voice to a whisper. "Things ended with gonorrhea."

"That'll do it."

"But if you really need me to ask him, I will. I can send him a text or email. See if he responds."

"I would appreciate it."

"Only because you're the one asking."

A glass broke somewhere near the pool table and Jenny disappeared. When she returned she yelled, "Rabbit."

"Rabbit what?" Quags asked.

"That was the name of the hide-and-seek spy game they were playing. Rabbit."

"Rabbit, huh?"

"For sure. You got me curious, Quags. Why the sudden interest in The Farm?"

"No reason."

"Really? Nothing?"

Quags smiled. "Let's just say I'm hunting rabbits."

CHAPTER 16

CHIEF GATES WALKED across the backyard under a waxing moon and bright stars. He stepped under the small portico and knocked on the door to the former slave quarters behind the main house. A moment later, Chief Gates's father opened the door to the Dad Shack. Dressed in jeans, work boots, and a flannel shirt, Gates Senior resembled an LL Bean catalog model. A full head of white hair rested above green eyes and a weathered face.

"Got a minute, Dad?" Chief Gates asked.

"Always. I keep saying I don't know why you knock. Just come on in."

The chief entered and sat down on a love seat. His father took the matching chair opposite his son. Behind him a TV was on, the sound on mute. Myriad family pictures hung on the wall.

"What's on the agenda?" Gates Senior asked. "Looks like something's bothering you."

"What gave me away?"

"Only takes a glance to know your mood. One of the advantages of watching you since you were a little boy."

Chief Gates searched for words to break the ice, then spoke. "I got a call from the Richmond PD a few days ago. They hit on a partial fingerprint match to the one pulled off of Heather's Walkman."

"Richmond?"

"Yes. But that's where the story started. Currently it ends at The Farm. Camp Peary." Chief Gates explained the chain of events, their assumptions, and the lack of concrete evidence.

"If all we have is the partial print match, we'll still need more. As of now, the Williamsburg Police Department doesn't have anything that could get a conviction. We think our suspect is employed on The Farm but I'm not sure how we're going to identify him without assistance. All we have is a montage of less-than-ideal photographs without a name. We have a request in for personnel files with the chief of security at the base."

"What about a subpoena?"

"That's the next step if our request is denied. I spoke with the commonwealth's attorney for the east district and he gave me the lay of the land. We may have limited options if they choose not to cooperate."

"And what happens then?"

"I'll find another way."

"Such as?"

"I've been kicking around a few options. We met with Dell White earlier to confirm a few details on the bus. That visit got me to thinking. Do you know anyone who works on base?"

"Most of the folks I knew are long since retired or dead. But all types work on The Farm. During the nineties, they had quite a construction boom. Built all kinds of stuff. Dormitories. State-of-the-art gym. New docks down on the river. I can ask around and may be able come up with a few names. It's been twenty-some years. Give me a day or two and let me think about it."

"I would prefer to keep it quiet if we can."

"You don't know anyone?"

"We've all met Agency types over the years, as you do growing up in this area. But I don't know anyone who's going to be helpful in identifying a particular individual on base. Hopefully our request for information on our suspect will bear fruit and I won't have to look at another avenue to get what I need. When the chief of police starts asking questions, folks have a tendency to gossip. I'm trying to avoid that."

"I'll poke around and see what I can find out."

"On the down low."

"Yes, Charlie."

Chief Gates began to stand and his father motioned him back into his seat. "Son, you have to promise me something."

"What's that, Dad?"

"If you find out who killed Heather, you let me know. I don't care if there's enough evidence for a conviction or not. If you know, you tell me. I'm getting old. I'll take justice any way I can get it."

"I'm going to pretend I didn't hear that."

"Pretend all you want, but I've been waiting for a long time. Too long to let it slip away now. If you can ID the killer, you need to tell me. Evidence or not."

Chief Gates sat in silence, staring at his father. Moments later, he stood. His father showed him to the door. Chief Gates could feel his father's eyes on his back, watching him as he crossed the yard in the direction of the main house.

*

Chief Gates reached the porch as his wife stepped through the kitchen door with a joint pinched in her left hand and a glass of wine in her right. The trilling of insects echoed across the vast darkness of the back field. A lone light shone through a window in the Dad Shack. Barbara lowered herself into a porch chair and placed her wineglass on a small table.

"You know, if someone would have found out a couple of years ago that the police chief's wife smoked marijuana, I would have been out of a job," Gates said.

"Times have changed. And so has the law. Besides, if a fifty-year-old history professor can't smoke pot every once in a while, who can? I'm not driving anywhere. There are no kids around. I'm sitting on my back porch. And sometimes this little bit of plant helps the chief of police get laid."

"You should do pro-marijuana commercials."

"Yes, I should," Barbara said, a smile lighting her eyes as she took a drag off the joint. "We didn't have much of a chance to talk last night. Anything new on the investigation?"

Chief Gates provided an update on the case, finishing with, "So today, we paid a visit to Camp Peary."

"Well, how'd *that* go?"

"The jury is still out. After Camp Peary, I went to visit Sean Bramble."

"Bow Tie Bramble? What did he have to say?"

"He indicated that he expects resistance to our investigation. I'm considering other options."

"What do you have in mind? Wait for this suspect to leave the base, pull him over, and fingerprint him?"

"Camp Peary is two miles outside of Williamsburg city limits. My jurisdiction doesn't allow me to pull people over in York County. It would be thrown out of court immediately." Charlie waited for the crickets in the field to quiet after an intermittent crescendo. "Who do you know who works at The Farm?"

"I know Maria Pacheco caters special events on base. Usually when big wigs come to visit. I know Deana Ray works in the dining hall, though I haven't seen her in forever. Silvia's husband works for York County Sanitation. I remember her saying they pick up trash from certain areas of the base. She once said her husband has to go through periodic security reviews."

Chief Gates committed the possibilities to memory as his wife continued.

"Every year there's a group of W&M history students who spend a week on The Farm, researching and excavating the remains of Bigler's Mill and Magruder, two lost towns that were relocated when the base was built. There's not much left beyond a church, a graveyard, and a few houses, but students are allowed to spend time on the base once a year. I could put you on the list. Maybe you could spot your guy. If you know what he looks like."

"Even if I knew what he looked like, I'd have to be incredibly lucky. The base is 10,000 acres."

"I'm just throwing it out there as a possibility."

"Thanks, but I'll see what else I can come up with."

"As long as it isn't sneaking onto the base without an invitation. That would be a good way to get shot."

"I hadn't considered that route."

"Then forget I mentioned it," Barbara said, taking a sip of wine. "You know, most people in these parts are good neighbors and patriots, and protective of The Farm and what goes on there. And I get that. But, Chief, you also have to realize you have an ace in the hole."

"I do?"

"Yep. You're a Williamsburg native and the Matoaka case has been stuck in the craw of a lot of people for a long time. Ask for help from the right person and you'll probably get it."

"I'll give your advice its due attention."

"Good. Now, come inside and give your wife her due attention."

*

Chief Gates rolled over and took a sip of water from the glass on his nightstand. "Who do you know in the Computer Science Department at work? Maybe they can help enhance some of the images of our suspect taken from surveillance feeds in Richmond."

"Jesus, Chief. You could at least pretend you enjoyed the sex you just had."

"I did. And unless you were faking it, you seemed to enjoy it as well."

"Have you ever heard of afterglow? What if I just rolled over after sex and asked some unrelated question like, 'Do you like ham'?"

"I'd say 'Who's making the sandwiches?'"

"You're hopeless."

"Does that mean you won't set me up with the Computer Science Department?"

"I'm friends with Christine Lui. She's the department chair. You've met her before. Twice."

"You'd think I'd remember a woman in charge of the Computer Science Department."

"I'll assume that comment was a function of poor memory and not a question of qualification based on Dr. Lui's gender."

"Of course."

"Good answer. Blood must be returning to your brain. Your decision-making is improving. I'll ask her and see what she says."

*

Gates Senior sat on a wooden chair, staring into the hall closet. The revelation of a lead in his daughter's death had led him to two large footlockers stored in the back. The footlockers were all that was left of his daughter, outside of memories and photographs. Lids still open, his eyes roved over the contents. Framed achievements bestowed upon one Heather Gates were stacked neatly in the corner of the nearest footlocker. Her high school graduation cap partially covered her first pair of shoes. A jewelry box housed far more trinkets than treasures. A stack of birthday cards were spread across an old cassette carrying case.

Gates Senior wiped a tear from his eye and stood from the old wooden chair. He left the footlockers open for the time being and moved to the small kitchenette to pour a glass of bourbon. He stared up at the family photos on the wall, his eyes finally coming to rest on a photograph of Heather sitting on the saddle of a horse. Tilting the glass upward, Gates Senior swallowed the drink in one gulp. Staring back at the photograph, another tear ran down his cheek.

CHAPTER 17

THE WHEELS OF the Gulfstream G450 touched down just beyond the large number 23 painted on Camp Peary's sole runway. The small jet with seating for fourteen taxied to the end of the blacktop and came to a halt. Minutes later, the plane door opened and lowered to the ground, the internal portion of the door providing a staircase from the fuselage to the tarmac. Devon Childress pulled his Toyota Land Cruiser to the edge of the runway, collected his two guests and their bags, and drove toward the main administration building.

"How was your flight?" he asked Paulsen, Camp Peary's chief counsel from Langley.

"Uneventful," Paulsen responded, his slight Boston accent seemingly more pronounced in person.

"Uneventful is good."

Childress looked in the rearview mirror at the polygraph examiner, whose gaze was focused through the window at a gun range in the distance. "First time to Camp Peary?" Childress asked.

The polygraph examiner shook his head. "No. I was here twice before, but it was dark both times. There wasn't much to see."

"You didn't miss anything. Seeing things here is a lot like not seeing things at all."

The polygraph examiner didn't respond, and Childress turned back toward Paulsen in the passenger seat.

"Did you find anything interesting in the files?"

"That's a conversation for the SCIF," Paulsen replied.

"We'll be there in five minutes."

*

Childress opened the door and let the examiner enter the room first, the back of the man's suit wrinkled from the day's journey. "We have a water cooler in the corner. The thermostat is on the wall. Feel free to change the temperature," Childress offered.

"It should be fine."

"How long will it take you to set up your equipment?" Childress asked.

"Thirty minutes should be enough," the man replied, resting two briefcases on the floor. "Is there a restroom nearby?"

"Next door," Childress responded. "We'll be down the hall. Last room on the left. We have coffee and donuts."

"Thank you. Right now, the only thing I need is a lavatory."

*

The sensitive compartmented information facility was in a windowless room on the second floor with the least enviable view on base. Resembling a clear cargo container laden with high tech equipment to prevent electronic eavesdropping, the box also housed a metal table with four matching chairs. The smooth walls and bright lights added to the ambience of the confined space. Straitjackets were the only thing missing.

Paulsen followed Childress into the SCIF, placed his leather bag on the smooth table, and sat down. As Childress settled into his seat, Paulsen removed a series of manila folders from his bag. Flipping through the files, Paulsen selected one and rotated it so that Childress could read it.

"Based on your confirmation of the subject from the security videos taken in Richmond, we limited our print analysis to the individual you identified as Ken Zara. As you are probably aware, his true name is Kirk Zambrano."

"And?"

"The fingerprint comparison analysis was determined to be inconclusive."

"The Richmond Police were wrong?" Childress asked.

"When it comes to prints, wrong and inconclusive are subjective. There's no official universal standard for comparing prints. The analyst noted similarities between the prints from the Williamsburg PD and those on file with the Agency, but not enough to provide a definitive answer."

"Did we compare Zambrano's fingerprints the Agency has on file to the prints from the original Matoaka crime scene thirty-five years ago?"

"The Agency decided that the partial print analysis from the recent print in Richmond was sufficient."

"What does that mean to us, exactly?"

Paulsen looked around the soundproof room as if seeking verification of its ability to keep a secret. "The Agency's official position is that the print analysis was inconclusive. That assessment was approved by the seventh floor."

"We have families here on base. If there's something I need to know to maintain security, I would like to be informed. Even off-the-record, unofficial guidance would be appreciated."

"In our business, there are times we should read between the lines and follow orders. Rest assured, your position is clear."

"I hope it is."

"I will make a note of it again. Now let's take a look at Zambrano's personnel files. The lawyer highlighted the employee's background as Childress followed along. "Zambrano applied for employment with the CIA in 1985 and joined the company in 1986. His training period on The Farm began in the fall of 1986 and ended in the spring of 1987. Please note this timeframe coincides with the Matoaka murders."

"Unfortunately, it does."

"After his training here, and a short stint back at Langley, his first posting was in Tokyo. His second posting was Bangkok. He spent two years in Kuala Lumpur. After that, he was in Beijing for four years, and then Seoul, where he's been ever since. He speaks Japanese, Korean, and Chinese, based on his last language evaluations. Those three languages make a very unique case officer. The fact that he is white makes him even more rare."

"And now he's here at Camp Peary as an instructor with his sights set on retirement."

"I cannot speak to his motivations, but it wouldn't be out of the norm."

"What are our expectations for the polygraph?"

Paulsen pulled out another file and opened it. "In the last twenty years, Zambrano has undergone thirteen polygraphs. He's never indicated deception. That includes questions about past criminal behavior. On several occasions, he has been asked whether or not he has ever intentionally hurt another person, up to and including murder."

"And he showed no deception?"

"None. But there is a caveat. Before his assignment to Beijing, he was trained in polygraph countermeasures. Standard protocol for all case officers serving in China, Russia, and Cuba."

"And how many polygraphs has he taken after we trained him how to beat the machine?"

Paulsen grimaced. "Four."

"Someone needs to explain to me why we train someone to beat the polygraph and then continue to polygraph them for security updates."

"Rules are rules. Requirements are requirements. Checkboxes are checkboxes. And we're both aware of the limitations of the polygraph. But as I said, the previous nine polygraphs, those taken before his countermeasure training, covered criminal behavior and consequently the years of the Williamsburg murders. He should have flagged as deceptive on one of those nine exams. "

"Or maybe he's equally gifted as a liar and a murderer."

"That's not an opinion the Agency is willing to embrace at this time."

Childress seemed to consider the implications of the conversation. "And if our suspect took a polygraph pertaining to the murders, and he somehow failed that polygraph, those results would be counterproductive to plausible deniability."

"That was discussed as well."

"Is the seventh floor aware this is an active police investigation and that one of the victims is the sister of Williamsburg's chief of police?"

"Everyone is aware. I was present in the meetings and subsequent legal discussions."

"And what is your opinion? What do you think?" Childress asked.

"God knows we don't need the black eye of a CIA career employee being involved in a series of murders."

"I concur."

"But if there's one thing I've learned in my time with the Agency, it's that some individuals are inherently better at concealing deception than others. History tells us there are natural born liars out there. The question is whether Kirk Zambrano is one. "

CHAPTER 18

"HOW DID YESTERDAY'S meeting with the commonwealth's attorney go?" Quags asked, catching up with Gates as his boss headed toward the elevator.

"He offered you a guest lecturing opportunity if you want it. Or a mock trial. He's teaching a class at W&M law school."

"Does it pay?"

"Only in good karma."

"I might need some."

"The commonwealth's attorney seems to think you're right about our friends at Camp Peary. He doesn't believe they're going to help with our investigation."

"I would gloat about being right, but I'd rather know about our suspect and his fingerprint."

The elevator doors opened and Quags and Gates stepped in. Gates pressed the button for the garage and the doors closed.

Gates continued to summarize his conversation with Bramble. "He also cautioned us about revealing the identity of an undercover intelligence officer. He reminded me that it's a felony. He went on to say the US government will show greater enthusiasm for charging someone who reveals the identity of an intelligence officer than it will to prosecute an intelligence officer who perpetrates a felony."

"*Coño*. Was there any good news?"

"He indicated he's willing to sign off on a subpoena if we don't get what we want from the Camp Peary Liaison Office."

"That's promising."

"Anything new on your end?"

"I went to Richmond to find a spy."

"Your booty call partner-in-crime?"

"Yes. Turns out he actually was at Camp Peary, but he was terminated. He moved to the West Coast and is now a pot farmer."

"You must be kidding."

"I'm not."

"What did the pot farmer say?"

"Nothing. We didn't talk. I asked *mamacita*'s roommate to let him know I wanted to speak with him. We'll see how it goes. I'm not holding my breath."

"I can see how a pot farmer may not want to speak with a police detective."

"It's legal there. It's legal here."

"Yes, it is. As my wife likes to remind me."

"Really?" Quags raised an eyebrow.

"I don't want to talk about it."

"Fair enough."

"On the topic of my wife, I asked her to hook us up with the Computer Science Department at the college. I was thinking they could help us enhance some of the images of our suspect. It may not amount to anything, but I thought it was worth a shot."

"Good idea."

"A great idea if it works."

CHAPTER 19

THE FOURTH AND final polygraph subject of the day, Instructor Zee, sat motionless in the chair. Two straps wrapped around his midsection to monitor his breathing. A blood pressure cuff rested snugly on his left bicep. Additional sensors were attached to his fingers to measure perspiration. Another sensor was embedded into the seat cushion of the chair, designed to detect clenching of the anus, a countermeasure employed on control questions.

"Feet flat on the floor, fingers spread," the polygraph examiner said as he typed the necessary parameters into his computer. Confirming the connection between wires for a final time, he probed his subject with preliminary chitchat.

"When was your last polygraph?"

"In the spring."

"How did you feel it went?"

"Identical to the previous twelve times."

"Is that the actual number?"

"It is."

"Is there any particular reason you keep count?"

"Is there any particular reason I shouldn't?"

"It's just a curious observation. I've been doing this a long time. I don't recall anyone who has taken so many exams to know the exact number."

"Recollection is paramount in my line of work. I also recall that we met briefly in Beijing nine years ago. You came to perform an exam on a potential asset."

"Then I apologize for not remembering you."

"No apology necessary."

"I usually recollect the faces of people I've administered exams to."

"Then next time we meet, you'll remember."

"Hopefully," the examiner said. "I think we're ready to begin the exam. Please try to relax and we'll get you out of here as quickly as possible."

"Will do."

"Here we go."

"Fire in the hole."

An hour later, the polygraph examiner shuffled around the SCIF, preparing to present the results of the exams to his two-man audience. A modest spread of build-it-yourself sandwich components sat on a corner table outside the SCIF. A pot of coffee stood near the condiments and a tower of Styrofoam cups. Childress paced the floor while Paulsen worked on his laptop, scribbled on a yellow legal pad, and stuffed deli meat into his mouth.

"I'm ready when you are," the polygraph examiner said, poking his head out of the SCIF's doorway.

Paulsen balanced his sandwich on his legal pad and Childress retrieved a fresh coffee. Stepping back into the SCIF, Childress gave the examiner the green light to proceed.

The examiner took a sip of water and cleared his throat. "I ran all four subjects through the standard security update covering loyalty to the US, loyalty to the Agency, disclosure of state secrets, drug usage, drinking habits, agency procedures, ownership of foreign assets, recent foreign contacts, current finances, criminal behavior . . ."

"We can skip the standard explanation. What are the results for the last instructor?" Childress asked.

The polygrapher shuffled through his paperwork. "I determined the last test subject was DNI."

"Deception not indicated?"

"That's correct. He was nondeceptive. He was truthful in his responses. As were all the other three instructors."

"I would like to stick with the last instructor for a moment."

"As you wish."

"Did you ask him about the Matoaka murders?"

"I asked if he was familiar with the Matoaka murders, and he confirmed he had heard the name. I asked if he was involved in any way with the murders, and he replied in the negative. I asked if he had ever been involved in any murder, and he also replied in the negative. No deception was indicated on any of those questions. He also indicated no deception when I asked if he'd been truthful on all the questions posed to him during the exam and during all past exams."

"In summary, he passed," Childress confirmed.

"Convincingly. The subject's biometric response was unwavering. His breath held steady at sixteen per minute. His heart rate ranged between fifty-nine and sixty-two beats per minute. Minimal perspiration was detected. He didn't respond in any way that would make me believe he was untruthful. By all measures at my disposal, he was DNI. As I said, all four test subjects were."

Childress studied the examiner's face. "How confident are you?"

The polygraph examiner took off his glasses and rubbed the bridge of his nose. "As confident as I can be in this profession."

"Thanks for your time and for coming down on such short notice," Childress said.

"It's the job. I'll have a complete written summary prepared before we leave. All I need is a desk in a corner somewhere."

*

Alone again in the SCIF, Childress locked eyes with Paulsen. "What does legal counsel think?" Childress asked.

"My initial thought is 'Thank the Lord.' The polygraph examination indicated no deception. The fingerprint analysis was inconclusive. Officially and legally, we have no reason to do anything. But we have options."

"Such as?"

"We could run him through additional polygraphs with different examiners and see if the results change."

"If Zambrano's been trained on countermeasures, the polygraph doesn't mean much. Additional tests won't change that."

"We could also play it safe and have him reassigned to some far-flung location. Perhaps Kyrgyzstan. We could make the reassignment as posh or as full of hardship as we choose. Or we could do nothing."

Childress sighed.

"What about you?" Paulsen asked. "What are your specific concerns?"

"As I said previously, what concerns me more than anything is the possibility of having a bona fide criminal here on The Farm. Living on base. We have a good number of families here."

"That's a valid concern. Maybe a better-safe-than-sorry alternative is prudent in this instance. I'll expedite discussions back at Langley. In the meantime, continue to keep an eye on him."

"I'll arrange for surveillance," Childress answered. "What about the Williamsburg PD's request for records? As I mentioned before, the chief of police's sister was one of the victims. He's not going to let it go."

"Direct their inquiry to my office. I'll handle all of the correspondence with law enforcement from here," Paulsen patted the top of the personnel records. "If you want to keep Zambrano's personnel files, I need a release signature on the dotted line and they're yours. You are ordered to keep them under lock and key and to put them in a burn bag when you're done with them."

"Destroy after consumption. Got it."

CHAPTER 20

MCGLOTHLIN-STREET HALL WAS a three-story brick building on the campus of William & Mary. The building's exterior architecture did little to reveal the nature of its tenants, the traditional brick facade more suitable for a library than a state-of-the-art Computer Science Department.

"What's the name of the professor we're going to see?" Quags asked Gates as they approached the front steps.

"Dr. Christine Lui."

"Do you know her?"

"My wife says I've met her a couple of times."

"But you don't remember?"

"I don't. Who knows, maybe she won't remember me either. That would put us on even footing."

"Oh, I'm sure she won't remember meeting the chief of police."

"Third floor," Gates said, scowling and pointing at the tenant board on the lobby wall.

Quags pressed the button for the elevator. A minute later they stepped into an open space filled with tables, computers, and the requisite geek accoutrements. An Asian woman in a business suit stepped around the corner and introduced herself.

"Hi. I'm Christine Lui. Nice to see you again, Chief Gates. It's been a while."

Gates winced almost imperceptibly and Quags stifled a grin.

"Likewise, Dr. Lui. This is one of my detectives, Luis Millares."

"It's a pleasure, Detective. And please call me Christine."

"Yes, ma'am, and please feel free to call me Quags," he replied, giving her a polite nod.

"It's my understanding that you come bearing gifts. We've never had law enforcement ask us for assistance, so this is a first. We're excited to help."

Gates handed Dr. Lui a high-capacity thumb drive. "Everything is on this."

"Let's see what we've got," Dr. Lui responded, taking the device and heading in the direction of a glass-walled corner office. Inside the room, she shut the door and plugged in the drive. A screen on the wall sprang to life.

"What am I looking at?" Dr. Lui asked.

"This is an attempted robbery at a Walgreens in Richmond last week," Gates informed her.

"Richmond?"

"Yes. But we believe one of the individuals in the video is responsible for a crime here in Williamsburg. Hence, our jurisdictional interest."

"I see." Dr. Lui never took her eyes off the screen.

Quags stepped forward and pointed to their suspect. "We're trying to get a better idea of what the guy in the hat and beard really looks like. We have multiple views of him from different angles. But in addition to the inherent low quality of surveillance videos, we had other complications."

"Such as?"

"The man altered his appearance," Gates said.

"How?"

"Different hats. Glasses. Facial hair."

"Interesting."

"We were wondering if you could work some magic and get us a better look at the man behind the disguises. We're also interested in whether that man actually touched the weapon in the course of an altercation that is central to the case."

"First of all, we don't do magic here, Chief. We do coding," Dr. Lui responded with a wink.

"I stand corrected."

"We have software that can extrapolate an existing image, or in this case, multiple images, and provide alternatives that may be more accurate. We can also enhance the video to try and determine whether or not your man touched the weapon."

"Sounds promising."

"It's not perfect. But it should get us closer to some answers."

"How long will it take?"

"How many hours of video are we looking at?"

"Over a hundred, but that's the total amount of surveillance feeds we received. Videos with our man in them are only a couple of hours in total."

"I'll have one of my grad students get started on it. First we'll enhance the images, and then we'll run them through the software for extrapolation. It should only take a day or two."

CHAPTER 21

EXITING MCGLOTHLIN-STREET HALL, Chief Gates checked his voice mail and deleted the first two. The third voice mail grabbed his attention, and he stuck his finger in his opposite ear to isolate his concentration. A half minute later, he hung up.

"Childress called."

"What did he say?" Quags asked.

"That he has news and we should call him."

"Let's return his call when we get back to the station. We don't need to have a public conversation with the CIA."

Gates cranked his neck in each direction, noting the students that were crisscrossing the lawn and sidewalks of the college campus. "Good idea."

*

Back in his office at police HQ, Gates called Childress's number, left a message, and hung up.

"Five bucks says he calls back within sixty seconds," Quags said.

"You're on," Gates replied, extending his hand to seal the deal. Before he could release his grip, his phone rang. "*Coño*," he swore.

"Nice Spanish, Boss. There's hope for you yet."

Gates answered the call and informed Childress he was putting him on speaker.

"Who's on the line?" Childress asked, his voice echoing.

"It's just Detective Millares and myself on this end," Gates said. "We're anxious to hear what you've learned."

"Well, it's not good news, I'm afraid. Not for your investigation. The print analysis came back as inconclusive."

"For all of the middle-aged white males who were in Richmond on the day in question?" Gates asked.

"For those who fit the bill."

"I'll take that to mean you recognized the man from the surveillance video and you only ran his prints," Quags surmised.

Childress ignored the summation. "The individual whose prints we analyzed also took a polygraph. He passed with flying colors. No deception indicated."

"Did you match the prints from the personnel file to the partial print from Walgreens? Or did you match the prints from the personnel file to the print from the Matoaka crime scene?" Gates asked.

"The details of the print analysis are classified. However, suffice it to say, our analysis is state-of-the-art."

"I'm sure it is, and I wouldn't want to insinuate anything to the contrary," Quags said, keeping the frustration out of his voice.

"Thank you for your understanding."

"I know we asked before, but would it be possible to have this individual's full prints so we can run the comparison ourselves? You can even redact the name."

"That's not my call to make."

"Whose call is it?"

"I have been instructed to inform you that all future communication and requests on this subject will be handled by Paul Paulsen in our legal department. I can provide you with his number."

"You're blowing us off."

"I understand your frustration. That being said, legal is the point of contact for all future inquiries regarding this investigation. I'm sure you can appreciate the chain of command, given your profession."

"We can," Gates replied, then hung up the phone and looked over at Quags.

"*Puta*," Quags said.

"Looks like we're going the hard route." Gates grimaced.

"Which is?"

"Back to the commonwealth's attorney. Time to officially rock the boat."

"I asked before and I'll ask again. Do you want company?"

"Nope. Time for you to get in touch with your detective roots."

"I can't wait to hear what that means."

CHAPTER 22

CHIEF GATES, IN full uniform, stepped into the sprawling office that occupied the third floor overlooking Monticello Avenue. A mix of lawyers, interns, paralegals, and administrative assistants buzzed across the floor, cubicle to cubicle and conference room to conference room, supporting the legal efforts of the commonwealth's attorney for Williamsburg and James City County.

Gates bisected the open lobby, strolling across the blue carpet with the state's seal woven in the center. He approached the young woman at the receptionist's desk and spoke, letting his uniform provide the bulk of the introduction. "I'm here to see Sean Bramble. He's expecting me."

"Yes, sir, Chief Gates. Follow me."

The woman rose from her chair, walked down a short hall, and pulled open a pair of wooden doors that stretched to the ceiling. Gates stepped into the smaller vestibule and peeked into the office on his right. The receptionist knocked quietly on the doorframe and nodded, motioning toward Gates with her other hand.

"Come in, Charlie," Sean Bramble said, stabbing a piece of lettuce with his fork.

"Thank you," Gates said to the receptionist as she disappeared through the double doors, returning to her position in the main lobby.

As Gates entered the office, Bramble continued to shovel salad into his mouth. A bib attempted to protect his bow tie from splashing dressing. A stack of unprotected files lay splayed across his desk, drops of errant oil and vinegar soaking into the legal documents.

"Sorry to interrupt your lunch. Thank you for making time."

Bramble waved his hand in front of his face as if to dismiss the interruption. Swallowing hard, he wiped his bib on his mouth and used his tongue to dislodge a piece of food stuck between two teeth.

"Hard to get coffee or lunch with you lurking around," Bramble joked, hoping to lighten the mood.

Gates sat down without an invitation. "We heard back from Camp Peary."

"And?"

"You were right. It doesn't appear as if they're inclined to help. In fact, they may prove to be an additional hindrance."

"How's that?"

"They've identified our suspect. They claim to have performed a print analysis between this individual's prints and those from the weapon recovered in Richmond."

"And it would be difficult to match prints to an individual without knowing who they were."

"Exactly."

"What did their print analysis show?"

"It was determined to be inconclusive."

"Of course it was."

"And they refused our second request to run the comparison on our side. And when I asked them whether they compared the prints they have on file to the original print from my sister's crime scene, they claimed it was classified."

"Not surprising."

"They also claim to have run our individual through a polygraph. The suspect passed."

"That's not good."

"If you believe them."

Bramble made a low growling sound and patted his hand on his chest.

"You all right?"

"Fine. Fine. Looks like the ball is back in your court, Chief. What do you want to do?"

"Let's go ahead with the subpoena."

"It's ready to be signed. And we're still looking for the personnel files for all of those individuals currently on base who were in Richmond last week, or any individual who was in Williamsburg during the time of the Matoaka murders and is now on base. And we would like access to their fingerprints."

"It's pretty straight forward."

"It is, but unfortunately, simplicity doesn't equate to success."

"I'm aware."

"And if the subpoena doesn't work?"

Gates took a deep breath and shook his head. "Let's just say I don't think the commonwealth's attorney needs to know what I'm thinking."

"Maybe we can have a drink and a chat about it when it's all over with."

"This investigation is only going to end one way. Someone's going to jail."

"I hope it's not you," Sean Bramble said matter-of-factly. "Let's get your subpoena."

CHAPTER 23

PARKED ON THE exit ramp, Quags sat behind the wheel of his unmarked police cruiser, stakeout staples littering the car. His dash camera was in full-record mode. A second camera was on the passenger seat, next to a bag of pork rinds. Water bottles and a Red Bull can lay on the floor. A cup of cold coffee sat in the console. His phone charger cable ran across his legal pad, the first few pages filled with a combo of doodles and detective notes.

The morning's coffee filled Quags's bladder, and he exited the vehicle, traffic on the highway racing by unabated fifty yards away. Stepping into a grove of short pines on the embankment, Quags relieved himself while trying to maintain one eye on the ramp. Precarious footing and divided attention resulted in wet shoes and Spanish expletives. As Quags finished, a black SUV pulled in behind his vehicle and came to a stop. Pulling up his zipper, Quags appeared from the tree line. Two men in dark suits and darker sunglasses stepped from the SUV.

"Williamsburg, PD," Quags announced, reaching for his badge and holding it out. Stumbling down the embankment and finding his footing on level ground, Quags assessed the situation and moved to the front of his vehicle. The two men followed Quags, one on each side of the police cruiser.

"How can I help you gentlemen?" Quags asked, successfully luring the men away from their SUV to the front of the police car.

"What are you doing out here?" the taller man asked.

"Investigating."

"Investigating what?"

"Murder."

The two men seemed surprised and Quags turned the tables on his visitors.

"Who sent you out here? Childress?" Quags asked.

"That's not a name we are familiar with."

"Really, the chief of security? You don't know him?"

"That's classified."

"It's not classified if I'm telling you."

The shorter of the two men attempted to flex his jurisdictional muscle. "In the interest of national security, we would kindly ask that you move the location of your current investigation."

"On whose authority?"

"National security."

"Who decides what's a matter of national security?"

"We do."

"That's not how the constitution works. I'm standing on public property investigating a series of murders."

"You're out of your jurisdiction."

"And so are you. We've contacted the York County Police and informed them of our intent to investigate from this location."

"We don't take direction from York County law enforcement."

"Apparently you guys don't take orders from anyone. But your jurisdiction ends at that big fence on the other side of the highway. I'd say from where we're standing, you have to be at least a quarter of a mile off base."

"Protecting national security allows us considerable leeway on jurisdiction."

"Says you."

The shorter man repeated his request. "We're going to kindly ask that you move your investigation to a more suitable location."

"Are you planning to arrest me? Detain me?"

"If we have to."

"If you're going to arrest me, I want the two of you to do me a favor. Look at the windshield of my car. Say hi to the dash camera."

The men cranked their necks toward the police vehicle. "You don't have permission to film us."

"I don't need permission. That's the idea of public property. And Virginia is a single-party consent state."

The two men looked at each other, turned, and walked back to their SUV.

"I guess that means we're done here," Quags said, raising his voice over the din of the highway.

Seconds later the SUV drove up the ramp and turned in the direction of the base. As the vehicle crossed the bridge over the highway, the driver stuck his hand out the window and gave Quags the middle finger.

"*Pendejo*," Quags said aloud.

*

Quags carried his legal pad into Chief Gates's office and shut the door behind him.

Gates peered over the screen of the laptop on his desk.

"How did the stakeout go?"

"The jury's still out. I did get harassed by two guys from the base. It was a brief conversation."

"Were they SPOs?"

"I don't know. No uniform. Dark Chevy SUV and sunglasses. I told them they were being recorded by my dashcam. It seemed to terminate their interest in me."

"Let's hear what you found," Gates said, closing his laptop.

"What I found is that stakeouts get harder with age."

"Doesn't everything?"

"Napping gets easier."

"I stand corrected."

Quags read the top page of his notes. "Here's the rundown. I arrived a little after eight this morning. Between eight and four thirty, I counted a total of fifty-nine vehicles heading up the exit ramp in the direction of the entrance to The Farm. I couldn't see the vehicles actually enter or interact with the guards, but they headed in that direction and the only thing at the end of the street is Camp Peary."

Gates nodded, agreeing with Quags's assessment. "It's a close-enough approximation for our purposes."

"Like I said, the total vehicle count was fifty-nine, but a majority of them were before 9:00 a.m. Between 8:30 and 9:00 alone, I counted thirty-two vehicles. Almost all of them had Virginia tags. All types of vehicles. Cars, trucks, work vehicles. Even a Mini Cooper."

"Sounds like civilians who work on the base," Gates stated.

"That's what I figured too. I wrote down every plate and got a photograph of each car."

"We only need one to pan out."

"There were a few companies who visited the base that may prove helpful. In order of appearance, we have Deer Park Water, Tidewater Landscaping, Vulcan Concrete, and the Virginia Department of Health. I contacted the landscaping company, and no one was interested in speaking about their business with Camp Peary. The president flat out told me he couldn't afford to lose his contract with the base and that he had signed an NDA. Local Deer Park distribution told me to contact their legal department. I still have a call in to the Virginia Department of Health and Vulcan Concrete. Oh, and a car carrier visited the base. It was registered to Tompkins Used Cars."

"Tompkins Used Cars?"

Quags confirmed the details on his legal pad. "Yep. It entered the base just before eleven this morning. Had a load of cars on it."

"Barry Tompkins?"

"Sounds right. A friend of yours?" Quags asked.

"I know him."

"Do you think he'd be willing to talk to us?"

"Depends on how much he's had to drink. Any chance you play poker?"

Quags grinned. "I've been known to. And if this investigation requires playing poker and drinking, rest assured, I'm your man."

"Barry Tompkins is a third generation used car salesman, which means he is genetically predisposed to talking shit. He's also a lousy poker player. But he is a great host."

"Is that good or bad?"

"We'll find out."

CHAPTER 24

THE RURAL END of Bush Neck Road terminated at a circular driveway in front of a simple brick rambler. To the left of the house a second gravel driveway extended toward the rear of the property.

"What's back here?" Quags asked as the car edged forward.

"The boathouse and poker room," Gates said, parking next to a line of trucks positioned in the dark shadow of thick trees. Quags got out of the vehicle and admired the moon reflecting off the surface of the water that stretched out into the darkness.

"What body of water is that?"

"Buzzard Bay. Just past the point is the Chickahominy River."

"I've fished the Chickahominy. Lots of bass and yellow perch."

"And loads of mosquitos," Gates added, swatting at the back of his neck.

"You said this guy hosts a regular poker game?"

"Like clockwork."

"They play for money?"

"Is there another reason?"

"Do they know you're coming? The chief of police could be a downer."

"I have a standing invitation. Once in a while, I take them up on it."

"Then everyone's going to be friendly when we get inside, right? No one's going to lose their cool because law enforcement crashed the party?"

"There shouldn't be a problem. Unless there are new faces. I know most of the regular guys pretty well."

Quags reached into the holster in the back of his waistband and touched his gun.

Gates looked over suspiciously.

"Call me cautious," Quags said.

"I'll call you more than that if you touch your weapon in there."

*

Cursing wafted through the screened porch on the back of the boathouse. Chief Gates knocked on the door and then pulled it open with a screech of rusted hinges. Thick pine beams ran across the ceiling of the main room, stretching over a sea of handmade wood furniture. Stepping across the threshold, a dozen chip-pushers at two tables greeted the chief in an uncoordinated chorus.

Barry Tompkins, homeowner and pit boss, rose from his seat and steadied himself on wobbly legs.

"You looking for a game, Chief?" Barry asked, ambling over to his guests, beer in hand.

"Not tonight."

Barry motioned with his eyes toward Quags. "Making an introduction for a friend?"

"No, this is one of my detectives, Luis Millares. We're here on business. You got a minute?"

"For you? Anytime."

Gates and Quags followed Barry through the back door onto the deck. A long pier jutted out into the water, disappearing into a cloud of fireflies. Halfway down the pier, two moored boats gently bobbed. Barry rested his back against the deck railing.

"What's on the agenda, Chief?"

"We want to ask you about The Farm."

Barry paused, took a sip of his beer, and then seemed to stammer. "Who says I know anything about that place?"

"I saw you drive a car carrier up to the gate yesterday," Quags said, piercing the man's flimsy initial defense.

"Even if I knew something, I couldn't talk about it."

"I know you're not supposed to," Gates replied.

"I signed an NDA."

"We're not looking for state secrets."

"Then what are you looking for? The Farm isn't within Williamsburg city limits, so it's outside of your jurisdiction. Unless I'm missing something."

"You're not missing anything. We believe a suspect from a crime here in Williamsburg may work on The Farm. That's the focus of our investigation," Quags said.

"What did they do?"

"Killed four people. In a single year," Gates responded.

The gravity of the revelation seemed to suck the wind out of Barry's lungs. "Damn, Chief. Matoaka?"

"That's right."

Barry turned to face the water of the bay, finished his drink, and wiped his mouth with his arm. "Well, Goddam, Charlie. Not beating around the bush, are we?"

"I've been waiting for thirty-five years. There's no time left for foreplay."

Barry shrugged and sighed. "I'll deny telling you anything if I'm ever asked."

"Fair enough. I'll deny I ever asked."

Barry glanced over Chief Gates's shoulder and eyed the screened porch door. "What do you want to know?"

"What kind of business are you doing with the base?"

"I take clunkers in and junkers out."

"What does that mean, exactly?" Quags asked.

"The base uses a lot of cars in training. They total most of them. A lot of them are shot to hell. Some are blown up. Rolled over. You name it."

"What kind of cars?"

"All kinds, but they prefer the bigger sedans. I get the impression they like them because they can take a lickin' and keep on tickin'. Like the old Timex commercial."

"How often do you make runs?" Gates asked.

"When they need them. Once a month, give or take."

"Where do you get your inventory?" Gates asked.

"I get a lot of cars at auctions, including police auctions. I know most of the used car dealers in the area and they know what I'm looking for. It's an easy sale."

"Who do you deal with on the base?" Gates asked.

"As far as contacts at the base go, I have a number for the public liaison officer. He's also the chief of security. He places the orders for the cars and deals with any payment issues."

"Childress?" Quags asked.

"That's right," Barry responded, seemingly surprised.

"And you contact him via phone?"

"I do. But when I call, it *always* goes to voice mail and he calls back."

"Who else do you deal with?"

"When I deliver the cars, I meet with someone at the driving school."

"Why do you call it the driving school?" Quags asked.

"Because that's what's written on the sign in front of the building. Not that you'd need the sign to figure it out. The building has a car track running behind it and a couple dozen parked cars. All black, red, and white."

"They only want vehicles of certain colors?" Quags asked.

"No, they'll take whatever color I can get, but they paint them. Either black, red, or white. That's all you see, cars arranged by color. I figure they must have a paint shop on the premises."

"Do you have a name for your contact at the driving school?"

"This year it's a guy named Putnam. It changes from time to time. Ditto for the base security officer."

"And this Putnam character lets you know when he needs vehicles?"

"I think the way it works is that Putnam contacts Childress and Childress contacts me. Then Childress arranges for the delivery. He provides a day and time. I arrive with a load of cars, the SPOs at the gate check my credentials, confirm my appointment, and escort me to the driving school. I unload the cars and the dogs give each of them a good sniff. After the dogs give the all clear, they're driven to a lot on the other side of the building. Once I'm done, I get a signature from Putnam and the SPOs escort me back to the gate."

"What about picking up cars?"

"If there's a pickup of junkers, I load them. If they can roll, that is. Sometimes these cars are so damaged, a flatbed is the only alternative."

"Do you go around the base and pick up the ones that can't roll?"

"Nope. I assume they have a flatbed on base to move the wrecked cars. When I pick up one that can't roll, it's just sitting in the usual area near the driving school. From there, I winch it up with my flatbed."

"Where do you take them?"

"I use a few different junkyards."

"How do you get paid?"

"Direct deposit from the Department of Defense."

"Anyone else you interact with?"

"I've met someone who I assumed was a mechanic. But he's not there every time."

"Do they ever refuse a car?"

"Not yet. Knock on wood. I make sure all of the cars run before I deliver them. But when you're going to blow up a vehicle, it doesn't have to be in perfect condition."

"Have you ever seen other parts of the base? Ever get a tour?"

"A tour? No. The Farm doesn't do tours for outsiders. My interaction with people on the base is limited. And I'm always escorted. In the eight years I've worked with them, I've spoken with exactly five people outside of the SPOs at the gate. I see other people, mind you. A lot of green bicycles. They must be free on base. I also see a good number of joggers. I've heard gunshots and explosions."

"You ever see anyone else coming or going? Any other civilians with business on the base?"

"Sure. Plenty of folks. Landscapers and such. But people with jobs on The Farm don't talk about it. You know how it is."

Gates seemed to digest the information. "Okay, Barry. Thanks for your time."

"Remember what we said about this conversation."

"What conversation?" Quags replied.

"Exactly."

CHAPTER 25

CHIEF GATES LOOKED at the name on the screen of his cell phone and stood. He strolled away from the dining room table and answered the phone as he entered the kitchen.

"Charlie speaking."

"Hey, Charlie, it's Sean Bramble. I've got an update on your subpoena."

"Fast news is not good news."

"We delivered a subpoena to Camp Peary and to the Agency's legal department in DC. Your request for records was moved to federal court for a hearing."

"That's awfully fast for removal of jurisdiction."

"I've seen cases bounce from state court to federal court before the prosecutor was even notified the subpoena had been served."

"So much for the government moving slow. And?"

"It's probable your request will be denied under state secrets privilege. The only hiccup on their side is that all claims of state secrets privilege have to be signed by the director of the CIA. I'm sure it's a formality, but it may take a day or two to get that signature."

"So, in a day or two, we're officially screwed."

"Not officially. There's still hope."

"Until there isn't."

"I also received a call from the Governor of Virginia. I'm an elected official, so he's not my boss, but he called to warn me that I was treading in the deep end of the pool. I thought I would pass that friendly warning on to you."

"Thanks."

"Given the current direction of the subpoena, if you have an ace up your sleeve, get ready to play it."

*

The annual pig roast was a Millares ritual. Quags poked a knife into the crispy skin of the pig on the *caja china* and declared it ready for consumption. The sixty-pound roasted swine was removed from the charcoal and placed on a long table covered in aluminum foil. Greedy fingers assaulted the swine, shreds of crunchy skin and steaming meat disappearing as if attacked by piranhas. Quags's mother, in her official *lechon* apron, stepped onto the patio and shooed the crowd swarming around the pig back to their chairs.

"Who took the tail?" she asked a moment later, suspecting a confession wasn't forthcoming.

Quags lowered himself into a rickety patio chair and handed a beer to his father who was seated next to him. "Happy birthday, Papi," he said, raising his own bottle in the air. "Salut."

"Salut."

Setting his beer on the lid of a cooler, Quags felt his phone vibrate and pulled it from his pocket. "What's up, Chief?"

"Bad news from the commonwealth's attorney. It looks like our request for records will be officially quashed by the courts in the next day or two."

"I hate to say I told you so, but I told you so."

"You did."

"What's the next step?"

"We keep going. We identify our guy. In the meantime, I'm thinking about poking the bear."

"You know I'm on board with that."

"Good. I was hoping you would be. How's the birthday party going?"

"The pig is done and we had a good run at the dominoes table. That's a winning birthday when you're Puerto Rican."

"And you're still going fishing tomorrow?"

"All day on the bay. I'll be out of pocket. Probably no phone reception."

"Then I'll hook up with you the day after tomorrow. Good luck, fishing."

"Sounds like I should say the same thing to you."

CHAPTER 26

NESTLED AMONG THE storefronts and business offices in Newport News's revitalized city center, the *Daily Press* occupied a one-story brick building, sharing prime real estate with the best shopping and restaurant options between Virginia Beach and Williamsburg.

Inside, the editor of the *Daily Press*, seventy-two-year-old Fred Hanlin, had the most envied view on the block. Not that he cared. He spent his days with NPR in the air and the written word on his mind. Not to mention that enjoying his view would require him to stand and peer over the tower of bound volumes that occupied the long window sill.

Gates popped his head through the threshold of Hanlin's office and announced himself. "Hey, Fred. It's Charlie Gates."

Hanlin straightened from his permanent stoop, flipped his combover back into position, and took off his reading glasses. Books littered the floor. A stack of newspapers teetered in the corner. Hanlin climbed from his seat, old knees creaking.

"Chief Gates. How are things in your neck of the woods? It's been a while."

"It has."

"If you ask me, it's a good sign when the chief of police doesn't have any news. Means things are going right."

"That's an optimistic view."

"Optimism is a badly needed currency these days. How's your father doing?"

"He's well."

"So, what brings you down the road today? Something going on in Williamsburg the press needs to know about?"

"Not exactly. I have a favor to ask."

"I'm at your beck and call."

Gates stepped back toward the open door and shut it.

Hanlin moved books from the tabletop onto an empty chair and offered Gates a seat on the other side of the table. "I apologize for the lack of organization."

"No problem. Tell me, what's the circulation of the *Daily Press* these days?"

"Physical or electronic?"

"Either. Both."

"Physical is around a hundred thousand. Electronic is about a quarter of that, but going up. We bought the *Virginia Gazette* a couple of years back and that added another thirty thousand. But, as you know, it's only published twice a week, on Wednesdays and Saturdays."

"I want to run something in the *Daily Press*."

"The *Gazette* still has its audience."

"I'm not interested in waiting until Saturday."

"I can run whatever you have in the *Daily Press* before the weekend and then again in the *Gazette* on Saturday."

"That'll work."

Hanlin wrote a note on a pad of paper next to his laptop. "What's the subject matter?"

"I want to run an article about the Matoaka murders."

Hanlin's eyebrows jumped, the topic seeming to catch the seasoned newspaper man off guard.

"The Matoaka murders?"

"That's right."

"Now I understand why you shut the office door. Did you catch a break in the case?"

"We got a potential fingerprint match. Unknown perp."

"You want the public's help finding the guy?"

Gates considered his response before offering it. "Not at this time."

"Meaning?"

"I just want to rustle the bushes a little."

Hanlin stared at Chief Gates. "See if you can get a snake to slither out?"

"I can't get into the specifics, but we'll need to be careful with the wording."

Hanlin again swiped his hand across his combover. "Well, if your UVA law degree and my fifty years as a journalist can't split hairs with a dictionary, who can? Let's see what we can pound out."

"I was thinking we set up the article as a cold case update. Remind the public that the crimes are still unsolved and that the police investigation is still active. Then I want to mention that law enforcement has recently discovered a new lead related to a fingerprint from one of the original crime scenes."

Hanlin nodded, his hands beginning to tap the keys on his laptop. For the next hour, the two men batted verbs and adjectives back and forth, crafting and fine-tuning a six-paragraph update that offered very little substance beyond the fact that a potential matching print had been discovered and is undergoing further analysis.

When they were finished, each man read the article in silence.

"Is that along the lines of what you had in mind?" Hanlin asked.

"That should do it."

"Any preference on where you want it? I was thinking about the front page, but below the fold."

"How does that work with an online newspaper? There is no fold."

"We call it, 'without the scroll.'"

"Clever. When can you have it in?"

Hanlin looked at the clock on the wall. "It can go out tomorrow if I get the wheels in motion."

"Tomorrow is perfect."

CHAPTER 27

FROM THE BOTTOM of the staircase, Chief Gates could hear his father talking to Barbara in the kitchen. The smell of coffee mixed with the sound of scrapple popping in the frying pan made his mouth water.

"Good morning," Gates said, entering the kitchen. "I see we have company for breakfast."

"Watch your mouth, son. I'm doing the cooking. If I were company, I'd be planted in a chair."

"To what do we owe the honor?"

Gates Senior snatched the morning edition of the paper off the counter and tossed it onto the table. "There's an interesting read on page one."

Chief Gates glanced down.

"It's been a long time since your sister's case has been in the newspaper," his wife said.

"Too damn long," Gates Senior added.

"For the record, as far as we're all concerned, we don't know anything about that article or where the information came from," Chief Gates admonished.

"The article claims an unnamed source," Barbara responded.

"And we all know the unnamed source is about to set the table for breakfast," Gates Senior snapped.

*

Barbara Gates passed the butter to the left and lifted two pieces of scrapple off the serving plate in the middle of the table.

"I thought there were laws against outing an intelligence officer," Gates Senior said.

"There are. But no one was mentioned by name, there was no insinuation that a suspect has been identified, and there was no solicitation to the public for help in identifying a potential suspect. And no part of the article was related to the intelligence community in any way," Chief Gates informed his father.

"Then what's the point?"

"It's just a reminder."

"Who are we reminding?"

"The person responsible for Heather's murder."

"You know more than you're letting on."

"We don't know what we don't know," the chief insisted.

"Oh, Jesus. Don't start with that shit. You know what you know. Period. Everything else you don't know, for Christ's sake."

Barbara Gates averted her eyes and added more cream to her coffee.

Chief Gates's phone vibrated on the table, offering a merciful pause to the conversation. Standing up, Gates took the call as he walked into the living room.

"Sorry to call you so early, Chief. But there's an incident you may want to be aware of."

"What is it?"

"They found a body near Lake Matoaka."

CHAPTER 28

CHIEF GATES STOPPED his car behind two ambulances and a fire truck. A pair of police cruisers were parked facing the opposite direction. The combination of emergency vehicles effectively blocked Mill Neck Road, a stretch of pavement without lines, curbs, or sidewalks. Gates stepped from his cruiser and a chill ran up his spine. He spotted Quags twenty yards away as the detective ended his conversation with a Williamsburg EMT who disappeared down the trail into the woods.

"Good morning, Chief," Quags said as his boss approached. "I was surprised to hear you were heading over."

"Any other location and I wouldn't have come. How did yesterday's fishing expedition go?"

"It was good. I was on my way back from my dad's when I heard dispatch mention Lake Matoaka."

"How long have you been here?"

"A while."

Gates peered at a brown wooden sign with a map of the lake's trails, and his gaze faded into a blank stare as memories swamped his thoughts.

"Are you all right, Chief?" Quags asked, pulling him back to the present.

Gates nodded. "I've only been to this area a couple of times in the last thirty-five years. We shut down a large homeless camp a few years back. Every now and then we get calls for illegal hunting. Campus police deals with most of the issues that arise. Kids partying in the woods. That type of thing."

"Harmless stuff."

"For the most part. What do we have this morning?" Gates asked, pointing in the direction of the trailhead.

"Female. Student. Julia Flossinger. Age nineteen. Avid runner. Looks like suicide. Campus police arrived on the scene first, then the EMTs. I brought up the rear."

Chief Gates looked down the unpaved path as two EMTs approached, pushing an empty gurney back toward the street.

"Where's the body?"

"Still at the scene," Quags said

"I assume we're walking."

"We are. The path is too narrow for emergency vehicles."

The two men began down the path, heading north. Moving out of the morning sun, the shade of the trees dropped the temperature a few degrees.

"Has anyone found a suicide note?" Gates asked.

"Not yet. Campus police have already spoken to her roommate and they're searching her room and computer. Understandably, the roommate is quite upset."

"I'm sure she is."

"All indications are that it was a suicide. The body had been moved by the time I got here, but the scene is pretty straightforward."

"How many suicides does that make this year?"

"Four students this calendar year. Three so far this semester."

Gates shook his head. "They always come in waves. One student takes his own life and then ten others start thinking about it. Who found the body?"

Quags checked his notes. "Oscar Guerrero. A junior. Studies architecture. Lives off campus with two roommates. Says he runs the paths every morning. He left his apartment at seven, passed by the body twelve minutes later, and called 911."

"Did anyone check his alibi?"

"It's in the works."

"Any criminal record?"

"None."

"What was the time of death?"

"Best guess puts time of death near seven last night."

"And no one saw the body until this morning?"

"Sunset is around seven thirty this time of year. Once the sun goes down, there's not much light on the trail. Especially in the pines. The body would have been hard to spot in the dark."

"Did anyone report the victim missing last night?"

"Not that we know of. But we're talking about college students. They don't always sleep in their own beds."

"No, they don't," Gates agreed.

Between the trees, Gates caught his first glimpse of the scene. A gurney was parked on the trail. A vertically challenged forensic photographer with bright red hair took pictures. Yellow police tape stretched in a large arc, wrapping around several tree trunks. Gates stood on the edge of the scene and digested the details. An overturned park bench was on its back, its legs protruding outward at ninety degrees. A rope gently swayed in the wind, dangling from a branch above the bench.

"I assume the girl was on the rope?"

"She was."

"Not many females hang themselves, statistically speaking."

"That bothered me too. But at first glance, I'd agree with the original assessment of suicide."

"And second glance?"

Quags wrung his hands together. "On second glance, the rope got me thinking."

Gates measured the scene for a second time and noticed excess rope coiled on the ground. "There's a lot of it."

"Good eye, boss. Probably thirty feet on the ground and another fifteen over the branch. So I ask you, did this girl go out for a run with forty feet of rope looped over her shoulder? I don't think so. The only alternative I can come up with is that the deceased stored the rope in the bushes, planning to use it later."

Gates pursed his lips but said nothing.

"I agree with your silence. It's not much of an explanation," Quags confessed.

Gates motioned toward the overturned bench. "Looks like the girl used the top of the bench to step off. Probably knocked it over in the process."

"That's what it looks like. But I'm still considering other explanations."

"While you're contemplating, let's take a look at the body."

"Right this way."

Gates followed Quags as he bisected the small group of EMTs, the victim visible in a body bag, zipper open. Gates moved closer to the gurney for a better view while Quags conveyed his thoughts.

"Death by hanging leaves a telltale V-shape on the neck. Compared to strangulation with a rope, which will leave a straight line. As you can see by our victim, the line is a V."

"So, she hanged."

"As opposed to being strangled, yes."

Gates tried to imagine the victim upright, going about her day. Classes. Lunch. Maybe a date. His second assessment of the body on the gurney was performed with a more discerning eye. "Based on her attire, she looks like a runner. Athletic top, pants."

"She does."

"No sign of any sexual malfeasance?"

"She was fully clothed. But I want to show you something about her attire that I can't figure out. I'm going to roll her over and you tell me what you see."

Quags struggled to roll the body onto its side, pushing the body bag open. Chief Gates pointed at the back of the girl's running pants. "What's on the back of her legs?"

"Exactly. It looks like dirt. Mud. But it's not the what that bothers me. It's the location. How did she get dirt on the back of her knees?"

"Maybe she sat down somewhere along the way."

"Dirt on the back of the knees but not on the butt? That's tricky. Unless you're trying out for Cirque du Soleil."

"Maybe you're a decent detective after all."

"I'm going to take that as a compliment, even if it wasn't one."

"Why would this girl get all dressed up in running gear just to come out here and kill herself?" Gates asked.

"I don't know about her attire, but coming out here could have been her attempt at being considerate. Maybe she didn't want her roommate to find her body."

"Did the deceased have any belongings with her?"

"Two keys and a university ID."

"What about a cell phone?"

"Nope."

"A nineteen-year-old without a cell phone? Now *that's* suspicious."

"She could have left it in her room."

"Put it on the list of items to confirm."

"Will do," Quags said, checking his notes. "One more thing. According to the deceased's roommate, she was on Zoloft for depression and anxiety."

"That's not good," Gates responded. "Stick around and help process the scene. Then see if you can locate her cell phone and find out where she got the rope."

"You got it, Chief."

CHAPTER 29

GATES PRESSED THE talk icon on his mobile phone as he put his car into drive.

"Is this Chief Gates?" a male voice asked.

"Speaking."

"This is Paul Paulsen. I'm an attorney for the Central Intelligence Agency. I represent legal inquiries into all things related to Camp Peary. I'm their chief counsel, of sorts."

"Good morning."

"And a good morning to you. I hate to be a bother, but I have to inquire about a serious matter."

"I assume this is pertaining to our subpoena."

"No, I'm afraid not."

"I didn't realize there was another matter to discuss."

"There is. Any chance you had an opportunity to read the local paper down in your neck of the woods?"

"Which paper would that be?"

"The *Daily Press*."

"I haven't had time to read it yet. I've been on the site of a suicide this morning."

"I'm sorry to hear that," Paulsen offered before continuing. "According to the article I read this morning, you have new evidence in the Matoaka murders."

"It's the same evidence you are already aware of."

"Our legal team is interested in the source of this news article. And we would like to remind all parties involved that intentionally revealing the true identity of a career intelligence officer is a punishable offense."

"I'm afraid I don't understand," Gates replied. "Devon Childress informed us the fingerprint we discovered wasn't from anyone at the Agency. We're taking you at your word. Are you saying that the chief of security at Camp Peary lied to us? Are you saying that one of your intelligence officers could be responsible for a series of cold case murders?"

Paulsen fell silent, seeming to realize the dilemma he'd created. "I think we're finished here, Chief Gates. Consider this a friendly reminder of the law. Have a good day."

CHAPTER 30

CHIEF GATES KNOCKED on the doorframe of Dr. Lui's office.

"Please come in," Dr. Lui replied, waving her hand while hanging up her phone. The professor motioned for Gates to sit, and he chose a chair with a view of the monitor on the wall. A stack of papers stood on the corner of Dr. Lui's desk. Gates's eyes wandered and he counted five framed diplomas in various locations throughout the office.

"I hear you have some good news," Gates said.

"We do. We ran the images from your security feeds through our enhancement algorithms and have come up with a couple of possibilities with regard to your suspect's true appearance."

Dr. Lui clicked her remote-control mouse and opened files on the screen. A second later the large screen divided into four smaller quadrants. Each of the four sections contained an image of the good Samaritan.

"Given that your suspect implemented several disguises, and given the surveillance video quality, enhancement was somewhat more challenging than anything we've tried to date. But it was a good exercise for us. We think it enabled us to refine our code a little, which is always positive."

"Glad to hear it."

"The four images you see on the screen are the most likely possibilities for your suspect's face, as seen from the front. You may notice that each one has a resemblance to the other, but they're far from identical."

Chief Gates put on his glasses. "The four images look like they could be brothers."

"Exactly," Dr. Lui answered. "And when we take these four images and run a separate algorithm on them, the system produces this image."

A single face popped onto the screen, an odd mix of computer graphics with photographic qualities.

"Looks like a middle-aged white male who misplaced his razor."

"We can alter anything you see with regard to the specifics of the face. We can add a goatee, change the color of his eyes, alter his hairstyle. Any options that might interest you. But the face on the screen is our baseline."

"I'm going to have to trust you on that. You're the professional."

"We've run trial subjects through the same process. As a tool for identification, it shouldn't be too far off."

"Thank you for your effort."

"Our pleasure. Now, moving on to the next topic. You indicated particular interest in whether your suspect actually touched the gun during the attempted robbery. I had one of my grad students dissect the Walgreens security video in extreme detail."

Dr. Lui again clicked the wireless mouse. "The image on the screen was captured in the reflection of a small mirror on the sunglasses display at the end of the aisle three. You can see in the reflection that your suspect does indeed touch the gun. Mind you, this is zoomed in five hundred percent. It would be virtually impossible to catch this image with the naked eye."

"Awesome," Chief Gates replied, thoroughly impressed.

"Yes. Catching the image in the reflection of the small mirror was quite remarkable. But then again, the student who worked on the analysis of the drug store video is a natural. Her name is Bisa, and she's the perfect combination of common sense, intense focus, and a genius IQ."

"Please pass on my appreciation."

"I will. There are two more items I wanted to show you."

The image on the screen changed yet again and Gates found himself staring down from one of Walgreen's overhead shoplifting cameras.

"I'm sure you recognize the perspective of the view now on the screen," Dr. Lui said.

"I do."

"Enhancing the video shows new details about your suspect and his shopping basket. As you can see from this first image, your good Samaritan had a birthday card, an energy drink, and a bag of trail mix in his basket."

"Drug store staples."

"Certainly nothing unusual. But the next discovery is . . ." Dr. Lui paused while she clicked her mouse and the image on the screen expanded into a blur of hair with distinct tuffs of uniformity. Among the tuffs of hair, bald patches formed neat rows. Dr. Lui drew Gates's attention to the relevant section of the screen. "This is a still frame that captures the top of your suspect's head after he loses his cap in the altercation with the robber."

"That's the top of his head?" Gates confirmed.

"It is."

"Are those gridlines a byproduct of the image enhancement software?"

"No, those gridlines are what I wanted to show you."

Gates leaned in toward the screen.

Dr. Lui continued. "Let me preface my interpretation of this image with a story. When I was in college, I blew out my knee playing volleyball. ACL, MCL, and meniscus. I ended up needing reconstructive surgery. I spent several months on crutches and my summer doing rehab."

Gates glanced in the direction of Dr. Lui's legs.

"Thankfully my father went out of his way to ensure I had the best surgeon available."

"And how does this relate to the image on the screen?"

"Because the surgeon who worked on my knee had the same pattern on the top of his head."

"I don't follow."

"The gridlines you see are hair plugs."

Gates pulled away from the screen for a different perspective.

"When you have a serious knee injury, you spend a lot of time looking at the top of your doctor's head. During examinations and assessments, the doctor is often nose to knee. As the patient, when you look down at the doctor, that's the view. And the lasting impression I have of my surgeon was that he had really bad hair plugs. In a perverse way, I looked forward to my doctor appointments just so I could check them out." The corners of Dr. Lui's mouth curved upward in amusement.

"And they looked like these?" Gates asked, pointing at the screen.

"My doctor's plugs were even more pronounced. But this was twenty-some years ago. I imagine hair plugs have improved over the years. Most technology has. I have no reason to think hair plugs would be exempt."

"Hair plugs?"

"Yep."

"Son of a bitch."

"That's exactly what Bisa said. She'd never seen hair plugs before."

"Anything else?"

"We enhanced everything in the video that seemed pertinent to your suspect. That said, we aren't law enforcement, so we don't know exactly what's important. There could be a number of other points of interest relevant to your investigation in the enhanced videos that we didn't catch. It might be prudent for someone on your team to go through the enhanced videos again."

"I'll have my detective take a look."

*

Gates sat in his car and called Detective Millares. "Check your email. We have an image of the suspect that we can work with. Courtesy of the William & Mary Computer Science Department."

"I'm on it. Give me a sec to pull it up," Quags replied.

"Let me know when you have eyes on it."

Silence fell over the connection until Quags responded. "It's an improvement over the surveillance videos, that's for sure."

"We can also tweak this image anyway we want."

"Very cool."

"Let's pull together some composite options. Hairstyles. Eyes. Facial hair."

"Definitely."

"Dr. Lui shared some other interesting information. It looks like our man has hair plugs."

"Hair plugs?" Quags raised his eyebrows at the unexpected detail.

"Yep. One of Dr. Lui's students did an extensive enhancement and analysis of the Walgreens surveillance video. Our good Samaritan has hair plugs. Not very good ones, apparently. When you get in tomorrow, I want you to take a look at the enhanced video and see if there's anything we missed on our initial pass."

"I'll get on it first thing."

"Any update on the suicide from this morning?"

"We made a few inquiries about the rope that was found. I'm waiting for confirmation, but it looks like it's one that's sold by nearly every sport and outdoor company on the East Coast."

"Any record of the girl purchasing some?"

"Not yet."

"Let me know if that changes."

"Will do."

"Good. Keep on it."

"On a separate note, I was told to expect a call this evening from a former spy."

"So the bartender pulled through for you?" Gates asked.

"She did."

"Let's regroup in the morning after you've had a chance to look at the enhanced video and you can tell me about your call."

"Roger that."

CHAPTER 31

EYES SHUT, QUAGS felt a vibration through the sofa cushion next to him. Sitting up, he grabbed the phone, checked the screen, and didn't recognize the number.

"Detective Millares," he answered.

"Good evening, Detective. This is Grant. You probably remember me as Jenny's boyfriend. Now ex-boyfriend."

"Intelligence officer turned pot farmer."

"Not exactly. My brother and I opened a dispensary. We don't grow it. We buy our product from a few different suppliers."

"My mistake."

"And in the state of Washington it's legal to grow *and* sell marijuana."

"Don't forget smoke it."

"It would defeat the purpose otherwise. Put a dent in demand."

"That it would."

"Jenny said you were looking for some information. I assume it isn't on the marijuana business."

"It's not. I'm looking for insight that may help solve a thirty-five-year-old cold case. The murder of four people in the nineteen eighties."

"And what information would I have that could help? I wasn't even born yet."

Quags laid out the chain of events from the Walgreens to The Farm, hitting on the Blue Bird bus and the partial fingerprint.

"A serial killer from the eighties?"

"Yep. And one of the victims was the sister of the current chief of police of Williamsburg. My boss."

"I can see your interest."

"It goes beyond interest."

"Technically, I'm not allowed to discuss anything related to the Agency or what I did there. That includes Camp Peary."

"Not even to find a murderer?"

Grant was silent for a long moment. "I guess it depends on the type of information."

"I'm not looking for state secrets. Just anything that can get us closer to the guy who left the fingerprint behind. We're working on a hunch that he's an instructor on The Farm."

"Getting your hands on information about an instructor is going to be tough. No one even uses their real name there."

"So we've heard. We met with the base's chief security officer and he laid out some of the obstacles."

"Childress?"

"Yep."

"He always seemed like a fair man. A bit of a stickler for the rules, but fair. You always knew where you stood with him."

"How well did you know him?"

"I was on The Farm for five months. He taught a couple of classes and regularly spoke to us as a group. I also had a few one-on-one conversations with him. Like I said, he seemed decent."

"How about the other instructors?"

"In what way? Most of them knew what they were talking about. A few were difficult. One was a dick. If you believe what you hear, back in the day, most of the instructors on The Farm were intelligence officer failures. Disciplined and banished to The Farm. A lot of them were rumored to have drinking problems."

"And the present-day instructors?"

"They didn't strike me as flunkies. Even the difficult ones seemed to be very gifted in certain areas."

"Such as?"

"Are you familiar with the courses at The Farm?"

"Just what I've read. Why don't you give me a quick rundown?"

"Basically, The Farm is a program where trainees receive the equivalent of a graduate degree in spycraft. Firearms, lockpicking, explosives, parachuting, cryptology, hacking, passing information. Even boating skills. Pretty cool stuff. Most of the time. Heck, they're still teaching how to open and reseal envelopes without leaving evidence behind."

"Jenny mentioned you didn't like writing reports. Anything else you didn't enjoy?"

"Waterboard simulation wasn't fun."

"Were you on the giving or receiving end?"

"The wet end."

"That wasn't mentioned in any of the material I've read."

"When it comes to The Farm, you can't believe what you read. Or see. I checked out The Farm on Google Maps once. It was mostly fiction. Almost nothing on Google Maps was located in the correct place on The Farm. The runway was in the correct location and some of the housing for the instructors was in the right place, but everything else was altered or deleted. The Farm has a baseball and soccer field that's not on the map at all. The dorms have been moved. For everything the public has heard about The Farm, there is a grain of truth wrapped in a secret and blurred by disinformation."

"I'll keep that in mind," Quags replied. "It's my understanding you were asked to leave the program."

"I was terminated. In Camp Peary parlance, I washed out. Ten to fifteen percent of every class doesn't graduate from the program."

"What happened in your case?"

"I ended up at the bottom of the murder board."

"What's the murder board?"

"A scoreboard for all the trainees in a given class. Updated every week. If you find yourself in last place on the murder board three times, you're out."

"And this murder board led to your departure?"

"It did. Twice I ended up in the basement because of poor scores from one instructor. The aforementioned dick."

"Jenny mentioned you didn't follow some rule and that was the straw that broke the camel's back."

"I got caught breaking a rule, which isn't hard to do. The Farm has lots of rules."

"There's a long list of rules on the sign at the entrance to the base."

"That's the tip of the iceberg. Trust me."

"I'm not much of a rules man myself."

"They don't make it easy. The course at Camp Peary is six months long. Visitors aren't allowed. Personal mobile phones are not permitted. Free time off base is severely limited. By design, it's a course in loneliness, isolation, and pressure. In fact, the old Agency name for The Farm was 'Isolation.' The place offers few release outlets. The rules are meant to push you to the edge."

"Doesn't sound like fun."

"It doesn't leave a lot of free time or options for things to do. Study, exercise, and sex. Those are the top three activities of CIA trainees on The Farm."

"Sex? With who?"

"Other trainees."

"With all those rules, I'm surprised you're allowed to have sex with each other. I assume they don't allow conjugal visits."

"You can't take *everything* away from people. On The Farm, trainees live in dormitories. Coed dorms. Everyone has their own room. And if you put men and women together under one roof for extended periods of time, sex is going to happen. When everything else is banned, it happens often. Of course, the rooms are under audio surveillance, so someone is probably listening to you knock boots."

"They bug the trainees' dorm rooms?"

"They do. And each trainee also has a small cubicle to serve as an office. But everything is monitored. The phones. Internet usage. The grounds."

"Nice. I would think promiscuity would be frowned upon."

"Not in and of itself. As long as you keep it in a room, everyone looks the other way. Sex in your office, the woods, or in common areas will get you thrown out. And having an affair would raise concerns about a trainee's trustworthiness and loyalty. But it wouldn't necessarily result in termination. Apparently it is well-known that a fair amount of sexual hijinks has occurred at Langley among high-ranking officers."

Quags thought about Jenny's gonorrhea comment but stifled the urge to broach the subject. Instead, he said, "Sex in dorms sounds like college."

"There was an element of college to it all. Without the keg parties. But they do have a little sports bar for the trainees on base. It's self-serve and you have to clean up after yourself. I personally think it's there to monitor how much the trainees drink."

"I assume everything was provided for you at The Farm?"

"The basics. A roof over your head. Three meals a day. There's a small country store on base. Laundry service. Access to medical care. The Farm has its fair share of injuries. We had a guy break his leg on a night parachute jump. Compound fracture. Two bones right through the skin."

"And if you needed something that wasn't provided by the base?"

"You could usually pick it up over a long weekend or while you were out in public practicing spycraft skills. Entering and exiting stores and other establishments is necessary to spot tails. In spy parlance it's called a cover stop. It's easy enough to grab small items like deodorant or toothpaste while performing an SDR."

"SDR?"

"Sorry. Surveillance detection run."

"Interesting," Quags said before segueing into his next topic. "Let me ask this. Did any of the instructors strike you as someone who could be capable of murder?"

"I think we're all capable of murder, given the right circumstances."

"That's a depressing outlook."

"You disagree?"

"I do. And I know for certain that we're not all capable of dealing with the feelings that come with killing a person."

"That's probably true. As far as The Farm is concerned, the only guys who struck me as psychopaths were the SOG guys."

"What is SOG?"

"Special Operations Group. All of them are former Special Forces. They used to be called the Special Activities Division, but the Agency changed the name. Doesn't really matter. Regardless of their name, they are the proverbial tip of the spear. And the US military doesn't spend that kind of money and time training them to be nice. Most of them teach weapons instructions on The Farm. No surprise."

"So if I were looking for a killer, I should start with people who have a military background?"

"Not necessarily. There are plenty of CIA case officer trainees who were previously in the military who aren't weapons instructors. I think something like twenty percent of CIA trainees have a military background."

"What about them? Any likely candidates for a murderer?"

"No more likely than anyone in the general population. Keep in mind, all of the teaching staff—outside of the weapons instructors—were former CIA case officers or tech officers who directly supported case officers."

"And does that make them less likely to murder someone?"

"I think you may have a misconception about what a CIA case officer actually does."

"Enlighten me."

"The job of a CIA case officer is to recruit other people to provide intelligence. Managing assets, a.k.a. other people who are willing to spy, is what case officers do."

"So I've heard. But you're also taught weapons, explosives, and self-defense."

"Yes. But most of that falls into the 'Break-Glass-In-Case-of-Emergency' category. If a CIA case officer has to kill someone, something has gone seriously awry. The vast majority of CIA case officers don't even carry a weapon. Most are never issued a firearm. The reason is simple. Case officers supply info to the people pulling the trigger or setting off the explosion."

"And you said that all of the instructors on The Farm were once case officers."

"That's right. Or tech guys who worked in the field supporting case officers. The Farm only wants instructors who have hands-on, real-life, in-the-field experience. Theoretical knowledge isn't held in high regard."

"Does that mean Childress was a case officer?"

"He was. At least until 9/11. From what I heard, 9/11 was the impetus for a lot of organizational change at the Agency."

"And you said that Childress taught classes?"

"He taught Picks and Locks. He was good. Really good."

"I have pictures of an instructor and a potentially married couple who we believe are trainees. We'd like to identify all three of them. We believe they are currently on The Farm. Can I text you some images and see if you recognize any of them?"

"Sure, but like I said, I won't be able to provide any real names. Everyone uses a pseudo on The Farm. Some people have more than one."

"Jenny mentioned you used a different name while in training."

"I was Gavin."

"Which is close to Grant."

"Choosing a pseudo that's close to your own name is a trick we learned from the Russians. If you choose a pseudo that's similar to your real name and someone calls you out when you're undercover, you can either acknowledge them or blow them off without too much explanation."

"Sounds kind of silly."

"The Agency loves its secrets."

"Apparently. Stand by for a text."

*

"The image of the instructor you sent isn't a photograph," Grant said into the phone minutes later.

"All we have is a computer representation, a facial composite. It's a rendering from several separate views taken from surveillance videos. It's been enhanced. Any chance you recognize him?"

"Nope. I don't know him. But instructors rotate through The Farm all the time. They stay for a few years and then move on. I washed out about seven and a half months ago, so the guy in your photo likely came to the base after that."

"This instructor was caught on surveillance cameras wearing multiple disguises. Is that par for the course?"

"They call it identity transfer."

"A fancy term for 'disguises'?"

"Yes. But you need to understand that a large part of a case officer's success is predicated on their ability to lose a tail. It's hard to meet with your assets if the home country's security or counterintelligence is watching. Identity transfer is one way to shake a tail."

"And the disguises are good enough to fool foreign intelligence officers?"

"Without a doubt. I'll give you an example. Thirty years ago, an exfiltration expert from the CIA met with President Bush face-to-face while wearing a full mask disguise. The first President Bush, not George W. Halfway through the interview, the CIA employee, whom President Bush had met on prior occasions, removed her disguise, much to the president's surprise. And that was thirty years ago. Technology has only made things better. In the seventies, the Agency was able to produce disguises sufficient to fool border guards. A black man could become white. A white man could become Asian. This was in the 1970s. With practice, a case officer can change appearance in twelve seconds. At least, that's the goal. And every case officer is issued a disguise kit designed specifically for them."

"Jesus," Quags replied. "In the incident at the Walgreens, why was the instructor wearing a disguise?"

"Part of the training. Spotting an adversary who has undertaken identity transfer is almost as important as perfecting one's own disguise."

"I can see that."

"For years, the CIA hired professional magicians to teach trainees sleight-of-hand tricks and misdirection. Most of those tricks have been incorporated into the training. It serves as an additional element to identify transfer."

"That's going to make my job more difficult. What about the photographs of the couple I sent to you? Do you recognize them?"

"I don't recognize the woman, but the guy looks familiar. It could be from seeing him around HQ prior to training. Maybe even at the Starbucks in Langley."

"There's a Starbucks inside CIA headquarters?"

"Absolutely."

Quags paused. "So, you worked at HQ before you were trained at Camp Peary?"

"We all do. There's a waiting list to attend training on The Farm. Most of the people in my class served as analysts back at HQ while awaiting their turn."

"And you say the male counterpart of the couple looks familiar?"

"He does, but I can't tell you anything beyond that. Everyone I was with at The Farm graduated last spring. Anyone who's there now would be a different class."

"How many classes are on The Farm at any given time?"

"Three while I was there. One class of trainees starting, one finishing, and one somewhere in between. Each class has twenty-five students or so. But there are just over a hundred dorm rooms in three buildings, so the maximum number of students would be in that neighborhood. The Farm also trains members of the DIA and select foreign nationals."

"Do you have any idea why the couple in the photographs I sent would provide a fake name and address to the Richmond Police? They weren't involved in any crime. They only witnessed an attempted armed robbery."

"And they had fake IDs?"

"Yep. Official Virginia driver's licenses, issued by the DMV."

"Sounds like they were playing Rabbit."

"Jenny mentioned Rabbit. Some kind of hide-and-seek game for adults."

"It's more than that. It's spycraft practice. And part of playing Rabbit is maintaining your cover identity, no matter what."

"Even lying to the police?"

"They may have thought the police weren't police at all."

"You mean they could have thought the whole thing was an exercise? A charade? The attempted robbery and disarming of the suspect?"

"That's exactly what I'm saying. I once played Rabbit in Asheville, North Carolina, and as I was walking down the sidewalk, practicing countersurveillance, I was swarmed by a half-dozen men who jumped out of an SUV. I was accused of selling drugs and threatened with arrest. But it was all a sham. The DEA agents were fake. The drugs were fake."

"And now you actually sell drugs. How ironic."

Grant laughed. "I guess so. I never thought about that."

"Where else did you play Rabbit?"

"All over. We started in small cities and gradually worked up to DC, Philly, Atlanta, San Francisco, Seattle. Playing Rabbit is what washed me out of the program."

"How's that?"

"I used the Atlanta Convention Center as a cut-through."

"And that wasn't allowed?"

"Not during the annual car show."

"For shits and giggles, let's say I wanted to find the couple that presented the fake IDs to the Richmond Police. How would I go about it? Assuming they're still trainees and live on The Farm."

"A subpoena would be the easiest way. But you're law enforcement, so I assume you knew that."

"The subpoena option is working its way through the legal system. Any other ideas?"

"Hmmm," Grant replied. Quags heard ice crunching through the phone line before Grant offered a second suggestion. "You could follow the weekend bus."

"What's that?"

"On most three-day weekends, the bus takes the trainees back to DC on Friday evening and returns to The Farm on Monday afternoon."

"Three-day weekends?"

"Memorial, Labor, Columbus, and Veterans Days. Federal holidays. And then you have Thanksgiving, Christmas, Easter, and the Fourth."

"Where in DC does the bus drop off?"

"It actually doesn't go as far as DC. It stops in Arlington. Rosslyn. Five minutes from the White House. The bus stops in one of several secure locations. You won't have access to that location. But you won't need it."

"And why is that?"

"Because everyone who takes the weekend bus to DC either takes the Metro or catches a ride from the Rosslyn Station."

"How can you be sure?"

"Because trainees are not permitted to use Uber from a secure location. Ditto for cabs."

"So if the trainees are dropped off in one of these secure buildings, and I won't have access, how exactly am I supposed to follow them?"

"Like I said, you won't have to. Park yourself near the Metro station. You'll see the trainees head your way. They come out in small groups, every few minutes."

"Are they going to be wearing matching T-shirts? Because I'm not sure what a trainee is supposed to look like if I don't see them get off that bus."

"Keep your eyes peeled for a group of people that look like they just got their mobile phones back after a month without it."

"I'll assume that's a look I'll recognize when I see it."

"You're a detective. You should be able to handle it."

"What about people on The Farm who want to get away for the weekend but aren't going to Arlington?"

"Tough. As I mentioned, before coming to The Farm, all career trainees work at CIA HQ or one of their satellite buildings around the Beltway. Everyone has at least a room rented in the DC area. Some people own houses, some live in apartments. Some stay with family."

"What about you?"

"I had an apartment in Clarendon, a neighborhood in Arlington."

"If the bus runs between Camp Peary and Arlington, and you have an apartment in Northern Virginia, what were you doing in Richmond when I met you?"

"I drove down from DC."

"After you took the bus?"

"That's right. I took the bus back to DC and then drove down to Richmond in my own car."

"Why not just go to Richmond directly?"

"It's complicated. Trainees don't really have an option. Personal vehicles are not permitted on The Farm, so it's not like you can just hop in your car and go somewhere. And you sure as hell can't catch an Uber at the front gate of the base. As trainees progress through the course, the Agency provides rental cars for them to perform location assessment, to practice avoiding tails, and to set up meetings with make-believe assets. But the rental cars provided by the Agency are not permitted to be used for personal business. That will get you thrown out of the program. So for most trainees, a trip back to DC means a trip on the bus. It's just less hassle."

"Were you free on the weekends, back in DC?"

"For the most part. But you're in training and you can't really tell anyone anything. It makes hanging out with old friends a little awkward. I found that a lot of the trainees hung out with each other over the long weekends."

"What if you wanted to go somewhere? Like fly to New York for the weekend?"

"You would need to get permission in advance. Submit an official request to travel so that the Agency would know where to find you at all times," Grant said. "Or you could risk it, roll the dice, and hope you don't get caught."

"Did you ever roll the dice?"

"I didn't. But I know people who did. It was done more often in the past. So I hear."

"Are you from Richmond?"

"Not originally. I went to VCU for undergrad. I have a lot of friends in Richmond. And I was seeing Jenny."

"You mean you drove down for sex."

"Sometimes, yeah. I assume you came to Richmond for the same reason."

"Fair enough," Quags said. "Can I call you back if I think of any more questions?"

"Nope. I'm calling you from a burner phone. I got it just for this call."

"Paranoid?

"Hell yeah, I'm paranoid. The mobile phone is the greatest liability ever created for an intelligence agency. The greatest asset and greatest liability. Anyone with a phone can be tracked. Nowadays, the technology is so advanced that not only can you be tracked, but they can track anyone who is tracking you. If you knew what I knew about hacking and tracking with cell phones, you'd be paranoid too."

"I'll take your word for it."

"If you need to speak with me again, have Jenny send me an email. I'll call you back as soon as I can on another burner."

"For what it's worth, it seems to me you would have been a good spy."

"Case officer."

"That's what I meant."

CHAPTER 32

UNSURE OF HOW long he'd been asleep, Quags rolled over in the darkness and ran his fingers over his handgun before finding his phone. Eyes shut, he pressed it to his ear.

"Millares," he answered groggily.

"We need a detective for a suspicious death."

"What's the address?" Quags asked, opening one eye.

"It's 5917 Tyler Street. Backs up to the golf course on Golden Horseshoe."

"Any word on the victim?"

"Identified by the caller as Dr. Lui, Professor of Computer Science at William & Mary."

"*Carajo*," Quags replied, standing from his bed and reaching for his pants. "Please inform first responders not to touch anything until I get there. And call Chief Gates and wake him up. Relay the information you just gave me."

"Yes, Detective."

*

Chief Gates arrived on the scene first, dressed in jeans and a Williamsburg PD windbreaker. A gaggle of EMTs and firemen stood in the yard. He took long strides across the manicured lawn and stopped at the front door to speak with a trio of first responders.

"I guess it's a little late to avoid waking up the neighborhood," Gates said, observing the crowd in pajamas who had gathered in the middle of the street. "Anyone inside other than the deceased?"

"The boyfriend is in the dining room, speaking with one of your officers. We were told to stand down until Detective Millares arrived."

"What's the boyfriend's story?"

"He said the victim was expecting him to come over but he couldn't reach her on the phone. When he arrived, the front door was unlocked and the alarm wasn't engaged. He entered and found the victim in the bathtub."

"What time was this?"

"After eleven."

"Kind of late to visit someone."

"It was probably a booty call."

"Did you check the body?"

"We ran through a preliminary assessment before we received the call to stand down. The victim is on the floor in the bathroom. The boyfriend said he found her in the tub and dragged her out of the water."

"No resuscitation efforts?"

"None were attempted by emergency personnel. The victim was dead before we arrived, sir."

The four men turned their attention toward the street as Detective Millares's car approached the scene at a high rate of speed, momentarily dispersing the group of pajama-clad rubberneckers. Seconds later, he bounded across the grass and joined the group on the front porch.

"Have you been inside yet, Chief?"

"Nope."

"Let's get gloved and booted," Quags said, before calling out for the forensic photographer. Minutes later, Quags entered through the front door and the EMT on the porch offered directions to the master bathroom. "The deceased is up the stairs, to the left. Back corner of the master bedroom."

*

Quags led Gates and the forensic photographer into the foyer. "We have an alarm system."

"The boyfriend said it wasn't on when he arrived," Gates replied.

"Where's the boyfriend?" Quags asked.

"In the dining room."

Quags stepped into the living room. Magazines were lined neatly along the edge of the coffee table. The mirror over the mantle shined with clarity. The pillows on the sofa had been fluffed, placed with care and precision in their respective corners. Quags ran his gloved finger along a bookcase and retracted a spotless digit. The sound of the forensic photographer snapping photos continued to his rear.

Entering the kitchen, Quags realized the cleanliness of the living room was not an anomaly. "Either Dr. Lui didn't cook, or she had OCD," he muttered. He opened the fridge and admired the perfectly organized shelves of food.

"So much for not cooking," Gates replied.

"A model home has nothing on this place," Quags replied, moving toward the back door and a deck that overlooked the yard. He pulled on the door handle and it slid open without protest. "The back door was unlocked," Quags said, bending at the waist to examine the door tracks and lock.

Turning left out of the kitchen, Quags stopped at the entrance to the formal dining room and observed its red walls, a glass table with six seats, and a chandelier. He assumed the young man seated at the head of the table with a box of tissues was Dr. Lui's boyfriend. He recognized Officer Bly sitting in uniform next to the boyfriend, whispering quietly. When Quags and Gates entered the room, Bly stood and stepped to the side to huddle with his boss.

"Good evening, Chief," Bly said.

"What's the story with the boyfriend?" Quags asked.

Bly ran through the same explanation Gates had received before Quags arrived. Quags looked over at the younger man dressed in blue jeans and an old William & Mary sweatshirt. "How old is he? He looks young."

"Name is Hank Gallows. He's a twenty-six-year-old PhD student."

"Let me guess, computer science," Quags said.

"That's right," Bly replied.

"Did he say anything incriminating?"

"He didn't. He seems genuinely upset."

"Take a break," Quags said. "The chief and I are going to have a few minutes alone with him."

*

Quags sat down and offered introductions, a business card, and credentials.

"So tell us, Hank, how do you know Dr. Lui?" Quags asked.

"We're dating."

"And she's the head of the department where you're earning your PhD."

Hank Gallows nodded. "I know what it sounds like. . . ."

"Let's be straight with each other, Hank. We don't care about your personal relationship with Dr. Lui. As long as you tell us the truth. The moment I think you're not being honest with us, the gloves are going to come off. Got it?" Quags said gently but firmly.

"Yes, sir."

Quags pulled out his notepad and began asking questions. "What time did you get here?"

"Around eleven."

"Kind of late for a visit, isn't it?"

"It's not that unusual for Christine and me. We're both night owls. We're both busy. Thursday night is sort of a standing date. Friday mornings are quiet for both of us."

"Were you planning on staying the night?"

Hank nodded.

"How long have the two of you been dating?"

"Five months or so."

"How would you characterize your relationship?"

"What do you mean?"

"Did you refer to Dr. Lui as your girlfriend? Did you go out in public?"

"Given her position at the university, we kept it as hush-hush as possible. We went to Virginia Beach for the weekend once. We also spent a couple of days in Charlottesville."

"And what happened when you arrived here tonight?"

"As I told the other officer, I came over, the door was unlocked, and I entered. I had tried to call several times."

"Was it unusual for the door to be unlocked?"

"A little. It's usually locked. But I have a key and the alarm code."

"You do?"

"Yes, sir." Hank pointed at his key chain. "The code to the alarm system is 9577621."

Quags wrote the code down in his notepad.

"After I arrived, I walked through the downstairs to look for her, then went to the second floor. I found her in the bathtub. It was awful," Hank said, his voice cracking and tears welling.

"Did you perform CPR?"

"I tried. I pulled her out of the tub. But I was sure she was dead."

"How did you determine that?"

"She was cold," Hank Gallows replied, trying to stifle deeper sobs.

"Okay, Hank. Hang out here for a little while longer. We're going to investigate and when we're done, I'd like you to take a look around the house with an officer. See if you notice if anything is missing or out of place."

"Yes, sir."

*

Lights illuminated the second floor of the two-story home. Beige carpeting ran from the landing at the top of the stairs, down the hall, and into three bedrooms. Quags paused at the doorway to the master bedroom and motioned for the forensic photographer to enter first. The photographer snapped photos of the made bed. He moved to the desk on the far side of the room, taking pictures of neatly stacked papers and folders. A dresser stood next to the desk, all its drawers firmly shut. An elliptical machine was in the corner.

"Doesn't look like there was any type of struggle," Quags said, still in the doorway. He stepped slowly forward, absorbing every detail as he made his way toward the bathroom. From the bathroom entrance he looked down at Dr. Lui's naked body lying on the white bathmat in front of the tub. A towel had been placed over her torso, from her chin to her thighs. A pile of athletic clothes sat on the floor, underwear on top, as if the victim had undressed, layer by layer, the clothes landing where they fell. Water filled the tub.

"I was holding out hope that there'd been a mistake. But it's her," Quags said.

"Yes, it is," Gates confirmed. "My wife is going to be upset."

Quags crouched down and peeled the towel off Dr. Lui's body. He examined her fingers and neck. "No visible wounds." He gently moved her left arm and noted the slight rigor mortis. A moment of silence fell over the men, each caught in their own thoughts. Quags opened and shut the cabinet under the vanity and then did the same with the drawers. Glancing over, he pointed toward the toothbrush holder.

"We've got two toothbrushes," Quags said. "Let's see if one of those belongs to the boyfriend."

"And if it doesn't?" Gates asked.

Without answering, Quags exited the bathroom and Gates followed. The detective opened each dresser drawer and examined the walk-in closet.

"Help me out Millares, what are you looking for?"

"There's nothing else here to indicate that Dr. Lui had a serious boyfriend. All the drawers and hangers are spoken for. All women's attire."

"Meaning?"

"Maybe nothing. But I'd expect a boyfriend of five months to have at least part of a drawer. Maybe some deodorant. A clean pair of underwear."

"Or Dr. Lui was so anal retentive she wouldn't allow it. People have quirks. Especially single people. Probably because there's no one around to tell them when they're acting strange."

"I'm single."

"Oh, I know."

Quags stepped back into the bathroom and motioned toward the clothes on the floor. "Did you get photos of this?" he asked the forensic photographer.

"I did."

Quags reached down with his gloved hand, picked up the long sleeve athletic top, raised it to his face, and inhaled.

"Anything?"

"Doesn't smell like clothes that had been worn to exercise."

"Maybe she was wearing them to be comfortable."

Quags walked into the center of the bedroom. His gaze fell on the elliptical in the corner. "I wonder if the manufacturer of that elliptical can tell us when it was last used. Pull data off its computer."

"That's a solid idea."

"It would solve the debate as to whether or not she'd been exercising and how that coincides with the decision to take a bath."

Quags reentered the bathroom, crouched down, and put his hand in the water. "Room temperature."

"That fits with the timeline."

"But it's curious. No soap in the water. No washcloth within reach." Quags stood up and perused the collection of shampoo, conditioners, and body washes on the shelf in the corner of the bath. He plucked a half-empty bottle from the front row and showed it to Gates. "And she has bubble bath. But she didn't use it."

*

Gates watched his detective work the collection of evidence for the next hour before Quags gave the green light for the body to be removed. "Any final thoughts?" Gates asked, heading out the front door.

"We'll know more when we get the forensic results back. We've collected a couple of prints, multiple hair samples, and we need to run a comprehensive toxicology screen. We have to analyze her phone and social media. We need to talk to family, friends, and coworkers. Someone other than the boyfriend. We also need to dig into his background a little. But on the surface, I don't think the boyfriend had anything to do with Dr. Lui's death."

"Follow the evidence. See where it leads," Gates said, feeling a vibration against his thigh.

As he pulled his phone from his pants pocket, Quags chimed in. "It's one in the morning. I hope that's your wife calling."

"Unknown number," Gates replied.

"At this hour? It's either a Nigerian prince who wants to give you ten million dollars or your car warranty has expired."

The phone continued to vibrate and Gates answered the call. Before he could speak, music blared from the phone's speaker.

"What the hell?" Quags asked.

Gates raced to silence the music. "Odd. Not sure exactly what that was. Reminds me of an old-school prank call. The sort of thing we'd do when we were kids."

The phone began vibrating anew and Gates moved toward Quags so the detective could also see the screen.

"Same number," Gates said.

"Give it another shot."

Gates answered for a second time and the same song began to play. The two detectives listened until the song faded into silence and the call ended.

"Do you recognize the music?" Gates asked, scowling.

"I don't. Should I?"

"It's by Paul Simon. Off the album titled *Graceland*. I can't remember the specific name of the song, but it was one of my sister's favorites."

"*Carajo*," Quags replied.

"Maybe it's a coincidence."

"I told you I don't believe in coincidences."

"We need to run a trace on this phone number."

"I'm on it. Give me a few minutes. I may have to wake up some people."

CHAPTER 33

GATES PARKED HIS car in front of his house and waited for Detective Millares to pull in behind him. The officers stepped from their vehicles into the trilling of crickets, the stars shining bright in the clear night sky overhead.

"This way," Gates said, flicking his head in the direction of the side yard. Quags followed in his boss's footsteps as they rounded the house and beelined for the Dad Shack in the backyard. A red pickup truck was parked in the grass next to the old slave quarters. The rear lift gate was off the vehicle, resting on a pair of saw horses. The left rear corner panel was damaged, the glass encasing the brake lights and turn signals smashed.

"Looks like your father hit something."

"It won't be the last time."

"You sure you don't want to wait until morning to check whatever it is we're checking?" Quags asked. "It's awfully early for a wake-up call."

"My dad will get over it when he hears why we've come."

"He's your dad."

"He is. And he owns a couple of guns, so let me go first."

Chief Gates knocked slightly on the front door of the Dad Shack, turned the knob, and entered.

"Dad," Chief Gates announced into the darkness of the small living room. He repeated his announcement, waited, and a light clicked on at the end of the hall. A moment later his father appeared as a shadow. Between mumbled curses, Gates Senior progressed down the hall. With the illumination of light in the kitchenette, all the occupants of the room became visible.

"What the hell's going on, son?"

"Dad, this is one of my detectives, Luis Millares."

Quags extended his hand. "You can call me Quags. It's a pleasure to meet you. Sorry to disturb you so late."

"We need to go through Heather's stuff," Chief Gates stated.

"It must be important."

"I hope so."

"Well, you know where the closet is. I'll get some coffee started."

"Thank you," Quags said.

*

Chief Gates pulled boxes from the closet and pushed them into the hall while Quags fished for information.

"What's on your mind, Chief?"

"Remind me what you know about my sister's Walkman?" Chief Gates asked as he tugged on the leather strap of the nearest footlocker.

"Your sister owned a Sony Walkman 983403. It was on her person when she was killed. It also provided the lone fingerprint of the suspect."

"Anything else about the Walkman?"

"It was a red AM/FM cassette player. You could listen to either the radio or cassettes."

"Exactly. And up until this evening, all the investigative work pointed to the likelihood that my sister was killed while listening to the radio. If you recall, she was killed before noon on a Sunday. That was typically when Casey Kasem did his American Top 40 countdown. We used to listen to it religiously growing up. I always assumed that's what she was listening to when she was killed. The fact that no cassette was found in the Walkman after my sister's death was another obvious indicator."

"And now you think she was listening to a cassette," Quags surmised.

"Bingo. I know my sister had a lot of cassettes and they're around here somewhere. I want to go through them."

"I'm game."

Chief Gates dragged the second footlocker out of the closet and opened the lid. On the right side were two large black cases with zippers. He removed both cases from the footlocker and took them to the small dining table. Gates Senior delivered two cups of black coffee and sat in an empty chair.

"I'll go through this case, and you go through that one. See if we can find a cassette of Paul Simon's *Graceland*. I know she owned it."

The two officers unzipped their respective cases.

"How many do you have?" Quags asked.

"A full case," Gates replied, his eyes dancing and his mind doing a quick calculation. "Eight rows, twelve in each row. Ninety-six in total."

"I have the same count, but a lot of them are mix tapes," Quags said, reading the labels on the side of the cassettes. "Summer of '85 Mix. Dance Party. Aerobics music."

"That was a big thing back in the day. Make your own mix tape. Make one for your friend. Make one for your girlfriend."

"For sure. We did the same thing. Back then, the world was divided into those who could afford CDs and those who couldn't. We couldn't. But the advantage of the cassette was the ability to mix and record your own music. That was a lot harder to do with the early versions of CDs and CD players."

"It was."

Quags took a sip of coffee before removing the first row of cassettes and placing them on the table next to the case. For the next several minutes, the officers opened each cassette tape and examined its contents. When they finished, most of the cassette tapes were back in their respective carrying cases. Two short stacks remained on the table, one sorted by each man.

"So, what do you have?" Quags asked.

"Four empty cassettes cases. Bryan Adams. The Police. Prince. U2."

"I have three empties. The Eagles. Steve Winwood. Led Zeppelin."

"No Paul Simon?"

"Nope."

Silence engulfed the two and Gates Senior spoke. "I think there's a smaller case in the closet somewhere. These cases here were from your sister's room. She had a smaller case of cassettes in her car."

Chief Gates returned to the closet and came back with a smaller carrying case. He placed it on the table and unzipped the side. All three men eyed the contents and Chief Gates reached for a cassette midway down the second column. He held up the cassette cover for Quags and his father to see. "We have a winner."

"Is there anything in it?"

Chief Gates flipped the cassette case open with a flick of his thumb. "Nope. Empty."

Quags rifled through remaining cassettes and their contents. "That's the only empty one in the smaller carrying case. Paul Simon's *Graceland*."

"Son of a bitch," Chief Gates said.

"What's the story here fellas?" Gates Senior asked.

"The story here is that whoever killed your daughter may have taken a cassette from her Walkman," Quags said.

"How's that going to help us?"

"That makes him a trophy keeper. And that means evidence is out there. We just have to get our hands on it."

*

Quags was outside smoking a cigar. He paced the grass in front of the Dad Shack, eyeing the damage to the old red truck. He held his phone to his ear and nodded and whispered his way through the brief conversation before hanging up. He placed his cigar on the edge of the concrete of the porch and reentered the Dad Shack. Chief Gates and his father were still at the table, staring at two hundred cassettes.

"The trace is done, Chief. The phone number that played the music for you is registered to John Flossinger. The phone was used by his daughter. Julia Flossinger."

"Our suicide from the park the other day?"

"The same."

"You're kidding?" Gates's eyes widened in surprise. "What's the connection between the girl and Dr. Lui?"

Quags shrugged. "Us. We're the connection."

"I hope that's not true."

"Either way, our suicide wasn't a suicide, and the killer took the victim's phone."

Gates paused. "Can we locate the origin of the call?"

"If someone gets sloppy and we get lucky."

"That hasn't been the case so far."

"No, it hasn't. I also got a call back from the guys finishing up at Dr. Lui's. The boyfriend, Hank, thinks that a gold necklace with a jade pendant is missing. He gave it to Dr. Lui. It wasn't in the house."

"Another trophy?"

"Possibly."

Gates held up his phone. "I found the name of the song that was played for us tonight. Do you want to take a listen?"

"Shoot."

Chief Gates pressed the screen on his phone and a video on You-Tube began to play. The opening music was identical to the snippet they'd heard earlier.

"That's it," Quags said. "That's the song. What's it called?"

"Are you ready for this?"

"I'm ready for anything."

"The name of the song is 'I Know What I Know,'" Gates said.

Quags considered the implication of the revelation. "Someone is taunting us. And that fucking pisses me off."

"You and me both," Gates Senior said.

"May I see your phone?" Quags asked, picking it off the table. He scrolled through the recent calls, tapped on the screen for a minute, and handed the phone back to Chief Gates.

"What did you just do?" Chief Gates asked.

"I sent him a message. On the off chance he'll be checking messages on a stolen phone."

"What did the message say?" Gates Senior asked.

Chief Gates opened the sent message and read it aloud. "That's your first mistake, asshole. Thanks for the lead."

Gates Senior smiled. "Son, I gotta say, I like this detective of yours."

"That makes one of us," Chief Gates replied.

Before Quags could respond, Chief Gates's phone chimed. "We have a response."

"And?" Quags asked.

"It says, 'Let sleeping dogs lie.'"

CHAPTER 34

THE YELLOW TURN signal on the rear of the bus indicated it was exiting onto Lee Highway from Interstate 66. Georgetown stood in the distance as the road descended downhill toward the Potomac River. Overhead, blocks of high-rise buildings under construction were dotted with cranes, the unofficial bird of Arlington, Virginia.

Quags kept his distance as the Blue Bird bus turned the corner two blocks south of the Rosslyn Metro Station. A moment later the bus slowed to a crawl and disappeared down a narrow street on the right. As Quags nudged the car forward, he and Gates peered down the narrow stretch of asphalt and noted the security presence and the barricade blocking the road. Still at a crawl, the law enforcement duo from Williamsburg watched the bus pass through the security checkpoint and vanish into the abyss between two identical buildings.

"And somewhere down there is our secure location," Quags said.

"Without a doubt."

"I'm going to take a ride around the block and see if we can't get a spot near the Rosslyn Metro station."

The car followed Lynn Street, a stone's throw from the Iwo Jima Memorial, then turned left as Key Bridge lurked ahead. Another turn completed their relocation and Quags pulled to the curb under a No Parking sign.

"No attempt to find a legitimate parking spot?"

"Not when I'm on a case and I have a badge," Quags replied.

"That's right. Protocol isn't your strong suit."

"This is my protocol. This spot should give us the best location to see the trainees as they head this way."

"Assuming the pot farmer wasn't pulling our leg."

"So far, he's been right about the weekend bus."

Light rain started to fall and Quags put the wipers on intermittent. Minutes later a group of young men and women trickled down a staircase from the direction of the secure location a block away.

"I think we're in business," Quags said, reaching into the backseat and grabbing his camera and telescopic lens. He scanned the faces of each individual and announced, "We have seven people coming down the stairs and they're all strangers to me. But every one of them has their mobile phone out."

"And a second group is on its way," Gates said between wipes of the windshield.

Quags readjusted the focus of his lens to the next group at the top of the stairs. "Bingo. Blonde. Third one down in the second group. That's our girl from Walgreens."

Quags handed the camera to Gates, who confirmed the identification. "If that's not her, it's her twin."

"Final decision, who do you want to follow? Our guy or girl?" Quags asked.

"Doesn't matter to me."

Quags and Gates continued watching from the car as another group of likely trainees appeared and descended the staircase like ants.

"I got our guy. Jeans. Dark shirt. Blue umbrella."

"And it looks like our girl isn't going into the Metro. She's probably going to catch a ride from in front of the station. Either a cab or Uber."

"This is where I get out," Quags said. "You follow the girl. I'll follow the guy. Keep your phone on."

*

Quags crossed the street and sat on a bench near the Metro entrance. Gates continued to watch the female suspect as she approached the curb in front of the station, her eyes never moving off the screen of her phone.

Still observing the girl, Chief Gates's phone rang.

"Looks like our male suspect is going to take mass transit," Quags voice said. Gates scanned the bench where Quags had been sitting a moment before.

"Did you get a good look at him?"

"He passed within ten feet. It's him. I'll let you know where I'm going once I figure it out," Quags said.

"Roger that. I have eyes on the girl. Keep me posted."

Gates ended the call and turned his attention back to his mark as the woman threw her bag into the back seat of a small hybrid, climbed in, and shut the door. As the driver pulled into traffic, Gates noted the large U sticker on the side window of the vehicle. Then he put the cruiser into drive and began his first tail in fifteen years.

The Uber crawled through traffic on Wilson Boulevard, heading uphill, away from the Potomac River. Gates concentrated on not losing the car as the Uber driver weaved in and out of traffic, ducking and dodging through the most well-heeled section of Arlington. At a stoplight in Courthouse, Gates's phone rang again.

"What's the word, Millares?"

"On the Metro. I almost lost him. I didn't have time to figure out the Metro pass vending machine. I had to badge my way through. I'm on the Orange Line. Heading west. If I'm looking at the map correctly, Vienna is the last stop on this line."

"Okay. I'm also heading west," Gates said, confirming his direction with the compass reading on his rearview mirror.

"Stay tuned."

Fifteen minutes later, the Uber pulled into the driveway of a condominium near the corner of Glebe Road and Washington Boulevard. The female witness climbed from the car, removed her bag from the back seat, and walked into the outer foyer of the building. She swiped an ID on the interior door and disappeared across the lobby, waving to the concierge behind the desk as she passed.

Gates waited a full minute before exiting his car. The outer doors of the building slid open as he approached and the concierge behind the desk looked up. Gates perused the resident list on the touch screen on the wall, and then knocked on the interior door, pressing his badge to the glass. The doors opened and the concierge stood from her stool behind the front desk.

"Thank you," Gates said, entering the lobby. He crossed the open tile floor and the concierge smiled.

"Charles Gates," he said, introducing himself with his badge and credentials.

The concierge showed no interest in confirming his identification. "How can I help you, Officer?"

"Do you know the woman who just entered?"

"I know all the tenants. It's part of the job."

"What's her name?"

"Her name is Wendy Cravello. She lives in 312."

"What can you tell me about her?"

"She's not here very often. But when she comes back into town, she usually has a few boxes to pick up. She didn't have anything today."

"Is there a husband or a boyfriend?"

"She had an engagement ring on her finger the last time I saw her. I'm pretty sure I met her fiancé a couple of times. Or, I assumed it was her fiancé. He was a tall guy, dark complexion. Good-looking."

"And her name is Wendy Cravello?" Gates confirmed.

"That's right, 312. Do you want me to ring her?"

"Not now. Maybe later."

"No problem. If you change your mind, I'll be here until six tomorrow morning."

*

Gates slipped back behind the wheel and checked his phone. The series of texts from Quags were short and sweet. *Leaving Courthouse Station.*

Arriving in Clarendon. Leaving Virginia Square. Arriving in Ballston. Getting off the train.

Gates remained in his car, deciding on his next move.

Coming out of Exit 9. Heading down Fairfax Boulevard.

Give me an address, Gates typed. *I'll meet you. I have a potential name for our girl. Followed her right to her door.*

As Gates sat in the illumination of his cell phone, an uptick in the rain covered his windshield. To his left, a man walked down the sidewalk, eyes glued to his phone. A second man with a familiar gait appeared behind the first man. Gates quickly typed a text.

I'm parked straight ahead.

Gates watched as Quags received the message on his phone and raised his eyes. As the male witness walked through the same doors the female witness had entered five minutes before, Quags approached the parked cruiser.

"How did you find me? I didn't give you an address," Quags asked as he settled into the passenger seat.

"I didn't. You found me. I followed the female witness to this apartment building."

"*Carajo.* They live in the same apartment building? What are the chances of that?"

"I don't think it's chance at all."

*

"You're back?" the concierge said, smiling.

"I was waiting for my partner to catch up," Gates said, nodding his head in Quags's direction. "Now that he's arrived, we're going to pay Wendy Cravello a visit."

"She just buzzed up a visitor."

"I know. And he didn't look very tall or dark."

"We don't get involved in the personal lives of our tenants. We have a strict no pillow police policy."

"I like that one."

"You can use it. Apartment 312 is at the far end of the hall. Turn right when you get out of the elevator."

CHAPTER 35

THE AROMA OF curry welcomed Gates and Quags to the third floor. Turning out of the elevator, they followed the dark carpet toward the end of the hall. The sound of music, television, and conversions faded in and out as they passed closed apartment doors.

"You think they'll talk?" Quags asked.

"We'll see," Gates replied. "Why don't you let me take the first swing at them. I'll be the good cop. If we need a bad cop, you can jump in."

"Works for me."

Moments later they stopped in front of unit 312 and knocked. They both heard shuffling on the other side of the door before the light coming through the peephole was momentarily extinguished.

"Who is it?" a woman's voice asked.

"The police," Gates replied, holding his badge up to the peephole.

A second later, the deadbolt lock clicked and the door opened.

"Are you Wendy Carvello?"

"I am," Wendy replied. She was wearing a long sleeve shirt, yoga pants, and no socks or shoes. Her blonde hair looked unbrushed.

"My name is Charles Gates. I'm the chief of police for Williamsburg, Virginia."

"Williamsburg? Can I ask what this is about?"

"Last week, you were a witness to an attempted robbery at a Walgreens on Broad Street in Richmond. We're here because you provided false statements to the police investigating that crime."

Wendy stared at the officers. "Why would the Williamsburg Police be interested in a robbery that occurred in Richmond?"

"A separate but related investigation."

"Would you mind if I took a minute to verify your credentials?"

"Of course," Gates replied.

Wendy shut her door halfway and typed into her cell phone. Several flicks of her finger later she opened the door again. She turned her phone toward Gates, showing him a photograph of himself from the Williamsburg PD website. "That's you all right."

"Perhaps it would be better if we discussed this inside," Gates said.

Wendy Carvello stepped back into her apartment and Gates and Quags entered.

"Please, have a seat," she said, motioning to the dining room table just beyond the kitchen. Quags's eyes danced over the photos on the wall as they followed their host's instructions. The sound of a toilet seat hitting porcelain caught his attention before they found their chairs.

"Are you alone, Ms. Cavello? We'd like to avoid any potential surprises," Quags said.

"I have a guest. A friend is here."

"Can you have your friend come out?" Quags replied.

Wendy disappeared around the corner and spoke in a whisper before returning with her friend in tow. With a glance, Gates and Quags recognized her visitor as the male they'd seen on the Walgreen's surveillance video. He was dressed in a plain T-shirt and running pants. Bare toes in need of a pedicure protruded from the cuffs.

"This is Matthew," Wendy offered.

"Do you have a last name, Matthew?" Gates asked.

"Spagnola."

"Okay. So, for the record, we have Wendy Carvello and Matthew Spagnola. Is that right?"

Heads nodded.

"Do you have identification?"

"We do."

"May we see them?"

Matthew produced his wallet and Wendy stepped to her purse resting on the kitchen counter. A moment later, Gates looked at the IDs and passed them to Quags.

"As I mentioned, my name is Charles Gates and I'm the chief of police for the city of Williamsburg, Virginia. This is one of my detectives, Luis Millares. We have a few questions for you."

The nerves in the room were palpable as Gates conveyed the series of events that had led them to Northern Virginia. When he finished providing the relevant pieces of the puzzle, Gates stated his request. "We are aware that both of you are career trainees at Camp Peary, also known as The Farm. We would like to ask you some questions about your training and one of your instructors."

Wendy quickly interjected. "We can't discuss details pertaining to our training. If you have questions, you'll need to contact the base liaison office. We can provide the number if required."

"Is that a memorized response?"

"It's our official response," Matthew replied.

"We've already spoken to Childress."

"And did he give us permission to speak freely? If he did, that's great. But we'll need to confirm."

"No, unfortunately he didn't. So we've come directly to you."

"I don't think we can offer you anything that isn't classified. As you know, our employer takes its secrecy very seriously," Wendy said.

"No argument there," Quags replied.

"I wish there was more to say," Matthew added, as if the statement would end the Q&A.

Quags shook his head. "Tell me, Wendy, how long have you been engaged? It's a beautiful ring, by the way."

Wendy Cavello flushed as Quags motioned toward her hand.

"Eight months."

"Congratulations. I would offer Matthew here congratulations as well, but I don't believe he's the man posing with you and your engagement ring in the picture on the wall. I think the photo speaks for itself."

"I'm not her fiancé. We're friends."

"Friends with benefits, or just friends?"

"I don't think that's an appropriate question," Wendy replied.

"Well, you just arrived back in the DC area from The Farm and the first thing the two of you do is get together. After spending all that time together on the base." Quags made eye contact with Matthew. "You haven't even been home yet. And you took separate modes of transportation here. Probably to ensure you wouldn't been seen together by other trainees."

Matthew didn't reply.

"The man in the photograph on the wall is my fiancé," Wendy confessed, breaking the stalemate.

"And you and Matthew here are also romantically involved?" Quags asked, making it sound like a statement.

Wendy nodded and Matthew lowered his gaze.

"It just happened. We didn't plan on it. The Farm can be a lonely place," Wendy replied, her voice on the verge of cracking.

"Does your fiancé know?"

Wendy shook her head.

"Does your employer know?"

"No," Wendy replied. A tear slowly ran down her cheek as if coaxed out for an on-time appearance.

"How's that going to go over?"

"I'm not sure."

"Sounds like it could be construed as an untrustworthy characteristic for a CIA trainee."

Another tear followed the first.

"But I don't see why anyone needs to know anything about what's going on. That can remain between the two of you, your employer, and the odd man out."

"What's the catch? I don't think you came all this way to tell us we shouldn't be in a relationship."

"You're right about that. We just need you to answer a couple of questions for us. Then we will be gone. We can all go on with our lives as if this conversation never occurred. Though I'm not sure what you're going to do about your next polygraph with regard to your current, um . . . circumstance."

Wendy considered the offer for several long seconds. "What kind of information are you looking for?" she relented.

"Information on one individual. I assure you it has nothing to do with the spy business. We're trying to find a serial killer. We'd like to start with what occurred at the Walgreens and your perspective of the attempted armed robbery."

"What's the connection between the robbery and a murder?"

"We believe the perpetrator of a thirty-five-year-old cold case was on the scene in Walgreens. We believe he was involved in the attempted robbery."

"Oh. And that's all you're interested in?"

"Yes."

Wendy paused, exchanged glances with Matthew, then answered. "We didn't even know it was a real robbery until later."

"What did you think it was?"

"A test. We were in training. Our instructors were running countersurveillance. They were wearing disguises so as to not be easily recognizable. We, the trainees, were given cover identities and told not to break cover, no matter what. We assumed the whole incident at the Walgreens was part of the exercise."

"Even after the clerk was pistol whipped and an entire row of merchandise was displaced? Not to mention the man who received a broken arm?"

"I understand where you're coming from. I'd probably doubt our story, too, if I were the average Joe. But we've spent the last few months pretending we live in a country that doesn't exist, recruiting imaginary spies, and practicing deceit in nearly every facet of our lives. We've run through mock border crossings with real guns and angry dogs, and have been locked up and interrogated. A displaced aisle of merchandise at a drug store didn't seem difficult to orchestrate as an exercise in deception. And on top of that, our instructor left before the police arrived. We just assumed it was par for the course, so to speak."

"And what did your instructor say about the incident?"

"When we returned to The Farm, he commended us for our professionalism and for maintaining our cover."

"Did he tell you it was an exercise? That the attempted robbery was staged?"

"He didn't comment one way or the other. But we received high marks on that day's exercise."

"And when did you find out the attempted robbery was real?"

"When the chief of security came to question us later that week. Then we became concerned because we had provided the police with false information. Childress said he'd speak with Richmond PD and sort it out on our behalf. He assured us we were not going to be in any trouble."

"Was anything said after that?"

"No. We assumed it was taken care of."

Gates produced the images of the instructor that had been enhanced by Dr. Liu. "Is this an accurate portrayal the instructor who was with you at the Walgreens? We had some quality issues with surveillance videos, but we believe this image reasonably depicts the individual in question."

The two leaned in.

"That's him," Wendy confirmed.

"What can you tell us about him?"

"Not much. His name is Ken, but everyone calls him Zee or Instructor Zee. "

"What does he teach on The Farm?"

"He's a floater."

"What does that mean?"

"Some instructors have a well-defined specialty. For example, the gun guys only teach guns. They may stand in as border guards or potential assets at mock cocktail parties, but as instructors, the gun guys are all about the weapons. Other instructors teach a couple of different courses. Or they take turns. It seems they teach whatever they're good at."

"What courses did Ken teach?"

"He was the lead instructor for negotiations."

"What kind of negotiations?"

"Basically it's how to probe for the appropriate carrot before asking a potential asset to spy on their own country. To spy on their friends. On their family. All for the US government. The course is very similar to corporate sales training and negotiations. Some people are just plain better at it than others. The rumor on Ken is that he ran more assets than any intelligence officer in the last twenty years. Rumor also has it that he spent most of his career in Asia."

"So he was a salesman."

"That's one way to look at it. He's also into martial arts. They have full-time hand-to-hand combat instructors on The Farm, but Instructor Zee was better than any of them."

"Any idea what kind of martial arts?"

"He didn't say. But he was good. One afternoon he taught us how to fight with improvised weapons."

"Such as?"

"A variety of garden tools. A rake. A spade. He also liked to screw with the students a little. He was fond of telling us that his daughter hit harder than we did."

"Did he teach you how to disarm an assailant with a gun?"

"It's a standard lesson on The Farm. One of the basics. It's probably a lot harder to do in real life than it is in practice. But he showed us how it's done."

"Indeed, he did. Up close and in person. Anything else about him?"

Wendy shrugged. "He is remarkably unremarkable. Brown hair. Brown eyes, or at least hazel. He's usually clean shaven. Probably five ten or so. Average weight . . ."

"And he lives on base," Matthew added.

"Do you have an address?"

"Nope. Trainees aren't allowed in the resident section of The Farm. We just know he lives on the base because he comes to work on a base bicycle."

"Out of curiosity, did you ever notice the top of his head?"

"I'm sorry?" Wendy asked.

"The top of his head. Did you ever get a view of the top of his head?"

Wendy and Matthew seemed to consider the question before answering. "He wears a lot of baseball caps," Wendy replied.

Maybe there's a reason for that, Quags thought.

CHAPTER 36

QUAGS CLICKED THE mouse, scrolling through the surveillance video from the Walgreens that had been enhanced by William & Mary's Computer Science Department. Frame by frame, he moved through the images in front of him until the overhead camera provided an unobstructed view of the good Samaritan's Walgreen shopping basket and its contents.

"Trail mix, an energy drink, and a birthday card," Quags said, reminding himself what they'd previously seen in the shopping basket. He leaned into the screen, his focus on the visible portion of the birthday card, the rest hidden by the pink envelope that accompanied the card. Slowly, the highly pixelated image seemed to give up its secret.

"Sweet," Quags read aloud before adding a string of expletives.

*

Quags knocked on his boss's office door and waited to be invited in.

"I think we got him," Quags said, crossing the floor and placing an enlarged image of the card from the good Samaritan's shopping basket on his chief's desk.

"What am I looking at?"

"You tell me. You're my sanity check."

"It's fairly grainy."

"But you can still read it."

"All it says is 'sweet.' That could be anything."

"I don't think so. We know that the good Samaritan was in the card section of Walgreens before the altercation. Specifically, he was in the birthday card section. And there's only one birthday I can think of that uses the word 'sweet.'"

"Sweet sixteen," Gates said, grasping the revelation. "You think the good Samaritan has a child who's sixteen."

"About to turn sixteen or just turned sixteen. And the envelope is pink. So I'm guessing it's for his daughter."

"It could be for a niece. There are any number of possibilities."

"There are a few possibilities, but only one likelihood. The card is for his daughter. And we know the amorous couple from Walgreens said one of Instructor Zee's favorite sayings was 'my daughter hits harder than that.'"

Quags could see his boss teetering on the edge of being convinced. He turned the screen of his phone and held an image in front of Gates. "I called the Walgreens in Richmond and asked them to look for a Sweet Sixteen card for a daughter that comes with a pink envelope. That's the image they sent back to me. As you can see, it's the same."

Gates's eyes widened and he leaned back in his chair. "Son of a bitch."

"You got that right."

"Sooner or later, I may have to admit you're a better detective than I even hoped you would be."

*

"Good afternoon, Charlie," Sean Bramble announced into the phone.

"Good afternoon. Any movement on the subpoena for Camp Peary?"

"Nothing so far. We're still anticipating that the director of the CIA is going to sign off on the secrets privilege assertion."

"Then our odds haven't changed."

"Not yet. Any progress on your end?"

"That's why I'm calling. We made some headway in identifying our man. We have confirmation that he's an instructor on The Farm. A career CIA officer who has spent time in Asia. He teaches negotiations and is a martial arts expert. And we think he has a daughter."

"No name?"

"He is known on the base as Instructor Zee."

"Age, address? Anything beyond a pseudonym?"

"No, but I think I can get that information."

"How?"

"I want to serve another subpoena."

"In this case, two subpoenas are not going to fare better than one. The resistance from Camp Peary and the legal department in Langley is going to be the same on a second subpoena."

"I don't want to serve the Agency again. I want to subpoena the York County School Division."

Sean Bramble stared up at the ceiling of his office, imagining the dots that Chief Gates was trying to connect. "York County?"

"That's right. A simple subpoena duces tecum."

"Simple is a relative term."

"I want to subpoena access to student records. If we can identify our suspect's daughter, then we'll be able to identify our perp."

"Anything more specific than that?"

"I'm looking for a girl somewhere around sixteen who lives on the base."

"How soon do you need it?"

"As soon as you can."

"Give me an hour."

CHAPTER 37

JAY MILLER, DIRECTOR of personnel for the York County School Division, read the subpoena while Gates and Quags sat in a matching set of chairs positioned on the other side of his desk. When he finished, his eyes moved back to the top of the page for a second pass. A minute later, Miller spoke, a stoic expression on his face.

"Well, Chief Gates, we can certainly help you with your investigation. Not that we have much of a choice."

"We appreciate the assistance."

"Follow me, gentlemen. I'll hand you off to Gladys Young. She knows everything there is to know about our student database. She also seems to know every soul in York County."

Miller stepped from his office, strolled past his secretary, and entered a sea of cubicles. "But fair warning, Gladys can be a little rough around the edges," the director added.

"Perfect. Detective Millares here can also be rough around the edges," Gates replied.

Miller glanced quickly at Quags as the three walked. At the end of the aisle, he motioned to his left, and the three men turned the corner. Several cubicles down, the director stopped and poked his head around the wall. Gates noted the nameplate on the outside of a cubicle. Then he noted the stench of cigarette smoke permeating the air.

Miller made introductions and explained the subpoena to his employee. "Get the chief and detective here anything they want."

"Yes, sir," Gladys responded. Thick wrinkles creased her cheeks, and Quags wondered how many of them were the result of smoking.

"Please, stop by on your way out," the director said to the officers before disappearing.

"Grab a chair," Gladys said. "There's one in the corner here and one in the empty cube across the way. Drag it over."

The officers did as they were told, and Gladys pulled open the bottom drawer of her desk. "Can I offer you a snack? See anything you like? Most of it's junk food, but I have some raisins and trail mix in here somewhere."

"No, thank you," Gates replied.

"Very well. Let me know if you change your mind," she said, closing the drawer. "So, you're looking for some information on a student?" she asked.

"That's correct," Gates answered.

"Do you have a name?"

"No name. But we have other parameters that should help us get to a name."

"Okay. I'll drive the computer and you guys tell me where you want to go," she said, hacking a cough into her elbow.

"We're looking for records related to a student who recently turned sixteen or would be approaching sixteen."

"Which school?"

"We assume the student lives in northern York, so probably Bruton High."

"I know it well. Most of the county's high schools are down here in Yorktown, but I'm from northern York myself."

"Do you have any idea how many students attend Bruton High?"

"Currently, the student body size is 622."

"You know the number off the top of your head?" Quags asked.

"Are you surprised?"

Quags shrugged. "A little."

"The number changes. New kids arrive. Some kids move on. We have a lot of military families in this neck of the woods. They move a lot. But the number I just gave you is the most recent head count as of Monday last week."

"Can you search your database by sex of the student?" Quags asked.

"I can. Which are you looking for? And don't give me any of that gender identity nonsense. I'm talking about the plumbing they were born with."

"Female."

Gladys provided commentary as she began her database search. "Okay. A sixteen-year-old female would in all likelihood be a sophomore. Obviously that's not exact, but it's a good indicator. So if we look at Bruton . . . the school has 141 people in the sophomore class and slightly more than half of them are females. There are 76 in total."

"Can you tell us how long each student has been enrolled in the York school system? We're looking for girls who recently enrolled. New to the school either this year or last."

"Why is that?" Gates asked Quags in a whisper.

"Because our pot farmer mentioned he didn't recognize the composite of our guy, which meant he was probably new and started on base after Grant had washed out."

"A pot farmer, you said?" Gladys asked, her interest in the conversation piquing.

"It's a long story. Can you search for girls who recently enrolled?" Quags asked.

"Hmmm. I don't know if anyone has ever asked for that parameter. Give me a second."

Gladys banged away on her keyboard and clicked her mouse while Quags took inventory of the walls of her cubicle.

"Okay," Gladys said. "Now all I need to do is look at enrollment dates and then perform a quick VLOOKUP and . . . presto. We have eight female sophomores who meet those criteria."

"Eight?"

Gladys confirmed her answer, pointing at the row count on the screen.

"Can you pull up the addresses for those students?"

"Yes, sir. Give me one second."

Another moment later the list of names with their associated addresses populated the screen.

"Two of those girls have the same PO box address," Quags stated, perusing the screen. "Different last names but the same PO box."

"Yes, they do."

"Is that unusual?"

"That PO box is used for base kids," Gladys said. "At least, that's what we call them."

"Base kids?" Quags asked, playing naive.

"You'll have to excuse my detective. He's from South Florida," Chief Gates explained.

"He must be from somewhere," Gladys retorted. "Around here, when someone says base, it means Camp Peary. And don't try telling me you've never heard of it. I'll call bullshit on that."

"He's heard of it. How many students in the York County School System live on base at Camp Peary and use that PO box?" Gates asked.

"The last time I checked it was just over sixty. That's all grades, all schools."

"Who would have guessed that many kids lived on The Farm?" Gates asked, rhetorically.

"I hate to state the obvious, but I think that's the point," Gladys replied. "The Farm doesn't want anyone to know how many families live on the base. They don't want you to know anything about anything. But the York County School Division can't have kids attending school with no names or addresses. Even we have minimum standards."

"And according to your database, two sophomore girls from Bruton High currently live on The Farm?"

"Newly enrolled sophomores," Gladys clarified. "Yes, that's what it looks like. Two girls. But there could be other kids in the age group you're looking for that I'm not aware of. Some kids on The Farm go to private schools. I wouldn't have that information."

Gates nodded. "How does the PO box on the base work?"

"We send all our correspondence to the PO box and I guess it gets sorted and delivered by base personnel. They have street names on base, but they don't use them for outside correspondence. They asked us to use the PO box, so we use the PO box."

"You said they have street names on base?"

"That's right."

"How do you know?" Quags asked.

"My cousin was married to a fireman. Before he retired, which was before he died, he worked at the Camp Peary fire station."

"They have their own fire station?" Quags asked.

"They do. They have houses on base and when there's an emergency, the fire department needs a street name and address to get there. But from what I heard, most of the time, they're putting out fires that start from explosions and the like. I gather they blow up a fair amount of stuff."

"Do you know the street names?"

"Every once in a while a parent will put their complete address on the emergency contact form. Which never makes sense to me. Is anyone going to send mail in the case of an emergency?"

"Not if they want help to arrive. Do either of the two new sophomore girls on base have their street address listed?"

Gladys double-checked her query results. "Nope. It would be here if they did."

"What else can you tell us about the two girls?"

"One is named Alice Hall. The other is Audrey Zambrano. I may have their parents' names. Or what they told us their names are."

"Zambrano," Quags repeated aloud.

"Zambrano could easily be shortened to 'Zee,'" Gates added

"One hundred percent chance a Puerto Rican would shorten that to 'Zee,'" Quags said. "Can you pull up the full names?"

"You have a subpoena and a badge. I'll pull up whatever you tell me to."

Gladys worked her next query and Quags asked questions. "Hypothetically, how would you know if a student or their parents were using a fake name?"

"We have a pretty good idea of our students' real names. We collect proof of immunization. And we ask for copies of birth certificates. As far as we know, they use real names on those types of medical records."

"Do you verify anything?"

"We don't double-check medical records or call every emergency contact, if that's what you're asking. Over the years we've never had a problem with the validity of the list. But they are in the spy business, so I assume if they wanted to, they could create forgeries for everything." Gladys paused for a long moment. "You know, if you told me what you're looking for exactly, I might be able to help you get there more quickly. I know a lot of parents."

Quags nodded in the direction of the screen.

Gladys spoke. "As I said, the first girl is Alice Hall. Her parents are listed as Oliver and Tammy Hall. She has no blemishes on her school record. Good grades."

"And the second girl?"

"The second girl is Audrey Zambrano. Father is Kirk Zambrano. Mother is listed as Lilly. She also has really good grades."

Time seemed to freeze for Chief Gates as he stared at the name on the screen. "Kirk Zambrano," he whispered, digesting the possible name of his sister's killer for the first time.

"Kirk Zambrano," Quags repeated. "Kirk is close to Ken."

"I think we have our guy," Gates said.

"Do you want me to make a couple of telephone calls for you guys? See if there's anything else about these girls that may help you out? Things that aren't necessarily in the York County School computers?"

"We'll take any information that you can get us," Quags quickly answered.

"Let me take a smoke break and make a few calls. I'll be back in, say, fifteen minutes or so."

"Can we get a coffee around here somewhere?"

"There's a Keurig in the kitchen. Creamer is in the fridge. Sugar and Splenda on the counter."

*

Quags added a splash of creamer to his cup and joined Chief Gates at a white table in the corner of the office kitchen. The chief of police scrolled through several screens of his phone and stood up.

"I'll meet you back at the station later. I need to check a few things and touch base with the commonwealth's attorney. Hang around here long enough to see what Gladys finds out. Get printouts and soft copies."

"Roger that, Chief. I'll fill you in later."

For the remainder of Gladys's smoke break, Quags sipped his coffee in the silence of the kitchen, perusing the internet for information on Kirk Zambrano. Unfruitful on his cursory attempt for intel, he quickly reached the conclusion that CIA case officers don't have much of an electronic footprint. "*Coño*," he said aloud, swirling the last swig of coffee around the bottom of his cup.

"Are you ready for round two?" Gladys asked, poking her head into the kitchen.

"I am."

"Come on. I found out a few things that may interest you."

Quags followed Gladys back to her cubicle, choking in the wake of her latest cigarette. At her desk, Gladys sat down and turned her chair to face Quags.

"The first girl on the list, Alice Hall, plays the piano for Bruton High. She was in a concert last month. Rumor has it that she grew up in Europe and was trained by a classical virtuoso. At any rate, she's a gifted piano player. She's also in the German Club. They're new to the area and her parents seem to keep to themselves."

"I bet they do," Quags whispered.

"The second girl is named Audrey Zambrano. Her father is Kirk Zambrano. Her mother Lilly Youn Kim. She's Korean, which makes Audrey half Asian. She plays on the Bruton soccer team. Apparently she's good. She started on varsity as a freshman. She's the leading goal scorer this year. She's dating a seventeen-year-old named Dean Stokes. He's trouble by all accounts."

"What kind of trouble?"

"Vandalism. Underage drinking. Fighting. Shoplifting."

"I'm sure the girl's parents are happy about the relationship."

"I bet they are," Gladys said sarcastically.

"Can I get a printout of everything you've queried?

"Sure. Give me a minute."

"And put whatever you can on a thumb drive?"

"Absolutely."

Gladys returned several minutes later and handed Quags a stack of paper and a thumb drive. In exchange, Quags offered Gladys a business card. "If you can think of anything else that may be important, please give me a call."

"You can count on it, Detective."

CHAPTER 38

QUAGS KNOCKED ON the front door of the Gates's residence. A shadow crossed the living room window, the knob rattled, and the door opened.

"Good evening, Mrs. Gates," Quags said.

"It's Barbara."

"Yes, ma'am."

"Come in, Detective. Charlie is in the kitchen. Just head on back."

Detective Millares passed the entrance to the living room and noticed the pile of papers and folders on the coffee table in front of the sofa.

"Ignore the mess. I'm putting together a new lesson for one of my history classes," she said.

"I didn't notice any mess."

"From what I understand, you notice everything."

"That's flattering, but not true."

"I'm only repeating what I've heard. I also heard you enjoy a good cup of coffee. You want me to make some? I could even whip up an espresso. It's no trouble."

"No, thank you. I'm good. I just wanted to drop a few things off. I won't be staying long."

"Suit yourself."

Quags entered the kitchen and Chief Gates pointed at the phone pressed to his ear, sticking a finger in the air to indicate he was almost done. Quags sat down on the opposite side of the kitchen table. He placed the printouts from the York County School Division on the table next to a bottle of twelve-year-old Macallan scotch and a nearly empty glass.

"What did you bring me?" Gates asked as he ended the call and put his phone on the table.

"I wanted to drop off copies of the queries we ran today. Compliments of York County public schools."

"What did you learn after I left?"

"Gladys provided a little more information on our two girls at The Farm. The first plays the piano and grew up in Europe. The second plays on Bruton High's varsity soccer team. A bit of a phenom, apparently. She's rumored to be dating a local bad boy. Dean Stokes."

"I know the name. His grandfather was a pastor. The family tree wilted from there on out. What else did you find on the girl?"

"Her mother is Korean."

"That fits with our fake married couple's statement that instructor Zee had worked in Asia."

"You can get an Asian wife in the US these days too."

"You know what I meant."

"I did."

"So it seems that Instructor Zee's real identity is Kirk Zambrano."

"That's right. And I poked around a bit on him."

"I figured you would."

"Kirk Zambrano may well be a clandestine officer for the Central Intelligence Agency but I can't prove it. The only DMV record for him is from the early 1980s. His home address was in Massapequa, which is on Long Island, New York. He graduated from Massapequa High School. I have a high school yearbook photo, a group photo from the track team, and the photo off his driver's license. The pictures sort of resemble our composites, but we are talking about photography from the early eighties."

Quags placed both images on the table.

"Certainly could be our guy."

"For now, I'm running with the assumption that it's him."

"Anything else?"

"There's nothing on Kirk Zambrano after high school. I assume he went to college somewhere, but I can't find a record of it. He has no Facebook account. No Twitter. He's not on LinkedIn. He shows up in Fairfax County real estate records for a house in Reston, Virginia. It's been a rental since it was purchased sixteen years ago. Beyond that, our guy is a black hole. No marriage records. Nothing."

"In this case, nothing means something."

"I agree. The question is what do we do next? Do we call our contact in the Agency's legal department and let them know we've ID'd the guy?"

"I'm not ready to tip our hand just yet. Besides, they damn well know who he is. I still want fingerprints. I want this guy dead-to-rights."

Quags paused to think. "Are you a fan of soccer?"

"Sure. UVA is a seven-time NCAA National Champion."

"Really? Virginia?"

"We love our soccer and lacrosse."

"Well, this coming Friday night, Bruton High is playing an away game against Jamestown in soccer. Boys and girls. I say we go. Maybe our guy shows up to watch his daughter play."

"And if he does?" Gates asked.

"I'll think of something."

CHAPTER 39

QUAGS PEERED THROUGH his binoculars, the cord hanging around his neck, his eyes scanning the faces in the bleachers on the far side of the field. The twenty-two players chasing the ball across the grass was nothing more than a distraction to the task at hand. When Chief Gates climbed the bleacher steps and blocked his view, Quags lowered the binoculars from his eyes.

"Sorry I'm late," Gates said.

"No problem, Chief."

"Why are we on the home team bleachers?"

"Easier to see the faces on the visitor's side."

"You should have told me to bring binoculars."

"You can use mine. I need a break." Quags slipped the lanyard from his neck and handed the heavy pair of visual aids to Gates.

The chief of police sat down and focused his view through the two lenses. "Did I miss anything?"

"Our girl Audrey Zambrano scored twice already. Gladys from the school district had good intel. The girl has skills."

"See anyone in the stands who looks like our guy?"

"No. We have a couple dozen middle-aged white men in the stands. Mostly fathers with kids on the team. And the boys' team plays after this one, so there are probably a few extras. I've looked at every face and none of them resemble our guy."

"Have you gone in for a closer inspection?"

"I did. And it's almost halftime. I was going stretch my legs and take another look. Visit the Porta-John."

"I'll hold down the fort."

"Do you want anything from the concession stand?"

"A bottle of water."

"Roger that."

*

Forty-five minutes later, the referee blew the whistle and pointed to the middle of the soccer field, indicating the game was over.

"Five to one. Audrey Zambrano had a hat trick," Quags said.

"And we didn't see our man in the stands."

"A serial killer who's not up for Father of the Year? Imagine that."

"When's their next game?"

"There's an away game next week against Deep Run High School. The next home game is in two weeks."

"Are we coming back?"

"If we need to."

Quags shoved the paper tray from his hot dog into his empty Coke cup. The two law enforcement officers followed the crowd down the bleachers and around the track that encircled the soccer field. At the far end of the field, the girls' team exited as the boys' team entered, heading in opposite directions. In the midst of the cacophony of cleats clicking on asphalt, Quags pointed with his nose.

"Zambrano, number seven, straight ahead," he said.

Chief Gates peered around the crowd in front of him. "I see her. Still no father. But it looks like her boyfriend is here."

Gates and Quags watched as a young man put his arm around the soccer star's shoulder and kissed her.

"He doesn't look like a bad boy," Quags remarked.

"He would if he were dating your daughter."

"Probably."

"You heading home?" Gates asked as Quags slowed his pace.

"In a few. I'm going to observe for a minute or two."

"Let's touch base at lunch tomorrow. I have a budget meeting with the city council in the morning."

"Sounds good, Chief. Have a good night."

*

Quags stood near the concession stand and watched Audrey Zambrano as she crossed the parking lot, arm-in-arm with her boyfriend. The couple stopped next to a red open-top Jeep Wrangler and the boy leaned his back against the fender of the car. Audrey Zambrano wrapped her arms around the boy's waist and began kissing his neck until her lips found his. Quags noticed the boy's grasp on half a butt. The make-out session ended when a car full of girls stopped in front of the Jeep, offering a high-pitched chorus of hoots and hollers. Audrey Zambrano planted a final kiss on her boyfriend and climbed into the back seat of the car with her friends.

As the girls departed, a group of boys joined Dean Stokes at the Jeep. High fives ensued as the group of young men piled into the doorless vehicle. After another moment of observation, Quags weaved through the vehicles in the parking lot and approached the driver's side of the red Jeep.

"Are you Dean Stokes," he asked.

All four occupants of the vehicle looked up from their phones.

"That depends on who's asking?" Dean answered.

Quags presented his badge. "I'm asking."

"Oh, here we go again," Dean replied.

"Gentlemen, I'd like to have a word with Dean," Quags said to the boy's friends, who bailed from the vehicle in a flurry of legs and arms.

"What did I do this time?" Dean asked.

Quags noticed the peach-fuzz mustache over the boy's lip and the bottom edge of a tattoo on his left arm.

"I just have a few questions for you."

"I want a lawyer."

"You're not under arrest."

"I haven't done anything. I don't have to talk."

"No, you don't. But if I were you, I'd consider my options. Unless you want a permanent BOLO out on you, with all the benefits that come with it. You can either answer my questions or get pulled over every time you're within Williamsburg city limits."

"That's abuse of power. You know I didn't do anything."

"I just have a couple of questions and you'll be on your way."

Dean Stokes clenched his teeth and winced a bit. "What do you want to know?"

"I want to know about your girlfriend."

"Audrey?"

"That's right. How long have you been dating?"

"A few months."

"What can you tell me about her?"

"She's the best player on the girls' soccer team. And she's hotter than hell."

"Anything else?"

"She's real interesting. She's lived all over the place. And, man, I mean all over. She's half-Korean, but she grew up in China and Japan. Australia. Middle Asia."

"Middle Asia? Do you mean the Middle East?"

"No, Middle Asia. Near Thailand."

"Malaysia."

"Whatever." Dean rolled his eyes.

"Have you met her family?"

"Why does that matter?"

"It matters because it's one of the questions I want to ask."

"I've met the mother once. She was picking Audrey up from practice after school. She has an accent but her English is good. She's a tiger mom. She makes Audrey study hard. School first, soccer second, and nothing in third."

"Where does that leave you?"

"On the outside looking in. Her mother doesn't like me."

"What about Audrey's dad?" Quags asked. "What does he look like? Have you met him?"

"I haven't. And I don't think I'm going to. Both of her parents are against Audrey and I dating."

"Maybe it's because you keep having run-ins with the law."

"I haven't done anything recently."

"Anything that you've been caught for," Quags said, fishing for a reaction.

"That's not cool. I've been turning my life around."

"I hope you have."

"It won't matter to Audrey's parents. She told me her dad ran a background check on me. He knows everything about my past, what I've done, who my parents are. She told me some stuff her father found out that even I didn't know."

"I don't doubt it."

"He also tracks his daughter on her phone. Her parents monitor her texts. I had to buy both of us burner phones just so we could talk."

"I guess you haven't been invited to dinner."

"To say the least."

"Do you know her address?"

"On base?" Dean Stokes paused for a moment, a wave of suspicion seeming to wash over him.

"Yeah, on base."

"Nope. I've been to her house a couple of times when her parents weren't home. But Audrey had to meet me at the main gate and escort me to her house. You hear all kinds of stories about that place, but from what I saw, it was just a neighborhood. Regular houses. Regular streets."

"And you don't know your girlfriend's address?"

"Nope. And there's no reason to. It's not like I can drop by when I'm in the neighborhood."

"Could you get it for me?"

"I could ask."

Quags reached into his pocket, pulled out a business card, and handed it to Dean. "Give me a call and let me know."

"That's it? Are we done?"

"Not yet. Tell me about your girlfriend's house on base."

"I don't know what to tell you. It was a house. A living room, dining room, kitchen. The bedrooms were upstairs. They had interesting stuff on the walls from all over the world. I wasn't sure what most of it was, but it was cool."

"What about the outside?"

"A normal two-story house. The backyard is on the river. They had huge stone slabs that made a walkway down to the water behind their house."

"Sounds nice."

"It was. They had a little dock and a firepit in the backyard. Audrey showed me a garden. It was full of buried pots with lids."

"Buried pots?"

"That's right."

"Curious," Quags said.

"You know something else that's curious? It's curious that the police would need to ask me for an address. What's up with that?"

"None of your business."

"And what do I get for doing this favor?"

"I'll make your next speeding ticket disappear."

"All right. Now, are we done?"

"Yes. We're done. Drive carefully."

CHAPTER 40

CHIEF GATES SAT on the bench of the twenty-five-foot Grady-White fishing boat. To his rear, behind the wheel at the center console, Quags gently steered the boat out of the Wormley Creek Marina. Passing the channel buoys, Quags headed westward on the York River. The shadow of the Coleman Bridge cast the boat into momentary shade as Quags pushed the accelerator, the dual outboard motors propelling them forward, leaving a wake behind.

Fifteen minutes later, Quags slowed the boat to a crawl. Pointing to his left, he identified the beginning of Camp Peary as seen from the water.

"The airstrip is right over there. Just beyond the marsh. The last time I was out here, there was a parachute entangled in the canopy of those trees over there."

"How close can we get to the shore?"

"You'll see the signs in the water."

As advertised, the boat approached the first warning sign affixed to a post that disappeared beneath the water's surface.

"They have signs every couple hundred yards. Keeps boats away. Too bad, really. The edge of the marsh is probably jumping with fish."

"I assume there are more than just signs to keep people away."

"You know it," Quags replied.

"Just stay on the legal side of the warning signs."

"Roger that, Chief. Keep your eyes peeled for houses on base."

The boat went upstream for another fifteen minutes, with Chief Gates pointing out several clusters of houses along the shore of the base. Beyond the far side of the base's property, Quags dropped anchor. Chief Gates pulled out a map and spread it on the console. The two men pinpointed their location using the map and the boat's GPS.

"I was thinking we start here on the west end of the base and crawl along the coast going eastward. The current should keep us moving at a nice, slow pace. We can do some fishing while we work our way downstream. With the camera lens we have, we should get a good look at the group of houses we saw."

"Sounds like a plan. As long as the boyfriend was right about the house being near the river."

"He was pretty specific. A garden. And a stone path down to the water's edge. A deck. A firepit."

"Let's see if we can find a winner for that description," Gates said. He flipped up the bench and removed a camera bag from the storage compartment under the seat. Sitting back down, Gates attached a super telephoto lens. He put the camera to his eye and adjusted the focus before taking a series of snapshots.

To the rear of the boat, Quags added bait to the hook of his rod and cast it toward the shore.

"I don't think I've ever seen someone bait a hook that quickly. You're not messing around."

"For a second, I thought you were going to call me a master baiter."

"No, I wasn't."

"At any rate, I figured one of us should be fishing. Makes us seem less suspicious."

"The size of this camera lens may give us away. It's overkill for trophy fish photos."

"They say size doesn't matter."

Gates ignored the comment and snapped more photos. "What bites around here?"

"Bass. Mullet. Rockfish. My brother caught a sturgeon last year. The ugliest fish I've ever seen. Rare, but prehistoric looking. They only come this far inland to spawn."

"They used to have sturgeon up to eight feet long in both the York and the James. Now they're a protected species."

Quags motioned toward the shore with a nod of his head. "Speaking of protection. We've got company."

Chief Gates turned his camera in the direction of a gray boat moving away from the shoreline of Camp Peary. "You're not the only one who moves fast."

"Indeed."

Gates put his eye back on the rear of his camera. "We've got three men approaching. The boat captain is armed with a handgun, holstered on his waist. One SPO with an automatic weapon to his left. Another to his rear."

"That's a Zodiac. It will only take them a minute to get here." Quags put his fishing rod in one of the tubular holders at the rear of the boat. "Just to be on the safe side, why don't you put that camera down for a minute? And keep your hands in plain sight. Limit any big gestures."

Gates set the camera on the bench and moved toward the center of the fishing boat. Standing next to Quags, the law enforcement duo watched the large inflatable boat approach, its camouflaged hull contrasting against the water in full daylight. The boat's engines churned the water white as the driver put it in reverse to counteract its forward momentum. When the boat was twenty feet away, the engine idled. One of the SPOs moved to the front of the boat. The other took a seated position near the rear, weapon at the ready.

"Good afternoon, gentlemen," the driver of the boat said in a commanding voice.

"Good afternoon," Gates responded. "How can we help you?"

"We'd like to know what you're doing. This is a secure military installation. Photography is prohibited."

Chief gates raised his badge and held it in the air. "My name is Charles Gates. I'm the chief of police for the city of Williamsburg. This is one of my detectives. We're on public land, or rather, public water. Photography is allowed."

"Not of the shore."

"According to who?"

"The US Government."

Quags interjected with notable venom in his voice. "What law enforcement agency are you employed by?"

"The US Government."

Chief Gates reached for Quags's arm and gently squeezed.

"I think you should talk to Devon Childress before you continue down this path," Quags responded.

The mention of Childress's name brought the aggressive tone of the boat's driver down several notches.

"My detective is right. Go ahead and give Childress a call. See if he would like you to impede a police investigation."

The driver of the boat reached for a radio on the console and turned his back on Gates and Quags. The two other armed SPOs maintained their positions and the direction of their weapons. After several long moments of silence, the driver returned the radio to the console of the boat.

"You're free to carry on."

"You bet your ass we are," Quags said aloud.

*

Quags chewed on a cigar as he eyed the shore through the lens of the camera. The camouflaged boat shadowed them, maintaining a position between their fishing boat and land. The SPO's attempt to impede their photoshoot was easily overcome by the super telephoto. Slowly moving downstream, Quags anchored where gaps in the trees on the shoreline offered a view of the base residences.

"I've seen the same tanker truck come down the street twice. Followed by a black SUV similar to the one that escorted us from the base's main gate to the visitor center."

"What kind of tanker?"

"I can't tell you. I only caught a glimpse of it. Maybe some kind of lawn service? A sprayer truck for weeds?"

"Any more houses that fit our description?"

"We have another possibility in the next cul-de-sac. A house with a stone walkway leading down to the river. A deck and a firepit . . ." Quags paused. "And an Asian woman just opened the gate on a short wooden fence."

"A garden?"

"That would be my guess. The boyfriend didn't mention a fence around the garden, but everything else fits."

As Quags continued to watch, the woman reached down, out of view of the camera lens. A moment later she stood with a dirt-covered pot in her hand. "We'll, I'll be damned. She does bury pots in the yard."

"Pots?"

"That's sure what it looked like. You want to take a peek?"

"Yes, I do."

Gates looked through the camera lens and then put it down on the seat. "Let's see if we can pinpoint our location."

The two men again referenced the map on the steering console of the boat. Dragging his finger along the shoreline, Quags checked the boat's GPS. "According to my calculations, those houses over there are located right about here," he said, dropping a finger on the map.

"I concur."

"Now what?"

"We keep fishing."

"Fishing or *fishing?*"

"Both," Quags responded, lighting another cigar.

"How do you know which cigars to chew and which cigars to smoke?" Gates asked, jokingly.

"They're all for smoking. I chew on some because my doctor told me to smoke less. But I decided I wasn't going to let my little incident with drug dealers dictate the rest of my life."

"And by little incident you mean being shot five times."

"That's what I meant. One of my injuries was a collapsed lung. My doctor advised me against smoking."

"Most people don't inhale cigar smoke."

"You're not supposed to. But once in a while, I can't help myself. I think it's genetic."

"You should heed your doctor's advice."

"I have very few vices left. No one is going to want to be around me if I lose any more."

"Fair enough. I'm not sure anyone wants to be around you now." Gates chuckled.

"Thanks for that."

"And they never found the guys who shot you?"

Quags paused as if to consider his response. "Neither the two gunmen nor the driver of the vehicle were ever arrested."

Chief Gates stopped taking photographs of the property on shore. "What happened to them?"

"They were found murdered six months later."

"Six months?"

"Yep."

"Any leads on who killed them?"

"Not that I was aware of. The drug business in South Florida is danger-ous. It has been since the eighties. That's partially why I survived."

"I don't follow."

"After I was shot, I was airlifted to Jackson Memorial in downtown Miami. Fortunately for me, the surgeons at Jackson Memorial have a lot of experience with gunshot wounds. And that's thanks to the drug business. If I'd been taken somewhere else, I might have succumbed to my injuries."

"And how long were you in the hospital?"

"About a month."

"And recovery?"

"Another four or so."

"So five months after you were shot, you were up, walking around, all that?"

"I was. I still had some aches and pains, but I was fully functional, for the most part."

"And then a month later, the three men involved in your shooting incident were found dead."

Quags took two long puffs on his cigar and stared up at the sky. "That's right. Quite a coincidence, really."

"I thought you didn't believe in coincidences?"

Quags flashed a quick smirk. "I don't," he replied as the drag on one of his reels let out and started to whine.

*

For the next hour, Quags and Gates took turns manning the camera in silence. The SPOs in the boat were still guarding the coast and the driver was now observing them through binoculars. Quags waved intermittently and waited for a reply. No response. When he gave them the bird, the driver immediately returned the gesture.

"Assholes."

"Why do you have to rile them up?" Gates asked, the effects of hours in the sun visible on his forearms.

"Because they deserve it," Quags said before relaying his latest observation "Our tanker truck is back."

Gates looked over with unaided eyes. "I can't see it."

"It's in the cul-de-sac on the other side of the house. I saw it pull in and haven't seen it leave. The house is blocking my view but I should get a shot when it leaves."

"I'm going to start cleaning up the tackle," Chief Gates said, folding the map he had unfurled hours before.

"Gotcha," Quags blurted.

Chief Gates glanced over. "Who did you get?"

"The tanker truck. It's not what I thought it was. It's a takeaway tanker, of sorts."

"What's it taking away?"

"Shit."

"What kind of shit?"

"Human. The name on the door of the truck is Wilkins Water and Septic."

"I'll be damned."

"You know it?"

"I do. I've known Tony Wilkins forever."

*

Back at the marina, Chief Gates sat on the hood of the car and made a series of calls while Quags finished securing his boat in its slip.

"Any luck?" Quags asked as he approached the car, his pants wet around the cuffs.

"I tried to call Wilkins Water and Septic, but there was no answer. I know his daughter works as the office manager. But I heard she had a baby not too long ago."

"And if he's working on The Farm, he may not have his cell phone on him. It was on the long list of prohibited items."

"The same thought occurred to me. Wilkins Water and Septic is on the way back to town. Not far from Duncan Pond."

"Okay, then. Let's go to see a man about a honey wagon."

CHAPTER 41

THE SIMPLE GRAY warehouse resembled a large shoebox. Duncan Pond, considered by most locals as nothing more than an industrial catch basin, lurked in the weeds at the back of the property. Small planes flew overheard at steady intervals, on approach to Williamsburg's Regional Airport.

Stepping from the vehicle, Quags winced and turned his head. "*Coño.* That smells awful."

"A close second to a decomposing corpse."

"I hope the money's good in the septic business, because it smells like a shitty job."

"I'd laugh, but I'm trying not to breathe."

Gates buried his nose in the crux of his elbow and both men headed for the door on the left side of the building. Inside, a lone male employee sat behind a desk. Paper of different sizes and colors clung to a corkboard on the wall in a hodgepodge of messages and notifications. A framed business license hung on a rusty nail.

"Is Tony around?" Gates asked, removing his sunglasses. "I tried to call earlier. My name is Charles Gates."

"He's cleaning up. He should be out in a minute. Please feel free to take a seat," the young man replied, barely taking his eyes off his computer.

Gates and Quags sat on a pair of old wooden chairs with squeaky metal wheels and occupied themselves by catching up on the day's texts and emails. Heads down, thumbs flailing, neither man noticed when Tony Wilkins stepped through the doorway on the side of the office.

"Charlie Gates," Tony said, stretching out the pronunciation of the chief's first name. A mop of wet hair dripped from Tony's head onto his shoulders.

"Tony. It's been a while," Gates said, standing. "This is one of my detectives, Luis Millares."

"You can call me Quags."

"Nice to meet you, Detective. Sorry to keep you waiting. But to be fair, I also didn't know you were coming."

"You got a few minutes?" Gates asked.

"Always."

"Let's get some air."

Tony Wilkins, owner, driver, and employee number one, turned to his lone office staff. "We're going to take a walk. Be back in a bit." Stepping outside, Tony headed in the direction of a weed-strewn trail that encircled Duncan Pond.

"Your office help is a man of few words," Gates said.

"That's because he's my son-in-law and he's afraid to say anything."

"I heard you became a grandfather. Congratulations."

"Thank you. My daughter gave birth to a healthy boy three weeks ago. Unfortunately, she was also my office manager. My son-in-law is helping out until she starts working again."

"Good for you," Gates said.

"Thanks. It's been a blessing so far. How's Barbara? How's your Pops?"

"Everyone's good."

"Glad to hear it."

The trail weaved along the bank before opening to a patch of green grass. Empty plastic bags skirted across the ground. Tony pointed toward a circle of stumps surrounding the remains of a makeshift fire pit. "Grab a stump."

The three men sat and Tony coaxed the conversation forward. "What brings you around with one of your detectives? I haven't done anything to warrant police attention since we were in high school."

"I don't think we need to rehash our past," Gates said, shaking his head.

Tony winked at Quags.

"We were fishing today and saw your truck over at Camp Peary," Gates said.

"Were you working or fishing?"

"Both," Quags said.

"Um-hmm," Tony replied, clasping his hands together. "What kind of work were you doing?"

"A murder investigation," Gates said.

"And how is my truck involved?"

"It's not. But maybe you can help answer a couple of questions."

"About what?"

"The Farm."

"No offense, Charlie, but even if I wanted to, I wouldn't have anything to tell you. It's a temporary gig. Been there for a couple of weeks and should be done by the end of the month."

"What's the job?"

"The official work order is environmental leaching remediation."

"Meaning?"

"The septic tanks are leaking into the York River. The Virginia Department of Health has been monitoring the shellfish sanitation on the York and some of the creeks that run from the base. They ordered an environmental cleanup. The base, in turn, hired me. When I'm done, I'm done."

Quags interjected. "That explains the Virginia Department of Health truck I saw heading onto base during my stakeout."

"Yes, it does," Gates said. "I wouldn't have thought the base was on septic."

"From what I gather, most of the base hooks into the main sewer line. When they did all that construction back in the nineties, they upgraded. But the residential area of the base was never connected to the sewer. Most of the houses have septic fields and tanks, which I'm emptying. Spending my days shuttling shit out and coming back for more."

"We saw you at the houses down near the water."

"That's where the leaks were discovered. And, as a public service announcement, I wouldn't eat the shellfish from around here for a while."

"Good to know," Gates replied.

"What's the neighborhood like?" Quags asked.

Tony paused for a split second. "You said you saw it from the river. It's pretty much what you think. Houses. Housewives. Kids. Dogs. Cats."

"From the boat, the houses didn't look like military housing."

"That's for sure. The houses I've seen were built for families. They even have a swim and tennis facility at the edge of the neighborhood. But driving a septic truck doesn't get me close to any secrets. I'm escorted the entire time I'm on the premises."

"The entire time?" Quags confirmed.

"Every second. Honestly, I can't imagine a worse assignment. Sitting in a vehicle watching a guy suck excrement from septic tanks. But the smell is pretty awful once things get churned up, so the escorts don't get too close. They usually keep a bit of distance."

"I'll bet," Quags said.

"What exactly are you after, Charlie?"

"I think my sister's killer may be living on base at Camp Peary. Working as an instructor."

"Good God."

Gates nodded.

"Has this guy been hiding out on The Farm for the last thirty-five years?"

"We don't think so. We think he was a new recruit undergoing training when the Matoaka murders occurred. We believe he recently came back as an instructor."

"And you think I'm privy to some kind of information that could help nail this guy?"

"We're throwing darts at a board we can't see," Gates said. "But we heard the houses are for the instructors or long-term base residents."

"Like I said, from what I can tell, the houses I service are for families. Basketball goals in the driveway. Toys in the yard."

"Anything else stand out?"

"The only other thing I can tell you is that whoever lives on base shits in a toilet like everyone else."

"How many houses are on your work order?" Gates asked.

"I had thirty-one at the start of the job."

"Do the houses have addresses?"

"They have house numbers and street names. Owl Creek Circle, Portobello Road, Cactus something or other. I'm primarily only working on Portobello. Owl Creek Circle is one of the cul-de-sacs."

"Can you choose which house to do next?" Quags asked.

"I suppose. I've had to skip two houses already."

"Why's that?"

"I couldn't find the lid to the septic tank. The base claims they don't have maps of the location of the septic tanks. Maybe it's true. Maybe it ain't. But without a map, finding a septic tank and its lid can take a bit of digging around. If I can't find a lid in an hour of looking, I'll move on to the next house. That's happened twice."

"Do you ever see any cars on base? Anything that could identify an individual?"

"One thing the base doesn't lack is cars. I see a large number of unmarked four-door sedans and SUVs. The kind you would expect to see on a base full of secrets. The private vehicles I see are different. Subaru Outbacks. Minivans. Those aren't government vehicles."

"Have you seen any other service vehicles out there?"

"The base has their own maintenance personnel. I've seen their trucks."

"But the base doesn't have their own septic truck?"

"No, they don't. If they had a septic truck, they wouldn't have called me."

"When's your next service visit?"

"I'm out there every day, except Sunday, until I finish."

"So you're going tomorrow?"

"If it's not Sunday."

"Do you think you can help us out?" Gates asked.

"Tell me what you have in mind, and I'll see what I can do."

"We want the address of one of the residences. It may help with a subpoena. The house backs up to the water. We think it's one of them on the cul-de-sac you were at today."

"There are two cul-de-sacs by the river." Tony seemed to count in his head. "Four houses on one and five on the other."

"The house we're looking for has large stone steps that lead down to a small dock," Quags said. "It has a garden on the side of the house with a short fence around it. And there should be some pots buried in the garden."

"What do you mean, pots?"

"Ceramic or clay pots about the size of a bucket."

Tony seemed taken aback. "That's pretty specific information you got there. How do you know that but don't know the address?"

"It's a long story," Gates said.

"I hope it's one with a happy ending."

"So do we."

"I'll get the address. Shouldn't be a problem. I just have to compare what you told me to the list."

"Thank you," Gates said.

Quags pulled out his phone, ran his finger across the screen, and handed it to Tony. "This is what our guy looks like. You can swipe through the photos and see a couple of examples."

Tony did as suggested. "Doesn't look like a killer. Doesn't look like much of anything."

"That's a killer's secret to success," Gates said.

"Out of curiosity, do you ever go inside any of the houses?" Quags asked, considering more than the address.

"Oh, hell no. Septic workers don't even get offered a glass of water. But I will use a hose if the house has one. Wash down the end of the vacuum tube, my shovel. Clean up any splashes."

"What do you do when you have to use the bathroom?"

"For most jobs, I go off-site. More often than not, I wait until I'm back here at the office."

"It's pretty ironic that you drive around with a truck full of shit, but have trouble finding a john to use."

"I've thought the same thing myself. Many times," Tony said with a hint of exasperation.

"And while you're on-site at Camp Peary? Where do you use the john?"

"They have a visitor center. I use the bathroom there."

"Have you ever dusted for fingerprints before?" Quags asked.

Tony Wilkins and Chief Gates turned their heads in the detective's direction. "No, I haven't," Tony said.

"Forget it, Millares," Gates added.

"What's the harm in asking?" Quags said. "I was just thinking out loud."

"I've warned you about that," Gates retorted.

"It would be hard for me to take prints off anything while I'm on the job. I have to keep one hand on the vacuum when it's running. That limits how far I can wander. And I wear gloves, for obvious reasons. Not to mention, I have security chaperones on this particular job."

"But you said they don't get close. That they watch you from afar."

"They do. But I think they'd notice if I pulled out a fingerprint dusting kit."

"Maybe there's another way," Quags said, his voice trailing off.

CHAPTER 42

TONY WILKINS SCANNED the lawn, his hand on his long metal probe, looking for the telltale sign of a dip in the earth that hid the lid to the septic tank. The first two jobs of the morning had topped off his silver four-thousand-gallon truck. He was hoping the next two houses would follow suit and provide enough excrement for another full load.

Tony walked around the property in a grid pattern, poking every depression in the ground. As he did, he surreptitiously assessed the yard next door. Chills ran up his spine as he digested the possibility the next address on his work order was the residence of a bona fide serial killer. When a jab of his probe produced the familiar sound of metal hitting concrete, Tony's thoughts returned to his work. He headed back to his truck for his shovel and crowbar, crossed the yard again, and began removing soil to expose the septic tank's hatch.

An hour later, the concrete lid was returned to its original position and Tony used his shovel to move the pile of the earth back from where it had come. He stomped his boots on the ground and headed to his truck for the journey next door. Less than a minute later, he crossed a section of cul-de-sac pavement and parked at the edge of the curb.

Getting out of the cab of his truck, he again grabbed his probe and began his search of the backyard for the septic tank. The hood of his chaperones' black SUV shimmered in the sun, the two-man security team watching him from behind the vehicle's tinted windows. As Tony continued to probe, he committed the details of the property to memory. Large stone slabs led to the water's edge. A small dock. A firepit. A garden with a short fence that seemed to be sprouting ceramic pots with wooden lids.

Fifteen minutes later, with the septic tank located, excavated, and opened, the vacuum on the truck sprang to life again. With the pull of suction came the initial wave of stench. Tony, immune to the smell, scanned the property near the house. Next to a small shed, a garden hose wound around a wheel-like dispenser. He cranked his neck to his left, checked on the location of his base escorts, and wondered if the large bushes near the house would obscure the hose and shed from the street.

Tony worked the vacuum until it sounded like a kid sucking on a straw that had reached the bottom of a milkshake. He turned the vacuum off, returned the septic lid, and replaced the displaced turf. He approached the house and unwheeled several yards of garden hose. For the next minute he sprayed water onto the grass near the septic lid and rinsed off his boots. He showered his shovel with a solid stream of water, and then placed the hose on the ground. With a quick glance around, Tony considered his options. He eyed the hose handle for several long seconds and then placed his shovel on the ground and rewound the hose on its dispenser. Calmly, he stepped toward the shed on his right and cracked opened the door.

"Can I help you?" a man's voice bellowed from Tony's rear.

Tony spun around, attempting to shut the shed door with flailing arms. "You scared the living shit out of me."

"And I asked if I can help you with something."

Panicking, Tony's mind raced. "I was just curious about the pots in the garden. I thought maybe there was something in the shed that would tell me what was growing in them. I apologize."

The man stared hard at Tony, glancing at the pots in the garden and then back into Tony's eyes. "There's nothing growing in the pots. The pots are for fermenting cabbage. It's known as kimchi. It's a Korean dish."

"Never heard of it."

"You can get it at most stores these days."

"I'll have to give it a try. I apologize again for being nosey."

"Are you done with the septic system?" the man asked.

"I am. I should be out of here in a couple of minutes."

"Then don't let me stand in your way."

Hands shaking, Tony grabbed his shovel and returned the vacuum hose to the brackets on the side of his truck, preparing for departure. As he pulled out of the driveway to take away another load of honey, he noticed the owner of the home still standing in the yard, watching as his truck turned down the street with his base escort in tow.

*

Gates and Quags stepped into the office of Wilkins Water and Septic and reintroduced themselves to the man behind the lone desk in the room.

"Tony told me you'd be coming by. He should be out in a minute."

As advertised, Tony appeared, again with wet hair as if he had just showered off the day's excrement. Tony turned to his son-in-law clerk and motioned toward the clock on the wall. "Why don't you go ahead and get out of here a little early today. Pick up some dinner on your way home. I need to have some time alone with our guests."

"Are you sure?"

"Don't make me ask twice."

Without another word, the young man turned off his computer, grabbed his cell phone and a set of keys off the desk, and disappeared out the front door.

"You called. How did it go?" Gates asked.

"How did it go? I almost shat myself. That's how it went."

"Given your profession, no one may have noticed," Quags remarked.

Tony glared at Quags with one eyebrow raised.

"Where you able to learn anything?" Gates asked.

"Depends on how you look at it. I didn't get any prints. I thought about cutting off the end of the hose that I was using to clean up. I figured I could've taken my shovel and lopped off the last foot of hose with the nozzle still attached. And maybe get you your fingerprints."

"Not a bad thought."

"But then I noticed the shed next to the house was in the perfect location. A row of tall hedges obscured my base escorts' the line of sight. So I changed my plan of attack."

"What was in the shed?"

"I don't know. Your man surprised me. Popped out of nowhere."

"You met our suspect?" Gates asked.

"You're damn right I did. He looked a lot like the composite photos you showed me."

"Did he say anything?" Quags asked.

"Hell, yeah. He asked what I was looking for in his shed. I told him I was curious about the pots in his garden and wondered if there was something inside the shed that would tell me what he was growing."

"That's good thinking," Quags replied.

"I didn't put much thought into it at all. I just blurted it out. And in case you're wondering, the pots have something called kimchi in them."

"Did he buy your cover story?"

"It was hard to tell."

"And you're sure it was our guy?"

"Absolutely. House by the water, stone steps, firepit, dock, garden with pots."

CHAPTER 43

"CHIEF, THERE'S A call for you. It came through on 911," his admin said from the doorway.

"On 911?"

"Yep. You want it in here?"

Gates, dressed in full uniform, glanced at Quags, who was seated across from him. Quags nodded.

"Patch them through."

"Yes, sir," his admin said, heading back to her desk.

"How often do you get 911 calls?" Quags asked.

"Not often. Probably someone who went off their meds."

"Or someone who wants to taunt the chief of police."

Chief Gates pressed the button for the speaker and answered. "This is Chief Gates. You're on speaker. One of my detectives is also here. How can I help you?"

"Good afternoon, Chief Gates. We've never met, but my name is Bisa. I'm a student at William & Mary. I helped Dr. Lui enhance the security feeds from a robbery in Richmond last week."

"You're from the Computer Science Department, yes?"

"That's right."

"Your photographic enhancements have been very helpful. Great work."

"Thanks. I was wondering, are you still looking for your guy from the video?"

"We are. Why? Do you have another image for us?"

"No. I just saw the man in the flesh."

"Where?"

"At the visitor center."

"Which visitor center?"

"Colonial Williamsburg. I work at the visitor center part-time."

"And you think you saw the same person from the images you worked on?" Quags confirmed.

"I know I did. I spent a lot of time looking at those videos and creating composites. I'd know him anywhere. Right down to his hair plugs."

"Did you see his hair plugs?"

"You're darn right, I did. He was sitting on a bench, tying his shoe. Even before he sat down, I thought he looked familiar. But when he was tying his shoes, I got a good view of the top of his head. It's definitely him."

"Is he still there?"

"Not in the visitor center. He was with a few other people. They all provided season passes and headed in the direction of Nicholson Street."

"How long ago?"

"A couple of minutes. Five tops."

"What was he wearing?" Quags asked.

"Jeans. Some kind of brown leather shoes with laces. He had on a gray sweatshirt with Virginia Beach across the chest in red letters. We have surveillance video here in the visitor center. You can see for yourself."

"Did he have a backpack?" Quags asked.

"He did."

"Then he's not going to be dressed like that for very long."

"We'll be right over," Gates said, hanging up the phone on his desk.

Heading for the door, Gates swiped the screen of his mobile phone and waited for an answer. Seconds later, he hung up. "We gotta go. My dad's working at the blacksmith shop today. He's not answering his phone."

"Are we driving or walking?" Quags asked.

"We're running," Gates replied.

*

The Colonial Williamsburg visitor center was less than a half-mile from police HQ. Quags entered the lobby at a full run, cutting in front of a line of tourists. He approached the nearest ticket window with the chief of police in tow. Quags leaned into the speaker hole on the security glass.

"We need to speak with Bisa," he said, simultaneously flashing his badge.

"She's in the manager's office," the middle-aged woman responded, pointing to a door at the end of the counters.

Bisecting the crowd of visitors, Quags pulled open the manager's door and held it for his boss. The presence of the chief of police in full uniform electrified the atmosphere of the small office.

"Where's Bisa?" Gates asked a woman at her desk in the corner.

The woman motioned to another door on the opposite wall. "She's in there with security."

Quags and Gates entered the adjoining room. Two security guards stood next to Bisa. Standing, she provided Gates and Quags with an update. "We've printed out a photo of your man and security tracked him to the main area of the park."

"How many surveillance cameras do you have?" Quags asked.

"One at every intersection and one at every establishment that has a cash register," one of the guards replied.

"Which one shows where our guy is now?"

The security officers and Bisa pointed at the screen on the lower left. "That one," Bisa said. "He's still in the Virginia Beach sweatshirt and jeans. He's standing outside of Chowning's Tavern."

Quags grabbed a pen off the desk, pulled a notice off a bulletin board, and wrote his cell phone number on the back of it. "Keep track of him with the cameras you have," Quags said. "Call me if you need to."

Quags turned around to see Gates leaving the room. Speed walking across the main ticket floor, Quags caught up with Gates at the visitor center's entrance.

"You want to form a plan, or should we just shoot on site?" Quags asked, falling into step.

"I'm going to get my dad," Gates said, checking his father's location on the screen of his phone. "You head to Chowning's Tavern and locate our guy. Keep your phone handy."

*

The man in the Virginia Beach sweatshirt entered the Geddy House with a group of tourists at ten before the hour. A tour guide pontificated on the historical significance of the exhibit while the visitors perused the signage scattered around the first floor of the centuries-old residence. As the group headed up the steep staircase to the second floor, the man in the Virginia Beach sweatshirt lagged behind. Glancing around, he quickly removed his long-sleeved outer layer to reveal a navy blue T-shirt. Maintaining his position at the rear of the group, he placed a cap on his head as he reached the small landing on the second floor. By the time the tour group stepped into the garden at the rear of the house, a mustache and sunglasses had been added to his disguise.

Zambrano continued to follow his pair of trainees out of the garden. So far, the young couple in their mid-twenties hadn't spotted their tail. Scanning his surroundings, Zambrano noted nothing out of the ordinary. Another day. Another round of Rabbit. It wasn't until he saw the uniformed police chief jogging across the gravel street that Zambrano's spidey sense tingled. Keeping one eye on his young targets, Zambrano ratcheted up his observations. He meandered to the far side of the gravel road and took shelter behind a rotating postcard display. Ten yards away, he noted a man in a suit with a phone pressed to his ear, standing all alone, scanning the crowd.

Peeking between postcards, Zambrano watched as the man in the suit seemed to lock his attention on something in the distance. The man put his phone in his pocket and began swimming through a group of Asian tourists. In the blink of an eye, the man in the suit grabbed a taller man in a gray Virginia Beach sweatshirt and corralled him off the main street. A moment later, the man was spread legged, hands against the wall of a log cabin. The man in the suit and tie performed a pat down, culminating in the examination of the man's wallet. A short conversation ensued, and the suspect was set free before the man in the tie returned to scanning the crowd.

*

At the intersection of Botetourt and Gloucester, Gates, with his father behind him, caught up with Quags coming out of the old post office. As the three men converged, Quags threw his hands up in the air in defeat.

"I lost him. I'm going to head back to the visitor center's security office and see if the feeds can pick him up again."

"I'll meet you later. I'm going to walk my dad over to the station for safe keeping."

"I told him I don't need safekeeping," Gates Senior stated, as if pleading for Quags to overrule his son.

"I'm not getting involved," Quags replied. "I've got a killer to catch."

An hour later, Gates joined Quags for a final loop of Colonial Williamsburg on foot. Neither man noticed the elderly colonial soldier walking in the opposite direction, the gridlines in the man's scalp hidden by a wide brim hat.

CHAPTER 44

QUAGS SWALLOWED HIS last bite of barbecue chicken and pushed his plate forward. Empty plates, silverware, and glasses littered the top of the four-seat dining room table.

"I hope you saved room for dessert," Chief Gates said. "My wife makes a mean apple pie."

"Sounds like an offer I can't refuse."

"You can refuse if you want," Gates Senior replied from one chair over. "More for me."

Chief Gates helped bring the dirty dinner dishes into the kitchen. Barbara Gates pulled dessert plates from the cupboard and the pie from the oven. A moment later, Gates felt his phone vibrating. Fishing his phone from his pocket, he leaned back against the counter to avoid the hot pie as it passed. Pressing the talk button, Gates was greeted by an unfamiliar male voice on the line.

"Is this the chief of police, Charles Gates?"

"It is."

"I'm glad I got through to you. I think it's time for us to meet face-to-face."

"Who is this?"

"I'll give you a hint. We almost met today in Colonial Williamsburg. Your detective passed within ten feet of me, twice."

Gates felt his blood pressure rise. "Come down to the station. We'll have that face-to-face. Bring an attorney. You're going to need one."

"Don't put the cart before the horse. Let's meet for a civil conversation first and take it from there."

"Civil?"

"That's correct. Someplace quiet."

"Where did you have in mind?"

"The end of Carters Neck Road. Ten o'clock. Bring your detective and come in his unmarked car."

Gates committed the information to memory.

"Did you get all that?" the voice asked.

"I got it. Carters Neck Road, ten o'clock."

"Be on time," the voice said before the line went dead.

"Is everything all right, Charlie?" his wife asked as she came back to the kitchen for the dessert plates.

"It's fine."

"You don't look fine."

"I've been thinking, after all that went down today, I don't want Dad working in Williamsburg for a while."

"He's not going to like that."

"I'll talk to him later. I don't need him making a big deal out of it in front of Millares."

Gates Senior cleared his throat, standing at the entrance way to the kitchen. "What am I going to make a big deal of?"

"Nothing. That's the point," Chief Gates replied.

Barbara handed her father-in-law the stack of dessert plates. "Take these to the table, please. Then we'll all have some pie."

"Now I'm being bribed with pie like I was two years old."

"Yes, you are," Barbara said. "And if you want your dessert, you need to run those to the table."

Gates Senior scowled, grabbed the plates, and left the room.

"I'll talk to him," Chief Gates repeated. "But before we have dessert, I'm going to step out back and have a quick word with Detective Millares. Looks like we have some work to do after dinner."

"Your sister's case?"

"Yes. It may be coming to a head."

*

Chief Gates leaned his shoulder on a porch post and took a deep breath.

"What's going on, Chief?"

"You're not going to believe this, but our suspect just called. He wants to meet. Tonight."

"*Coño*. Are you sure it was him?"

"He mentioned something about seeing you in Colonial Williamsburg today."

"He was on to us."

"So it seems."

"Where are we meeting?"

"Carters Neck Road. Ten o'clock."

"I don't know it."

"The other side of Camp Peary. York County. Carters Neck is a residential street that dead-ends near The Farm. Back in the day, there was a security gate, if I remember correctly. He also said to bring you along and for us to come in your unmarked car."

"He's got an agenda."

"Yes, he does."

"Could be an ambush."

"Anything is possible. Bring our vests, just in case."

Quags checked his watch.

"You still have time for pie," Gates said.

"And a coffee," Quags added. "I'd hate to get shot again without a full dose of caffeine."

CHAPTER 45

QUAGS STOPPED THE police cruiser near the end of the asphalt. Gravel tracks continued for thirty yards straight ahead before narrowing into a single path, the surface overrun by weeds. The two officers exited the car and darkness engulfed them. Gates glanced back in the direction of the houses they had passed on their way down the street and estimated the nearest residence was a quarter mile away. Quags stepped to the rear of the vehicle and popped the trunk.

"A vest for you," Quags said, handing the heavy material to his boss before picking up his own. Reaching into the trunk a second time, Quags removed a shotgun. "Just in case," he said, racking the slide on the Remington 870.

"You're forever the optimist."

"I also have my Glock and an ankle .38."

"Of course you do."

"Better too many guns than too few."

Quags handed Gates a flashlight, grabbed an identical one for himself, and shut the trunk. Heading off the asphalt, the footsteps of the two law enforcement officers became audible as they crunched across the gravel toward the towering chain-link fence ahead. As the path narrowed, their rendezvous came into sharper focus.

"You were right about this location. It's an old gate," Quags said, pointing toward an abandoned guard house.

An overhead light strained to illuminate the bald patch of ground near the former gate, its rays swallowed by the shadows of the surrounding woods. Peering down the fence line, Gates noted additional lights in the distance, tiny dots every few hundred yards. Quags glanced upward to the rolls of razor wire perched atop the fence. A series of signs made it clear that the fence line marked the beginning of government property and visitors were not welcome. *Use of Deadly Force Authorized*, written in large black print, emphasized the point.

Gates motioned to the parallel grooves in the earth on the other side of the fence. "It looks like vehicles patrol the perimeter."

"Noted," Quags replied.

The snapping of sticks caused both men to freeze before Quags raised his gun to his shoulder. The officers watched as a human outline emerged from the woods, the man's dark green camouflage pants and black shirt providing cover against the shadows. Slowly the man approached the fence line and his face crept into view.

"Do you see this?" Quags asked in a whisper, as the man continued toward them.

"I do."

"Septic Tony and Bisa were right. Our enhanced images weren't too far off," Quags said. "Better than the old photos from the DMV and his high school yearbook."

"Indeed," Gates replied. "Lower your weapon. Let's hear him out."

"Fine, but if anything goes fishy here, I'm dropping him," Quags said, aiming his gun toward the ground.

"Good evening, gentlemen," the man said, seeming to eye Quags's grip on the shotgun. "Thank you for being on time. We only have ten minutes until the next security patrol passes."

"We noticed the tire tracks. What happens if we're here when the security patrol arrives?"

"We won't be."

"Humor us," Quags said.

"Neither of us are breaking any laws. But our security personnel does have a tendency to overreact. All things being equal, I'd prefer to be gone by the time they arrive."

"Fair enough," Gates said. "And I assume we're under surveillance as we speak."

"We are. There are motion-activated cameras at regular intervals along the perimeter. They're designed to detect intrusions. They provide very limited coverage outside of the perimeter. With the exception of the base's main gate. But the camera focused on this location can see us where we currently stand."

"We were told it's sixteen miles around the base. That's a lot of cameras."

"It is. And as law enforcement, I'm sure you're aware there's a limit to the number of cameras that can be effectively monitored in real time. The wildlife around here is responsible for triggering the vast majority of security breaches."

"If the wildlife could read the signs, they would stay out," Quags said. "I assume there are other security measures on site."

"Of course. But as long as you stay on that side of the fence, none of them will concern you."

Gates and Quags seemed to digest the information.

"And I noticed that you're armed," the man said.

"We are. Any surprises up your sleeves?" Quags asked.

"I'm clean."

"Do you mind verifying?" Gates asked, twirling a finger in the air.

The man lifted his shirt with both hands and spun around slowly. "Good enough?"

"It'll suffice," Gates responded.

"I wouldn't be opposed if you placed your shotgun on the ground. For safety," the man suggested.

Gates nodded at Quags who did as he was asked, pointing the barrel in a safe direction toward thick brush.

"And with that pleasantry behind us, shall we make proper introductions?" the man asked.

"As you probably know, my name is Charles Gates and I'm the chief of police for the city of Williamsburg. This is one of my detectives, Luis Millares."

Quags nodded.

"We assume your name is Kirk Zambrano," Gates said, measuring the suspect.

"Kudos to you. That must have taken some effort. I barely use that name myself."

"It wasn't easy. But we are curious about the name you use on base. We know it's Ken, and that the trainees call you Zee."

"Zara," the man said. "But you can call me Zee as well, if you'd like."

"We'll stick with Zambrano," Quags replied. "And before we head down the avenue of more charades, in addition to your name, we know where you live. A nice house down on the water. You're married and have a daughter who plays soccer for Bruton High."

"I'd prefer that you keep my family out of the conversation."

"Maybe you can tell us what brings us out here this evening?" Gates said soothingly.

"Obviously we have something to discuss."

"You could have come to police headquarters."

"I think this location provides us with the chance to speak more freely."

Distant gunfire made Gates and Quags stiffen. Quags eyed the shotgun on the ground.

Zambrano stood motionless. "That's just a training exercise. No cause for concern. It's an everyday occurrence around here. Neighbors who live near the base don't even notice the noise."

"Maybe they don't, but that can't be good for resale value," Quags said.

"I understand that you've been investigating me," Zambrano said.

"We have," Quags replied. "For the murder of four women thirty-five years ago. As well as a student and a professor last week."

"I don't know anything about a student and a professor being killed. And from what I've gathered, one of the victims from thirty-five years ago was your sister, Chief Gates."

"That's correct. Which means you've been keeping up with the investigation."

"Not exactly. During a recent polygraph, I was asked if I had knowledge of the Matoaka murders and if I was involved in any way."

"And what was your answer?

"I answered in the negative."

"It's our understanding that you passed this polygraph."

"I did."

"Were you surprised by the question regarding the Matoaka murders?"

"Not entirely. It seems that question was asked to all of those who underwent polygraphs that day."

"How would you know what other people were asked?"

"Because the four of us who took polygraphs that day discussed it."

"Isn't that against the rules?"

"We're instructors. It's a gray area. We actually discussed it without directly discussing it."

"How does that work?"

"It's an acquired skill."

"I would think being questioned about a specific murder would come as a shock. Unless, of course, you were involved," Quags said.

Zambrano smirked.

"Something funny?"

"You'd be surprised at the questions I've been asked during polygraphs over the course of my career."

"For example?"

"During one of my earlier security polygraphs, I was asked if I had sex with animals."

"How did you answer?" Quags asked.

Zambrano scowled. "I responded in the negative. But my response didn't stop the examiner from delving deeper into the topic. For over an hour, he maintained that the machine indicated I was being deceptive."

"Any disgruntled pets at home?" Quags asked.

Zambrano stared hard at Quags for a long moment. "At the end of the day, that polygraph was just an attempt to rattle my cage. At some point, most Agency employees get pressed for being deceptive about something related to drugs, sex, gambling, or drinking. Pornography is a favorite target."

"So, going back to your most recent polygraph and the questions related to the Matoaka murders. I still don't understand why these questions didn't raise red flags," Gates said.

"Simple. I wasn't involved in the murders. Just as I didn't spend much time thinking about whether I had sex with animals. But after hearing the name Matoaka murders, I did a little research. I was surprised to learn that the current chief of police was the sibling of one of the victims."

"So you do remember the murders?"

"I remember the news. My time here on The Farm as a trainee overlapped with the murders."

"We assumed that was the case. Did anyone from the Agency explicitly inform you that the Williamsburg Police Department was looking at you as a suspect in multiple murders?"

"No. I had to piece that together myself."

"And how did you do that?" Quags asked.

"My first indication, beyond the polygraph question, was actually a septic worker who was poking around in my shed."

"He could have needed to borrow a rake."

"We both know he didn't. My second clue was our near meeting at Colonial Williamsburg earlier today. I watched Detective Millares here question a guy wearing a sweatshirt identical to one I had been wearing five minutes earlier. That's a coincidence that's hard to overlook."

"You're observant," Gates said. "I doubt most people would have noticed."

"An unobservant clandestine officer is going to have a very short career."

"What else?" Gates asked.

"Those two incidents made me suspicious. My suspicions were further confirmed this afternoon when I asked my wife and daughter whether they had seen or heard anything out of the ordinary regarding our family, our house, or the base. Initially, my daughter denied knowing anything, but eventually admitted that her boyfriend had been questioned by the Williamsburg PD and that the police had specifically asked her boyfriend what

I looked like. My daughter was reluctant to share this information with me because she wasn't supposed to be in contact with this so-called boyfriend."

"Teenagers can't be trusted," Quags said.

"No one can. At any rate, those pieces of the puzzle pushed me to poke around a little more. Then I discovered that the chief of police of Williamsburg attended high school with Tony Wilkins, now the owner of Wilkins Water and Septic."

"Nice detective work for someone who's not a detective," Quags replied.

"And those discoveries led you to call this meeting?" Gates confirmed.

"Actually, there was one more clue. I stumbled upon an article in the local newspaper about the recent discovery of a fingerprint in the Matoaka investigation. That tidbit, combined with the others, compelled me to reach out to you."

Zambrano paused. "Now, may I ask a question?"

Quags looked at Gates and shook his head.

"Sure," Gates answered.

"I'm curious as to how I ended up on your radar as a suspect?"

Gates briefly summarized the chain of events from the Walgreens to the Blue Bird buses. Zambrano listened. "Subsequently, we were told your employer obtained your fingerprints from your personnel files and compared them to that from the Walgreens. We were told the comparison analysis was inconclusive. This contradicted the results of the Richmond Police. Unfortunately. Your employer is making that difficult to confirm."

"The Walgreens in Richmond . . . " Zambrano mulled aloud. "I knew that altercation was going to be trouble. The surveillance camera feeds were bound to garner some interest. Everyone likes a good hero story."

"I don't think many are going to enjoy the ending to this one," Quags said.

"I would have preferred to avoid the entire incident. But I have a visceral reaction to someone shoving a gun in my face."

"I can't blame you there," Quags said. "Though it does indicate a level of uncontrolled anger. Something a murderer may also exhibit."

"Or I'm simply someone who doesn't like to be threatened," Zambrano said.

Gates moved on to his next question. "There's something I can't figure out. Why did you leave the scene at the Walgreens without speaking to the police? It was apparent you committed no crime," Gates asked.

"I didn't plan to leave without making a statement. My actions were a direct result of a mistake on my part."

"A mistake?"

"I forgot to bring my credentials with me."

"Doesn't sound like a big deal."

"To you, probably not. Rest assured, that mistake could get you killed in the field."

"But you weren't in the field. It was a training exercise. You could've provided your real name to the police for verification."

"I could have. But that would have required involving base management and an official incident report, which would have included the fact that I didn't have my credentials on me. Not to mention it would have slowed down the training exercise that day. The path of least resistance and least paperwork was to leave. It was also the safest path."

"How's that?" Quags asked. "What do you mean the safest path?"

"If that security video went viral and my identity was leaked, a lot of people could have been put in harm's way. A lot of assets that produce valuable intelligence could have been compromised."

"So leaving the scene was a calculated decision?" Gates asked.

"I considered my options and acted. As you said, I didn't break any law. And, as it turns out, the incident provided an opportunity to assess how our trainees would deal with adversity. How they would handle an unplanned complication."

"Okay. For the sake of argument, I'll consider that a plausible explanation," Gates said. "Now, where do we go from here?"

"Did you come in the detective's car, as directed?" Zambrano asked.

"We did."

"And I assume you have a print kit in your vehicle."

"I am a detective," Quags said.

"Would you mind retrieving it?"

"Are we taking prints?" Gates asked.

"That's exactly what we're doing."

Quags pointed to the shotgun on the ground as if to remind Chief Gates a weapon was readily available. Gates nodded in confirmation and Quags broke into a jog. Minutes later he returned, print kit in hand.

Quags prepared the fingerprint kit on the ground near the fence line, not far from his shotgun. "I assume we're doing this one finger at a time, through the fence."

"Unless you have another idea," Zambrano responded, checking his watch. "Under five minutes before the patrol comes through."

"Are you ready?"

"When you are."

One by one, Zambrano pushed his fingers through the chain-link fence and Quags rolled the suspect's digits to capture the evidence. When he finished, he held the paper up and Gates shined his flashlight on prints.

"What do you think?" Gates asked.

"They look good. Should work fine."

"Then we're done here?" Zambrano asked.

"Actually, I had a couple more questions," Quags said.

Before Zambrano could respond, a gunshot from their rear sent Williamsburg's finest scrambling for cover.

CHAPTER 46

GATES ROLLED IN the direction of a gulley on the far side of the path as the sound of the gunshot reverberated through their location. Quags hunkered down behind a stump on the opposite side of the clearing. A second shot rang out, and Quags lowered his head further. Glancing back toward the fence, he caught a glimpse of Zambrano as he reached the woods, running full speed.

"You okay, Chief?" Quags called out.

"I think so. Can you get eyes on the shooter?"

"Not from where I am," Quags said, pulling his handgun from his rear holster. "But I'm about to fix that."

In a muted voice he counted down from three in Spanish, stood, and broke into a sprint through the brush adjacent to the path. Approaching the gravel between the path and the asphalt, Quags paused behind a large tree and listened, a firm grip on his gun. The sound of car door slamming shut echoed down the street. Quags broke into another sprint, and as he reached asphalt, he saw the rear of a vehicle as it accelerated away from the scene.

"*Coño*," he said, trying to catch his breath. He holstered his weapon, put his hands on his knees for a moment, and then began running back to the fence line. He arrived at the clearing to find Chief Gates holding his left shoulder, branches and leaves stuck to his boss's clothing.

"Are you okay, Chief?"

"I will be," Gates responded, pulling his phone from his pocket. "Time to call it in."

Quags stepped toward Gates and put his hand over his boss's. "Don't."

"Don't what?"

"Don't call it in."

"Why not?"

"You're going to have to trust me."

"You're going to have to give me a reason."

"I'll explain in the car, Chief. Let's go."

Quags stooped to gather the fingerprint sheet and his shotgun from the ground.

"We need to report this," Gates repeated as the men jogged toward the car. "At the very least, we need to call our friends in York County. Report shots fired in their jurisdiction."

"In the car, Chief. Please. No one was injured. I saw our guy running into the woods."

Reaching the police cruiser, Quags placed the shotgun and the fingerprint sheet into the trunk. Peering down the residential street, he noted that not a single neighbor had stepped outside to investigate the two gun blasts. He took another glance back at the fence near the old gate and estimated the distance from their location. Shaking his head and cursing quietly, he climbed behind the wheel and started the car. Driving out of the neighborhood, he kept the car's lights off and his eye's glued to the rearview mirror.

Phone still in hand, Gates pressed Quags for an explanation. "We have a duty to report what occurred. Even if a crime wasn't committed."

"The person who fired the shots at the fence was driving a red pickup truck that's missing a tailgate and has broken rear lights on the left side."

"That's impossible."

"I wouldn't joke about a thing like that."

Gates swiped at the screen of his phone. "My father is at home," he announced, holding the screen toward Quags.

"You mean your father's phone is at home. My guess is that he's nowhere near it. Call him and find out."

Gates did as suggested, and the call went straight to his father's voice mail. "Goddammit. Millares, you better be wrong about what you saw."

*

Quags stopped the car in front of the Gates residence. The front porch light was on and fainter light shone through a thin curtain in a second-floor window. Gates exited the car, walked along the front of the house, and turned the corner. Quags quickly caught up with his boss and fell into step next to him. Between the main house and the Dad Shack, the old red pickup with the missing rear gate and broken tail light stood in its customary position. Gates peered into the cab of the truck as Quags put his hand on the hood.

"It's warm," Quags said.

"Son of a bitch," Gates replied, heading for his father's abode. Grabbing the doorknob, he twisted and pushed to no avail. He pounded on the door and the lights inside of the apartment came on. Locks clicked and the door opened.

"What's the noise about," Gates Senior said, wearing pajamas.

"Knock it off, Dad."

"Knock what off?"

"Detective Millares saw you."

"I don't know what you're talking about."

"Enough. Just stop it. What the hell were you thinking?"

"Watch your tone, son."

"No. What in the hell was going through your mind? I'm the chief of police and an attorney. I worked hard for those titles. And you show up to take a potshot at an instructor standing on the grounds of Camp Peary? Are you kidding me?"

Gates Senior stared at his son.

"Where's the gun?" Quags asked.

Gates Senior pointed toward the corner of the room on the other side of the small dining table. "Over there."

Without asking, Quags stepped around the table, unloaded the weapon, and confirmed the chamber was empty. He placed the rifle on the floor near the front door, the muzzle leaning on the wall, pointing toward the ceiling.

"How did you know where we were?" Gates asked his father.

"The window was open when you were talking on the back porch."

"You were eavesdropping?"

"No. I said the window was open."

"Tell me you didn't bring your phone with you when you were out there."

"Hell, no. Give me a little credit."

Chief Gates rolled his eyes. "You want credit for not bringing your phone? This is what you want credit for?"

"I see your point," Gates Senior replied sheepishly.

"Jesus. You've put me in an awful situation, Dad."

"You? You didn't do anything. Blame it all on me. What are they going to do, put me in jail?"

"Yes. That's exactly what they'll do."

"They can't do anything to me worse than what's already been done. Waiting thirty-five years for justice."

"I'm going to step outside and give the two of you a moment," Quags said.

As the two Gateses bickered, Quags deftly plucked the rifle from its position near the door and exited the Dad Shack.

CHAPTER 47

CHIEF GATES CONTINUED to lay into his father. "Seriously, what were you doing out there tonight?"

"Taking care of business."

"Bullshit. You were interfering in *police* business. And I'm the chief of police!"

"You're also the brother of Heather Gates. Don't forget it."

"You've put me in a bad position, Dad."

"Don't worry. Your suspect is fine. I missed high on the first shot and left on the second. I didn't hit him."

"Millares says he saw the guy running into the woods. But that doesn't change the fact that you shot at him. It doesn't change the fact that you tried to kill him."

"I guess we should be thankful I can't shoot like I used to."

"We'd better hope you and Millares are right. If you're wrong, I'll be fired and you'll be behind bars."

"I missed. High on the first shot. Left on the second."

"That's what you said. I fully expect the York County Police, Virginia State Police, or FBI to be at our door within the hour."

"I'll tell them what happened."

"You won't tell them anything. You were never there."

"I was."

"No, you weren't."

"That's the plan? Tell them I was at home the whole time?"

"Yes. That's the plan. You're not going to answer any question other than your name, age, and address. The only thing coming out of your mouth other than your name, age, or address is 'I would like to confer with an attorney.'"

"Is that you? Are you my attorney?"

"Until I'm arrested, it's me."

"Sounds like our problem is solved, then."

"I assure you it's not."

A long silence fell over the two. Chief Gates could feel his heartbeat in his neck and temples.

"I don't think you have any idea what you've done."

"I know exactly what I've done. My only regret is I failed."

"Let me be very clear. I want you in your bed and I want you to stay there for the remainder of the evening."

"Or I get spanked?"

"Dad, I'm serious. If we get visitors, you stay put."

"Well, I'm sure as hell not going to let you take the fall for me."

"Stick to the plan. If it comes down to it, you provide your age, name, and address. Beyond that, what do you say?"

"I want my lawyer."

"Right."

"And what are you going to do, son?"

"Have a drink, listen to the police radio, and wait for the authorities."

*

Chief Gates was on the front porch, staring out at the darkness, when headlights appeared at the end of his driveway. The lack of flashing lights or additional cars kept the chief of police in his chair until his visitor arrived in a cloud of driveway dust. Quags exited the vehicle covered in sweat. Without a greeting, the detective climbed the front steps and sat in the chair next to his boss.

"Where did you head off to? I called multiple times."

"I took a ride," Quags said. "What's the word?"

"Nothing. Not a word. Nothing across the radio. No word from the York County Police, state police, or the FBI. No call from Childress. Nothing."

"Maybe our suspect didn't mention the shooting to anyone."

Gates shrugged. "Can I get you a drink?"

"Please. I don't care what, as long as it's a double."

Chief Gates went inside, fetched a full bottle and a glass, and returned to the porch to find Quags lighting a cigar.

"That was quite a show out there," Quags said, smoke wafting from his mouth into the sky.

"I apologize for my dad."

Quags took a long sip from his glass.

"Should I ask what you did with the rifle?" Gates asked.

"What rifle?" Quags replied, cigar smoke swirling around his face.

"Uh huh," Gates replied, taking a sip of his own drink. "You still have the fingerprint sheet?"

"It's in the trunk."

"Why don't we take a ride?"

"Where are we going?"

"Richmond."

"At this hour?"

Gates shrugged. "If we're not going to be arrested, we should see if those prints are a match."

"I'm game."

"I guess it's my turn to make a few calls and wake some people up. Starting with Detective Brooks."

"I'm sure she'll love you for it."

CHAPTER 48

"A PENNY FOR your thoughts," Gates asked as Quags stared trancelike straight ahead into the darkness of the highway. The clock on the dash read 12:05 a.m.

"Make it five bucks and you've got a deal."

"Or you could tell me for free and keep your job."

"Persuasive argument. What I was thinking is that we've been played."

"Why?"

"Probably because our suspect is a member of the intelligence community. Physical and psychological sleight of hand is what they do."

"Maybe, but for now we got our prints."

"Prints that our suspect willingly gave us."

"So?"

"Maybe the only reason he gave us his prints is because he knows they aren't going to match. What if the guy we met at the fence was wearing some kind of alternative print over his real fingertips? I don't think it would be hard for an instructor on The Farm to pull that off. We know they are the master of disguises. The lighting at the fence line wasn't great. It was a location our suspect chose. We could have easily missed it. I should have examined his hands more closely before taking his prints."

"Let's run these prints and see what the results are before we beat ourselves up."

"Do you want to put a twenty on whether these prints will match?"

"No," Gates said.

Quags returned to his trance for a few long moments before breaking his silence. "When we get to Richmond, I need to stop off at a bar. I have a question for a pot farmer."

*

Chief Gates waited in the car while Quags cut the line in front of the bar. He pressed through the crowd between the bar and the three-man band playing in the corner. Bellied up to the metal counter, he waited for Jenny to notice him. Pouring shots into six glasses, Jenny spotted him out of the corner of her eye and winked.

"I didn't expect to see you again so soon," she said, talking over her shoulder as she returned a bottle to the shelf behind the bar.

"Neither did I."

"Can I get you a beer?"

"Not this time around. My boss is waiting for me in the car."

"Then what brings you in?"

"I need to speak with Grant."

"He told me that he called you."

"He did. And he told me if I needed to reach him again that you'd send him an email and he'll call me back on a burner phone."

"Did he?"

"Yep."

"All right. Let me step outside for a smoke break in a couple of minutes and send an email. Anything special I should tell him?"

"Let him know it's a matter of life and death."

"Really?"

"No. But it's urgent."

"I'll let him know."

"Thanks, Jenny. I owe you one."

"Two. You owe me two."

Quags made his way back through the crowd to the police cruiser and climbed behind the wheel.

"How did it go?"

"The message will be sent shortly. We'll see."

"Detective Brooks called. She's waiting for us."

*

Detective Brooks met Gates and Quags under a metal arch that stretched over the entrance to Richmond Police Headquarters.

"Thanks for meeting on short notice," Gates said.

"Happy to help," Brooks replied.

Quags handed the envelope with the print cards to his Richmond counterpart. Brooks peaked into the envelope as if it were going to divulge secrets.

"And these are prints from the good Samaritan at Walgreens?"

"They are. Hopefully they'll confirm he's more than that."

"I have my forensic tech waiting for us downstairs. Let's see if we can solve this mystery, once and for all."

The trio of law enforcement officers made their way to the basement and weaved their way to the far corner. Seated at the large L-shaped desk was the young tech with the large ear gauges who had performed the original print analysis.

Detective Brooks made introductions. "Jimmy here is the forensic tech who ran the prints the first time. He was gracious enough to come in late and assist."

"We appreciate it," Gates said.

"The opportunity to help solve a thirty-five-year-old cold case involving your sister? I wouldn't have missed it."

Brooks handed the prints to the Jimmy. "How much time do you need?"

"Not much. I have the prints from AFIS and the original crime scene. All I have to do is scan these in. I should have preliminary results in a few minutes."

*

Brooks, Gates, and Quags sat in a semicircle, staring at the backside of the latent print expert as he worked his magic.

"Any word on the gun that was used in the robbery attempt at Walgreens?" Quags asked Brooks.

"We haven't turned up anything concrete. Does that still matter to you?"

"If this analysis shows that the prints don't match, we could be back to square one," Quags replied.

"I'm curious how you found the guy," Brooks asked.

"It wasn't easy," Gates admitted. "The intelligence community holds its secrets close to the vest."

"Is the suspect aware he's a suspect?"

"He is. And he volunteered his prints."

"That must have come as a surprise."

"It did. And if the prints match, it'll be an even bigger one," Quags answered.

"You're not an optimist."

"Find me a detective who is."

Gates warned Brooks. "He's just looking for someone to bet with him. The offer on the table is twenty bucks the prints won't match."

"I'll take that bet," the Jimmy the LPE replied, spinning in his chair to face his audience. Quags, Brooks, and Gates stood to see the screen over the tech's shoulder.

"Are you telling me it's a match?" Quags asked.

Jimmy vacated the space in front of his dual-screen workspace. "The only print from the Matoaka murders is a match to the suspect's right thumb. I can identify twenty match points, including a small scar, which gives it even more certainty."

"How certain are you?" Brooks asked.

"Nearly one hundred percent. Four nines."

"*Puta madre*," Quags said.

"Our killer is confirmed as Kirk Zambrano," Gates said aloud, clapping his hands together with force.

Quags nodded in approval. "Hopefully he's still alive."

CHAPTER 49

"HE'S EXPECTING YOU," the administrative assistant said as Gates and Quags crossed the large carpet with the Virginia state seal woven in the middle. "You can head on back."

"Thank you," Chief Gates and Quags replied in near unison. Down the hall, Gates knocked on the frame of the open office door. Inside, Commonwealth's Attorney Sean Bramble stood from his seat and waved in his guests.

"Chief Gates and the prescient Detective Millares, I assume."

"Good morning," Gates replied. "Thanks for the time, as always."

"I understand we have movement on our Matoaka murder suspect."

Gates responded. "We do. We've officially identified the suspect. Kirk Zambrano. We got his full legal name from the York County schools and now we have matching fingerprints."

"And were these prints legally obtained?"

"The suspect offered them voluntarily."

Bramble's eyebrows jump. "So you met him?"

"Through a fence."

"The big one that runs around Camp Peary," Quags added for clarification.

"Interesting."

"Unusual. No doubt," Gates replied. "Given what we've learned, I want to issue an arrest warrant. In addition to another subpoena that is specific to our suspect."

Bramble nodded. "We can do both, but before you get your hopes up, know that the Agency isn't going to allow you to serve an arrest warrant on their property."

"No, they won't. But someday our guy is going to have to leave that base. Retire. Live his life. And I want that arrest warrant hanging over his head. Down the road, he may get pulled over for a moving violation or, if we're really lucky, another crime. When they run his name or his prints, he'll be detained for an outstanding arrest warrant related to a murder."

"I understand the goal. I just didn't want anyone to believe the Agency would cooperate."

"Unlike a subpoena, an arrest warrant doesn't require their cooperation."

"No, it does not."

"Then let's pull the trigger," Gates said.

"If both of you are amenable to the suggestion, I would like to call Paulsen to inform him that we have officially identified the suspect and are planning another subpoena. As a courtesy."

Gates and Quags exchanged nervous glances. "Fine."

"Good. Let's make a phone call."

*

Bramble, Gates, and Quags sat around the small table, staring at the phone, listening as it rang, ninety miles north on the other end.

"Paulsen," the voice responded tersely, followed by several heavy breaths and a cough.

"Good morning, Mr. Paulsen. This is Sean Bramble, commonwealth's attorney for Williamsburg and James City County."

"Yes, sir. How are you this morning?"

"Very well, thank you. I'm here with Chief Gates and Detective Millares of the Williamsburg City Police Department. You are on speaker."

"Good morning, gentlemen. How can I help you?" Paulsen asked.

"This is a professional courtesy call," Bramble said.

"I never turn down one of those. Even if most of them don't turn out as courteous as advertised."

"And I'm afraid that's the case this morning as well. We wanted to provide an update on the Matoaka murder investigation. Per the Williamsburg Police, the suspect has been positively identified. In addition to obtaining his full name, the suspect voluntarily offered his prints to the authorities. One of those prints has been confirmed as a match to the print found at the Matoaka murder scene in the eighties."

"I see," Paulsen replied.

"As I'm sure you're aware, the suspect is an instructor on The Farm. His name is Kirk Zambrano," Gates said.

Silence followed.

"Are you still there, Mr. Paulsen?" Bramble asked.

"I am."

"Any response to these new developments?"

"I'd prefer any further discussion on this topic to be face-to-face. And as luck would have it, I'm getting ready to leave the office and catch a flight down your way. I should be at Camp Peary before lunch. If you're available Chief Gates, perhaps we can meet."

"I'll clear my schedule" Gates said.

"Good. How about later this afternoon? Say around four o'clock? Childress and I will meet you and Detective Millares at the Camp Peary visitor center."

"We'll be there," Gates replied.

"Good. Looking forward to meeting you in person."

All parties offered brief parting salutations and the call ended.

"Well, gentleman, it seems as if you've hit a nerve," Bramble said. "A face-to-face meeting at Camp Peary is a change in the trajectory of this case."

"Yes, it is," Gates stammered.

"You feeling all right, Charlie? You look a little ashen," Bramble asked.

"I'm fine."

"Give me a call later and fill me in on what happened."

"Will do."

*

In the parking lot in front of the brick building, Gates stopped before getting into the vehicle. He checked his surroundings for eavesdroppers and spoke to Quags over the roof, both men leaning on the side of the car.

"That call was not a positive development," Gates said.

"No, it wasn't. Something's up."

"My gut's telling me the same thing."

Both men considered the possibilities, staring at each other over the car from opposite sides.

"You know, maybe we can get one step ahead for a change," Quags said.

"What do you have in mind?"

"Just a hunch. Give me a couple of minutes," Quags said, stepping away from the car and pulling a cigar from his breast pocket. "I need to make a few calls."

Ten minutes later, Quags opened the door to the cruiser and sat down, a mauled cigar between his teeth.

"What's the word?" Gates asked.

"Sentara Regional has a gunshot victim in their morgue. He arrived this morning. We need to head over there and see if it's our guy. See if your father's aim is better than he thinks it is."

CHAPTER 50

SENTARA WILLIAMSBURG REGIONAL Hospital sat north of a stretch of outlet malls in the middle of an open swath of land that had remained untouched for the previous two hundred years. The impressiveness of the modern exterior of the building was nearly equal to the state-of-the-art medical equipment brimming within its walls. If Colonial Williamsburg embraced the historic charm of yesteryear, Sentara Regional was a symbol of how to reach for the future.

Quags parked in an emergency vehicle spot adjacent to the front doors, and the two officers crossed the black top of the circular driveway. Inside, a trio of sleeping bodies lay like fallen Jenga blocks in chairs along the wall. Two floors below, they stepped from the elevator and proceeded through a series of corridors. Outside the morgue entrance, they pressed the call button on the wall and waited.

A big-bellied, bald man with a walrus mustache opened the door and greeted them. "Chief Gates. Detective Millares. Come on in."

Gates spoke to the medical examiner's backside as the man walked past two empty stainless steel tables.

"Detective Millares says you got a body this morning. A shooting victim," Gates said.

"I did, indeed. I was told it was an accidental shooting."

"Who brought him in?"

"Camp Peary Fire and Rescue."

Gates felt his stomach sink. "We'd like to see the body."

"I figured as much. Follow me."

The bank of refrigerators held a total of twenty guests, stored at a constant thirty-six degrees Fahrenheit. Numbered in rows from left to right, the ME checked the chart on the wall to confirm the correct location. He stepped to the middle of the wall and tugged on the handle of a waist-high drawer.

"Here you go," the doctor said, unzipping the body bag and unveiling the naked corpse of a middle-aged man with a very large exit wound in his chest. "As you can see by the extent of the injury, there's not much of a mystery. Bullet entered the victim's back and blew out the chest cavity."

"No argument there," Quags said.

The ME grabbed the file for the deceased and offered a summary. "Okay . . . let's see. We have a fifty-two-year-old male. Kirk Zambrano. Five foot eleven. One hundred and eighty-five pounds. The victim arrived at the hospital DOA."

"What time was he brought in?"

"At 6:37 a.m."

"And time of death?"

"Based on temperature and rigor mortis, he died between ten and twelve last night. He was brought here for refrigeration until further arrangements could be made."

"So he was shot last night and discovered this morning?"

"That's right."

"What can you tell us about a potential weapon?" Gates asked, getting to the meat of the discussion.

The ME's eyes returned to his summary. "Something in the 0.25- to .30-inch range, 7mm. Hunting ammo. Could be a 243 Winchester, a 7mm Remington, a 270. Maybe as large as a 308. All of those would fit the bill. It's hard to determine the exact caliber given the elasticity of the skin, among other factors."

"Distance of the shot?"

"Also hard to determine without a caliber. Within a few hundred yards. But the cause of death is clear. A bullet blew a hole through him."

"Was an autopsy requested?"

"No. Neither requested nor required."

Gates moved to the pale feet of the deceased and Quags moved toward the head.

Quags bent over for a close up of the scalp and announced his findings. "We've got hair plugs."

"I noticed them during my preliminary examination," the medical examiner said. "Quite pronounced, really. Makes me think twice about getting some."

"Roll with the bald look, Doc. It suits you," Quags said without looking up from the corpse.

The ME ran his hand over his own head.

"Anything else you noticed?" Quags asked.

"I think the guy practiced martial arts."

"Why do you say that?"

The doctor moved to the dead man's nearest arm. "If you look at his hands, you can see the first two knuckles are pronounced. Thick skin. Off color. A lot of martial arts focus on striking with the first two knuckles."

"We watched this guy break someone's arm on a surveillance video, so whatever he knows, it works."

"I also noticed the deceased is quite fit."

"Except for the hole in his chest," Quags said, almost under his breath.

"Unlike most of the other doctors here at Sentara, there's something terminally wrong with all of my patients."

"I guess there is."

"Would you mind if we take prints?" Quags asked.

"I don't. And neither will he. There should be a kit on the counter to the right."

Quags followed the doctor's direction, returned to the body, and began taking prints from all ten fingers. "We took prints off this guy last night, but I want to make sure there hasn't been a switcheroo."

"A switcheroo?" the ME asked, curiosity spreading across his face.

"I've been wondering if the fingerprints he provided to us are really his, or if he performed some sleight of hand. If he somehow concealed his real prints."

"Well, I can attest he's not wearing gloves. For what that's worth."

"How often do you deal with Camp Peary?" Gates asked as Quags continued to take prints.

"Not very often. I've been working here for eight years and I've only had two other bodies from the base."

"How did the previous two die?"

"One was a parachuting accident. The individual broke his neck landing in a tree after his parachute malfunctioned. The other was a woman. Shrapnel hit her femoral artery. She bled out. The emergency room gets people from Camp Peary on a regular basis. Training to be a spy involves a fair number of injuries. The morgue, obviously, has fewer visitors than the ER."

"Anything else about the victim that could be relevant?"

"His boots had mud in them, and he showed signs of having walked in the woods."

"We saw him in the woods last night," Gates revealed.

"Then you've corroborated some of the evidence." The ME removed a handkerchief from his white lab coat pocket and wiped perspiration off his dome. "The problem is we're talking about Camp Peary. They can tell us whatever they want."

"You're preaching to the choir, Doc," Quags said.

"Based on the evidence, do you have reason to doubt their story?" Gates asked.

"I tend to doubt most things. But I have no evidence whatsoever to prove it. I wish I could tell you more, but I've shared all I know. I can order a toxicology without raising too many eyebrows, if you're interested, but those results wouldn't be available until next week."

"We'll pass. Any idea how long he'll be here?" Gates asked.

"I was told a transport will arrive by the end of the day."

"I'm done here, boss," Quags said, holding up the fingerprint sheet.

"Thanks for your time," Gates said.

"My pleasure, Chief."

Gates took a step toward the door. "Hey, if anyone asks, we were never here."

The ME nodded. "I get the feeling I may hear that a few times today."

CHAPTER 51

GATES DROVE HIS official chief of police vehicle east on I-64, heading for the four o'clock emergency meeting with Paul Paulsen, chief counsel for Camp Peary. A steady stream of tractor trailers drove through a light rain, mist escaping under their mud flaps, covering the car's windshield.

Quags checked the screen of his phone and then lowered it to his lap. "Brooks in Richmond says their tech is running the copies of the print from the morgue."

"I'm running with the assumption they're going to match."

"We'll see. What's the game plan on this meeting with Paulsen and Childress?" Quags asked.

"I'm counting on Paul Paulsen being a government attorney."

"Meaning?"

"He likes to talk. So I'm going to let him."

"And if he asks if we know anything about a shooting along the fence line last night?"

"We can admit we were at the fence to meet our suspect. And we had nothing to do with the discharge of a weapon in that proximity."

"We were as surprised as anyone. That's the truth."

"Exactly. Our real advantage in this meeting is that we know something he thinks we don't."

"That our guy is in the morgue."

"Yes."

"What if they've figured out it was your father who fired the gun?"

"If they had that information, some form of law enforcement would have come to the house."

"You'd think. But then again, these spooks are unpredictable."

"The correct verbiage is *case officers*."

"I like *spooks*," Quags insisted.

"*Come mierda.*"

"Nice Spanish, Chief."

"Thanks," Gates replied, exiting the highway and climbing the exit ramp toward Camp Peary.

"And here we are again," Quags said. "The gate to hell."

*

Gates and Quags endured a second round of the security protocols at the main gate. The process, in its entirety, was a mirror image to that of their first visit, right down to the dog sniffing his way across the back seat of the cruiser.

Finished with the security procedure, an SPO approached the driver's window. "Follow your escort to the visitor center. Stay inside your vehicle until your escort indicates it's safe to exit. Your hosts are waiting for you inside. Follow your escort's directions until you're handed off to your hosts."

"Will do," Gates replied, rolling up the driver's side window.

"I bet these SPOs are a ton of fun at parties," Quags said.

"People might say the same about you."

"They don't. I'm damn fun."

"I'll take your word for it."

"When this is all over, we'll have a party."

"I hope it won't be a party behind bars, in general population."

"You know they don't put cops in gen pop. We'd have our own cell together, isolated from everyone."

"Sounds wonderful."

Quags pointed through the windshield at seven identical black SUVs. "Looks busy at the visitor center."

Gates followed their escort's directions and parked in the spot farthest from the door. He cut the engine and waited for his SPO escort.

"This way, sir," the SPO said, arriving and standing stoically outside the vehicle with perfect posture.

Gates and Quags walked down the sidewalk, entered through the main doors, and noted another pair of SPOs standing at attention. Childress stood near the middle of the room speaking to another man whom he dwarfed by at least a foot. Additional SPOs stood at attention in the far corner of the room. As Quags and Gates approached, Childress leaned down, whispered to the shorter man, and then offered introductions with the sweep of his hand.

"Paul Paulsen," said the short attorney with an off-center toupee, introducing himself and extending his thick, pudgy hand. "It's nice to meet both of you."

"Likewise. Thank you for the offer to meet face-to-face."

"Our pleasure. We do have a nondisclosure agreement for you to sign before we proceed," Childress said.

"What's the nature of the NDA?" Gates asked.

"Everything you see or hear is classified. It's required of everyone who proceeds beyond the visitor center."

"What exactly are we going to see and hear?" Quags scoffed.

"Sign the NDA and you'll find out," Paulsen replied.

Gates and Quags took a moment to sit on the sofa in the reception area to sign their NDAs. Finished, they passed the documents to Paulsen while Childress handed them visitor badges.

"These badges are to be kept visible at all times."

"Understood," Gates replied, slipping the lanyard over his head.

Paulsen sat down across from the two officers, clasped his hands together, and licked his lips. His toupee leaned forward, threatening to fall.

"Thank you again for coming out. I also wanted to express my appreciation for the courtesy call and the commonwealth's attorney's time earlier this morning. I thought you'd be glad to know that I've been authorized to share some information with you about your suspect, the instructor whose name you mentioned on the phone earlier. We've had a development that may be of interest to you and your investigation."

"Do tell," Gates forced out.

"The instructor you referred to was found dead earlier this morning. It appears to have been an accident. It's still under investigation."

"What kind of accident?"

"An accidental shooting. We're looking into the possibilities. Camp Peary is a live-fire training facility. It could have been an errant shot, an unintended discharge, or even a hunting accident. The latter is worrisome because a hunting accident could have been prevented if safety protocols had been followed. The victim was not wearing a hunting blazer."

"Any information on the bullet?"

"Not as of yet. It hasn't been located."

"For the sake of clarification, the instructor you're referring to is named Kirk Zambrano, correct?" Gates asked.

"Yes. He's a career officer who had been serving as an instructor on The Farm."

"We would like to see some verification around his death."

"As I mentioned, I've been authorized to share Zambrano's personnel files. With redactions, of course."

"Of course."

"And, if you're interested, I've been authorized to take you to the scene of the accident. Let you and your detective have a look around."

"We accept," Quags interjected.

"Chief Gates?" Paulsen asked.

"Absolutely."

"Then, without further ado, this way, please."

Childress, Paulsen, Gates, and Quags exited from the rear of the visitor center and followed Childress's lead to a parked SUV.

"Where's our escort?" Quags asked, glancing around.

"Paulsen and I are your escorts," Childress replied. "It's a ten-minute drive followed by a short walk. The terrain is uneven and it's been raining off and on, so be careful when we get out of the vehicle," Childress stated.

Gates looked down at his leather shoes.

"We'll manage," Quags said, eyes glued to the scenery on the secret side of the base.

The SUV followed the main entrance road and took a left at the first stop sign. It passed what looked like an administrative building and a baseball field before turning onto a single-lane road shaded by towering pine trees.

"Any traffic lights on base?" Quags asked.

"That's classified."

"Unless we see one."

"You won't."

The SUV followed the meandering stretch of asphalt through the trees until it reached the end of the pavement. Slowing, the SUV turned right onto a dirt road, a set of potholes sending the occupants of the car bouncing in their seats. A quarter of a mile down the dirt road, the first glimpse of an open field came into view. The SUV veered left at a fork in the road, and the perimeter fence appeared through the woods.

"Straight ahead is the security perimeter that sits adjacent to several long-standing residential neighborhoods," Childress said. "There's an old gate in this location. It was closed decades ago. Back in the day, some of the career trainees were rumored to have used the secondary entrance as a location to escape the confines of the base. Some rumors included instances of trainees enjoying momentary freedom in the bars near the college."

"I'm familiar with this area," Gates said.

"I would think so. You grew up around here."

"I did."

The SUV took another right and stopped. Childress put the car into park and pointed out the window. "From here, we walk."

Exiting the car, Quags had an unobstructed view of the previous night's rendezvous location, no more than a hundred yards away. He tried to imagine where he lost sight of Zambrano in relation to his current position. The doors to the vehicles closed with resounding thuds, snapping Quags out of his detective trance.

Gates and Quags fell into step behind Childress and Paulsen as they left the car on the dirt road and shuffled toward the first line of trees near the top of a small ridge.

"I'm interested in your theory that the shooting could have been a hunting accident," Gates said in the direction of Childress and Paulsen.

"The body was found in an area that is restricted to a limited number of base personnel and residents," Childress explained. "It also serves as one of the three established hunting zones. We had hunters in the area last night and, as Paulsen indicated, the deceased was not wearing an orange vest. Blaze orange outerwear is a requirement."

"Is hunting popular on base?"

"Extremely popular," Childress responded.

"And, as it were, quite necessary," Paulsen added. "Culling is the only way to control the deer population. State wildlife officials estimated the total number of deer on base to be north of two thousand."

"That's a lot of deer," Gates agreed.

"It is. And that many deer can be a problem when the personnel on base spend so much time in the outdoors."

"And did the hunting group in the area last night report firing a weapon?"

"That's classified," Paulsen answered.

The four men made their way through the woods, down the short slope of the ridge, sticks snapping underfoot. Low branches reached out, clawing at the men's clothes. At the bottom of the ridge, Childress pointed toward the field.

"This clearing is a favorite among the hunters. I bagged a twelve pointer here, myself. A spring-fed creek bisects the field, providing a year-round water source," Childress stated. "Our victim was found on the left side of the clearing, just past the midway point."

Quags slipped back into detective mode, calculating the distance across the field, eyes moving in steady increments.

"Was the victim also hunting?" Quags asked.

"He was unarmed."

"Any guess what he was doing out at night, if he wasn't hunting?"

"That's part of the investigation. He was known to be an avid runner, so that's one possibility," Childress stated.

The four men worked their way down the short slope and halfway across the field. Gates, Quags, and Childress jumped the bisecting stream with ease while Paulsen pussyfooted his way over the water, narrowly avoiding a splashdown. In a grove of trees near the edge of the field, four small flags were stuck into the ground, marking the patch of land where Kirk Zambrano had taken his last breath.

"This is where the body was found," Childress said.

Kneeling down, Quags felt the earth with his fingertips. He assessed the scene, eyes darting across the ground before looking up at the branches above. He noted the blood-soaked leaves on the ground, partially rinsed by the rain.

For the next ten minutes, Gates watched as Detective Millares plied his craft to the remote location. When Quags finally stood again, he put his hands on his hips, and glanced back over the field they had crossed. "How was the body taken out?"

"Ambulance," Paulsen replied.

"Did they come across the field?"

"No, they came from the opposite side. It's a longer trip, but it's flatter and closer to a paved road," Childress said.

The four men stood over the crime scene until Childress pulled his cell phone from his pocket. Turning away, he spoke quietly into his phone before hanging up and facing the group.

"If you can excuse us, I need to have a minute with Paulsen," Childress said.

"Please," Gates replied.

The two Agency men stepped away and Gates noted the quartet of camouflaged SPOs lurking in the woods.

"We have company," Gates said.

"I saw them," Quags replied. "Did you notice our proximity to the fence?"

"I did."

"How far do you figure it is?"

"A hundred and fifty yards. Maybe less."

"That's what I figure too."

"What do you think happened out here?" Gates asked.

"Hard to say for sure. A hunting rifle could easily kill a man in this location if it was fired from the fence line near the gate. Even if it were fired from the residential road beyond the gate. And you know what that means."

Gates peered back at the gate over Quags's shoulder. "How sure are you about my father's shot missing our suspect?"

"I saw Zambrano running when the second shot was fired. I didn't see the suspect go down. He vanished into the woods. But the location of the body is making me reconsider what I saw."

"It was dark."

"But a deer round from a hunting rifle would drop a man where he stood. Or put an end to any running."

"It would."

Quags stared toward the fence. "There's another question at hand here. A simple question. One that's more for you than it is for me."

"What's that?"

"Do we care who shot him or if it was an accident? I know you're going to disagree but a large part of me thinks we should be satisfied with this ending. We identified our suspect. Now he's dead. The rest of the story is noise."

"It's not noise. It lacks justice. It lacks closure. It's like putting an asterisk next to a professional sports record."

"Sometimes justice wears a disguise. And the conclusion we're looking at here offers a degree of compassion. It saves a lot of people from having to reopen old wounds."

"Those old wounds never closed. Just look at my father."

"It also saves the taxpayers of Virginia from the expense of a trial."

"We're going to have to agree to disagree on this one."

Paulsen interrupted the ongoing conversation, reapproaching the crime scene, his toupee seemingly more askew. "How is everything? Can I answer any questions for you?"

To Paulsen's rear, Childress was marching across the field in the direction of the SUV.

"Where's Childress going?" Quags asked.

"Childress has a private matter he has to deal with. He'll meet us back at the car," Paulsen said. "Do you have any additional questions? Anything I can clarify?"

Quags focused on the ground again and slowly shook his head. "And no one has found the lethal bullet?"

"As I said before, not as of yet."

"Have you tried using a metal detector?"

"We have. Thus far, to no avail."

"It would be helpful."

"I cannot disagree. It's a vital piece of the investigation. Rest assured we will keep looking."

"Out of curiosity, who found the body?"

"An SPO on patrol duty."

"On foot patrol?" Quags asked.

"Yes."

Quags cranked his neck around as if to silently imply the location was far off the beaten path. "I guess we'll have to wait and see what your investigation uncovers. But for now, I'm satisfied. At least until the bullet is located."

"And you, Chief Gates?"

"If my detective is satisfied, so am I."

"Okay, good. Let's head back."

*

The three men trounced through the field and traversed the stream in the opposite direction, Paulsen successfully navigating the hurdle with more finesse than on his previous crossing. The sun made an appearance through the day's rain clouds and Quags noticed the outline of the SUV's roof glistening over the small ridge ahead.

"Gentleman, if you don't mind, could we hold up here for a second?" Paulsen asked.

Gates stopped. Quags slowed his pace.

"Are you all right?" Gates asked the pudgy, out-of-breath attorney bringing up the rear.

"I'm fine. But there is something else we need to discuss."

"Here?" Quags asked, coming to a halt. He suspiciously eyed the edge of the field in all directions.

"Not to worry. Hunting has been temporarily suspended on base. Until the investigation is complete."

Quags assessed his surroundings for a second time and came to the same conclusion regarding the safety of the location. "I'd prefer to hear what you have to say when we get back to the visitor center."

"I'm afraid the visitor center may not provide the privacy necessary for this conversation."

Quags raised an eyebrow in his boss's direction.

"I'll cut to the chase," Paulsen said. "We're aware of your presence at the fence yesterday evening. We know that you met with instructor Zambrano. The three of you were captured by the motion-activated security camera near the gate. We know that your rendezvous ended rather hastily. We believe shots were fired and those shots led to a premature conclusion to your meeting. Unfortunately, the cameras at that location are video only. There's no audio. Given that, we had to make a few assumptions on our end about what occurred."

"For the record, we never stepped foot on base property. We didn't break any law," Gates said. "And neither of us fired a weapon."

"The video footage clearly shows that neither of you were holding a gun when the alleged shots were fired. The only rifle seen on the video appears to be a shotgun, and it is on the ground. But Detective Millares did unholster his weapon and aimed it away from the base. If you combine Millares's reaction with the scramble that preceded it, it could be interpreted as a nefarious incident at the fence. Unfortunately, the cameras have limited visibility beyond the perimeter. We were hoping to get your perspective on the incident, given your front-row seat."

"We don't have another perspective to offer you," Gates said.

"I can appreciate your position. That said, your perspective would be helpful in determining which course of action we take from here."

"What is that supposed to mean," Gates asked.

"As of now, the death of Kirk Zambrano is being tentatively classified as an accident. We are still open to other possibilities," Paulsen said, pausing for effect.

"Such as?" Gates asked.

"I'd rather not speculate. But we have discussed pulling the satellite imagery from last night to determine if any other vehicles were in the vicinity of the fence line at the time of the presumed shooting. We could use that as the starting point for a satellite image scan of the broader region. By piecing together multiple satellite images over time, we could track any vehicles that exited the adjacent neighborhood. With enough persistence and effort, we could see where any vehicle from the area ultimately parked for the remainder of that evening."

Gates swallowed. Quags remained frozen.

"But as I said, it would be a lot of work. Time. Effort. Cost."

Paulsen again paused for effect and then released a long, exaggerated sigh. "Or we could end this investigation, right here, right now, in the middle of this field."

"How's that?" Gates asked.

"We officially close the investigation. Chalk it up to an accidental shooting and we all move forward. We provide you with a death certificate, as well as Zambrano's personnel files, and everyone gets closure."

"What's the catch?"

"You cannot go public with any information pertaining to Zambrano, even if he is deceased. Regardless of what the evidence proves."

Gates turned toward Quags and back toward Paulsen. "Can I have a minute with my detective?" Gates asked.

"Of course. I'll step away for a few moments and enjoy the view."

"Thoughts?" Gates asked Quags, dropping his voice.

"I'd like to shove his toupee down his throat."

"Anything else?"

"They're offering a deal. We get our documents, and they get to close the door on Zambrano. If satellite imagery is truly in play, well, I don't need to elaborate on the implications for your father. Or for me, for that matter. I drove to your house in my cruiser."

"No, elaboration is necessary."

"This is their backyard. They can manipulate the story and evidence in any fashion they want. My suggestion is to buy some time. A couple of days. Let's take a look at the personnel files. If we like what we see and there's enough in the files to prove Zambrano is our killer, we can agree to the offer of an official conclusion of the investigation."

"Some of the families will not be satisfied with that conclusion. I've met with all of them over the years. Most of them want a lethal injection, the electric chair, or even an old-fashioned rope around a neck."

"I don't disagree, but justice comes in many forms."

Gates took a deep breath of air. "Okay, let's go with your suggestion."

Gates motioned to Paulsen, who stepped back toward the officers with bated breath.

"We'd like to take a couple of days to go over Zambrano's personnel files. We'll touch base with you after we've had a chance to dig around a little on our suspect's background."

"Sure, sure," Paulsen responded. "That's perfectly acceptable. But I must stress that we believe the proposed conclusion to this case would be a relief for everyone involved. I'm sure most would be happy to have this incident behind us and to close these long-standing cold cases. I'm equally sure your father will find both solace and relief in the conclusion of this investigation."

Gates stared hard at Paulsen. "How soon can you get us Zambrano's personnel files?" Gates asked.

"I'll arrange for them to be delivered first thing in the morning."

"Good, we'll be waiting," Quags said, turning back in the direction of the SUV.

CHAPTER 52

CHIEF GATES STOOD at the entrance to the small conference room serving as the Matoaka nerve center and observed Quags in silence as he flipped through pages of Kirk Zambrano's heavily redacted dossier and scribbled a note on a legal pad before rolling the top sheet back, exposing a clean page.

"Find anything in the files?" Gates asked into the room.

Quags looked up and put his pen down on a stack of papers. "I'm plodding along. Trying to fill in the blanks. A lot of the material was redacted. All things being equal, I'd like to find something in this guy's background to indicate he was the monster we thought he could be."

"We matched his prints, twice. And we confirmed it was him from the morgue."

"We did. And yet his background is clean."

"Not unusual for a serial killer. Or a spy."

"Or this file is fictitious. According to the documents from Paulsen and the Agency, our man Zambrano began his clandestine career in Tokyo, Japan, followed by Bangkok, Kuala Lumpur, Beijing, and Seoul. In total, he spent twenty-six years in Asia working for the Agency. What exactly he did for the Agency is anyone's guess. He served as the second secretary in both Tokyo and Malaysia. Apparently that title is a real position within the diplomatic ranks. It is also often reserved for members of the intelligence community working under the diplomatic cover of the State Department. Those were the only employment titles listed anywhere in his files. And I'm guessing the reason they were included is because it's such a common title it has very little value with regard to secrecy."

"I'll take your word for it."

"When I attempted to cross-check things about this guy, I came up empty-handed. We know when Zambrano was overseas, but when I searched for multiple unsolved murders of young women during the time he was in these locations, I couldn't find any. I found unsolved murders, but not a string of them."

"He was a trained clandestine agent. He was trained not to be caught. He just chose to apply those skills to murder."

"Maybe."

"Another explanation could be that crime isn't reported in the same fashion in the countries where he was stationed."

"I don't buy that. We're talking about major international cities. Four of the largest capitals in Asia. They have English language papers and English editions of local papers."

"It wouldn't be the first time crime reports were intentionally suppressed."

"I don't think that's the case. Believe it or not, these countries seem to share the United States' perverse obsession with serial killers. Another American export. Right up there with Coke, McDonalds, and KFC. But my point is that I don't believe for a second this guy only killed women in Williamsburg, Virginia."

"That would be highly unusual."

"I also can't shake what you told me after your first visit with the commonwealth's attorney."

"Which was?"

"The Agency would never allow one of their officers to be named publicly with regard to a high-profile cold case that's over three decades old."

"That's what he said."

"Well, there are two ways to accomplish that. One of which would be to kill him on base and label it as an accident."

"Killing one of their own on base? Other people would have had to sign up for the lie."

"Maybe they did."

A quiet fell over the men and lasted until Chief Gates's secretary tapped on her boss's shoulder.

"Chief Gates, you and Quags have a visitor."

"Who is it?" Gates asked, turning around at the doorway to face his secretary.

"She says her name is Audrey Zambrano."

Gates flashed a look of surprise. "Give us a minute and then escort her to my office."

"Yes, sir," his secretary answered.

Gates turned back toward the conference room and locked eyes with Quags.

"Let's see what the girl has to say," Quags said, pushing his chair away from the table and standing.

*

Audrey Zambrano entered Gates's office and Chief Gates stepped around his desk to shake her hand. Gates motioned toward Quags and introduced his detective to their visitor.

"Shall we take a seat?" Gates asked.

Audrey lowered herself into the leather chair across from Gates and placed her backpack on the floor. Her black hair was pulled back into a ponytail, leaving her face fully exposed. Her mixed ethnicity was evident in her features.

Quags rested his butt on the top of a short bookcase along the wall.

"We'd like to extend our sincerest condolences on your loss," Gates said.

"Thank you."

"How are you holding up?"

"It's been a rough couple of days. My mom isn't taking it well."

"I can understand."

"I wasn't sure you'd know who I was," the high school student said with an air of confidence that belied her age.

"We recognized your name," Gates replied.

"I was hoping you would. Detective Millares questioned my boyfriend about my father. After a soccer game against Jamestown High School."

"Yes, I did," Quags replied. "It was part of an open investigation."

"That's why I'm here."

"How can we help you?" Gates asked.

"I really don't know if you can. I don't know if I'm helping you by coming here or if I'm helping myself. Or if I'm helping my dad."

"Why don't you tell us what's on your mind and maybe we can all figure it out together," Gates said.

"All right. I have a couple of things in my backpack that I want to show you." As Audrey Zambrano reached down for her bag, Gates and Quags exchanged furtive glances.

"I found some items on the desk in our study after my father's accident." Audrey placed a stack of papers in front of Chief Gates. "These are notes my father took the day he died."

Quags leaned in and perused the top page. "How do you know when these notes were taken?"

"I don't know exactly when the handwritten notes were made, but he printed off some articles from the internet. They had the date and time printed on the bottom of each page. Those pages were printed the day he died. It looks like he was researching a series of murders in Williamsburg thirty-five years ago. From what I've read, your sister was one of the victims, Chief Gates."

"That's right. She was my younger sister."

"I guess it's my turn to offer condolences."

Gates nodded.

Audrey seemed to turned red. "I don't know how to say this, so I'm just going to come straight out and ask. Was my father a suspect in these murders?"

Chief Gates tried to remain stoic. Quags winced, then responded. "Based on fingerprint evidence, your father was a person of interest. Charges were never filed against him."

"Is that because he died before he could be charged?"

"Not entirely," Gates lied.

"The reason I ask is my father's research notes listed the victims, their causes of death, the dates they were killed. That kind of stuff. And I know from TV that a lot of criminals chronicle their crimes. Follow their crimes in the press."

"They do," Quags admitted.

"Which made me wonder if that's what my father was doing. Was he following these murders because he was involved, or was it something else?"

Audrey flipped several pages in the stack, reached into her bag again, and removed a DVD in a plastic case. "I found this on my father's desk along with all of his notes."

"What is it?" Chief Gates asked.

"It's a copy of my uncle's wedding. It was on VHS originally and copied onto a DVD at some point. It's not the quality of today's videos. It's a little choppy in places."

"Have you watched it?"

"Many times over the years. It's the only video I've ever seen with my paternal grandmother in it. She died not too long after it was recorded. I think that's why my dad kept it around. It was the last time he saw his mom."

"And is there a connection between the video and the murder investigation?" Quags asked.

"I think there is. Can we watch it?"

"Grab your things and let's head down the hall," Quags said.

*

The trio settled into an office three doors down. Quags wiped the top of a dust-covered DVD player, plugged it in, and inserted the disc.

"You can fast-forward a little. The first few minutes are from the rehearsal dinner. My dad wasn't there for that. He showed up late on Friday night. The part you need to see starts at the church," Audrey said.

Quags did as instructed and fast-forwarded until the camera opened with a view of the exterior of a stone church. Well-wishers filed in slowly, many pausing to wave at the camera as they stepped through the ornate wood-and-glass doors. As the camera moved to the inside of the church, guests filled the pews per their association with the groom or bride.

The video faded to black, and the next scene opened with the bridesmaids and groomsmen stretching from the step near the altar to the front pews. Sunlight filtered through the stained glass. As the organ began to play, the camera zoomed in for close-ups, including the groom and his entourage.

"Who are we looking at?" Quags asked.

"That's the groom. My uncle Jacob," Audrey said. "And the man to his immediate right is my father. He was the best man."

Quags paused as the video panned to the best man's face. "He's younger, but the face is the same," he said to Gates.

"It's him," Gates agreed. "Should we sit through the entire wedding ceremony?"

"We don't need to. We can skip ahead to the reception," Audrey replied.

Quags fast-forwarded again and the next break in the footage opened with a view of a three-tier wedding cake. The camera moved to the procession of guests, who took turns stopping at the elaborately decorated table to sign the wedding registry. On the wall behind the table was an enlarged replica of the wedding invitation.

"Look at that," Quags said, freezing the frame.

Gates read through the details of the invitation and his eyes opened wide. "Son of a bitch."

"If you keep watching, you can see my dad gives his best man's speech. After that, it's the typical wedding reception. Dances, the garter belt, the bouquet toss."

"We get the idea."

"The last chapter of the video is brunch."

Quags fast-forwarded again. A shot of a long table near a wall of windows overlooking the ocean filled the screen. The view panned left and right, showing the room was occupied by several dozen people in semi-casual attire.

"This is brunch the following morning on Coronado Island in San Diego. You can see some of the same characters from the wedding. I heard that a lot of them were hungover."

"Looks beautiful."

"It is. I've been."

The camera made a three-hundred-and-sixty-degree pass of the room as everyone found their seat. Half of the room filled one side of the long table, the other half on the opposite side.

"That's my dad with the blue golf shirt," Audrey said.

Quags again paused the recording.

"Not much happens from here on out. Those were the parts of the video I wanted you to see," Audrey added, tears welling in her eyes.

"And this video wasn't doctored in any fashion?"

"Not that I know of. But as you can see, the day after my uncle's wedding was the same date your sister was killed, Chief Gates. And my father was in California, having brunch with a few dozen guests. Including several marines, one of whom was my grandfather."

Audrey reached into her bag and placed a piece of paper on the table. "This is a list of all the guests in attendance that weekend. Or most of them. My aunt says a few names may be missing."

Quags reached over, plucked the list off the table, and perused the names. "Anything else in the video that we need to see?"

"Nope. That's the end of the important parts" Audrey said, wiping a tear from her face.

"That's quite a display of detective work you pulled together," Gates said.

"I just finished what my dad started. Put the pieces together."

"Well, the fruit doesn't fall far from the tree. Is there anything else that you think we need to know?"

"Not off the top of my head. I'm hoping the DVD speaks for itself."

"I think it does," Gates said.

"I have another question for you," Quags said.

"Sure."

"When was the last time you saw your father?"

"The night he died."

"Can you walk us through that day up until the last time you saw him?"

"Sure. The day was a little odd, to tell you the truth. I came home from school and my father asked me if I had seen or heard anything unusual with regard to our family or our house. He said something about a suspicious person in the yard who was doing the septic work. He seemed concerned for the safety of our family. I told him that the Williamsburg Police had asked my boyfriend about him."

"The same boyfriend you weren't supposed to be seeing."

Audrey nodded. "Yeah."

"And this was in the afternoon?"

"Yes. And based on the time stamp at the bottom of the computer print-outs, my dad then spent a few hours researching the Matoaka murders."

"What happened in the evening?"

"We had dinner together around six thirty, which is pretty typical. Then my father left the house around nine thirty, I didn't see him leave. I was in the shower. But when I got out, he wasn't home."

"Are you sure about the time?"

"I am. After my shower, I studied physics for an hour before going to bed. Sometime after ten, my father came back home. I heard him. He sounded upset. I heard him make a phone call and twenty minutes later Childress showed up at our door with two security officers."

"SPOs?"

"Yes."

"At your house?"

"Yes."

"Did you see them?"

"I peeked down the stairs. A few minutes later, my father left the house again with Childress and the two officers. I never saw him again."

Another tear ran down Audrey's face.

"So your father left the house at nine thirty, came back after ten, and then left the house again?"

"That's right."

"Son of a bitch," Chief Gates said in a whisper.

Quags seemed equally stunned by the revelation.

"What do you think happened to your father?" Chief Gates asked.

"He was accidentally shot."

"You don't seem surprised."

"You know where my father worked and what he did, right?"

"Yes."

"Well, living at Camp Peary can be dangerous. There's a lot of activity at night. Instructors like my father are constantly coming and going at all hours. You hear gunfire and explosions."

"So your father leaving at night, coming back, and leaving again wasn't unusual?"

"Not at all. He's been doing that my entire life. Even before we came to Camp Peary."

"And you think he was accidentally shot?"

"I do. There's no other explanation."

The conversation stalled and Quags suggested an end to the meeting. "Can we get your contact number? We may have some other questions for you at some point."

"Sure," Audrey replied. She retrieved a pen from her backpack and scribbled her name and number across the top of a printout on the table.

"And we'd like to thank you for coming in and bringing this to our attention," Gates said, standing again and extending his hand.

As Audrey stood, she said, "I did it for my dad. He was a strict father, but he was a man of integrity."

*

Chief Gates showed Audrey to the door and the two officers reconvened in Gates's office. Quags sat down and stared out the window, his mind racing. Gates closed the door and stood behind his desk, running a hand through his hair.

"Obviously we have a problem," Quags said.

"Indeed we do. If the girl is telling the truth."

"There's one way to find out," Gates said. "Run down the witnesses from the wedding."

"Assuming that pans out, and what she says is true, then Zambrano didn't kill your sister. He didn't leave a print behind on her Walkman."

"It also means that my father didn't shoot and kill Zambrano," Gates said.

"Not unless Zambrano somehow went home after he was shot, made a telephone call, met with Childress, and then went back to the field and died," Quags replied. "The massive bullet hole in his chest would have made that unlikely, to say the least."

"How long will it take to confirm his attendance with some of the wedding guests?"

"The wedding was thirty-five years ago. It may take a while."

"Recruit some help. See what you can find out."

"Roger that. And I want to arrange a meeting with Childress."

"You mean Paulsen?" Gates asked.

"Nope. Childress. I don't want to hear Paulsen's commentary on what Childress did the night Zambrano was killed. Paulsen wasn't there."

"Are we sure?"

"We called him in DC from Bramble's office. That was the morning we found out Zambrano was dead. Paulsen flew down later that day."

"I'm not sure Childress will talk, but it's worth a shot."

"See what you can do, boss."

CHAPTER 53

QUAGS STOOD ON Duke of Gloucester Street in Colonial Williamsburg and watched as the nose-in-their-phone public of today mixed with daily life from two centuries ago. He checked his watch and confirmed he was on time. He was also in the right place, his location unmistakable given its position between the shoemaker and the weaver.

A red horse-drawn carriage plodded down the street. The driver of the two-horse-powered vehicle sat high behind the beasts of burden, the enclosed carriage beneath him and to the rear. With a flick of his whip and a single "whoa" the driver brought the carriage to a halt directly in front of Quags. The door to the carriage opened and Devon Childress smiled toward the detective.

"Come on aboard," Childress said, motioning to the bench seat on the opposite side of the carriage. "I'm not sure how four or six people used to fit in these things, but the two of us should manage."

Quags climbed in and sat on the red velour seat. The two men's knees almost touched, their feet sharing the floor space between the two bench seats. Childress slid over and closed the door to the carriage. With another flick of the driver's wrist, the horses began to pull their load down the gravel road.

"Interesting choice for a meeting," Quags said.

"Let's just say I was in the area for work and this isn't my first carriage ride. For the next twenty minutes or so, we have it all to ourselves."

Two small speakers in the corner of the carriage began to play a recorded message, describing the surrounding buildings and their importance as the vehicle rocked and shimmied down the main drag. Childress reached over and turned the volume on the speakers to low.

"I'm all yours," Childress said. "What did you want to discuss? I assume the personnel records you requested were self-explanatory."

"As much as heavily redacted documents can be."

Childress shrugged. "I had no control over the content of the information provided."

"I don't doubt that. But there are things you did have control over. I wanted to discuss a couple of them."

"Please."

"Have you spoken with the family of the deceased?"

"Of course. Arrangements needed to be made, and as the chief of security, I had a hand in those preparations. I have spoken with Mr. Zambrano's widow on multiple occasions."

"I'm curious, was she aware that her husband was a murder suspect in an active investigation?"

"The topic never came up. And at this juncture, it doesn't matter."

"I think it does."

"Why's that?"

"It's come to our attention that Kirk Zambrano was out of town the day that Chief Gates's sister was killed in 1987. I spent most of yesterday afternoon confirming this with a rather lengthy guest list. As it turns out, Zambrano was the best man at his brother's wedding in San Diego that weekend."

A look of surprise washed over Childress's face and then disappeared.

"I was not aware."

"I cannot imagine you would be."

"If what you say is accurate, then Kirk Zambrano should have never been considered a suspect at all."

"That's the way it appears. Except for the mystery surrounding one of his fingerprints, which matched the lone print left at the Heather Gates crime scene."

"Obviously there has been an error in the print comparison."

"That is the most likely explanation," Quags said. "The Williamsburg PD is going to have the prints compared again. This time by a neutral third party. The Miami PD crime lab."

"Hopefully that will clear things up."

"It won't clear up who shot Kirk Zambrano."

"Kirk Zambrano's death was officially declared an accident."

"But the bullet was never found."

"No, it wasn't."

"Which leaves the door open for possibilities with regard to the shooter."

"If you want to look at it that way. If you wanted to pin the accidental shooting on one individual."

"I'd rather know the truth about what happened."

"We all would."

"I think you already do."

"Be careful with your accusations, Detective."

"Audrey Zambrano paid us a visit at police headquarters. She wanted us to know that her father was a good man with integrity. In the course of that conversation, we asked her when was the last time she saw her father. Do you know what she replied?"

Childress didn't respond.

"I'll answer for you. She said she saw her father sometime after ten o'clock, at their house on base, down by the river. She said that you and two SPOs came to their home shortly thereafter and left with her father. That makes you one of the last people to have seen Zambrano alive. It also makes you a suspect."

"In what?"

"In Zambrano's death."

"As I said, Zambrano's death has been declared an accidental shooting. That's how it will remain."

"I understand your position. But you're going to have to live with the fact that you had a hand in the death of an innocent man."

"An innocent man that you tried to convince me wasn't innocent."

"That I did. But it's never too late to make things right when new evidence surfaces."

Childress glanced out the glassless window of the carriage at a group of Chinese tourists invading a souvenir stand. Quags measured the man seated in front of him, his eyes running from head to toe. It was at the end of Childress's long legs where Quags's eyes froze.

"Is there anything else I can do for you, Detective Millares?" Childress asked.

Quags forced his eyes off Childress's shoes. "I'll let you know the results of the new print analysis."

"It won't change anything with regard to Zambrano."

Quags dropped his eyes again, staring at his counterpart's feet. "I expected more emotion from you. Some kind of human response. Zambrano was a colleague of yours."

"Zambrano understood the importance of the Agency's mission and the sacrifices that need to be made to maintain its secrets."

"I don't think Zambrano would have agreed that those sacrifices include murdering an innocent man."

"Once again, you were the one who insisted he wasn't innocent," Childress answered.

A moment later, without a word, the carriage magically came to a stop in front of Shield Tavern.

"This is where I'm getting off," Childress said. He unfolded his lanky frame from the confines of the carriage. Stepping down, Childress almost slipped in a small patch of mud on the side of the road. Quags followed suit, stepping off the carriage, aiming for drier ground.

"Have a good afternoon, Detective" Childress said in parting.

As the tall career clandestine officer turned and walked away, Quags's gaze fell to the footprint Childress had left behind. He stood on the side of the colonial road until the horse-drawn carriage moved on. Looking down, Quags intentionally stepped into the mud, placing his shoe directly next to the imprint that Childress had left behind. Removing his phone from his pocket, he took a photo of the two prints side by side in the mud. He confirmed the quality of the photos he had just taken and his phone began to vibrate in his hand. He ignored the incoming call, eyed the prints in the mud for a final time, and cursed.

CHAPTER 54

THE DISMANTLING OF the Matoaka nerve center had ground to a halt. A tower of boxes leaned precariously near the door. An unfolded map hung off the corner of the table. Quags sat among the packing debris, his mobile phone on the table next to a stack of legal pads. When it began to vibrate for the third time in as many minutes, Quags answered the unknown number.

"Detective Millares?"

"Speaking," Quags responded.

"This is Grant. Jenny's ex-boyfriend. The pot farmer. I'm returning your call. Sorry it took a while. I was out of pocket, hiking with some buddies for a few days. I got an email from Jenny that you wanted to speak, but they don't sell burner phones out on the trail. I had to wait until I got back to civilization. What can I do for you?"

"I'm not sure it matters anymore, honestly."

"How's that?"

"We identified our guy."

"The guy responsible for the cold case murders?"

"Our main suspect."

"That's awesome. Congratulations."

"It's closure. Of sorts. The guy's name was Kirk Zambrano. He was an instructor on The Farm. He was the man in the computer-generated images that I sent to you when we first spoke."

"I remember. He must have been relatively new on base. I didn't know him."

"And you never will. He's dead."

"How?"

"In a shooting accident. He was shot on the grounds of Camp Peary after we met him and took his fingerprints. We visited the body at the morgue. I can confirm he was shot. I can't tell you if it was an accident."

Quags proceeded to tell Grant about the encounter at the fence line and the collection of fingerprints from their main suspect.

"On our way to have Richmond PD perform analysis on the prints, I became concerned that perhaps we had been duped. That perhaps the man had provided fake or altered fingerprints. That's when I asked Jenny to reach out to you again."

"Fake prints?"

"Or altered prints. Is this possible?"

"Depends on what you mean."

"Is it possible for someone to have fake prints over their real finger-prints? Maybe a glove of some sort. Something not immediately visible to the naked eye. The kind of stuff you see in movies."

"As I told you the first time we spoke, the Agency had full rubber masks in the seventies."

"I recall. You referred to it as identity transfer."

"That's right. Good memory. Fingerprint transfer was a part of that repertoire. Early on, it was primarily used for disinformation. Plant some-one's fingerprint in a location where it shouldn't be and then make sure the print is found. Pretty simple."

"In theory."

"Once biometrics gained in popularity, fingerprints became part of the security breaching protocol. Most of the high tech security systems in the world now rely on some level of biometrics. Fingerprints, palm prints, retinal scans, voice scans."

"I've seen most of them in action."

"In its infancy, producing transferable fingerprints was a time-consuming process. But as technology and computers have advanced, it's become easier, and 3D printing technology has advanced the capabilities even further."

"Are these part of the current coursework at The Farm? Transferring fingerprints?"

"Absolutely. It has been for decades. Nowadays, it's a modern version of Picks and Locks. Picks and Locks 2.0 is what they jokingly called it."

"The first time we spoke, you mentioned that Picks and Locks was a class."

"Your recollection is spot on again. Picks and Locks, and its 2.0 version, was taught by Devon Childress."

A long silence fell on the conversation.

"Are you still there?" Grant asked.

"I am," Quags replied.

"Any other questions I can answer for you?"

"Not now. Thanks for the call back."

"You're welcome. Have Jenny reach out to me if you need anything else."

*

For the rest of the afternoon, Quags pored through the case evidence for the umpteenth time. To his left, Post-it Notes protruded from the side and tops of stacked documents, the colorful paper forming a collage of investigative artwork. To his right, the redacted personnel files were spread across the table and chair next to him. A knock on the door offered Quags a momentary break.

"You wanted to talk?" Chief Gates said, entering and shutting the door.

"I do. I met with Childress today. And I need a sanity check."

"Okay, but don't blame me if you don't like the answer."

"Hear me out."

Chief Gates sat down. "Let's have it."

"Imagine you're a case officer in training on The Farm in the eighties. You're also on the cusp of becoming a budding serial killer."

"Okay."

"And one long weekend break in October you head to DC from Camp

Peary on the Blue Bird bus. Then you drive back down to Williamsburg and commit your first murder."

"Why come down to Williamsburg? There are plenty of people in the DC area to kill."

"Cover. Alibi. You can say you went back to DC for the long weekend. Fifty people would confirm you rode the bus to DC on Friday and returned on Monday. It's not an airtight alibi, but it's an alibi."

"And we know for a fact it's a possibility."

"Right. As a newly minted murderer with my first kill under my belt, I follow the story in the press. This is before the internet, meaning I'm watching the local news and reading the local papers. And over the course of the weeks following the first murder, our killer learns that the police have a shoe impression from the suspect. Somehow it's leaked to the press and our killer sees it."

"Okay."

"As a case officer in training, learning to circumvent security as a profession, our suspect decides to ply his skills for his own benefit. He decides he's going to try to get his hands on the shoe impression he left behind on his first kill."

"By breaking into a police facility?"

"That's right. The article mentioned that the Virginia State Police were helping the Williamsburg Police Department with evidence analysis. We both know the nearest state police facility to Williamsburg is on Airport Road. From what I read, it's been there since the 1970s. More importantly, it's conveniently located within a couple miles of Camp Peary."

"So our man breaks in, steals the impression, and gets away without anyone being the wiser."

"Yep. That's what I'm saying."

"It's plausible."

"Do you remember the size of the shoe determined by the shoe impression? It was a Nike running shoe."

"Size nine," Gates replied.

"That's right. Nine. On the smaller side. Any chance you noticed the size of Childress's feet?"

"I didn't."

"Neither did I. Until today. We were in a horse-drawn carriage and our feet shared the common floor between the two bench seats that faced each other. At some point during the ride, I noticed that Childress had remarkably small feet for a man his height. Once I noticed, I couldn't divert my attention from his footwear. After we got off the carriage and parted ways, I took photos of my footprint next to his. I wear size eleven. Childress wears something closer to a nine."

"That's a small shoe for a tall man."

"Yes, it is. And those small feet got me to thinking. Childress is the chief of security on the base. He also serves as an instructor. Do you recall the class he teaches?"

"I don't."

"Picks and Locks," Quags replied. "Including biometrics and the transferring of fingerprints."

Gates seemed to digest the analysis. "I think we need to go back to the commonwealth's attorney and have another conversation."

"I have a better idea."

CHAPTER 55

VIENNA, AUSTRIA, HAS long been referred to as the spy capital of the world. As a result of its location, history, lax espionage laws, and large number of international organizations that call Vienna their headquarters, the city serves as a nexus for the exchange of secrets. And if Vienna, Austria, is the spy capital of the world, Vienna, Virginia, has more CIA personnel residing in its town limits than anywhere on earth. Sitting seven miles from CIA headquarters, Vienna's growth has mirrored that of the Agency's over the last fifty years.

The unmarked Williamsburg police cruiser exited the Beltway on Route 7, heading west. Weaving through the never-ending traffic and construction of Tysons Corner, the cruiser looped onto Route 123 south. Minutes later, signage for Vienna welcomed them to the well-heeled town.

"I hope you're right about this address and our lawyer friend."

"I am. Paul Paulsen is listed as an attorney for the Central Intelligence Agency in several public documents. He's also a member of the bar in multiple states, including Virginia. Ironically, he may have an odd name, but it's the one his parents gave him at birth. And the address I found is for the only Paul Paulsen in the DC area."

Gates checked his phone for directions. "In a mile or so, we're taking a right on East Street. Just past Westwood Drive."

"East Street and Westwood? Sounds like someone was direction-ally challenged."

Two more turns brought the car into a neighborhood featuring fifty-year-old ramblers and split-levels sitting in the shadows of newly con-structed ten-thousand-square-foot behemoths.

"It's down on the right," Gates said.

The unmarked cruiser came to a stop at the curb in front of a brick split-level on a small hill. Looking up at the residence from the street, they could see several rooms with lights on. As they observed, a shadow moved across the front window.

"It appears that someone is home," Gates said.

"Let's find out."

The two law enforcement officers climbed the incline of the driveway and followed the walkway to the front door. Standing on a doormat that read *All Are Welcome*, Quags motioned downward. "We're going to see if that's true."

Reaching up, he pushed the doorbell and waited. Several long seconds later, the doorknob turned and a woman in an apron opened the door.

"Good evening," Gates and Quags said simultaneously.

"Good evening," the woman replied, wiping her hands on her apron. Her gray hair was pulled back into a ponytail, dark eyes framed by a pair of black eyeglasses.

Quags let Chief Gates offer introductions and both men provided their credentials for verification.

"Is your husband Paul Paulsen?" Gates asked.

"He is."

"We would like to have a word with him."

"Please come inside. I'll get him for you."

Gates and Quags stepped inside, and their host closed the door behind them. The scent of dinner cooking wafted through the air. Quags stepped further into the room and admired the piano in front of the living room's main window. Photographs of Paulsen and his wife depicted them as world travelers with six of the new seven wonders on display in frames.

Mrs. Paulsen entered the room for a second time. "He'll be right up. May I offer you something to drink?"

"We're fine, thank you," Gates said as Paul Paulsen climbed a short staircase and arrived on the main floor.

"If you would excuse me, I'll get back to making dinner," Mrs. Paulsen replied before disappearing through a doorway on the far side of the room.

Paul Paulsen offered no greeting to his visitors. Above his stoic expression, his cockeyed toupee seemed to be hanging on by a thread.

"Sorry to visit unannounced," Gates said. "But we thought it would be the best way to get some truthful answers."

"You thought wrong," Paulsen replied. "You shouldn't have come to my home. This is not a place of work."

"It is tonight," Quags said.

"Do you have someplace we can talk in private?" Gates asked.

"There is no place more private than where we are standing. And my wife has a higher security clearance than I do. So, by all means, say what you came here to say."

Gates nodded for Quags to begin.

"We came here to inform you that we have evidence that Kirk Zambrano's death wasn't an accident. It was a cover-up. A failed cover-up. The only question that remains is how involved you were."

"What evidence are you referring to?"

"Zambrano's daughter paid us a visit. She provided evidence that her father was in California at the time of the Matoaka murder that produced the sole fingerprint in those cases. She further provided testimony that exonerates Chief Gates's father as a potential source of your accidental shooting theory. After the incident at the fence line, Zambrano went home and called base security. Shortly thereafter he left his house with three individuals from the base—two SPOs and Devon Childress. He was never seen alive again."

Paul Paulsen squinted. "Do you have any evidence beyond the testimony of a high school girl? She isn't even old enough to provide a deposition without a parent."

"And she only has one parent left," Quags said, pausing to let the statement sink in.

"Did you ever look into Zambrano's background?" Quags asked.

"Zambrano passed every background investigation the Agency required of him."

"I'm not talking about a polygraph. I'm talking about his time overseas. I used the documents you provided to research unsolved murders in the countries where Zambrano was stationed. During his tenure in each location, there were no known unsolved murders of young women. Either Zambrano was a serial killer on a thirty-five-year vacation, or he wasn't a killer at all. Which do you think is more likely?"

"I'm neither an investigator nor a detective."

"Do you know if Childress was at The Farm during the same period as the Matoaka murders?" Gates asked

"He never indicated that to me."

"If he was there, would you find it odd if he didn't mention it?" Quags asked.

"Agency employees are trained to be tight-lipped. Especially those serving at the premier training facility in the US."

"Fair enough," Quags conceded. "Did you ever notice the size of Devon Childress's feet?"

"I'm sure I didn't."

"Well, they're small for a man of his stature. Surprisingly small. Size nine, if I had to guess. The same size as the footprint that was left at the first Matoaka murder scene. The one that later went missing from a Virginia State Police evidence room."

"I'll take that as speculation."

"You can take it any way you like. Just look into him."

"Rest assured, I will."

"You'd better hurry. Because if Childress is what I think he is and he kills again before you get around to investigating him, I'll go public with what we know."

"That will put you behind bars for revealing the identity of an undercover agent."

"No, it won't," Gates interjected. "Because the only name we'll mention is yours. You're not a covert employee. You're not covered by any state secrets provisions. We'll let the whole world know exactly what you've done."

Paul Paulsen's face flushed. "You have a long drive back to Williamsburg ahead of you this evening. I think this meeting is adjourned."

"And you have work to do," Quags replied.

Paulsen showed his guests to the front door and opened it. "For the record, gentleman, there's something I don't want you to overlook. My position as legal counsel within the Agency is guided by a single principle."

"Which is?" Gates asked.

"Protect the Agency. At any cost."

*

"I think that went well," Quags said minutes later, the police cruiser stuck in southbound traffic on Route 123.

"We may have crossed the line."

"Which line is that?"

"Visiting the man's house without notice. His wife was there. I felt bad." Gates let out a sigh.

"That man is complicit in the murder of an innocent man."

"We don't know that for certain."

"At the very least, we know he was involved in the cover-up. He's also the same man who was willing to use your innocent father to blackmail us. Childress knew your father didn't shoot Zambrano. Paulsen must have known too."

"I'm not saying you're wrong, I'm saying that's an assumption. Childress could have told Paulsen anything and Paulsen probably would have believed him. Like you said, Paulsen was in DC when Zambrano was killed. He relied on Childress for information."

"He did. But I think our trip here made one thing clear. Paulsen needs to investigate Childress. Right down to his size-nine shoes."

The two officers enjoyed a bumper-to-bumper crawl down Route 123, stopping to consume chili dogs from a hole-in-the-wall called the Vienna

Inn. Back in the car after their pit stop, Gates broached the subject of the rifle used in the fence-line shooting.

"My father has been asking me about his rifle. The one you took from his place the night Zambrano was shot."

"That gun ceased to exist the moment I walked out of your dad's shack with it. Within an hour, the first three inches of the barrel sank to the bottom of the Chesapeake. The rest of the weapon followed suit. Nothing bigger than my palm. Dropped in different locations. All serial numbers removed. It will never be recovered."

"You weren't fooling around. I'd admire your handiwork if it weren't illegal to destroy evidence."

"As it turns out, the gun was only evidence of a bad decision by your father. He shouldn't have been shooting in the direction of a military base. He still doesn't understand how close that was to a fiasco."

"He knows. He doesn't care."

"That's when man is at his most dangerous."

"Indeed. By the way, my father is going to smoke some ribs tomorrow evening. You should stop by."

"What's the occasion?"

"My birthday."

"Happy birthday, Chief."

"It's not until later this week. But my dad has plans for this weekend and the weather looks promising tomorrow."

"I would love to, but I can't make it. I have a date with a new *mamacita*."

"Puerto Rican? Cuban?"

"No. American this time."

"Let me know if you need me to translate for you. From English to English. Puerto Rican to American."

"Thanks, Chief. I think I've got it."

CHAPTER 56

QUAGS FELT FOR his phone in the darkness and turned on the bedside light. Eyes closed, he groggily offered his name to the caller.

"Millares."

"This is dispatch. Sorry to wake you. Patrol called and is requesting your presence at an automobile accident."

"Where?"

"Colonial Parkway. Just past Merrimac Trail."

"Any idea why they're requesting me?"

"A vehicle with bullet holes and two fatalities. That's all I know."

"Tell them I'm on my way."

Quags hung up the phone and looked over at his date's brown hair on the pillow next to his.

"Is everything okay?" the woman asked without turning over.

"I have to go. Keep sleeping. I'll be back in a few hours. I'll bring coffee."

"Is this what dating a detective is like?" the woman asked, still facing in the other direction.

"Yeah. It's one of the perks."

"Coffee or having the bed to myself?"

"Sometimes you get both."

Quags grabbed his phone, wallet, badge, and gun. He turned off the bedside light and walked through his room in the dark. In the living room, he fumbled for his shoes, went out the front door, and locked the dead bolt behind him.

*

Quags saw the myriad flashing lights from the first responders and emergency vehicles blocking the road. A dozen rescue personnel stood at the edge of the road, staring down a steep embankment. Emergency floodlights aimed into the abyss. Repelling ropes trickled over the precipice, one end tied to carabiners that were attached to a firetruck. As Quags got out of his car, he approached the scene and joined the others in staring over the edge. Voices from below were intermittently drowned out by the din from the jaws of life.

Quags recognized the senior uniform patrol officer on duty and approached.

"How's it going, Officer Magnus?"

The thin officer turned towards Quags. "Just another night in paradise. Thanks for coming."

"What's the story? Why am I out here at three in the morning?"

Magnus flicked his head away from the scene. "Take a walk for a second." As the two strolled away from the commotion, the noise faded.

"We have an old Chevy Impala with bullet holes down its side resting at the bottom of an embankment. Two fatalities. The deceased were the only ones inside the vehicle, though someone could have been thrown from it since the windshield was completely blown out. We might not know for sure until morning light. You'd be surprised how far a body can travel with the appropriate inertia. We figure the car rolled four or five times before it came to rest where it is."

"How long will it take you to get it out?"

"It's going to be tricky. We're going to need some heavy equipment to get the car back to street level. But the height clearance for the tunnels on the parkway are going to be problematic. We may have to get creative."

"Were either of the victims shot?"

"We'll have a better idea of the injuries and what caused them once the bodies have been successfully extracted. Our rescue guys are doing their best."

"Did you run the tags?"

"The car didn't have any," Officer Magnus replied with suspicion in his voice.

"What about IDs?"

"The first responder down the rope was able to reach the driver. The deceased had a wallet in the breast pocket of his sportscoat. The only piece of identification found in the wallet was a business card with your name on it."

"My name?"

"Yep. Your business card. That's why I called. Any idea who it could be?"

"I'm not going to venture a guess," Quags replied stoically. "Any registration in the vehicle?"

"We haven't made that determination yet. Obviously, we'll have a better idea when we get the car up and have time to examine it. You can imagine what the interior currently looks like."

"I can."

"The driver of the vehicle should be out before long. Rescue is already cutting through the frame. The passenger is going to be a little more difficult. We haven't been able to reach him yet. The car is on its side, passenger door facing down. We'll have to finagle it a little."

Quags stared down the empty darkness of the Colonial Parkway and back toward the edge of the embankment. "I don't see any skid marks."

Magnus nodded. "It doesn't appear there are any. And the Colonial Parkway is unlined concrete. Skid marks would stand out. But lack of skid marks is typical of a driver falling asleep behind the wheel. Or maybe someone who's busier texting than paying attention."

"Or maybe a driver who swerved because someone was shooting at their car."

Magnus shrugged.

"Who called the accident in?" Quags asked.

"An anonymous driver."

"Did they see the car go off the road? Because if they didn't actually witness it, I doubt they'd be able to see the vehicle in its current location. Certainly not at night. Probably not during the day."

"I'll look into the details of the phone call."

Quags cranked his neck and looked down the road in both directions. "Do we have any cameras out here?"

"On the parkway? A few. A couple of the overpasses have cameras. I'll have the feeds pulled."

"Good. If it's all the same with you, I'm going to stick around here for a while."

"No problem. I'll keep you in the loop as we progress."

*

Quags sat on the edge of the embankment, ten yards out of the way but close enough to watch the recovery efforts unfold. He was nearing the end of his cigar when the red rescue stretcher began its ascent. Hoisted by a winch on the tail of the firetruck, the stretcher reached street level and came to rest on the concrete of the parkway. The body was removed from the rescue stretcher, placed on a mobile one, and then slid into the rear of an ambulance. Quags stepped on his cigar and walked to the rear of the emergency vehicle. Officer Magnus met with Quags in front of the open doors.

"Can I take a look?"

"Of course. But it could be messy."

Quags climbed into the ambulance and shimmied past the stretcher. At the head of the body, he unzipped the bag and exposed the battered and bruised face of the deceased."

Quags scowled. "*Coño.*"

"I don't know what that means in Spanish, but I get the feeling I agree with you."

"What the hell were you doing out here?" Quags asked rhetorically toward Paulsen's corpse.

"Do you know him?" Magnus asked.

"I do. He's an attorney," Quags considered expounding on Paulsen's identification and decided against it. His mind switched gears and he began to race through the possibilities surrounding the accident scene. "Can you make sure both bodies are taken to Sentara Regional?"

"I sure can. But I think we're still an hour away from extracting the second body."

"That's fine. I'll catch up with them in the morning at the medical examiner's office. And then I'll take a look at the car."

"It should be in impound by late morning."

"That'll work. Send me the VIN number when you have it."

CHAPTER 57

THE BIG-BELLIED MEDICAL examiner with the walrus mustache buzzed open the doors and invited Quags in.

"You're keeping me busy this week."

"My apologies. And despite what you may think, I prefer my suspects alive. They answer more questions when they're still breathing," Quags replied.

"You won't be getting answers from either of the two brought in this morning."

Quags tried to force a smile. "What can you tell me?"

"I've finished my preliminary assessment." The ME motioned toward two stainless steel tables on the far side of the room, white sheets draped over the bodies. "Which one would you like to hear about first?"

"Let's go with the driver."

The ME peeled back the sheet, exposing Paul Paulsen from the waist up. His white skin and soft physique indicated the man spent little time outside or in the gym. "The driver died of blunt force trauma. He sustained massive head injuries in addition to damage to his torso. X-rays indicated over twenty fractures. Ribs, vertebrae, skull. Both femurs."

"Any obvious indication those injuries could have come from something other than a car accident?"

"Obvious? No. Not for the driver. The body looks as if it were inside a vehicle that rolled a half-dozen times over rough terrain."

"Any indication he was drunk or under the influence of drugs?"

"I took a blood sample to determine his BAC. It will go out with the morning run. Results should be back tomorrow. A complete toxicology will take longer, as you know. If it's officially requested."

"Do it."

"Done."

"What about our second victim?"

Moving to the next table, the ME exposed the body in the same fashion he had exposed Paulsen's body. Quags stood stoically near the torso, recognizing the face of the long corpse as Devon Childress.

"As you can see, this victim also had severe head trauma. Skull fractures. His left orbital bone is shattered. Both sides of his jaw. Both arms. Most of his ribs." The ME paused and pointed to the victim's nearest hand. "In addition to the injuries sustained in in the accident, the second victim was also missing all of his finger and toenails."

"Accident victims don't lose their nails very often," Quags stated.

"No, they don't."

"I guess someone wanted to see what the victim had to say for himself before they killed him. Someone who owned a pair of pliers and wasn't afraid to use them."

"I can't imagine a scenario where that wasn't extremely painful," the ME said with a grimace. "This was the first time I've dealt with torture."

"And the last time for him."

Both men stared at the badly damaged body on the table in front of them.

"I'm assuming you can ID both victims," the ME said.

Without taking his eyes off Childress, Quags pointed to the other table. "That's Paul Paulsen. He's an attorney. He works for the Agency. He lives in Vienna, Virginia. He's married. He works on legal issues that impact Camp Peary."

The ME scribbled the name and hometown onto a clipboard

at the foot of the table. "That should help notify next of kin. And the second gentleman?"

"This is the chief liaison and security officer for Camp Peary. Or he was until early this morning."

"No effing way," the ME said. "Someone's got to be looking for him."

"You would think."

"Do you have a name?"

"His cover name is Devon Childress. I have no idea what his legal name is."

"What exactly is going on here, Detective?"

"I'll let you know when I figure it out. The simple answer is these guys work for the same employer as the accidental shooting victim from earlier this week." Quags checked the clock on the wall. "What's the estimated time of death?"

"Best guess is between one and three this morning. I assume that'll coincide with the time of the accident. I'm confident that's what killed them."

"And no further identification was found on either victim?" Quags asked.

"No."

Quags walked to the end of the far table and pulled the sheet away from Childress's legs. Dried blood covered the dead man's toes. "Any chance you measured his feet?"

"I did. They were size nine. A small foot for someone so tall."

"But the right size for a serial killer."

The ME shrugged. "Do you know anyone who can provide his legal name?"

"I have a number for the liaison office at Camp Peary. I'll call them, leave a message, and have them reach out to you."

"Thank you."

Quags's eyes ran over Childress's corpse as he circled the table a second time. "Can I get a pair of gloves, an evidence tube, and a swab?" he asked.

"Absolutely," the ME replied. He stepped to a drawer on the side of the room and produced the requested items.

Quags donned gloves, grabbed a swabbed, and bent over to get close to Childress's face. He inserted the buccal swab into the descendant's mouth and collected a mix of saliva and blood . He placed the swab in the evidence tube and stared at Childress's body for a final, long moment.

"Any other questions?" the ME asked.

"No. That does it for now. Let me know if you learn anything else on your end. I'll touch base with you later today."

"Sure, Detective. If someone asks, should I say you were never here?"

Quags cocked his head to the side. "I don't think it matters this time. Everyone I've interacted with at the Agency is dead."

"That's what worries me."

*

Quags exited the front doors of Sentara Regional Hospital, sidestepping a panic-stricken man helping a pregnant woman toward the entrance. Walking away from the building, he listened to his voice mails and then called Chief Gates to provide an update on the morgue's two newest guests.

"I'm just leaving Sentara. I met with the medical examiner and saw the bodies. The driver was confirmed as Paulsen. Want to guess the identity of the passenger?"

"Devon Childress."

"That's right. What gave it away?"

"It was a logical conclusion. Everyone else we've met with has turned up dead."

"That's what I just said to the ME."

"Great minds think alike."

"I'm on my way to the impound lot. I'm going to check out the vehicle from last night's accident. I got a message saying there's something I need to see."

*

Quags stepped from his cruiser, the hum of I-64 reverberating across Williamsburg PD's impound lot. Cars and trucks were parked in long rows across the worn earth and cracked concrete. Quags walked along the first line of vehicles and entered the side door of a metal garage. He checked in with the evidence officer on duty, signed his name, and stepped onto the garage floor. He immediately recognized the heavily damaged body of a Chevrolet Impala jacked off the floor in the middle bay. Officer Magnus from the night before was standing next to the vehicle. A pair of legs protruded from under the car. A metal bar slid out across the floor as Quags approached.

"I got your voice mail," Quags said. "I was at the hospital visiting the car's two occupants. I came over as soon as I could."

"No worries," Magnus replied.

"What do we have?"

"A fifteen-year-old Chevrolet Impala. After five and a half rotations down an embankment. In addition to the eleven bullet holes running down the driver's side."

"Any luck with the contents of the vehicle?"

"Yes and no. The car was clean. And when I say clean, I mean clean. Cleaned out. Bumper to bumper. No paperwork. No floor mats. No spare tire. No jack. Not even a penny in the console. In fact, the only thing we did find was a toupee and a briefcase."

"The toupee belonged to the driver."

"We figured. The other occupant had a full head of hair."

"Where is this briefcase?"

"Over on the bench," Magnus said.

"I'll check it out in a second," Quags said. "Any luck with the VIN number?"

"We're looking. The VIN tag on the dash and the door jamb are missing. Probably removed before the crash. But the VIN number is also on the chassis, the engine block, and a few other locations. Those are harder to get to when the car looks like crumpled foil." The officer pointed to the legs protruding from under the car. "One of our mechanics is currently working on it."

"Without the VIN, the car isn't going to help my investigation."

"I can't tell you much about the car, other than what you see in front of you. But I can tell you how it ended up at the bottom of the embankment."

"I'm all ears."

"I obtained the surveillance feeds from the Colonial Parkway. Right before I called you. There's an iPad on the workbench next to the briefcase if you want to take a look."

"You bet I do."

Officer Magnus stepped to the workbench and slid the iPad between himself and Quags. He swiped at the screen and queued two videos. Pressing play, he gave a brief description.

"This first surveillance video is from the east side of the parkway, heading west. The time stamp reads 2:07 a.m. At that time of night, there's very little traffic on the Colonial Parkway. In fact, between two and two thirty, the vehicle you're about to see is the only one traveling west."

As Quags watched, a flatbed truck entered the screen. "That's not our vehicle."

"No, it's a flatbed truck. A GMC T-6500. It's carrying some kind of cargo under a tarp."

"Hmmm," Quags uttered.

"At 2:23, the same flatbed is seen by a different traffic camera about a mile from where the accident occurred. As you can see in the second recording, the flatbed truck has lost its cargo. The tarp is still there. No outline of any cargo."

"What's the distance between the two cameras?" Quags asked.

"Three and a half miles."

"So in fifteen minutes the truck covers three miles and unloads a vehicle off the side of the road."

"That's how it appears," Magnus confirmed.

"How long does it take to unload a car from a flatbed truck?"

"If you don't care about damaging the vehicle, it can be done very quickly. A couple of minutes at most."

"Can we ID the truck?"

"We could, if the truck had plates. But it didn't. No plates on the front or rear. No name on the door. No distinguishing characteristics besides the fact that it's a flatbed truck."

"I'm not surprised by that."

"At this point, neither am I," Magnus said.

Quags took his eyes off the screen and motioned toward the briefcase. "Did you open it?"

"I took a quick peek. I wore gloves. Help yourself," Magnus said, pushing a box of gloves down the workbench.

Quags donned gloves and opened the briefcase. He stood over the open case, reading the top document. He flipped through several additional pages and then, without any elaboration, he closed the briefcase.

"I'm going to need to go over these documents back at HQ."

"Let's officially sign them over to you. Make sure we have a clear chain of custody for the evidence."

"Absolutely."

Magnus led Quags toward the door and offered a final observation. "I've processed a few hundred accident scenes in my time, but none of this makes sense to me."

Quags considered his response. "Someone is trying to close an investigation before the police can."

"That has to be pretty rare."

"The last time it happened to one of my cases, I ended up shot and in the ICU."

CHAPTER 58

DRIVING HIS POLICE cruiser with the briefcase on the passenger seat, Quags checked the screen of his ringing phone and put the medical examiner on speaker.

"Hi, Doctor. What did you learn?" Quags said.

"I learned you work fast."

"I do?" Quags asked.

"Some people from Camp Peary paid a visit. They said you contacted them."

"I was planning to, but I haven't yet."

"They said you did."

"I didn't."

"Oh."

"Oh, what, Doc?"

"They had credentials and they took the bodies with them. Loaded them into separate vans."

"How many people?"

"Five men and a woman. All dressed in suits."

"Hmmm."

"They also said you were no longer interested in running a toxicology on either the driver or the passenger."

"Also not true," Quags said.

"I had a sneaking suspicion I should have checked with you."

"It's all right, Doc."

"You want to know the really odd part about it? I never mentioned the toxicology. They brought it up. Said you requested."

"Curious," Quags said, the wheels in his head spinning and then gaining traction. "Can you still run the BAC?"

"That sample already went out. Unless it's intercepted along the way, it should produce results."

"Keep me posted."

"I apologize."

"Don't worry about it. Whatever is going on is bigger than you, me, and the chief of police."

*

Quags spread the contents of the briefcase on the table, then stuck his hands in every pocket and corner as if hoping to discover a final, elusive clue. He stacked the documents to his left and a legal pad to his right. For the next several hours, he read, took notes, searched databases, and sprinkled doses of creative Spanish curses into the air. Satisfied with his findings and tired of sitting, he stood from the table and rubbed his eyes. Then he grabbed the stack of documents in front of him and headed down the hall.

Seconds later, Quags knocked on the door of Chief Gates's office. "Chief, you got a minute?"

"Millares."

"I stopped by earlier but you weren't in."

"More budget meetings this week. The usual dog and pony show. Anything new on our car accident?"

Quags provided an update of his trip to the impound lot and the bodies that had been in the morgue. He finished with a summary of the video of the flatbed truck with its disappearing cargo.

"It was a staged accident?"

"Yes."

"Seems our intelligence friends have no qualms about killing their own."

"They remind me of a drug cartel. Ruthless."

"What did you find in the briefcase?"

"That's why I'm here."

"Sit down and walk me through what you've got."

Quags sat across from Chief Gates and put the stack of paper on the corner of his boss's desk. He flipped through several pages and removed one with a red Post-it Note attached to the side.

"This first document is the list of personnel currently on base who were also at Camp Peary during the period of the Matoaka murders. This was part of our original subpoena request. A lot of the details are redacted, but the names are there."

Quags passed the document to Gates, who read through the lengthy list of names. "The list is longer than I thought it would be."

"Me too. It came with names, but without any titles. Some of those people on the list could be administrative help. Or maintenance. Or cooks. It wouldn't be unusual for a government employee to work for thirty-five years in one location. And then, of course, there are clandestine officers on that list."

Gates perused the names again, eyes scanning down the page. "The only name I recognize is our man, Kirk Zambrano."

"That's right. But his cryptonym was Ken Zara."

"Which means?"

"Check out the fifth name on the list."

Gates focused on the name in question. "It says David Childs."

"Right, David Childs. If we apply what we learned about cover names and identities, Kirk Zambrano became Ken Zara. And David Childs became . . ."

"Devon Childress," Gates said.

"Very good, Chief. That means we have confirmation that Childress and Zambrano were both at The Farm together in the eighties around the time of the Matoaka murders."

"That's half of the mystery."

"I also ran a background search on all people named David Childs who fit the age parameters of being a clandestine officer trainee in the late eighties."

"David Childs sounds like a common name."

"It is. But I limited the search to those individuals over six foot two," Quags said. He turned over another document and handed it to Gates. "That's an image of David Childs from Maryland DMV in 1985. He lived in Rockville at the time. He was originally from Dayton, Ohio. He went to Belmont High. And he played on the school's basketball team. I also have a photo from the school's yearbook." Gates handed his boss another page with a second image on it.

"The photos look like Childress."

"Because they are. A young Childress. Before he became a murderer."

"Allegedly."

"Not allegedly. Unlike Zambrano, who didn't leave a trail of dead women behind as he worked his way through major cities in Asia, Childress did. According to his personnel files, he spent extended time in Caracas, Bueno Aires, Santiago, and Quito. In all four locations, during his tenure indicated in those files, there were multiple unsolved murders. All of the victims were women in their twenties."

"I'm sure the fact you speak Spanish was helpful in researching those cases."

"Without a doubt. And when you put it together, it leaves us with a nice little package of circumstantial evidence. Almost too nice. Too neat. As if it were all for show. The car accident that was conveniently located within Williamsburg city limits. The documents appearing in the trunk of that car. The fact that my business card was the only thing found in the driver's wallet. It was all orchestrated for my benefit. In an effort to close the murder investigation and wipe their hands clean."

"Have you considered that we actually may have to close the investigation? We're running out of options."

"You mean suspects."

"I do."

"I know. But I'd feel better with evidence. Real evidence. All the documents in the briefcase could be fakes. They could have located missing women cases in various locations and told us that Childress was stationed in those cities during the same time period. It could all be fabricated. Don't forget we are dealing masters of disguises and kings of disinformation."

"Forging documents with a backstory that matched would require effort on their part."

"It's in their wheelhouse. And if the documents are real and Childress framed Zambrano with a fingerprint transfer, what was his motive?"

"That secret may have perished with Childress and Zambrano."

Quags rubbed his chin, rolled his neck, and stared at the ceiling, deep in thought. "I'm not ready to fold just because they want us to. We're talking about evidence and a motive. It's hard to go to trial without them."

"And it's hard to have a trial without a suspect," Gates retorted.

"A trial . . ." Quags muttered, his voice almost a whisper.

"What do you want to do next?" Gates asked, as if calling his detective back from his trancelike state.

"I'll tell you what our next move is. If they want us to close this investigation, it's going to be on our terms. I'm going to give them an ultimatum. Either provide what we need or get ready to go to trial."

"Trial?"

"Yes. Someone is still working this investigation on their side. Someone who killed two Agency employees in a staged auto accident in our jurisdiction. Someone who picked them up from the morgue. Someone who canceled my toxicology request, which they couldn't have known that I ordered. Someone at the Agency is still on the case."

"I'll support whatever you have in mind, as long as it's legal."

"For now, my plan requires a phone call. I'm going to need to meet with Bow Tie Bramble and have him help me contact someone new in the Agency's legal department. Whoever is replacing Paulsen or handling the legal affairs of Camp Peary. And then I'm going to give that person a week to provide evidence for the murders Childress committed. As well as a motive for Childress transferring Zambrano's fingerprint to your sister's Walkman."

"And if that doesn't work?"

"Like I said. If that doesn't move the needle, then we're going to trial," Quags replied.

"What makes you think they'll capitulate?"

"Paul Paulsen. They killed him after we threatened to use his name in connection with this investigation. They killed an Agency attorney whose identity was already public. All because they didn't want further publicity."

Quags rubbed his hands together, pulled a cigar from his pocket, and inhaled, running it under his nose. "Let me take you out for drinks for your birthday and I'll tell you how it's going to work. Consider it a birthday present. A surprise."

"I hate surprises."

"You may like this one."

"Fine. Birthday drinks."

"Good. How's Friday evening? At Berret's. I'll let you know the exact time by the end of the day."

"Friday nights are busy at Berret's. You may have trouble getting a reservation."

"That's what our badges are for."

CHAPTER 59

QUAGS STEPPED INTO the Matoaka nerve center, sat down, and made a phone call. When he finished, he placed his mobile phone on the table, stood from his seat, and left the room. Ten minutes later he was on the brick sidewalk outside Berret's, a self-described seafood restaurant and grill, meaning they served everything that once walked, flew, or swam.

Quags followed the brick walkway to the front door and pulled it open. The sound of banging pots and pans emanated from the kitchen in the back. A group of business men, the only patrons still in the restaurant after the lunch rush, sat drinking iced tea in a secluded corner with a laptop open on the table.

As Quags approached the hostess podium, a blonde woman in her twenties wearing a tight black dress stepped forward. "Sorry, lunch service ended at 2:30. We open again at five for dinner."

"Is your manager around?" Quags asked.

"He is. But he's going to tell you the same thing."

"Just get him for me, if you will."

"Sure. Give me a minute."

Quags wandered into the first dining room and counted the tables. Then he stepped onto the covered patio and imagined what it looked like at full capacity—tables occupied, the chest-high bar lined with thirsty patrons. Quags finished his self-guided tour with a peek into the kitchen.

He returned to the restaurant's entranceway as the blonde hostess reappeared with three hundred pounds of man to her rear.

"Here he is," the blonde announced before departing.

Quags held up his badge long enough for the restaurant manager to verify its authenticity. "My name is Detective Luis Millares, I'm with Williamsburg PD. Are you the manager?"

"I am," the man said. "My name is Liam Glason. Everyone calls me Slim." The man extended his meaty hand, tattoos running up his arms before disappearing under his shirt at the elbows.

"Slim?"

"I know, it's ironic."

"I'm Puerto Rican. We love nicknames. Everyone calls me Quags. And if I were handing out a nickname for you, Slim would be about right." Quags offered him a friendly smile, putting the big man at ease.

"What can I do for you, Detective?"

"I'm looking to make a reservation for Friday at seven. On the covered patio."

"For how many?"

"Two."

Slim opened the reservation book on the podium and flipped several pages. He scanned the entries for Friday evening and scribbled onto an already full line. "I have you down for two people at seven under Williamsburg PD."

"Do you need a contact phone number?"

"Usually, but your badge trumps a phone number. You'll get a table."

"Thanks."

"We try to maintain a good relationship with local law enforcement. You never know when it will pay dividends."

"Then can I ask you for another favor?"

"Absolutely. Anything you need."

"For the rest of the day, can you keep a list of everyone who calls and requests a table on the patio between six thirty and seven thirty on Friday night?"

*

Fifteen minutes later, back in police HQ, Quags stepped from the elevator and headed down the main hall. He stepped back into the Matoaka nerve center and retrieved his phone from the table. Further down the hall, he poked his head into Chief Gates's open door.

"Chief, I got a reservation for Berret's on Friday at seven. On the covered patio."

"Don't tell me you really used your badge to get a table."

"Then don't ask."

Gates shook his head.

"We're on for Friday. I'll be your designated driver."

"Looking forward to it."

"Excellent," Quags said.

*

Quags walked across the carpet with the state seal of Virginia woven in the center and approached the administrative assistant for the commonwealth's attorney.

"I'm here to meet with Sean Bramble."

"He's expecting you," the administrative assistant said as she stood from her seat. A moment later she led Quags to the threshold of Bramble's office. She knocked on the door, turned the knob, and showed Quags into the room before closing the door and returning to her post in the main foyer.

Bramble, yellow bow tie around his neck, stood from his seat and extended his hand.

"Thank you for meeting me on short notice," Quags said.

"Not a problem. Anything I can do. What's on your mind and how can I help?"

Quags reached into his breast pocket and removed a single-page document. He handed the paper to Bramble. "I need your legal opinion on that document," Quags said, placing his finger over his lips in the universal sign for silence.

Bramble nodded and began to read.

Quags watched intently as Bramble's eyes moved down the page and then back to the top. When he finished his second pass, Bramble handed the paper back to Quags.

"Follow me," Bramble said, reaching into his pocket and placing his mobile phone on his desk. "Let's take a walk."

Quags rested his phone on the desk next to Bramble's and fell into step behind the commonwealth's attorney. A short elevator ride later, the two men were outside, sitting on a bench near the building's designated smoking area.

"I would like to hope you're wrong about your conclusion. But given the trajectory of this case to date, that may be misplaced hope."

"I don't think I'm wrong. And I can prove it."

"How?"

"I would like your help in locating the replacement for our deceased Agency lawyer. Someone took over for Paul Paulsen. I want to know who's in charge of legal affairs for Camp Peary now."

"And then?"

"Then I inform them we're still expecting evidence in order to close our investigation."

"We can do that."

"Good. Once that's done, I want to discuss your offer to speak with your law school class."

CHAPTER 60

AS A DETECTIVE with roots elsewhere, Quags went unnoticed in most Williamsburg venues. He received the occasional nod and the less occasional evil eye, but by and large, he vanished into public spaces with ease. As a homegrown chief of police, Gates garnered more attention. When Quags held the door open for his boss to enter the restaurant, the crowd of patrons in the foyer near the hostess podium parted. Without a word, the same blonde Quags had seen a few days earlier abandoned her post at the podium and led the two officers to their table in the corner of the covered patio.

Handing each man a menu, the blonde said, "Your server will be right with you. Enjoy your meal."

Quags and Gates perused the drink menu and settled on a Tidewater craft beer. They placed their orders with their server and read through the food options.

"You want to try some oysters?" Quags said. "The menu says they're local."

"I'll pass."

"Do you think Virginia Department of Health tells the restaurants the local oysters aren't fit for consumption?"

"I'm sure they do. But maybe it's only the oysters near Camp Peary that are bad. Either way, I'm going with a birthday cheeseburger," Gates said, shutting his menu.

"I'll have the same," Quags replied as his eyes were drawn to the large man now filling the doorway to the covered patio.

"I need to use the facilities," Quags said, excusing himself from the table. "I'll be right back."

Quags headed in the direction of the restroom before turning into the manager's office. Inside the windowless room, Slim stood next to a desk bursting with paperwork.

"What do we have?" Quags asked.

Slim handed Quags the seating chart for the covered patio. One of the tables was circled in red. "Just like you said. An hour after you visited the other day, we had a reservation request for the covered patio for 6:45. It's a table of four. Three guys and a woman."

"Are you sure?'

"Yep, took the reservation myself," Slim answered. "And you and the police chief are sitting right here," he added, pointing to a table with a blue square drawn around it.

Quags rotated the seating chart once to get his bearings and then returned it to Slim.

"You don't need this?" Slim asked.

Quags tapped his temple with his finger. "It's filed. I got it."

"If you change your mind, it'll be here in the office. Have your waiter ask for me."

"Will do. Thanks, Slim." Before Quags left the office, he turned back toward the manager. "Slim, can you do me another favor? Can you send the table circled in red a platter of the local raw oysters? I'll pay the bill, but don't tell them who it's from."

"Sure thing. I'll pass it off as a free appetizer promotion."

*

Quags returned to the table, glancing over at the group he'd just ordered oysters for. As he sat down, Chief Gates raised his glass. Quags picked up his beer and offered a toast. "To your health and a few more good years."

318

"Thanks," Gates said, taking a sip of beer. "Now, are you going to tell me your plan for going to trial without evidence, motive, or a living suspect?" Gates asked.

"I did promise that as your birthday present."

"You did," Gates said.

"Well, I met with Sean Bramble."

"You said you were going to. Did you get what you needed?"

"We made contact with the new liaison officer at Camp Peary. The jury is still out on our request for evidence."

The sound of clapping hands coming through the doorway attracted the attention of everyone on the patio. Before Gates could protest, a group of five servers dressed in white tops and black pants broke into an enthusiastic rendition of "Happy Birthday." A smattering of patrons at surrounding tables joined in and Gates gave the room a halfhearted wave of acknowledgment. At the conclusion of the song, one of the female singers placed a gift on the table in front of Gates.

The two officers stared down at the wrapped present as the group of well-wishers dispersed, exiting the covered patio in the direction of the kitchen.

Gates scowled at Quags. "I meant to tell you I didn't want anyone singing 'Happy Birthday' to me."

"I had nothing to do with it," Quags said earnestly. "I didn't tell anyone it was your birthday."

Gates ran his hand over the present. Deep blue wrapping paper was crisscrossed with a white ribbon. A small card was taped under the ribbon.

"You're the birthday boy," Quags said.

Gates removed the small card and unfolded it. He read the card, closed it, and slipped it back beneath the ribbon. "It's for you."

"What is?" Quags asked.

"The card says it's for you."

Quags pulled the present to his side of the table, removed the card, and read it. "Detective Luis Millares," was neatly typed across the small folded paper.

Quags shrugged and removed the ribbon from the box. He tore

through the blue wrapping paper, exposing a plain white box inside. He picked up the box, checked its heft, and set the box back on the table. "There's something in it."

"I hope so. Otherwise, what's the point?"

Quags pulled on the top of the box and it opened, revealing its contents. Cautiously, he reached into the box and pulled out a Ziplock bag. He held it up in the light, suspending it over the table between himself and Chief Gates.

"*Puta madre . . .*" Quags said.

Chief Gates peered through the side of the plastic bag and his eyes got misty. "A cassette tape. Paul Simon's *Graceland.*"

"I don't know what to say, Chief."

Gates put his palm out and Quags handed the cassette to his boss, holding the bag by the corner.

Quags glanced around the room, measuring how many eyes were on them. He focused his attention on the table that had been circled in red on the seating chart. Its chairs were unoccupied. A tray of uneaten oysters sat in the middle of the table.

"What else is in the box?" Gates asked, visibly rattled.

Quags assessed the remaining contents, each in its own bag. "We have one jade pendant. Probably the one Dr. Lui's boyfriend thought was missing from the professor's house. We have a cell phone, which I assume will turn out to be Julia Flossinger's, the runner found hanging near Lake Matoaka. We have a key chain in another bag, with the initials W&M. And in the final bag, we have what appears to be a hair band of some sort."

"Son of a bitch," Gates replied.

"I assume these are all trophies from our unsolved murders."

Quags began packing the contents back into the box when Slim arrived tableside, a cheeseburger platter on each arm. He placed the plates on the side of the table and offered Chief Gates congratulations.

"Happy birthday, Chief. We didn't know it was your birthday. We'd have gladly used our own employees to sing to you. We do it all the time."

"Those weren't your waiters?" Gates asked.

"No, sir. They did walk through the kitchen and out the back door, which was a little uncool. But you're the chief of police. I just figured it was a surprise."

Slim glanced down at the shredded wrapping paper and the contents of the box. "I'm going to let you enjoy the rest of your meal. Your bill is on the house. Stay as long as you like."

"If it's not a problem, we'd like to take these to go," Gates said. "We have an urgent police matter that needs our attention."

"Not a problem."

Slim took the plates back to the kitchen to box them and Gates dropped his voice to a whisper. "Start talking, Millares."

"I'm not sure, but I believe we just witnessed a game of Rabbit. Up close and personal."

"Are you telling me the people dressed as servers who just sang 'Happy Birthday' were clandestine officers in training?"

"That's exactly what I'm saying."

"How could that have been coordinated without you being involved?"

"Because the CIA has been listening to my phone."

"They've been surveilling you?"

"And then some. The CIA has been listening to me, even when my phone isn't in use or when it's powered off. They've probably been listening to and tracking both of us."

Gates patted the phone in his own pocket and Quags nodded.

"I'll explain in the car," Quags said. "Let's grab our dinner and take this evidence on the road."

"Richmond?"

"Yep. But I need to stop by the station to pick something up first. It'll only take a minute. While I'm inside, maybe you can give Richmond PD a call and tell them we're on our way. We're going to need access to their rapid DNA testing machine and someone who knows how to operate it," Quags said.

"Will do."

Ten minutes later, Quags came bounding down the front stairs of police headquarters. He opened the trunk and placed a small plastic bag on the carpeted floor near the unwrapped box of evidence they had received at the restaurant. Then he reached into his pocket, pulled out his phone and dropped it in. He walked to the passenger window and knocked.

"Were you able to reach the right people in Richmond?" he asked Gates.

"I tried Detective Brooks, but it went to voice mail. Then I called the captain. He said to head over to the Virginia Department of Forensic Science. Detective Brooks will meet us there. They'll have everything ready for us by the time we arrive."

"Good," Quags replied. "Now hand me your phone. It needs to ride in the trunk next to mine."

*

On I-64 heading east, Quags drove twenty miles per hour over the speed limit while Gates pried for answers.

"You want to start explaining?" Gates asked.

"Where should I begin?" Quags asked rhetorically.

"At the beginning."

"Well, as I said, I met with Bow Tie Bramble and we were able to get in contact with the attorney at the Agency who is now handling Paulsen's work. We explained the situation and what was required to close certain investigations relevant to the Williamsburg PD. We let them know that a body count without supporting evidence will not close the investigation."

"You gave them an ultimatum, which is what you said you were going to do."

"Correct. Then I asked Bramble about speaking with his law school class."

"I think you'd be a solid guest lecturer."

"That's not exactly what we agreed on."

"No?"

"No. We agreed that my experience as a detective may be better suited to a mock trial than to a lecture. I suggested we run a mock trial on actual murder cases from Williamsburg. Bramble thought his students would be very interested. In fact, he suggested we livestream the mock trial to the UVA law school class as well. Apparently the two programs have strong ties. They often observe and discuss each other's mock trials."

"Between UVA and W&M, that's over a thousand students."

"It is. And we have a complicated case of multiple murders on our hands. Bramble's law students could discuss what can be done, legally, to move the investigation forward. We discussed covering our four cold cases and the more recent deaths of a W&M student, a W&M professor, a CIA attorney, and Camp Peary's liaison officer."

"You would have to be very careful with what you're suggesting."

"As I discussed with Bramble, the only names I would use are Paul Paulsen and Devon Childress. One is a non-covert attorney and the other was a cryptonym used in a public-facing capacity. Both are legal to use in the public domain."

"And Bramble agreed to this?"

"He did. We also discussed having the testimony of the daughter of a deceased career intelligence officer whose father died in a supposedly accidental shooting. The same man who was framed for one of the cold case murders even though he was actually three thousand miles away at the time. We spent over an hour discussing all of the angles and implications. We discussed possible press coverage and the inclusion of the mock trial proceedings in legal publications. Maybe even a podcast."

"And when is all of this going to occur?"

"It's not. It was all bullshit."

"I'm not following you."

"Before our discussion, I gave Bramble a written note informing him that I suspected the Agency was listening to my conversations, even when my phone was powered off. He didn't take the information well. Apparently, if you want to piss off a commonwealth's attorney, tell him that a federal agency with no US jurisdiction is eavesdropping on a local law enforcement officer."

"I can see that sending Bramble over the edge."

"At any rate, I was hoping the Agency would eavesdrop on the ensuing conversations between Bramble and me. That the plans for the mock trial would give them some motivation to comply with our requests for evidence."

"And it worked?"

"It appears so. The results of the ruse being the trophies that Childress took from his victims."

"You played them with disinformation. Very clever."

"Perhaps. Another alternative is that we have a box of junk in the trunk and someone is out there laughing at our expense."

"Don't say that. It's my birthday."

"In a few hours, we'll have our answer."

*

Quags and Gates were standing shoulder to shoulder, watching the Virginia Department of Forensic Science's DNA analyst run through his laminated troubleshooting checklist. Seemingly compelled to break the silence, the tech with thick glasses gave a rundown on the equipment. "This machine is relatively new to us. The official name of the device is the Applied Biosystems RapidHIT ID System from Thermo Fisher Scientific. It cost a quarter of a million dollars."

"That's nice. Does it work?" Quags asked.

"So far, it's solved one murder and identified two bodies found in an advanced stage of decomposition."

The door at the rear of the room opened and Detective Brooks strode in. "Sorry I'm late, gentlemen."

"And we're sorry to drag you into work after hours. Again," Gates said.

"After hours? There's no such thing in the life of a detective. How's the fancy crime-busting machine?" Brooks asked the forensic DNA analyst.

"It'll take a couple minutes to calibrate."

Brooks turned her attention to the table on the side of the room that was lined with plastic evidence bags. "What do we have?"

"With any luck, we have trophies that were kept by the Matoaka killer. A cassette tape, a cell phone, a necklace, and a couple of other items."

"May I?" Brooks asked before picking up the evidence tube containing the swab of Childress's saliva and blood.

"That's a buccal swab from our suspect. The suspect who we believe framed and killed our previous suspect. We hope to match the DNA from the swab to the DNA on some of the trophies."

"I hope it works out."

"We're all set," the forensic tech announced, throwing the trouble-shooting checklist on a chair in the corner. "First we'll run the buccal swab, then we'll run the other evidence. We should have our first result in ninety minutes or so. Which piece of evidence do you want to compare to the buccal swab first?"

"The cassette tape," Gates replied instantly. "We'll be waiting right outside the door."

*

An hour and forty minutes later, Chief Gates was pacing in front of the glass door to the room.

Quags was on his back, stretched across three chairs arranged side by side. "Even if this pans out, I still have a problem."

"If the DNA pans out, we have no problems. It's done. Once and for all."

"We still don't have a motive."

"A motive? Serial killers don't need a motive. They're deranged."

"That, I know. I was referring to a motive that explains why Childress would attempt to frame Zambrano by using a copy of his fingerprint."

"Like I said, serial killers are deranged. Motive can be elusive for a psychopath."

Quags shook his head. "You're confusing motive with an understandable motive."

"In the back of my mind, I just heard my father's voice say, 'What in the hell are you talking about?'"

The sound of a door opening brought the conversation to a halt. Gates stopped pacing. Quags sat up and looked over. Brooks stepped from the lab room, broke into a smile, and gave two thumbs up.

"It's a match?" Gates asked.

"It's a match. The DNA swab off the cassette matches the DNA from the buccal swab."

"How sure."

"It's a match, Chief Gates. You got your man."

Chief Gates approached Brooks and embraced the short detective in a bear hug. Spinning her around, Brooks's feet left the ground. He returned Brooks to the safety of the floor and embraced Quags with an equally tight hug, sans spin. Laughter and celebratory curses filled the room as the three officers placed their arms on each other's shoulders and momentarily jumped like children.

"Wait here," Brooks said, extracting herself from the celebration.

"I couldn't have done it without you, Millares," Gates said.

"I'm glad I could help. I hope all the families can find some peace."

"Amen to that."

Brooks reappeared with three plastic cups liberated from a nearby water cooler. She reached into her purse and pulled out a small unopened bottle of Woodford Reserve. "We have a tradition in Richmond's Major Crimes Unit. We close all murder investigations with a drink. I brought this from home, hoping we'd have a reason to open it."

"Sounds perfect," Gates said, taking his cup and accepting a healthy pour.

Quags and Brooks then filled each other's cups and the three raised them toward the ceiling.

"To the wheels of justice that refused to stop rolling, and to the victims and their families," Quags said. "And may the guilty rot in hell."

"Hear! Hear!" Brooks replied, and all three emptied their cups in one smooth motion. "It will take ninety minutes for each of the other pieces of evidence to be processed. We'll be here most of the night. You guys should head back home and try to get some sleep. I'll stay behind and see it through. I'll call you in the morning."

"Are you sure?"

"I'm sure. I'll be right here, eyes on the evidence, making sure procedures are followed to a T."

"Thank you, Detective."

"It's my pleasure. That, and my boss will have my ass if I screw it up."

CHAPTER 61

THE DRIVE FROM Richmond to Williamsburg was a blur of excited conversation and cigar smoke. Quags and Gates rehashed parts of the investigation and the twists and turns of the past several weeks.

On the far side of Williamsburg, the police cruiser took a left onto Jamestown Road, heading southwest in the direction of the Gates residence. As the road darkened and downtown Williamsburg faded into the rearview mirror, the remoteness of the rural stretch of pavement engulfed the vehicle. Quags and Gates continued their banter, too engrossed in their conversation to notice the large black SUV until it had passed them. A second SUV appeared to their left and slowed down to match their pace. A third SUV quickly fell in behind them, effectively boxing in the unmarked police cruiser.

"Looks like we've got visitors," Quags said. Red brake lights from the SUV in front of them flooded the interior of the car. "They're forcing us to pull over."

"Don't," Gates replied.

"I may not have a choice. We're boxed in and they're slowing down," Quags replied. "I'm pulling over." Steering with one hand, he reached into his shoulder holster and removed his weapon.

Chief Gates followed his detective's lead and unholstered his own gun. Quags brought the car to a gentle stop, and both men checked their weapons.

"Locked and loaded," Quags announced.

"Ditto," Chief Gates replied.

"Keep your hand on your gun and your finger near the trigger," Quags said.

For ten long seconds, the cruiser sat unmolested in the darkness on the side of the road. In the sideview mirror, Gates saw the passenger door of the SUV behind them open.

"We have someone getting out of the rear vehicle."

"Hold steady," Quags replied, straining to see the approaching figure.

Gates watched as the figure closed in on the car. "It's a woman. And her hands are in the air."

"Roll down your window. I'll cover you," Quags instructed

Gates lowered his window and the woman stopped near the door, hands still in the air. She bent at the waist so the officers could see her face.

"I assume you recognize me."

"I do," Quags responded. "You're Paul Paulsen's wife."

"That's correct. May I get in the back seat?"

"As long as you realize I'll have my service weapon pointed at you at all times."

"Fair enough," the woman replied, opening the rear door and climbing into the back.

Quags checked the mirrors and confirmed the woman was the only one to exit any of the SUVs.

The woman moved to the center of the back seat so each man could see her more clearly.

Quags turned the ceiling light on for further illumination.

"Pulling over a law enforcement officer is a good way to get shot," Quags stated plainly.

"That's why I approached with my hands up. And if you'll allow it, I'll show you my credentials."

"Slowly, please," Quags said, steady hands aiming his gun at the woman.

The woman reached into her pocket, retrieved her credentials, and handed them to Chief Gates.

"Another attorney with the Central Intelligence Agency. It says your name is Paula Frushour," Gates said with a hint of surprise.

"That's correct."

"Your last name is Frushour, not Paulsen?"

"Correct. I kept my maiden name. For obvious reasons."

"You didn't like the sound of Paul and Paula Paulsen?" Quags asked.

"Would you?"

"It would be memorable," Quags said.

"Maybe in another line of business."

"And maybe you can shed some light on what we're doing here," Gates said.

"I'm here for closure. We can't afford to lose any more people to your case."

"Then you should stop killing them," Quags said.

"It's not that simple, Detective."

"Explain it to us."

"I assume you were able to recover DNA off some of the evidence we supplied."

"We were," Quags confirmed. "We have a positive match between the buccal swab taken from Childress and the DNA found on the cassette tape that was taken from my sister's murder scene. The other pieces of evidence are being analyzed as we speak."

"They will all match."

"Is that because you made them match?"

"No. Those objects were found in a secure safe in Devon Childress's home on base."

"I guess we're going to have to trust you on that."

"Yes, you are. But I have no reason to lie."

"With all due respect, we'll have to agree to disagree on that front," Gates said.

"I can appreciate that sentiment," the woman replied.

"Let's say we believe you. Let's say we believe that the documents you provided us regarding Childress's background are legitimate. And the evidence you provided was actually from a safe in Childress's house."

"If you believe that to be true, then your case is closed."

"Not exactly," Quags said.

"Oh, that's right. You still want a motive," the woman stated.

"Yes. I'd still like to have a motive. For why Childress, or David Childs if you prefer, would try to frame Kirk Zambrano."

"I can provide a motive. I spent the last two days hunting down and speaking with some of their 1986 classmates from The Farm. Several of them told a very similar story. But I have no evidence to prove what they said. You'll have to either believe it or not."

"Let's hear it."

"As you've learned, Kirk Zambrano and David Childs were both trainees on The Farm during the Matoaka murders. At some point during the course, Zambrano reported to security that Childress had been sneaking off the base after hours."

"I assume that means he was also sneaking back onto base. Which seems like a more difficult task."

"It was. But in the late eighties, security wasn't what it is today. Not to mention we specifically train our clandestine officers on how to circumvent security systems."

"Valid points," Gates said.

"I assume Childress was sneaking off base to commit murder," Quags said.

"We don't know that. But Zambrano allegedly reported that Childress had been sneaking off base after hours. Childress denied it and, without proof, the allegation was dismissed. But it led to bad blood between Zambrano and Childress. According to their classmates, this bad blood culminated in a full-fledged fight on the obstacle course several weeks later. Childress had five inches and thirty pounds on Zambrano. But Zambrano had been raised by a marine who taught hand-to-hand combat."

"We saw what Zambrano can do with his hands on a surveillance video," Quags said.

"As you can imagine, Zambrano gave Childress a serious beating. In front of their classmates and instructors. It was humiliating. Combine that with the fact that oversized egos are rampant among case officers and trainees, and you can imagine the impact. But at the end of the day, it was determined that Childress had instigated the incident. So life went on."

"Why was fighting between trainees permitted? Why wouldn't they be forced out of the program at that point?" Gates asked.

"Because this was the nineteen eighties. Training was rougher back then. Physicality between trainees and instructors was common place. Thirty-five years ago, as part of the program, trainees were subjected to several days of detention and interrogation, with limited food and water. Physical assault was often part of that interrogation. In fact, trainees had to sign release forms absolving the Agency of any liability regarding injuries incurred during the experience. Today, that kind of physicality between instructors and trainees would never be allowed. The interrogation portion of the program was substantially altered in the nineties."

"And Childress was so pissed and humiliated that he decided he'd plant Zambrano's prints at one of the Matoaka murders?" Quags surmised.

"That's our assumption."

"His only mistake is that he didn't know Zambrano was going to be in California for a wedding the weekend he killed Chief Gates's sister and planted the print," Quags added.

"No one did. Zambrano never officially requested travel leave for that weekend. He took leave on his own. The ironic part is that unsanctioned leave would have been a valid reason to expel him from the training course."

Gates slowly turned toward Quags and the two locked eyes. Gates shrugged almost imperceptibly.

"It passes the sniff test," Quags said. "But why did Childress allow Zambrano to teach on The Farm if there was bad blood between them?"

"Childress had minimal input on the hiring process of instructors."

Quags considered the answer.

"I have one remaining question. Why was your husband killed?" Gates asked. "He wasn't a covert employee."

"My husband perished in a tragic car accident. The BAC test results will confirm that he was intoxicated at the time of the accident."

"This is the official story from the CIA?"

"It is."

"And the unofficial story."

"Have you ever heard the expression that the only way two people can keep a secret is if one of them is dead?"

"Of course," Gates said.

"Then further explanation is unneeded."

A long silence filled the car.

"What now?" Gates asked.

"I'd prefer we all go home and put this behind us. A step in that direction is the Williamsburg Police Department closing the case."

Gates considered the statement. "If the DNA proves a definitive match between Childress and the evidence provided, we can proceed in that direction."

"The Agency would see that as an amenable resolution," the woman replied. "And if it is all the same to you, I'd prefer if we never have to meet again."

"I think we all want that," Quags agreed.

CHAPTER 62

THE SMOKE FROM the half-barrel smoker billowed into the evening sky as Gates Senior pulled slab after slab of meat from the heat. His apron dripped with an amalgamation of grease, spices, sweat, and beer. The pork ribs were transported to the long picnic table in the yard, landing with a resounding thud.

"Smells awesome and looks even better," Quags said.

"Guaranteed to make you lick your fingers," Gates Senior replied.

Barbara Gates moved a roll of paper towels closer to Quags. "Or you can use a paper towel."

"I'll lick," Quags replied with a wink.

Everyone at the table waited for the chef to untie his apron, marking the official end of his cooking duties. He draped his apron over a plastic chair and ambled toward the table. Stopping at a blue cooler, he opened the top and then handed out cold beers.

With tears welling in his eyes, Gates Senior spoke. "I'd like to thank Detective Millares for his work in closing the case of my daughter, Heather. It's been a long time coming. Too long. May she rest in peace."

Everyone raised their beer and said, "Amen."

"Let's dig in," Barbara Gates said, motioning toward the spread of food.

*

A stack of picked-clean rib bones teetered in an aluminum pan with a pile of sauce-stained paper towels.

Gates Senior wiped his mouth and his hands and turned toward Quags, seated to his right. "Did my son mention that I want my rifle back? The one you stole."

"I don't know what you're talking about," Quags replied, taking a bite of rib meat. Chief Gates and Barbara both followed suit, leaving Gates Senior to watch everyone at the table chewing with their mouths full, acting as if they were unable to respond.

"Don't think I can't see what you all are doing here. You should be ashamed of yourselves. Stonewalling an old man."

"Maybe you can file a stolen property report with the police," Barbara said.

Gates Senior scowled at the ensuing fit of laughter. "You're lucky we're celebrating this evening. Otherwise, I'd walk away from this table right now. And I'd take my meat with me."

"I'd also like to say something," Quags said, standing. "I've been thinking about this for a while now, and I've decided it's time for me to retire from police work."

"If you think that'll get you off the hook for the gun you stole, you can forget it," Gates Senior grumbled.

"You can't retire," Chief Gates said, dropping a rib onto his plate. "You're the only detective I have with any murder experience."

"And, our recent investigation aside, you're the chief of police in a jurisdiction where homicides don't occur."

"They could."

"I'll tell you what. The next time you have a homicide, I'll help out with the case while I train one of your other officers. Or better yet, we can work with Brooks in Richmond to get one of the other Williamsburg detectives the experience they need."

"What are you going to do after you ride off into the sunset?"

"My brother and I are going to buy a bigger boat and start a charter fishing company."

"Do we get free trips?" Gates Senior asked.

"Sure," Quags replied. "Who knows, maybe you'll get lucky and catch your missing hunting rifle."

www.ingramcontent.com/pod-product-compliance
Lightning Source LLC
Chambersburg PA
CBHW031934110726
47902CB00001B/178